THE COLLINEAU COVENANT

Sam Clinton

ISBN-13: 978-1482365450
ISBN-10: 1482365456

Cover by Luise and Thomas Steinkellner

For Basia

PROLOGUE

His hands shook and were clammy as he gripped the haft of the razor-sharp sword, gritted his teeth and made a faltering cut into the side of the victim's neck. Bright red blood spurted at him, shocking his torso and head backward. He felt the life of the victim draining in the fading warmth of the blood dripping from his hands.

The leader screamed at him. 'Go on. Cut his head off.'

Hasan balked.

'Cut it off!'

Pulling back the head of the convulsing body and squirming, he hacked through the neck and then thrust the head violently away from him, splattering blood over his white, baggy *shalwarkameez*. The tethered lamb's body slumped to the ground, legs kicking out the last traces of life. Hasan groaned and pressed his clenched fist hard against his stomach.

'You've killed an enemy. Now you're supposed to hold up the head in triumph.'

'Sorry.'

'Never mind. Well done. See, you don't need training to cut off a head.' With a cynical smile and the casual voice of experience, he said, 'The real thing is easier.' He looked out toward the rocky desert and his eyes narrowed to serious reflection. 'This is just the beginning.'

Dressed only in his underpants, Hasan lay on his bed peering into the darkness of his small hotel room recalling that gruesome

4

moment at the training camp under the mountains of Pakistan's northwest frontier ten months ago. The training was hard: assault rifle, rocket grenades, hand grenades, dagger, hand-to-hand combat, personnel bombs and more. He'd done it all, even beheaded a living being.

That was training but today would be the real thing. Today he will demonstrate his courage and faith and sacrifice his young life – with a bomb. He had no fear. Death was the doorway to Paradise and Muhammad will take him swiftly to that wonderful place. Resurrected, he will meet his numberless brother fighters who had died courageously before him. Hasan's mind swirled as he re-created images of that place of spiritual and physical pleasures he had first seen as a young boy in his mother's captivating, melodious voice.

Now a six-foot, twenty-two year old fully trained, strong warrior in Islam's righteous jihad, he will kill the enemies of Islam.

'You'll feel no pain,' his imam had assured him. 'And you will have everlasting life.'

That thrilling prospect welled up excitement in him. A surge of adrenaline strummed his nerve ends and rushed exhilaration through his body.

This was his day of destiny and not a whisper of doubt entered his mind.

Italy was the land of his birth but he hated it. He hated its people too because they had supported Satan in his war against Islam. At eleven o'clock, he will pay them back for their great sin. His friends will then know and cheer and call him a *shahid* among *shuhada*, a brave martyr among martyrs, for his people's sake. And his father will know and be proud.

The hotel room was unlit, unventilated, and oppressively warm. He smoothed back his long, raven-black hair and went to the open window. There he breathed deeply to extract freshness from the sultry Rome air. His gaze swept across the rooftops to the massive dome of St Peter's Basilica, lifted into intricate relief against the dark sky by lights around its base. Behind St Peter's, the moonless night was giving way to a soft, brighter hue. A scorching hot day of death was drawing itself inexorably over the Eternal City.

A sudden, intense loud drumming pulled his gaze upward and his body stiffened as two small helicopters with flashing lights sped overhead like angry fireflies making haste toward the brightening horizon. In the street below, the headlights of a cruising police car reflected off parked cars crammed into the narrow street.

He stared at his bedside clock. When its lighted digits tripped over to 05:00, he pressed a button on his cell phone and listened for a curt response. One of his three bomber friends in another hotel whispered, 'Time to go'.

His heart started to race. 'With you in five minutes.'

He pulled on his jeans, blue denim shirt and trainers. The rest of his belongings were strewn about the room but they could stay where they were. He had no further need of them. He laid a neat fan of euro notes on his bed for the hotel bill. Forty-five euros for one night in a dingy single room with bathroom facilities in the corridor was not worth it but he would not complain.

He looped the shoulder strap of his deadly holdall over his head and adjusted the bag so the detonator button was to hand. Like a resolute soldier reporting for his last mission, he stood erect with shoulders pulled back proudly. He blew out the nervousness starting to gather in his chest and set off to join his brothers in faith.

The dim glow of daybreak filled the unlit reception area as he crept through to the main entrance. He pressed a switch at the side, pushed the glass door open to the buzz and click of the release mechanism and strode out into the relative cool of the morning air. Once outside, he could see his friends waiting just three houses away.

A car turned into the road and swept headlight beams across his back. Not really knowing how, he could tell it was the police car he had seen from his window. The officer in the front passenger seat, whom Hasan at first glance took to be a boy in uniform, stared glumly at him as the car drove slowly by. Farther along the road it stopped. Hasan slowed his step. The officer turned back and looked at him but then the car moved on and disappeared round the next corner. He stared at the corner for moments, heart pounding and cold sweat breaking on his forehead. Then he realized other early risers were on the street and he was just one of them.

Occasionally glancing apprehensively down the street to the corner, he greeted his fellow bombers with handshakes and embraces.

'We had fleas in our rooms,' one of them said.

'I had an elephant in mine,' said Hasan.

They all laughed. None of them mentioned the mission but by listening to their edgy small talk exchanges you could have detected the excitement of anticipation.

CHAPTER ONE

It was 9:30 on Pentecost Sunday. The *Meteo* presenter promised it would be a scorching June day.

Pope Boniface X crossed himself and uttered 'Amen', ending the service for the Christians and other poor souls slaughtered by the early Romans in the Colosseum behind him. The colourful masses surrounding him in the Piazza del Colosseo mumbled an echo.

'God protect us from evil,' said Sebastiani irreverently. *Colonello* Sebastiani stood alone by his Carabinieri Alfa Romeo in the cooling shadow of the skeletal Colosseum.

As Rome's anti-terrorism chief, his job was protecting Rome and its people from tyranny and he worked at it doggedly.

'Okay, let's get this over and done with.' These words inexplicably raised images of home and retirement. Since his divorce, thoughts of retirement presented a lonely and miserable prospect, but at his age, fifty-five, it was still years away and for that he was grateful. The demands of anti-terror work and his dedication to it had collapsed his marriage. He wondered where Linda was today and guessed she was in some European capital playing her violin. Wherever she was, she was gone from him. A citation at his last assessment said it all: A fine leader totally dedicated to protecting Rome and Italy from the evil of terrorism. It might have added: while totally dedicated to neglecting his family.

His only son, Roberto, was his only attachment to family and, deep in studies at Padua University, he rarely found time to make contact.

But at this moment at the Colosseum, all was submerged below an extraordinary foreboding. More than at any time in his career he believed Rome would suffer its first terrorist strike and doubted his measures could prevent it.

He followed the news daily and it scared him. Italy's open support of American middle-eastern policies had unnecessarily stirred up antipathy in Islamic countries. And, as if purposely to fan the flames of discord, the imbecilic prime minister had broadcast a tactless rant about Islam and the superiority of Western culture. This not only caused offence throughout the world but also gave rise to a direct threat on the Internet. It was a red-alert certainty. Hundreds of thousands filled the streets to celebrate the papal spectacle. In the inflamed mind of a jihadist, this was a ripe opportunity to strike at Italy and the heart of Christendom in a single blow. It was just a question of how many would die.

Constant contact with his unit leaders was important in this situation. Keep them on their toes. Scanning his heavily armed troops placed around the Colosseum and in its higher arches, he barked into his walkie-talkie, 'Topman to all unit heads. Stage 1 ending.'

Sebastiani smiled ironically and shook his head in disbelief as fawning clerical assistants moved to help the aged Pope Boniface from his dais. Their practiced, genteel hand movements reached superficially for the Holy Father but made no contact with him.

'Topman here. All units. Stage 1 complete. No incidents,' said Sebastiani.

No bombs or guns had materialized out of the blue to cast death all around, as he'd anticipated – but there was still time.

'Topman to unit leaders. Activate Stage 2. Pope returning to Vatican.' Against the noise of the suddenly applauding onlookers, he shouted, 'Pope moving to Vatican. Stand by.' And in case any of his listeners had any doubts, 'Get this man there alive. Do you hear me?'

The final stretch, the route leading the papal procession to that magnificence of High Renaissance architecture, St Peter's Basilica, for the pope's inaugural mass, was just two kilometres or so but crowded and difficult to protect.

As the papal procession began to assemble itself, he drove off to check the disposition of emergency service vehicles, crowd barriers and his troops along the procession route. At strategic points he stopped to confer with unit leaders, at times leaping out of his car to bark orders into his walkie-talkie to others involved all over the city, his sharpshooters in high places and those randomly checking people's bags and clothes with electronic security devices. In all a five-thousand strong security force was active over the whole of Rome's center.

Pleasant morning sunshine, not yet too hot, bathed the excited masses into good humour. Believers and tourists of all colors and nationalities strained and jostled each other for the best positions along the route, from the Colosseum all the way to St Peter's Basilica. Frantically waving national flags blended in colourful agitation, like a vast multitude of multi-coloured flowers in a lively, swirling wind. None of those cheering shared the turbulence filling his mind.

Nothing was spared in this celebration of the new Pope whose entourage reflected the height of extravagant papal grandeur. Incongruous amid the historical pageantry, a vanguard of six police motorcyclists, wobbly at the very slow pace, led the procession away from the Piazza del Colosseo and into the Via dei Fori Imperiali, that broad road Mussolini pretentiously commanded should run directly through the ancient imperial forums, those seats of absolute power of the Roman emperors Trajan, Augustus and Nerva.

A corpulent, proud bishop in an ostentatiously decorated green chasuble hoisted the Papal Crucifix aloft with the flair of a military band leader raising his mace and set off at the head of Pope

Boniface's colourful procession. More than a hundred brilliantly clad cardinals, thirty or so seemingly disinterested attendant boys in surplices carrying ornate crucifixes and gilded, bejewelled censers, and a large sauntering mix of lesser ecclesiastics, followed.

In the midst of all this, Pope Boniface himself, in glistening gold and white pontificals and secure in his white pope mobile, appeared to float majestically above all around him, the grand pontiff in all his aloofness. A phalanx of soldiers in traditional hussar uniforms – bright red tunics and white breeches, feathered helmets, thigh-high black riding boots, bayoneted rifles angled across shoulders – marched stiffly on either side.

Immediately following the Pope, the *sedia gestatoria*, the scarlet silk-covered, gemstone-embellished, portable throne was carried empty on the shoulders of eight young priests in scarlet robes. The white ostrich feathers of the traditional fans carried to the sides of the throne bounced lightly like foam in time with the movement of their bearers.

And at the rear, yet more slowly meandering police motorcycles.

Sebastiani got out of his car at the Monumento Vittorio Emanuele, Rome's much maligned wedding cake edifice. Native Romans hated this building, not only because its angular architecture clashed with the circles and arcs of most of Rome's Renaissance style, but also because they never forgot it replaced a lovely hill and the community that once lived upon it. But he liked it. He didn't know why he liked it; he knew only that he did.

Sebastiani, the still-fit badminton devotee, hurried nimbly up steps to a high terrace, a military watch point at the side of the building, and looked back at the colourful column weaving its way slowly toward him. The surge of noisy emotion pouring out from the crowds heaved a thrill in his chest. A cacophony of loud cheering, whistling and applauding followed the colourful pageant as it snaked its route. His racing mind was irritated by the slow progress of the parade.

His walkie-talkie communicator buzzed. 'Topman.'

'Deputy here, sir. Bad news.'

'What is it, Ferri?'

'Milan intelligence. Minutes ago. Islamic extremists, Italian nationals. Left Milan yesterday to bomb Rome. Duck-dived surveillance.'

'*Merda*. That's all I need. How many?'

'Four males. Could be here.'

'Details?'

'Still coming through.'

Sebastiani compressed his lips and drew air noisily through his nostrils. 'With you in two minutes.'

He paused to look back again at the procession and grimaced as it moved in front of the stand seating Italian politicians and other *prominenti* in the Via dei Fori Imperiali. They stood to applaud the pope. Sebastiani stared transfixed and rigid. But the explosion he imagined would blast them all down into the much-pillaged ruin of the Foro Augusto never came.

'What the bloody hell can I do?' If some mad beings were determined to attack Rome today he saw no way of stopping them, even with five thousand troopers on the streets.

Before the procession reached him, Sebastiani drove on to Largo Tassoni to meet up with his number two, *Maggiore* Luca Ferri.

Largo Tassoni, a popular, cozy triangle lined with wisteria-covered hotels, was filled with newsstands, street cafés and the pervasive, delicious smells of coffee and Italy's finest pizzas. It was also choc-a-bloc with a noisy, excited horde.

Ferri was a professional military man of – according to Sebastiani – the highest quality and therefore his own choice as his deputy. The young Ferri was always in touch and commanding, and arrogant with it. But as Sebastiani approached him, a dark frown framed his finely defined face and sparkling azure eyes. '*Buongiorno*, Colonel.'

'Right, Ferri. Milan bombers. What's happening?'

The chill breeze lurking in the shadows of Largo Tassoni was not enough to cool Sebastiani's agitation. The immediate threat of an explosion obliterated from his senses the noisy excitement of the swarms of people overflowing the pavements of the Corso Vittorio Emanuele.

'I've got their IDs,' said Ferri.

'Circulated?'

'All teams alerted.'

'Good.'

'We won't find them in this lot, sir.'

Resigned to that fact, Sebastiani shook his head. 'If they are here, why haven't they detonated already?' He bit on his lower lip as he checked his watch. 'Ten-thirty-five. I'll be glad when this is over.'

'Half an hour should do it, sir. I think it'll be okay.'

'Ugh? Then I suppose I can go home.' Sebastiani slowly shook his head. 'You surprise me. Do another check. All units. Make sure they've got their minds on the job. Put out a general. All travelling bags checked thoroughly. I want the pope and everyone else alive at the end of this. First, get that sorted out,' he said, pointing to two young *carabinieri* gassing with a pair of state police as though nothing could be more important than just being there and looking cool.

As Ferri approached the conversation, the two *carabinieri* shifted awkwardly and drifted off to some activity in the crowd.

The two state police officers stayed determinedly where they were, one with a foot resting on the top of the front wheel of his light blue *Polizia* car doing some form of leg exercise and the other slouched back against its door with his eyes shut, sunning his face, his wrap-round sunglasses set rakishly on top of his black, wavy hair.

Ferri returned three minutes later. 'Fine sir. All units confirmed okay.'

Sebastiani read his latest updates. Italy's internal security agency confirmed the Milan bombers were still at large. 'Okay, half an hour. Let's see if we can make it.'

A heavy, foul odour reminded Sebastiani the scum-laden Tiber was just a hundred meters away. A close friend with an anxious mind once warned him, 'If you fall into the river you've got one minute. If you don't clean off the bugs and acids in that time they'll kill you.'

Sebastiani and Ferri shouldered their way through the noisy, bustling crowd and onto the Corso Vittorio Emanuele. Together they walked without speaking along the barriers and scanned the crowds for the signs of the terrorist. They had trained to spot the anguished face amongst the happy celebrators or the agitation of the young man or woman gripping a travelling bag concealing instant death.

Sebastiani's communicator buzzed a message: *Prec. arrests. Eleven held on suspicion. No explosives. Air Force enforcing Rome no-fly zone.*

So far, everything was okay. Another fifteen minutes to complete the bursting Corso Vittorio Emanuele and start the majestic train along the sentinel obelisks of that hated creation of the Fascist Architecture movement, the Via Della Conciliazione, to the relative safety of St Peter's Basilica. The cathedral was fully prepared: one hundred voices of the Vatican boys' choir would herald the pope's arrival with Palestrina's *Tu es Petrus* and thrill the thousands of believers inside the Basilica and outside in St Peter's square.

He checked his watch again: 10:45. His churning stomach would settle only when the pope was safely in the hands of the Swiss Guard.

As the procession rolled its way ponderously past, his face creased into a smile. Not far now: only a bridge and ten or fifteen minutes at a slow pace. It's going to be okay.

Suddenly the world changed.

The percussion wave from the multiple explosions tore at the buildings of Largo Tassoni, sucking the air from Sebastiani's lungs and knocking him to the ground. His ears hurt and, at first, he could not hear the screams of the panicked crowd. Debris and body parts fell all around him as he forced himself to his feet, hands shaking and blood pouring from a cut above his forehead.

The bridge and the papal procession had been totally obliterated.

'*Porca puttana!*' he screamed.

Fighting the pain, he wiped at the grey dust and blood from around his eyes and mouth and fought clumsily to operate his walkie-talkie.

'Get your men to the bridge!' he shouted into the radio.

He stumbled toward the Tiber, shouting a commentary and orders into his walkie-talkie. 'Topman to all units. Emergency, emergency. Bomb attack Ponte Vittorio Emanuele. Bomb attack Ponte Vittorio Emanuele. Bomb squad and units local to explosions, Level 1 response. All units, full alert actions.'

The intense midday traffic forcing itself through the crowds at Largo Tassoni ground to solid congestion.

The sun was higher and hotter. Running through the pandemonium on the Piazza Pasquale Paoli toward the devastated bridge with Ferri and his unit, Sebastiani was wet through with sweat. Stone dust and blood filled his eyes and mouth.

He stopped in his tracks. 'For Christ's sake!' he screamed. A dead young man sitting curiously upright against a low wall stared into the distance with surprised, open eyes, a large nail protruding from his grit peppered face. He ran on. The nearer he came to the Tiber, the progressively more gruesome the scene. At first, bloodied, groaning, crying and confused, grey zombies, crawling and stumbling around and screaming for help. Brave fellow victims who had escaped the worst of the blasts aided others more seriously injured. At the river's edge, dead, indistinct forms lay among the detritus, slaughtered *carabinieri* identifiable among them.

He peered into the chasm where the bridge had been and into a dreadful boyhood flashback. The surging plumes of black dust and smoke that filled the abyss, the shattered, bloody corpses of punished humans in grotesque poses burning among the marble and concrete debris and on the jagged rocks engulfed in the tumult of the river, was an image burned in his memory. It was that picture of fiery hell in a religious book that had scared him sick.

The stench of the Tiber intensified his revulsion. He turned and faced the buildings lining the once-bustling Piazza Pasquale Paoli. The façades of its pizzerias, cafés, hotels and offices had been blasted away. They had taken the full impact of the explosions and only the outlines of what once had been rooms remained. The ever-full street cafés that filled the square were gone.

The areas on both sides of the bridge resembled war zones with bloody dead and severely wounded lying in the dense murkiness of atomized stone and marble.

Physical nausea gripped him. 'Fucking, fucking hell!' he screamed impotently.

Ferri, grubby but showing no signs of injury, shouted to him from out of the dusty gloom. 'Sir! You okay?'

'I'm okay.' In control now and brain ticking over orderly, he shouted, 'The bombs contained metal objects.'

'Bomb squad's here. State police are controlling traffic.'

'Good, good.' He patted Ferri's arm.

Sebastiani grabbed the arm of a *carabiniere* stooping over a body and screamed at him. 'Bodies away from the bridge. Barriers up. Do it now.' He pressed a button on his walkie-talkie, 'Scene of crime team…'

Explosions to his left and right flattened him to the ground again.

Within a minute his walkie-talkie crackled alarm. 'General alert. St Pio river unit. Explosions along the river. Explosions on bridges parallel to Vittorio Emanuele. Casualties. Emergency services called.'

'Fuck!' he screamed, heart pounding and mind filled with images of suicide terrorists detonating bombs in the crowds. 'Topman to Apollo. Devil on the loose, explosion sites.'

But he knew his elite commandos had no chance of searching out bombers from the terror-stricken, scattering hordes. He clenched his fists at his side and scanned hopelessly for bombers. 'Bastards! You bloody bastards!'

Suddenly, the dissonant howling and flashing blue lights of police cars, ambulances and fire engines intensified the chaos around the Piazza Pasquale Paoli and the deafening cacophony around him.

He caught sight of St Peter's dome and realized what was happening. 'The Vatican.' He shouted into his walkie-talkie. 'Topman to Vatican Unit. Evacuate the Basilica. Get them out of there fast. Clear the museum.'

Sebastiani feared the Vatican security unit, on the far side of the Tiber from him, would be drawn to the death and devastation at the bridges and leave St Peter's exposed. Hands bleeding, his walkie-talkie was difficult to grasp. 'Topman to Vatican Unit. Hold your stations.'

Running back to Largo Tassoni amid rescue service vehicles and personnel pouring into it, he called down one of three helicopters he had stationed for the event. 'Chopper Alpha. Topman at Largo Tassoni. Get me to the Vatican. Quick!' He pointed in the general direction of St Peter's as though the pilot could see him.

In a controlled, friendly voice, the pilot responded. 'Chopper Alpha. Topman, please identify.'

'Topman to Chopper Alpha. I'm in the middle of Largo Tassoni waving my bloody arms at you.'

'Chopper Alpha. We see you, Topman.'

'Get down here quick. Get me to the Basilica!'

'Chopper Alpha. Topman stand by.'

Rescuers scattered from the whirlwinds of stone dust blasted at them as the helicopter approached. Screwing his face against the fierce downdraft of blinding debris, Sebastiani threw himself through the open door of the chopper before it touched the ground.

'Move, move, move!'

The helicopter swept upwards, over the ruin of Ponte Vittorio Emanuele, and high enough for him to see the breadth of devastation. He reckoned about three hundred bodies on the sides of the Tiber once connected by the bridge. The Tiber's fierce current had swept other bodies downstream and onto rocks in the lower reaches of the river. No sign of the Pope's vehicle. The bridges to the left and right of the Ponte Vittorio Emanuele, although not so damaged, could not be used.

His walkie-talkie clicked an irritating text update: *Looters arrested at Pasquale Paoli.*

From above the river he could see the frantic attempts to evacuate St Peter's Basilica of congregated worshippers and priests.

A thunderous blow rocked the helicopter violently.

As he looked on, explosions tore away at the stone columns supporting Michelangelo's great dome. The massive cupola shuddered violently as if trying to free itself from the girdle of iron chains that had bound its base for the last four hundred years. Its supports cracked and shattered. Like a dying man, it collapsed downwards onto the high altar and Bernini's *baldacchino* that shaded it. In the main apse, the throne of St Peter was crushed beneath the rubble.

More explosions ripped at the roofs of the transepts and nave, crashing them down around their sturdy supports onto the seething body of the cathedral. Thick, choking dust charged with the taste of burnt chemicals filled the ruin.

'Fucking hell!' He ran a dirty, sweaty hand over his bleeding head. 'Topman to Central Control. Major emergency at Vatican. Full rescue services to Vatican.'

He stared at St Peter's grand portico expecting it to be shattered by bomb blasts but none came. While its beautiful glasswork had been blown out, the great entrance remained structurally intact and defiant against the wreckage of masonry flung against it.

'Topman to unit leaders. Confirm rescue services. Damage reports to Central Control.'

Sebastiani looked down into the Piazza San Pietro, a cauldron of carnage, panic and raging activity; a battleground. Grubby, dishevelled human shapes rummaged amid the devastation like demons in hell trying to extract the dead and injured but, so far, no sign of the rescue services.

Sebastiani estimated about four hundred dead on the bridges and about the same number of dead in the cathedral. Many more than that would have been injured and he wouldn't know for sure how many until the fire brigade and their helpers had removed the rubble. Five or six days of hard work, he guessed: risky work because of the danger of more collapse – and there could still be survivors under it all.

'Drop me where you can in the Piazza.'

'Sir.'

About to call the Vatican Unit chief, a shout from behind distracted him.

'Colonel Sebastiani, sir.'

Against the loud sirens of the fire engines and ambulances pouring into the Piazza San Pietro, Sebastiani yelled back at the young, dirty-faced *carabiniere* offering him his walkie-talkie. 'What is it?'

'*Generale* Conti, sir.'

'*Pronto*. Sebastiani.'

'Fabio. The media. We must do a press release.'

He rolled his eyes heavenward and shouted to counter the blaring sirens of ambulances arriving. 'What, now? I'm at the Basilica. We're digging out bodies.' He turned his head away and screamed, 'Fuck it!'

'Right now. The prime minister's issued a national state of emergency.'

'Yes. Yes sir, I know.'

'There's going to be uproar. Maderno's Fountain. Right away. I need just a minute.'

'On my way.'

A loud voice drew him round. 'You the senior officer here?' The RAI Uno reporter pushed a microphone under his nose and a cameraman behind pointed his camera at him.

Sebastiani thrust a hand against the lens. 'Wait. Just wait, will you? You…you…' His immediate intense rage at their intrusion turned quickly to weary acceptance of the need for the media to get their hot news out to the world. 'Press release, north fountain in ten minutes.'

Around him, TV and radio transmission units beamed the sickening devastation into the living rooms of a shocked world. Nothing would ever be the same again.

At the sight of General Conti, Sebastiani became curiously concerned about his dirty, untidy state, his conscientiousness about such things deeply imbued by a lifetime in the military.

The gleaming, urbane Conti carried his fifty-six years well. He was large and well proportioned, elegant in his silver and gold-embellished uniform. 'Christ, Fabio, you're a mess. You okay?'

'I'm okay.'

'Look, I know you don't need this right now. Quick as you can. Estimates, dead and injured. What measures you've taken since the explosions. Media wants details.'

Conti gave no sign of being emotionally affected by the horror surrounding him. UN peace-keeping in the Congo had shown him the worst excesses of man's hate and inhumanity: the bloody massacre of thousands of innocent villagers, the axed remains of women and children, the evidence of whole-scale raping and cannibalism. For him, today's disaster was clean by comparison.

Sebastiani ran a grimy forearm across his sweating forehead. 'National security services are now on high alert. Italy and western-friendly nations. Dead and injured, here's the tally.' He handed Conti a grubby printed telegraphic list:

20

Basilica, ca 750 dead, ca 400 injured.
All bridges ca 450 dead, ca 600 injured.

'Lot of bodies still in the river. It'll take time to get a clear picture. We've fished the pope's wagon out of the river. He's dead,' he added dispassionately.

A noisy shuffling of young *carabinieri* feet drew their attention from the destruction to a short but pompous-looking, much decorated officer making his way toward them, followed closely by a thirty-ish, attractive, bosomy, blond-haired woman in a colourful summer dress with just a little more décolleté than seemed appropriate for the situation.

'Oh God, no,' was Conti's response to the appearance.

They came to attention as the Head of the Italian military, *Comandante General dell 'Arma, Dottore* Daniele Franchi, stumbled, coughing and gasping for breath, over the rubble and through the sprawling vehicles, thick entangled cables and other hardware of media communications systems in the process of being assembled, his arms flailing the air, all the while doing his awkward best to scan the devastation.

Gathering himself together, Franchi came in all guns firing. 'Conti, you're responsible. Tell me who did this dreadful outrage.'

Franchi's uniform was his courage. In it, he overcame the complexes about his shortness, his Tweedledum (or Tweedledee) waistline and his less than polished articulation. In it, he was able to stand up to the lofty and intellectual likes of Conti. Franchi was not as conversant with Carabinieri matters as his position demanded. It was generally understood that he had risen to the top by virtue of his inherited wealth and his familial relationship to that other person of challenged stature, the prime minister.

'That is not clear,' said Conti. 'At this stage, we just don't know who did it.'

'What is clear,' said Franchi, sucking in a chest full of air to complete the sentence, 'is that the prime minister is blaming the ineffective Italian military for poor security. He's demanding

21

heads. Yours most likely, Conti,' he added swiftly with a splutter, implying his own head was safe.

Conti had dealt with Franchi's usual bluster of attempted intimidation many times before and responded calmly. 'All security for this event was properly carried out.'

Franchi's response was sharp, bordering on a screech. 'Like what?'

'All preparations were agreed with the Ministry of Defence.'

Franchi put a hand over his mouth, cleared his throat and said in a more conciliatory tone, 'Of course, Conti. Of course.' He then strained his eyes toward the grubby figure next to Conti. Condescending to identify the man but making no comment about his battered condition, Franchi said accusingly, 'You're Colonel Sebastiani.'

'Yes, sir.'

'Sebastiani. Yes!' Franchi's raised tone suggested he had found the solution to a long-standing problem. 'Head of Rome anti-terror.' He menacingly pinched together all the fibres of his small face and, in a high pitch, threatened again, 'You could lose your job over this. It's the biggest calamity to hit the world. Who knows what the effects are going to be.'

A curious silence ensued while all eyes fixed on Franchi whose own eyes fixed diligently on the activities of the rescue services. 'Outcries from all over the world. Dreadful. Could cause a war. Who knows? My God.'

For a whole minute, he stared silently – apparently subconsciously, but who knows? – at the woman's cleavage and then sternly at her face, which made Sebastiani believe he was about to reprimand her for her lack of decorum. Under his accusing gaze, her own self-conscious gaze dropped awkwardly downward. Then he said, as though addressing her, 'You have until this time...' He checked his watch and then appeared to study Sebastiani's eyes. 'Eight tomorrow morning. First report. In my office. General Conti, I want you with me at the Rome attack committee meeting at nine. Actually, it's the Operation Vatican

Attack Committee meeting. That's what it's called.' Placing a hand gently on the young woman's arm, he said, 'Ferdinando, arrange it with my secretary here. Make sure you're there.'

'Sir.'

Franchi perfunctorily scanned the devastation again. 'Dreadful political and economic repercussions for Italy. And the rest of the world. Dreadful.' Becoming aware of the media gathered en masse around him, he said, 'The world's press is anxious and waiting. Deal with them, Ferdinando.' He glimpsed his watch. 'I have an emergency meeting with the prime minister and the...um...um, Minister of Defence.'

With that, he smiled warmly at his female companion and, striking an air of grand importance, strutted off ahead of her over the rubble to his waiting limousine.

Conti's face loosened into a sarcastic smile. 'So, Fabio. Our beloved Franchi is blaming us for the bombing. *Stronzo*. And you did not hear me call him a turd.'

'Call him what?' Sebastiani smiled, his grime and blood-smeared face taking on the laughable expression of a clown.

'If I were boss of the Carabinieri, I would demand to know from you, you Sebastiani, how the hell they got on the roof of the Basilica. But he didn't want to know that.'

Sebastiani shaded his eyes against the sunshine and gazed at the smouldering ruin of the cathedral. 'Good thing he didn't ask. First, I don't know who did it. Or how they got on the roof. No way anyone could get up there. Not today. Vatican security is tighter than Da Vinci airport. The roof was locked and guarded. Suicide bombers? No. And no guns were fired.'

'Not jihadists then?'

'Can't be certain. But I'd say no. The explosions have been set up over time. That's not their way.'

'International anti-terror? CIA?'

'Too early.'

'Okay Fabio. The media. What do I tell them?'

'Not Islamic terrorists. If our suspects from Milan are involved, they're not alone. Somebody big has an almighty reason for doing this. We'll know a lot more when I debrief the bomb squad and forensics. Fontana promised me a provisional in three hours. For the media, we don't know.'

'Bomb squad report to me soon as you can.'

'Sir.'

'Fine. I got the figures and the general picture. Leave it to me. You get on with your work.'

'Yes sir.' Knowing he did not have to face the media lifted Sebastiani's spirits. He was not shy and could handle it but was pressed by the situation. He used his private mobile phone to contact Ferri. 'Drop whatever you're doing and get over to the Basilica. I want you around for my bomb-squad debriefing.'

'On my way. We've sealed off the roads leading to the bridges and Vatican.'

'Well done, thanks.'

Six hours since the last explosion. The early evening was still bright but stand lamps erected in anticipation of a long night drew focus to the corners where rescue teams struggled with life and death.

One blessing, at least: bottled mineral water was in great abundance and Sebastiani had at last cleansed his mouth, face and head of blood and grime. But his dusty uniform and the filth still around his neck and eyes gave him the appearance of a coal miner just ascended from the mineshaft. What's more, the water did nothing for his collapsed morale.

Needing a moment to regain strength, he crunched his beaten body onto the rubble just inside the portico of St Peter's, bent over and gripped his thighs in the way a marathon runner does at the end of a race.

He felt hopeless. His job was to protect Rome from terror attacks but he had failed and now felt responsible for the bloodshed. Fighting back the nausea welling up inside him, he looked around the desolated Basilica. Firemen, army personnel and members of the public worked feverishly in the swirling smoke, thick dust and crumbled stonework, still searching for the dead and injured. Paramedics stretchered victims into ambulances that then sped off to the blare of sirens in the hope of finding hospitals that were not already full. Emergency medical teams treated the more seriously wounded in blue field hospitals erected in the middle of St Peter's Square.

His head shot to the right. Michelangelo's *Pietà* was intact, covered with dust but complete. Mary's sadness portended the deep sorrow that would face the loved ones of those who had died here today. This sight of Mary sped his mind, compacting memories into mere seconds, obliterating from his senses the backdrop of frantic and noisy activity that enveloped him. He was in another time, to his only other visit to the Vatican, at least twenty years earlier. This is about as far as I got because the *Pietà* was just there, he remembered.

Then, he was stung by principle. The lavish opulence of the Roman Catholic Church compared with the abject poverty of many of its adherents in the world offended him, so he had turned and walked away from its portals. Now it was a ruin and many people had died in it today. Although nominally Catholic he was not a religious man. It was of great philosophical interest to him that people took such a strong position on God and the hereafter that they could kill themselves and innocent others so readily. He saw no end to the terror. Al-Qaeda's pursuit of a pan-Islamic caliphate was without compromise and its terror cells targeted masses of unsuspecting, innocent, unarmed civilians. They purposefully staged attacks to cause the greatest possible injury and death, and to bring the greatest possible outrage. How could there be conciliation?

He fumbled with his walkie-talkie and without pulling his gaze from Mary, said quietly, 'I guess the Sistine Chapel is okay?' Not attempting to hear an answer, he slotted the communicator into its holder.

'Fabio, I'll make this quick.'

The usual echo of words spoken aloud in the Basilica had disappeared with the roof. Captain Marco Fontana and three of his bomb-squad team, one struggling to control an excited sniffer dog, formed a loose half-circle in front of Sebastiani and Ferri. They wore jeans, short-sleeved shirts, navy blue plastic sleeveless tops with the word CARABINIERI across the backs, sneakers, and white, latex gloves.

'We've found no unexploded bombs.' Fontana, a short, stocky southern Italian, spoke slowly with a gruff, deep-throat resonance that made him clearly audible despite the clattering rescue activities.

'No more bombs then?' asked Ferri.

'I didn't say that. All Vatican buildings searched. Nothing found. The bombs were Semtex and all had the same tagging. All command detonated. The only difference, the bridge bombs contained metal objects to cause personal injuries.'

Ferri asked, 'Source?'

'We know from the residues picked up at the scene that it's C4 from the Czech Republic. Part of a consignment stolen from a production plant three years ago. Never traced.'

'Target, Marco?' asked Sebastiani. 'This doesn't fit any group I know.'

'Any clues?'

'None. The Mafia mine bridges but they don't operate against the church. Islamic extremists?' Fontana screwed-up his face. 'No evidence of that. Explosives on the roof? Locked and heavily guarded. We'll check it out when we can get up there. That won't be easy.'

'The Milan suspects wouldn't use Semtex,' said Ferri.

'No, they wouldn't. All other terror groups are foreign. Targets in their own countries.'

'And the Mafia don't operate against the church,' Sebastiani reminded himself.

26

'No, Fabio.'

Sebastiani summarized. 'Unknown terror group. Target, Roman Catholic Church or some of its people. Or both.'

Fontana pouted and nodded his head before answering. 'Looks like it.'

'How could anyone leave explosive around in the Basilica without being seen?'

Fontana looked back into the ruin. 'Good question. Could be explosives were laid where repair work was done. Not sure. Forensics will show more.'

Sebastiani played with the plaster a medic had stuck to the wound on his head. 'Nothing clear, then, Marco?'

'No. I would have expected support structures to be targeted. They weren't.'

'We've got to look at the repair work and who did it,' said Sebastiani, looking at Ferri to make the point.

'Fabio, your business. First report by midnight.'

Fontana and his team rushed off, leaving Sebastiani and Ferri looking at the devastation.

Sebastiani checked the time: coming up to seven o'clock. The dropping sun cast shadows of gloom into the upper reaches of the ruin. 'The Vatican's closed circuit TV system,' he said, scanning around for cameras. 'The control room wasn't touched so everything was recorded until the roof came down. Plenty of film. TV footage. But whoever set this up wouldn't stick around just to get on TV.' He wiped blood from his chin with a wet grubby handkerchief, examined it and then dabbed his chin again. 'Make sure TV channels put out requests for cameras from the public.'

'Building records, work documents. We need to check them,' said Ferri.

'Right. Set up a meeting with the Vatican's architect. Works boss. Whatever you call him. Do that as soon as you can.'

A young, anxious *carabiniere* rushed up to them, saluted and handed Sebastiani a note.

His eyebrows arched as he read it. 'A-ha! Do what you have to here, Ferri. I've got a suspicious death to look at.'

The young officer led him to a small huddle of paramedics in red overalls examining a scarlet-clad body.

Sebastiani approached the most senior-looking medic, a tall, thin, grey-haired man. Reading the name from the note, he asked him, 'Is this Cardinal Aldo Ricci?'

'Are you Colonel Sebastiani?' asked the senior medic.

He nodded. 'Ricci. What's happened to him?'

'Not sure. Just three hours ago he was helping with rescue work.'

'He wasn't killed by the explosions?' His response was shrill.

'No. Someone wanted it to look like that. Look at this.' The medic crouched by the body and moved its head from side to side. 'He's been roughed up and beaten to death.'

Islamic terrorists wouldn't seek out and kill an old cardinal after blowing the Vatican, he reasoned. Anyway, Islamic militants didn't bomb Rome, he was certain. If Ricci's knowledge of the people behind the explosions was a risk, they would have killed him long ago. A contract killing? But not Mafia.

He pulled on the flesh below his lower lip and walked around Ricci's corpse making mental notes about its condition. His death was not directly related to the attack on the Vatican, he concluded, so why was he murdered?

He peered toward the murky, smouldering ruin that surrounded him. A picture of a conspiracy was beginning to form in his mind – a powerful conspiracy.

CHAPTER TWO

Arms hanging to the sides of his chair and head lolling forward onto his chest, Sebastiani stared down into the sparkling pinpricks of coloured lights dancing in the darkness of his closed eyes. Bereft of any idea of what to do next, he sat there motionless. Then he tried to force his eyes open but couldn't.

It was raining hard. No, it had been raining hard because he remembered its spread-shot pellets thrashing against his window but he could no longer hear it.

A violent, dark figure was threatening him from behind but try as he might he could not turn his head to see it. Although he was certain this enraged being now occupying the outer edge of his field of vision was set on killing him, he had no fear of it, only the irritation that his head was fixed rigid, negating his will and denying him a glimpse of the being's face.

As he awoke, the cotton wool mists numbing his brain cleared away. He found himself at his desk in his barracks quarters, sweating profusely and looking at his bandaged left hand, wondering how it came to be bandaged.

Gradually, he became aware that the telephone on his desk was ringing. He flopped across his desk and pulled the telephone to him, pressed a button marked 'Loudspeaker' and rested back.

Mild panic accompanied his efforts to voice words through his sticky mouth and dry lips.

'*Pr...pronto*. Sebastiani.'

'*Colonello* Sebastiani?' The Italian title of address could not hide the distinctly French accent.

'*Si.*'

'My name is Elaine Bruneau. I'm calling from France.'

Decoding the voice he registered an educated and self-confident being at the other end. 'This is a secure phone. Are you French secret service?'

'*Oui.* I'm calling from our Paris office.'

'What do you want?' he snapped in French, expecting a French official enquiry about the attack.

'I am calling just to make sure you are okay.'

'What?' He stared at the telephone. 'Why would the French secret service be interested in my health?'

'It is a personal call. I have a special reason for wanting to know you are alive.'

He closed his eyes, inhaled deeply and huffed out noisily. 'It's late. Please get to the point.'

'Of course. You have been through unbelievable hell today. I will be quick.'

Sebastiani heaved his leaden elbows onto the arms of the chair and let his head sink back. 'Go on then.'

'You and my mother, Bernadette Bruneau, were once very good friends.'

On hearing this name he lurched forward in his chair and grabbed the telephone from its cradle. 'Did you say Bernadette Bruneau?'

'Yes'

'Bernadette Bruneau.' The words escaped his lips on a cheerful breath. Transported back to the joyous times of his university youth, he recalled the happy, carefree pretty face of the only girl he could ever truly love. That's how he felt now, in this instant of excited recollection. Bernadette Bruneau, the vivacious, chestnut-haired French exchange student was the embodiment of all that was exciting and pleasurable in his life back then. She was his soul mate. Then one day she vanished from his life without a word, leaving him desolate.

More awake now to be cautious, he said dryly, 'I know the name. What about her?'

'I am afraid she's dead.'

This stark declaration drove Sebastiani to silence. They both waited for the other to speak.

Elaine broke the pause. 'My mother died in a car crash a couple of years ago.'

'Sorry. I knew her a long time ago. I'd forgotten her.' He regretted his insincere tone.

'I understand. But she never forgot you. She told me all about you.'

He began wondering why he was engaging in such a ludicrous conversation but he let it ride. 'Why? Why would she remember me?'

'I am about to shock you, Colonel Sebastiani.'

'It's been a day of shocks. Just go ahead, will you?'

'When I heard about the Rome attack I thought you might have been killed. It would have been very sad for me personally.'

'Oh. Why?'

'Because, Colonel Sebastiani, you are my father.'

An unintentional grunt escaped the back of his throat as he shook his head, but he managed a controlled tone of honest enquiry to ask, 'What are you talking about? Your father?'

'My natural father.'

'Good God. Are you sure?' Sebastiani's mind played with images of the face on the other end of the line and gave Elaine Bruneau a pale complexion overhung with auburn hair, like her mother.

'Mother told me long ago that my real father is Fabio Sebastiani. Said I should know this. Fabio Sebastiani, from Rome.'

'Lots of Fabio Sebastianis in Rome.'

31

'I know. I have checked. Believe me, there is no doubt. I have to come to Rome to speak with your General Conti. Can we meet? I will bring proof. There is a lot to tell.'

He sat up stiffly in his chair. 'Why are you meeting Conti?'

'I cannot say.' She laughed. 'You are not on my need-to-know list.'

'He'll tell me, I'm sure.'

'I do not think so.'

Sebastiani was at first confused by the prospect then intrigued, realizing he might now discover why that beautiful creature had departed his life, leaving him totally sad. Then he imagined possible consequences if this woman's claims turned out to be true. And she did seem to be telling the truth. 'I can't talk now. Believe me I'm tied up for the rest of the night.'

'I understand.' She was secret service so she would know he'd be debriefing colleagues, superiors and politicians. She would understand this was not the time for personal chat. 'I will telephone you again before I leave for Rome. I'm not sure about timing yet. But fairly soon. In the meantime, I will send you photos. Is your barracks address okay?'

'Yes. Fine.'

'Do not worry. I will not ask you for anything. You have your own life. I realize that. And I won't embarrass you. I won't call you Father. I already have a very good father. I'll call you colonel.'

After the call, he realized he had not used his title, colonel; could not recall mentioning it at all. He wondered what else she might know about him.

Nostalgia engulfed him. Bernadette Bruneau. Highly intelligent and exciting Bernadette. She went so suddenly leaving no clues. But the activities of youth and demanding philosophy and physics courses had removed her to the back of his mind and the intervening years had passed by without him giving her another thought. But she was always there ready to be retrieved to his mind's eye in an instant.

A daughter. A tender smile of regret creased his cheeks as his mind churned his youthful past with images of Bernadette and her insistence on unrestrained and unprotected lovemaking. Roberto came to mind. He would need to know he's got a sister. Roberto would be excited. His mind swirled with the pleasure of his new discovery.

Then doubt gripped him. Why had she not troubled to contact him long before if she was so certain he was her father? She was meeting Conti so she was probably an agent, a French spy, and spies play deadly games. And why was she meeting Conti? What if she was a double agent operating for the organization that bombed the Vatican? There could be many reasons why this organization would want him watched. She had said she would bring proof but constructing proof is all part of the deadly game. These thoughts unsettled him.

Fully awake now, he stood by the window and was puzzled to see it had not rained at all.

Night activities, tying up operations with Rome State Police and negotiating additional military investigation resources from Milan and Naples sped dark night through to blinding sunny day. Sebastiani finished his shower, quickly wrapped a towel around his waist and grabbed the phone.

A saggy voice answered his call. '*Pronto*. Ferri.'

'Sebastiani here. Cardinal Ricci. Did you get my message?'

'Yes sir. I saw Ricci after you'd gone. No doubt about it, he was murdered.'

'I think so too. But I reckon it has nothing to do with the bomb attack.'

'Just a moment. If it had nothing to with the bomb attack then I don't understand. Do you mean, had nothing directly to do with it?'

'That's what I mean.'

'Then Ricci was a threat to someone. Knew something. I don't know. Killed him because the situation was right.'

'He was beaten up badly before he died. He was murdered.'

33

'No question at all.'

'All right. We'll let this one go. It's with the state police so leave it with them. Okay?'

'Umm, yes. Okay. Probably best.'

'More important, you're coming with me to the Vatican. This morning.'

'As already arranged, sir,' said Ferri with an edge of sarcasm that was not lost on Sebastiani.

'Pick you up in an hour.'

Sebastiani settled himself on the rear seat of the car, set his head back on the headrest and smoothed tired aching from his temples. 'Something's wrong. Our Milan suspects are not criminals. They wouldn't know we were tracking them, for Christ's sake. Somebody inside the force has warned them.'

Ferri was in a struggle with his leaden eyelids and trying to gather the full meaning of what Sebastiani was saying. 'I find that difficult to believe, sir.'

'So you trust in our brothers in the military?'

'In criminal investigations, I think we have to. Don't we, sir?'

'No, we don't. I think you're tired. I expected a more considered answer than that.'

'I'm tired, for sure.'

'Aren't we all?'

They spent the next five minutes silently looking out of the windows but Sebastiani's occasional fidget showed he was not at ease.

Sebastiani broke the silence. 'Do we have Muslims in the team?'

'In the Carabinieri, yes. Not a single one in anti-terror.'

'You've checked then?'

'Yes, sir.'

'Muslim converts from Christianity? Somebody who might have helped these guys?'

'I don't know, sir.'

Sebastiani slapped his thigh. 'Bloody Conti. Said a security failure has been identified and dealt with. National security matter. Nothing more to be said.'

'He said that?'

'National boss. Can say what he likes. Bloody nonsense, of course. Someone inside the force. Got to be. How else would they know?'

'Surveillance could just have failed. Even so, strange he'd want to block that information, especially from you.'

'Failed? I don't think so.' He jabbed Ferri's forearm with a finger. 'Conti's protecting someone. I don't know who. Anyway, it can't stay blocked forever. I won't let it. Ah, we're there already.'

The St Peter's end of the Via Della Conciliazione was a stirring mass of silent protesters with banners declaring the prime minister and his government must go, and weeping mourners lighting candles and building heaps of flowers before the gates. Just before his car turned off it and into Via Rusticucci, a short side street of Vatican offices, Fabio Sebastiani looked for the great cupola of St Peter's Basilica, even though he knew it was gone. His stomach lurched at the reminder of the devastation of yesterday, raising the heat of anger in his tired body.

'Christ sake. Who the hell would want to do that?'

Ferri pulled out his notebook and stared into it as though answers lay within. 'Someone with a need to demonstrate their power. Perhaps one religion over another.'

'Islam being the other religion?'

Ferri stifled a yawn with the back of his hand. 'Not necessarily. The cardinals. They'll know.'

'What d'you mean? Know what?'

'If the pope had serious enemies.'

'All popes have serious enemies. Political. Religious. But to bomb the Vatican is beyond reason.'

'I wonder if this particular one had to die.'

'Could have been just the pope in office, regardless of who it was.'

While Sebastiani was picking up on a brainstorming exchange, Ferri looked to be fighting sleep – and it showed in his answer. 'Yes.'

'What about the Church hierarchy? Could be an inside job. The cardinals?'

'Those still alive.'

'Yes, those still alive.' A discernible tone of wonder accompanied his words. 'Why weren't these people anywhere near the bombing? Lot of secrecy in the Roman Catholic Church so we'd be lucky to get a full and honest answer to that question. I wonder what excuses they'll have for not being among the dead. Names and positions: any information?'

The major returned to looking in his notebook. 'I tried to get a list of surviving cardinals from Vatican admin. No one could tell me who'd be at the meeting. Just these names.' He ran his finger down a list. 'Twenty-nine. No idea who the top people are. I'll flesh that out today.'

'The Minister of Defence met with Vatican people last night. Cardinals mostly.'

Ferri held his hand over his mouth and spoke through another yawn. 'What came out of that?'

'Very confused. Suddenly no leader. Yes, names and positions in the hierarchy. So many killed, that won't be clear.'

On leaving the car, they straightened themselves, stroked down their trousers and tugged down on their tunics in unison, as if by command. Their driver led them to a large, brown door in the Via Rusticucci and pressed the doorbell.

His cell phone rang. '*Pronto*, Sebastiani.' What he heard made him involuntarily grasp Ferri's arm as though to hold him in balance. 'Jesus Christ!' His incredulous exclamation was barely audible but very long.

'What's wrong, sir?'

'That was the state police. They've got three corpses and the IDs are positive. They're the Milan bombers.'

'Dead! Three? Not four?'

'No, three.' His mind raced seeking reasons for the absence of the fourth suspect. 'Look, I'll do the cardinals without you. Go to the north end of Via Francesco Sivori. Police and forensics are there with the bodies. I'll be with you in about an hour. Oh, and Ricci is ours. Complications, Major.'

The high-ranking Carabinieri officer closed the ancient wooden door behind him and considered the all-round gloominess of the priest's office he had entered. Dark brown wood and scarlet felt seemed to cover everything, but these drab furnishings fitted well with the nature of the man he was there to meet. He drew a long breath, laid his gold-braided cap on a side table and then sat down, uninvited, in a sad looking, high-backed armchair whose stout legs looked as though they had bowed under the weight of years.

'Can we be heard?' The police officer spoke in an urgent, secretive undertone.

'No.' The priest also spoke quietly but with exasperation.

Irritable exchanges: that's how the conversation continued.

'There's only the anteroom you came through. I'll know if anyone comes in.'

The room was lifeless with only its two items of religious devotion to break through its dullness: the pained Jesus nailed to the small crucifix above the heavy oak writing desk at which the priest sat with his arms folded and, on the opposite wall, a byzantine icon of mother Mary with the baby Jesus at her bosom.

Through the large sash window the officer could see, across the way, the grand residence of the pope, which was now without an occupant. He studied the great palace for evidence of damage from the blasts of yesterday but nothing had reached that far.

Slaves to the perfection of the pope had done their work well because everything about the house was impeccable, as though the building were completed new only yesterday. Its gardens too manifested flawless perfection. Precisely squared, meter-high boxwood hedges in a complex design of sweeps and circles enclosed startlingly green lawns and a large sparkling fountain alive with sparrows cooling themselves in the spray. Everything so perfect.

But he felt disgustingly imperfect, trapped and tainted by criminality. He was locked into crime because of his love for a young Carabinieri officer in his charge. The thought anyone might ever discover this secret worried him constantly. Filled with affection, he had soaked up Domenico's improbable arguments about the new pope's long-established plans to clean up the corruption in the Church. And the down payment on his agreement to cooperate gave him immediate, incredible wealth. Because of these things, he had allowed himself to be inveigled into an oath of silence when plans were laid. Love and the money on offer were irresistible. This is how it must be for arms dealers, he had thought: just close your mind and take the money. Anyway, he always believed they wouldn't go through with it. Rather, he made himself believe they wouldn't.

He despised this man he was here to meet, this authoritarian, puffed-up cleric, this hypocrite who had called him his partner in crime. That had hurt but he couldn't deny it. He scanned the room and its few items of furniture.

'Relax. The room is not bugged.'

'How would you know? Anyway, I wasn't looking for bugs.'

'You've come here to tell me what I already know. Your men fouled up a most important operation.'

'Nonsense. I'm here to remind you to be careful what you say at the meeting. Don't ask me any awkward questions. As for the Muslims, my men did the job.' The officer resented his perceived subordination to this dreadful person but he feared the cleric's blackmailing possibilities that held him firmly subordinated. 'They didn't foul up. The plan worked out.'

The cleric swept his hand across these words dismissively. 'You would say that.' Then, leaning forward and jabbing a finger at the table, he said, 'Not only did your men fail to hide the bodies for all time, something I expected, but one of them got away. Isn't that going to cause complications?'

38

'I never expected my officers to do more than just kill them. They were on the way to set off their bombs. Could have stopped the whole event. They had to be stopped. That's all. Timing allowed for nothing else. Yes, one got away. That's unfortunate but I'm confident I can sort it out.'

'The report suggests your men are sadistic psychopaths. The bodies were in a dreadful state.'

The policeman frowned wondering what report and how the priest had come by that detail, which was not made public. 'They left it like a religious execution. We, the Carabinieri, have intelligence their own brothers, Muslims loyal to Italy, murdered the men. That's the way it will be. Many murders by Islamic zealots have torture associated with them.'

'That does not sound very clever to me. I can see I decided wisely to have Ricci dealt with by others.'

'Yes. And who set you up with a hit man?'

'I have my contacts.'

'Who was it?'

'Do you honestly believe I would tell you? You promised a clean job. Such promises.' The cleric turned his gaze to Jesus and matched his sad countenance. He sighed. 'Oh dear, oh dear.' He moved his knees left and right so that his chair swivelled. 'The one who got away. Might you just happen to know if he is still alive?'

'He was left for dead but...'

'But he got away,' the priest cut in sarcastically. 'Where is he?'

'I don't know.'

'If he ever comes into your hands, what will you do?'

'If he's alive, he will come into my hands and he will be silenced.'

The priest linked his fingers in his lap and swivelled his chair again. 'I trust he will. How do you see it? The media, how will they see these murders?'

'They'll report what we tell them. We'll find evidence against someone close to these men. We arrest them. It's always relatives. That's how it will be reported. Simple.'

'Simple? Huh.' The priest swung his chair to face the window, showing the officer his back. He looked down to the side of his chair and asked, 'Who's the investigating officer?'

'Rome's anti-terror chief, Colonel Sebastiani. Why?'

'What are your plans for him?'

'What do you mean?'

The priest spun round to face the officer. 'He's running the bombing investigation. What if he's successful?'

The policeman shrugged his shoulders. 'We'll use diversions. It'll be impossible for him to get anywhere near the people who did this. Some of them are too close to him. He'll be looking elsewhere.'

'You seem very confident.'

'We're tracking him. If he gets close, my men will take action.'

'What action? What will your men do?'

'They could threaten his family. Force him to consider how his investigation could endanger their lives. Or just silence him completely. I don't know. He's a clever man. But then so are my men. He's being watched.'

'Is it a problem if someone were to see you here.'

'No.' He stood and snatched his cap from the side table. 'I'm a top Carabinieri officer investigating a major crime.' He glanced at his watch. 'We'd better go. We shouldn't be late.'

'Ah, come in, sir. My name is Casey. Monsignor Casey.'

The melodious lilt, the softness of his voice and his name betrayed to Sebastiani he was Irish. He wore a light grey suit with the typical matching light grey shirt with choker collar. 'I arranged this meeting with the cardinals. It'll be inside the Pope's Privy Council chamber in half an hour. General Conti is already here. Please follow me and we'll join him for coffee while we wait for Doctor Franchi. He phoned apologies for his lateness. He'll be here in fifteen minutes.' Casey's Italian was fluent.

A broad ray of late afternoon sunshine from the high windows imperceptibly scanned the princes of the church assembled before Sebastiani and his colleagues. Their number included, so he had been informed, one cardinal priest from France, four cardinal bishops from the seven Holy Sees of Rome, a collection of cardinal deacons and other priests.

The elevated rows of two hundred seats around the oval chamber provided for the ever-growing number of members of the College of Cardinals. Before the bomb attack, there had been one hundred and sixty. Today, only forty-two leaden faces glared down at the investigators standing before them at floor level. The large, ill-lit hall with its atmosphere of medieval gloom, recalled the setting of an inquisition.

Standing legs astride and arms akimbo, which embarrassed Sebastiani because he was sure everyone in the room had, like him, conjured up *Il Duce* in their minds, Franchi introduced his team and then said, '*Le sue eminenze*. The devastation has hit us all.' Affecting despondency, he breathed a deep sigh. 'Italy is in shock. The world is in shock. We don't yet know who committed this dreadful crime or why. We believe the attack was directed at the Church rather than Italy, per se.' Then, applying exaggerated emphasis, he said, 'We *must* bring the culprits in quickly before they commit yet more attacks.'

He looked round at his team members as though expecting some comment on his performance so far.

There he goes, thought Sebastiani. Bloody Franchi, the headline man. He introduces topics but can't deal with the discussion and analyses. Sebastiani wondered why the moron bothered to turn up other than to appear involved.

Conti intervened. 'Gentlemen, we need your formal authorization to investigate within the Vatican State. Who do we go to for that? Who is now leader of the Church?'

The question caused no surprise. The solemn faces looked toward the priest seated at the right side of the pope's seat of office. Dressed in a long, plain white garment and a white skullcap pressed

41

onto his straggly, long grey hair, he stood out from his brother priests, who wore black robes and red caps. The many folds on his long, colorless sixty-year-old face testified to years of meditation and study in places not blessed with sunshine.

Arranging the skirt of his garment around his knees, he leaned forward and responded in a French-accented voice filled with solemn, priestly gravitas. 'Well, yes, gentlemen. Things have changed. Authorization would normally come from the pope's office. I'm sure you can take it that it will be given. I'm not aware of any limitations to your access.'

Crossing one leg over the other, he sat sideways and slowly swept his gaze across the faces of the policemen standing below him. 'I must explain something. As you might know, a pope is elected in a conclave of qualifying cardinals, normally one hundred and twenty. Sometimes less.' He seemed to lose track for a moment and filled in by adjusting again the skirt of his garment. 'Only a few qualifying cardinals are now living. And they are not all here. Moreover, not everyone here in this room is qualified to vote in the election of a pope. The process is very complicated. We have an emergency. An enforced *sede vacante* gentlemen, *sede vacante*.'

As though to ease a headache, he dropped his forehead onto his hand and remained silent for thoughtful moments. Slowly raising his head, he continued. 'It's not just the pope. We also do not have a papal seat of office. It will take many years to restore St Peter's Basilica. So we who sit before you, and cardinals from other countries, will meet and decide the next steps.'

'It's important for the Carabinieri to know who to deal with and how,' said Sebastiani. 'Are your administration offices still functioning?'

'The various papal offices are still fully staffed. No individual from these organizations was lost so they will continue to function.'

'What's your name, please?'

'I am Archbishop Roger Collineau.' He stood. From his elevated position, his extraordinary height became exaggerated and presented a sense of dominance over the inquisitors, which seemed to have its greatest impact on the short Doctor Franchi, who fidgeted. A superior attitude took him over. 'I am now the most senior in the College of Cardinals, and the cardinals assembled here have today suggested I assume the papal role temporarily until a new pope is elected in the usual way. Except that, in the circumstances, it will not be done in the usual way.'

Sebastiani knew as much about the usual way of electing a pope as he had read in his newspaper. '*Eminenza*, who do you think was behind the attack?'

Collineau responded with the surprised look of total ignorance: the hunched shoulders and open hands of a Frenchman, and a dithering shake of the head, but no words.

'Were you at any time notified of any possible threats against the Roman Catholic Church or against the pope himself?'

'Sir, your own security services had informed us at least two years ago that the Vatican was not a likely terrorist target and we've received no change to that information. I'm afraid I can't even begin to guess who perpetrated this crime.' Collineau sat down. 'One thing I can tell you is that we now see ourselves as targets. For that reason, and because our Basilica is in ruins, we've decided it would be best for the Church if we move the papal seat to France. As soon as you agree we can go.'

Sebastiani's challenge carried an edge of aggression. 'France? Why France? Where precisely? How will you be safer there?'

'France has a pope's palace, a Catholic cathedral and all the related offices. In Avignon.'

'Those are public buildings controlled by the French government.'

Collineau peered stone-faced at the colonel. 'You are well informed. The palace directors are negotiating with the French government about our occupancy and, in time, purchase. In the circumstances, the French government is being very cooperative. In fact, when I spoke to their representatives this morning, I got the impression they'd be rather happy to have it off their hands.'

'Security?'

'Yes, our safety. Do you know the papal palace?'

'I know of it.'

'Then you'll know it is built like a fortress and safer than the Vatican. We've yet to work out the details. Over time, we'll close the Church's institutions in Rome and replace them with equivalent offices in Avignon.'

Then the clerics sat silently for moments with apparent deep interest, some leaning on their elbows as though expectantly awaiting the next act – which was Sebastiani again.

'Whatever your situation is here, we'd like you to stay in Rome so we can contact you. We need your help. So far, there are no obvious culprits, so maybe you can help us get on the right track.'

'Are we to be interrogated?' came a voice from an upper row.

'Not interrogated, sir. We will interview you individually. What happened has involved many hundreds of persons in many ways. There are many people to interview, material to analyze. We'll speak with each of you in turn over the next few days or weeks. As soon as possible.'

'That won't do. I have appointments in other countries.'

'Then cancel them. We need you here. I'm sure everyone will understand.' Sebastiani let that sink in as a general command.

He focused his eyes on those of Archbishop Collineau. 'I take it *Eminenza*, you'll be discussing the move to France with the Italian government?'

More quickly than Sebastiani thought sensible, Doctor Franchi moved to the front to end the meeting. 'I think that's enough for today. We'll get more out of the personal sessions with you. We'll call you and arrange times that suit us all.'

'I have just one more question before we go,' said Sebastiani. 'What was Cardinal Ricci's role in the pope's ceremony yesterday? Did he have a particular task?'

The clerics looked around at each other and shrugged but gave no answer.

'Did any of you know Cardinal Aldo Ricci personally?'

Pursed lips, raised eyebrows, more shrugs but absolute silence.

Sebastiani thought it odd that no one admitted to knowing Ricci but he didn't press the matter. 'I have a request before we go. Would you please give your names and contact details to this officer. This information is important for us to keep track of who we talk to.'

Franchi beamed his delight around the room as though to indicate that from his standpoint the meeting had been successful and useful to his military. Then he closed the session: '*Eminenze.* Gentlemen'.

Sebastiani and Conti walked out into the hot Via Rusticucci together. Although shaded in the afternoon, the pavement and walls had taken a scorching during the middle part of the day and now radiated the energy gained.

Conti put his hand on Sebastiani's shoulder. 'Fabio, come to my office in Via Nazionale right away.'

'Not possible right now, sir. State police have got the bodies of three of the Milan bomb suspects. Ferri's with them now. I'm on my way.'

'Who killed them? Carabinieri?'

'Don't know yet.'

'A breakthrough, Colonel?'

'We'll see.'

'Tell me about it this evening. Eight o'clock in my office in town. Bring Ferri with you.' He whacked his left hand with the white gloves he carried in his right hand and waited for his driver to open the car door.

Ferri led the way to the crime scene, a walled enclosure for large rubbish containers now cordoned off by red and white tape. Forensics personnel in white overalls searched, collected and marked.

'Looks like an execution.'

Sebastiani grunted his disbelief at this hypothesis. 'Three bodies. Where's the fourth? Went his own way, obviously.'

'No, sir. He was here. Forensics found blood from a fourth person.' He pointed to a chalk-encircled dark patch. 'There.'

'Umm.'

'Also, organic peroxide explosives in sports bags. The bomb squad took them away.'

The bodies lay face downwards, positioned side by side with hands bound behind them. Ferri pulled up the bloodied T-shirt of one corpse with his latex-gloved hand to show the horrific cuts covering its torso. 'They were also tasered. Look.' He half-turned a body, exposing marks on the chest. 'Gagged and tortured. Hands smashed, arms broken. Eyes gouged. A single stab into the heart from the back, all three the same. Something odd though. The blade was pushed in slowly and then twisted. Not a hard thrust.'

'Forensics said that?'

'Yes. Identical wounds. The same dagger killed all three. And the torture was brutal.'

'If they were being attacked why didn't they blow themselves up?'

'Could be they knew their killers.'

'Oh, come on,' said Sebastiani, his tone incredulous.

'A religious execution?'

Sebastiani scowled and shook his head. 'Religious execution? For goodness sake, Ferri. I don't think so.'

'Some Islamic groups wouldn't agree with what these guys were doing.'

'Oh that. Forget the Muslim connection. Someone in our organization has fingered them. They didn't duck surveillance at all. They've been killed by someone with friends in the military.'

Ferri's obviously disbelieving silence made Sebastiani wonder if he was speaking with less than good sense. 'TOD?'

'Corpses are about a day old. TOD early yesterday morning, somewhere between six and seven. Found today by corporation rubbish collectors.'

'Killed early yesterday. Before they could get to the celebrations to do their bombing. They've been murdered before they could stop the big show. Why would they leave their hotels so early? Not many people on the street to bomb at that time.'

'That's anybody's guess. To prepare at a buddy's house, maybe? Pray somewhere? Who knows?'

'And the bodies were here a whole day before they were found.'

Ferri laughed. 'People round here don't have rubbish.'

'Are our men calling on the neighbours?'

'No. State police are doing the rounds.'

'Fine. That'll do.' He dropped his head backward and closed his tired eyes. 'Why?'

'Sir?'

'For me, no question. They were killed to stop them bombing. But why? Whoever killed them had good reason and I think it was to do with the attack on the Vatican. Good intelligence. Military intelligence. That's how they were tracked and killed.'

'We shouldn't rule out Islamic vigilantes.'

'Fine but I don't think they did this.' Sebastiani crouched by the bodies. 'What's this?' He pointed to a small, blood-smeared card nailed to the back of one of the corpses, apparently as a casual afterthought. 'What does it say?'

'Righteous Sword.'

'Righteous Sword?' He stood and contemplatively rubbed his forehead with the back of his hand. 'Gladio.'

'Government sponsored subversion groups. All NATO countries had them. Not anymore though.'

These words unsettled Sebastiani and while Ferri looked down at the corpses he looked at him thinking he had a belief in people and organizations where he should be mistrusting them. Could this be a weakness? 'Do you believe that? Gladio. I'm not sure.'

'Ended by international agreement. Our *Propaganda Due* with it.'

'Right.' Sebastiani crouched on his haunches to study the three corpses, occasionally half-turning his head to throw questions. '*Propaganda Due*. P2 rebirth? Heard anything?'

'No.'

'Sons of P2? A Gladio attack. What d'you think?'

'The attack on Rome or the attack on these men?'

'Both. Yes, both. Gladio killed like this. Look at the hands.' Sebastiani flicked the binds with the tip of his finger. 'Plastic arresting loops. Police issue.'

'All state security groups have them.'

'Yes, Major,' he said ponderously while getting to his feet. 'Bomber number four. Do you have his ID?'

Ferri dug out a slip of paper from his pocket and read the name. 'Hasan Muhammad Al-Qali.'

'How the hell did he escape this? Or was he supposed to? Perhaps he didn't. He could be suffering a worse fate than his friends.'

'He'll turn up some time.'

'Maybe. We live in hope. How long you going to be here?'

'I don't know. A couple of hours yet. Until forensics have nothing new to give me, then I'll get some sleep at the barracks.'

'You had better be quick. Conti wants us both in his town office at eight this evening.'

'Oh, Christ.'

'One moment.' Sebastiani stood back and looked down at the three bodies. 'Listen, we can't exclude anyone from this. The bombing or these murders. If the Mafia's involved, you and I had better watch our backs. Right?'

'I realize that.'

Conti's out-of-barracks office, a suite of large, high-ceilinged rooms, one of them a conference room for seating fifty people, was his favourite place of work. It was his sanctuary: a place to which he could officially retreat from his lesser facilities at the barracks where the daily hurly-burly of military activities could be a distraction. His grand office and the secretarial and technical staff that breezed about in subdued and polite efficiency lent to his high station as chief of national anti-terrorism. It was his powerhouse for meetings with national and international military and political grandees with any interest in anti-terrorism.

His private office bore the clean, efficient lines of modern design, and boasted a large chandelier, a mid-air explosion of crystal glass shards whose sparkling prism colors he found restful and a useful talking point when official conversation faded into banalities.

Sebastiani had attended many meetings in the conference room but today Conti led him directly into his inner sanctum for the first time. He was indeed taken by the remarkable chandelier, though he feigned not to notice it.

'Fabio. Good to see you. Take a seat.'

'*Buongiorno*, Sir.'

When Sebastiani removed his cap Conti drew in a whistled breath at the sight of the antiseptic patch on his head. 'Does that hurt?'

'No sir,' he lied.

'You'll heal with sleep. I guess none of us has had much of that over the last twenty-four hours.'

'Forty-eight hours in my case.'

Conti smiled and changed the subject. 'Day of revelation. The cardinals are off to Avignon and the Milan bombers are dead.'

'Three of them.'

'Right. Three of them. Strange.'

'The card found with the bodies. Do you know about that?'

Conti nodded. 'What about it?'

'Righteous Sword. Could be Gladio, sir. P2 revival? If so, it's conceivable P2 attacked Rome.'

'Christ alive, Fabio! No. The card was obviously intended to distract. What are you thinking? Clandestine military operation against the Vatican? What purpose?'

'To cause tension in the masses? To stop Boniface doing something we don't know about? Was he soft on communism?'

'Out of the question. Deep state agencies were disbanded. You know that.'

'I know.' Sebastiani's tone lacked conviction. 'There's always the younger generation of the extreme right.' Realizing the dangerous direction he had taken, he backed off. 'It was an obvious question and I'll keep an open mind on it, sir.' Which meant – as Conti had inferred – that he would assign an experienced hand to investigate it.

'You know, Fabio, about a year ago, a retired ex-colleague of mine told me a funny thing. He was convinced the old extreme right of Italy was on the rise again. I told him he was a fool. But you never know. I read recently the Catholic Church's influence on Italy's economy is a contributing factor to its decline. Not doing my investments much good. Not a reason to destroy it, though. What have you got so far?'

'The Milan bombers,' said Sebastiani.

'Yes? What about them?'

'What if I told you our own men had a hand in their murder?'

'What the hell are you talking about? My God, man, you're testing the boundaries, today.'

'It's obvious to me that they were tracked and taken out. Our surveillance team lost them and you know how. I need to know that too.'

'Can't tell you yet. Let it be for the time being. I have reasons for secrecy here.'

'I have to know how they were traced by killers and the only explanation I see is someone internal passed on information about their movements.'

'Trust me on this one. When I can, I'll let you know.'

'If you say.'

'I do. What else have we got?'

'The bomb squad report.'

'Yes. The bomb squad report.' Conti picked up his copy and opened it at a marked place. 'Page 3, item 18. The Vatican roof. Is that what you're going to tell me about?'

Sebastiani swallowed several times to ease the soreness in his throat that his screaming and hollering of orders during yesterday's holocaust had caused. 'Yes. I was convinced this was not an Islamic terror raid because of the roof bombings. The roof entrances were reported sealed and guarded.'

'And they were not, Sebastiani. They were certainly not sealed and guarded.'

'That leaves it wide open. It's a screw-up.'

'Screw-up! Screw-up, my ass. It's a fuck-up, that's what it is. Who's responsible for that?'

'I've arrested the officer responsible. I suppose he will argue that by not being at his place of duty, he saved his life and those of his men.'

'You know better than to say that.'

'Just sarcasm, sir.'

A silence prevailed as Conti walked to the window while scanning the report. 'Damn. That's dreadful.' He half-closed his eyes and peered at Sebastiani. Then he shouted across the room. 'Where the hell is Ferri?'

'I sent him for information. He'll be here shortly.'

On cue, he entered, cap under his arm and a bunch of papers in his hand.

'Good,' said Conti, returning to his seat. 'Some things I want to know. Then you can push off and get some sleep. First, what's organized?'

Sebastiani sat forward and cleared his throat, which was beginning to fail him. 'The whole country, military and state police forces are on high alert and investigating locally. Our embassies and spies around the world are making contact but nothing yet. On top of that, the prime minister has asked friendly foreign governments for assistance. The major has already checked friendly intelligence agencies.'

'They've started investigating,' said Ferri. 'I've organized a team of specialists to coordinate their input.'

'Good to know your world network is buzzing,' said Conti. 'Foreign governments tell us their police forces are investigating locally.' He looked at the chandelier, pouted and patted his chin.

'Curiously, not all those governments you would expect.' He dug a finger into his cheek, thought silently for moments and then asked, 'Local resources, Colonel. Do you have all you need?'

'I've got three hundred anti-terrorism specialists in Rome linked into the national setup. Their normal anti-terrorist work dovetails with this investigation. But I've assigned one hundred of them specifically to this crime. Extra detectives from Milan and Naples will assist in interrogation of witnesses, investigation and analysis.'

'Is it enough?'

'Yes.'

'Do you agree, Major?' he said startlingly loudly.

'I do, sir. Also, we've put out a TV item with phone numbers that the public can call if they have information.'

Conti nestled his elbows on the cushioned arms of his easy chair and spoke above his knitted fingers. 'I have the go-ahead from the Minister of Defence to pull in whatever and whoever I want. You must tell me what you need, Colonel. Got that?'

'Understood, sir.'

'I have a question. What sort of organization could attack Rome in this way?'

Ferri answered. 'Well, a relatively small group of trusted people working over a long time. Two, three people. Four maximum. If they were suicide bombers the only trust needed is that they carry out their mission. But this was not a suicide mission.'

'A fact that seems to exclude Islamic militants. Go on.'

'A group would need to be a trusted circle of silence. Friends, family.'

'We can't rule out al-Qaeda.'

'Not totally, but no suicide bombers were found. A lot of explosives were used so time was needed to set it up.'

'Yes.' Conti sighed and frowned. 'Gentlemen, I hope to God al-Qaeda had nothing to do with this. What would that mean in the current climate? Another fucking war? It's all getting a bit world-threatening.' He raised surrendering hands to quit his theme. 'Just private thoughts. Anything else, Colonel?'

'Early responses from European anti-terror organizations all say the same thing. No expected direct attack on the Vatican. No information about suspects.'

'And what do the CIA say?'

Sebastiani turned to Ferri. 'You've read their report.'

'It's not helpful. They say al-Qaeda but they're under pressure from their own government to provide quick answers. In the US at the moment, al-Qaeda is blamed for any attack on the West, especially by their Department of Defense, regardless.'

This news stirred Conti in his seat. 'Did your contacts at the CIA say that?'

'Yes sir.'

'Don't repeat that outside this office. What other possibilities do you see?'

'Could be an internal Italian conspiracy to hit the government. The economy's nose-diving. That stirs up the extremists.'

Conti raised the palm of his hand to Ferri. 'We had that before you came in. But we have to keep open minds on the possibility.'

Overcoming his lassitude with a sigh, Sebastiani said, 'And then there's the Church itself.'

'A conspiracy within the Catholic Church?'

'Why not?' He held his neck and swallowed. 'Seizure of power. Remove the papacy from Rome. It's happened before. Way back, I'll admit. We'll need special expertise to chase this out.'

Conti got up strode across the room and shouted back over his shoulder. 'That possibility had occurred to me, too.' He opened the door and called into the adjoining room, 'Luisa, please come in.'

In the manner of an old-time gentleman, he guided a woman radiating a lustrous smile across the burnished floor. She was thirtyish, dark-haired, lithe and very attractive. She wore tight, distressed, light-blue jeans with rough-edged gashes across the thighs with tanned flesh showing through. Sebastiani struggled to look at her face against the pull of the sexy fashion decoration while Ferri mentally undressed her.

'Gentlemen, allow me to introduce Doctor Luisa Fabian. I've convinced her bosses at the Rome Institute of Religious History that we need her knowledge to advise us on matters to do with the Vatican and the Roman Catholic Church. She will work closely with you Fabio on such matters. I've worked with her before and I can assure you she is very good.'

She shook their hands confidently.

In prejudiced minds, women involved in religious history were of the long skirt and baggy blouse variety. Thinking about how things had changed and how young she looked suddenly made Sebastiani feel old. But Conti had said 'doctor'. Given that and her workplace at the university, he took her to be a professor and an intellectual. Grim, matter of fact and throaty, he said, 'I look forward to working with you, Doctor Fabian.'

She responded keenly. 'You'll have to explain everything you want me to do.'

He recognized the southern Italian accent but it was light and interesting, not the gruff voice common to women of Rome.

'Well, first thoughts.' His mind played with the patches of tanned thigh, which he could sense down there and close by. 'You'll be our guide to all things religious. The Vatican. The Roman Catholic Church. Right?'

'That's what I understand.' She drew together the very slightest strain on her face as she added, 'We can discuss the details.'

'Yes, we should get together in our ops room.' He rubbed at the crease just above his nose while turning to Ferri. 'Have you set up an ops room?'

'Being set up in the Vatican as we speak. *Stanza dei Segreti*.'

'Chamber of secrets? What's that? I take it you know the *Stanza dei Segreti*, Doctor Fabian.'

'Of course I do.'

Her smile was generous and affected Sebastiani in ways he had almost forgotten.

CHAPTER THREE

The siren from the car chauffeuring Sebastiani to the Vatican opened a way through the mass of mourners and the barrier at the main entrance to St Peter's Square. On the far side of the square, the noise and bustle of rescue work produced muffled echoes through St Peter's still-standing portico. In the square itself, small clusters of exhausted and bloodied medical personnel worked intensely on the recently uncovered victims while the occasional Red Cross van raced in, unloaded a variety of plastic and cardboard boxes, loaded up with emptied ones and raced out again.

Media hounds, bedraggled after a night at the site, lounged about chatting among themselves, smoking and drinking coffee. State police looked on as the City's cleansing department scooped up the debris from the frantic rescue activities of the last thirty hours.

Others just stood and stared earnestly at the wrecked Basilica with fading expectations of any more souls being extracted alive.

'*Caso*, same place in two hours.' This was Sebastiani's signal to his long-serving driver that he could fill the time in between how he wanted.

Ferri saluted. '*Buona sera,* sir.'

Sebastiani gave no greeting in reply but glanced across at the tragic scene and stood for a while listening to a group in the crowds singing a mournful hymn, which only served to reinforce the memory of his brush with death in the cataclysm.

He popped a throat pastille into his mouth and then turned to Ferri. 'Milan bombers. What's going on?'

'Their bombs would not have exploded, sir.'

'Their killers wouldn't have known that so they weren't given the chance to try.'

'Right. They stayed at hotels just behind the Vatican. Not far from where their bodies were found.'

'Their killers knew where they were staying.' And this confirmed – in his mind, at least – that expert surveillance tracked the Muslims all the way from Milan to their beds in Rome. 'Of course they did.'

Sebastiani stood for several minutes watching the mourners and the rescuers. 'Those poor, poor people,' he said quietly.

Ferri smiled sympathetically and nodded.

'And the hotels?' said Sebastiani, picking up on the topic again.

'Because of the hoo-ha about the bombing, the hotels contacted state police.'

'That's good of them. They don't usually bother.'

'The men had paid their bills and left without taking their possessions. Some clothes and passports.'

'They didn't intend going back. Our men there?'

'Yes, sir.'

'The fourth bomber?'

'Still nothing.'

'Sod it,' Sebastiani growled and looked around expectantly. 'Okay, where is it?'

'The ops room? This way, sir.'

Ferri led the way to the Vatican's mysterious *Stanza dei Segreti* but his boss set the fast pace.

'What else you got?' asked Sebastiani.

'Five suspects arrested here in Rome. Couple in Naples. All native Algerian Muslims. Arrested within the last two hours. No details. News from UK. Two al-Qaeda suspects skipped their net, believed to be in Rome or on the way here. So far, no contact with those. European countries all on high alert. Details later.'

56

Always on the ball. Typical of Ferri, thought Sebastiani. He wondered if he thought about anything other than chasing terror. 'Good. Ricci. Anything new?'

'Nothing, sir.'

'Listen, Major. It's very important I speak to Professor Fabian.' The thought of her raised an image of tanned thigh peeking through her jeans.

'She's in the ops room. I saw her earlier.'

They walked through large oak doors carved with the Stations of the Cross, and through Renaissance-decorated long, arched corridors that led into a magnificent room with high, vaulted ceilings painted with scenes from the Garden of Eden. Today, the peace of paradise echoed with the vibrant and noisy activity of *carabinieri* setting up the room for anti-terrorism activities.

Sebastiani raised a chuckle above his ire. 'So this is the Chamber of Secrets.'

'Yes. Enough room for the whole anti-terror department. We've got a lot of work to do at the Vatican so this is perfect. The computers are already connected into our main system.'

'System security?'

'Checked out by IT.'

'Physical security?'

'Twenty-four-hour guard already posted. Most of the people we need to interview first are in this very building.'

'Excellent. Where's Doctor Fabian?'

'She's in the room somewhere, studying the paintings.'

'Get her here right away.'

Sebastiani noticed that he pressed just one button to call and considered this was more than just professionalism.

'On her way, sir.'

Sebastiani saw her approaching. 'Right. We're pretty well set up. Good. Except for those actively monitoring communications at the Intelligence Centre, get everyone to the ops room for nine-thirty tomorrow morning. Briefing. Whole team. Confirm all roles filled. No vacations, no sicknesses. Do it right away.'

Luisa smiled and waved at the departing Ferri as she addressed Sebastiani. 'Hello, Colonel.'

'*Buongiorno*, Doctor Fabian.'

She heaved a sigh and looked around the room. 'Isn't this amazing?'

'It's certainly the most opulent ops room I've ever seen.'

'It's the only stanza Raphael Sansio painted on the ground floor. Do you know his work?'

'No, I don't.' His manner and tone closed the cultural excursion. 'I need your professional help. Do you have fifteen minutes?'

'Certainly. I'm working for you now.'

'Have you signed a confidential agreement?'

'Yes, I have. All that we talk about will be forever secret.'

He placed two chairs to face each other then held the back of her chair until she had sat before taking the one opposite.

'I was thinking about how you will work with us. For me and for most of my team, the Vatican is complex. What I had in mind was that you would help us in dealing with the Vatican's offices and people. Smooth our way.'

'That's what I understood from General Conti.'

'I want you to extend that role.'

'Okay. Just tell me what to do.'

He pulled his feet back under his chair and dropped his hands down between his thighs. Realising this made it look as though he was studying her knees he thrust his head and shoulders back. 'I… It seems clear to me… Damn. How can I best explain?' He drew the tips of his fingers over his eyes and down his cheeks.

His hesitation compelled her to kick-start his thoughts. 'It's about the bombing, yes?'

'You know, it was far too big. Bombing a bridge and killing the pope would have made a serious enough point. Why did they explode the Basilica too?'

She nodded attentively, grasped the sides of her chair and pushed herself a fraction forward on stiffened arms, which stirred

58

him inside. He looked at her face, her hair, to her right, to her left, to his troops across the room – everywhere but at her bosom, where his mind was.

'Did the bombers need to go so far? Do so much damage?' he asked.

'Depends on what they wanted to achieve. I've been thinking about the attack. My God, hasn't everyone? I can think of a few reasons why someone might want to attack the Catholic Church so badly. Some political, some religious.'

'Go on.'

'Well, the obvious one, to destroy the worldwide Roman Catholic Church. That would be stupid. Only mindless idiots would believe they could do that.'

'This was not done by mindless idiots so destroying the Church was not what the bombers intended.'

'No. I don't think so.'

'What would be a more likely reason?'

'To remove the Church from Italy. To establish the papacy somewhere else.'

'Both of these?'

She grinned and touched his arm. 'One goes with the other, Colonel.'

He dropped his head and drew his fingers along his eyebrows. 'Of course.'

'Dethroning popes has been done before. And the papal seat has not always been in Rome. It was in Avignon for a time.'

'A-ha!' In Sebastiani's mind, the lofty Archbishop Collineau raised himself up to full height. 'An attempted coup from within the Church. Could that be a reason?'

'Certainly. Been done before.'

'Tell me about it.'

'It was a bloodless coup. And it got rid of Pope Boniface the eighth.'

'Is that relevant to our crime?'

'You know, Colonel, I've made a discovery that really surprised me. The new Pope Boniface who was killed in the attack, Boniface the tenth. Last night I went through his biography and family history. He was a Gaetani. Emilio Gaetano.'

'What about it?'

'It's absolutely amazing. Same family as Boniface the eighth. Probably the reason he took the name Boniface as pope. Both from the same family. No pope has been forcibly dethroned and killed violently since Boniface the eighth. And now a modern member of that same family suffers a similar fate.'

'So?'

'I think you're trying not to see. The only other pope to be forcibly dethroned since then is also a Gaetani. Boniface back then made enemies in a big way so it might be that grudges still hold. A vendetta against the Gaetani. Otherwise the family connection would just be a remarkable coincidence. I don't believe it is just a coincidence.'

'Wait a minute. How long ago was Boniface the eighth killed?'

'Seven hundred years ago.'

'Oh, my God.' Sebastiani looked to the heavens. 'I think we can forget about that, don't you?'

Clenching her fists, she fixed her wide eyes on his. 'Absolutely not!'

'That's a devil of a long time. I would need some convincing.'

'I know the history. Let me explain.'

'I don't have the time for long explanations. I'm under pressure.'

'But I believe it's worth the time to tell.'

'How long?'

'Ten minutes.'

'Just ten minutes.' He looked at his watch.

'Colonel, in my work I look for historical events that tie with later ones. There are lots and some of them spread over centuries. If I find nothing, at least I have closed off possibilities. The Boniface case is special and astounding. I'd done the work on the Gaetani a few years ago, never expecting this would turn up.'

'Well, I'm listening.'

She sat again, crossed her legs and grasped her knee with both hands. 'Believe me, Boniface the eighth, Benedetto Gaetano, made lots of very serious, very powerful enemies.'

Anagni, 6 September, 1303

The troubled Pope Boniface VIII ambled out of his office chamber and onto the balcony. Looking west he could see the misty purple of the rolling Albani hills in the distance. Beyond them, dark clouds spread heavenly rays as the sun dipped out of sight after burning the day. A pleasantly cool, lively wind came from the sea.

Peering down into the palace courtyard he studied the animated exchanges between the stooping Cardinal Frederico Bocchini and a soldier seated astride a breathless, steaming horse. The old man's hasty withdrawal from the discussion increased the strain on Boniface's nerves. He returned to his private chamber anticipating the news would confirm what he already sensed: that an adversary was drawing near. The accursed Colonnas were closing in to unseat the Pope of Rome.

Bocchini entered the pope's chamber and scurried over its stone-slab floor as best he could, given the deformity of his back, the result of a spinal disease contracted when he was young. With his sunken, scrawny face transformed by the half-light of the chamber into a skull and the frantic movements of his grotesque body, he looked like raging death scampering to avoid the grave.

'*Vostra Santità! Vostra Santità!* Sciarra Colonna's army is near,' he cried. 'He will kill you. You must leave Anagni right away.' Dropping his head respectfully, he breathlessly grasped the pope's arm.

'Frederico. Please, please calm yourself.' Benedetto Gaetano took Bocchini's hand in his two and held it solicitously.

61

Both men were sixty-eight years old but life had been much kinder to the Pope, a relatively tall, upright man, with rounded features. His friendly eyes expressed the empathy he felt for Bocchini in his fight to form words through his choking excitement.

'My dear friend, Benedetto. Sciarra Colonna is ruthless. Go to Rome. Go quickly before he gets here.'

From 1260 until 1264, Bocchini and Benedetto Gaetano had pursued their doctorates in canon and civil law together. Although Gaetano's exceptional talents had granted him more prominent positions within the Roman Catholic Church, their oft-crossing paths had enabled them to maintain their strong friendship.

Immediately following his consecration and coronation in Rome as Pope Boniface VIII, he set about undoing the mistakes of his incompetent predecessor, Pope Celestine V. Celestine, an erstwhile hermit, had no understanding of the complicated laws and devious politics of the Roman Catholic Church and resolved difficulties by handing out privileges and favors to agitating cardinals, bishops, kings and princes. In righting these wrongs, Boniface had made bitter enemies.

'Now tell me, Frederico. What is all this about Colonna? Why should I leave Anagni?'

'Sciarra Colonna.' Pressing a hand against his chest he wheezed and mutely raised the other hand to bid for patience while he recovered. 'They accuse you of killing Pope Celestine.'

Boniface stood motionless, staring down at Bocchini's contorted face. With an air of unconcern, he said, 'That is not true.'

'He died after release from your prison.'

'That is immaterial.'

'They're after your blood. Go to Rome.'

'I'm staying right here.' The pope's demeanour swayed between aloof arrogance and hurt indignation. 'I see no reason to flee.'

'Sciarra's a killer.'

'He has that reputation.' The pope turned his stern, pensive face to the grey clouds darkening the hills visible out beyond the balcony. 'Isn't it incredible? These people who want me dead. My one-time loyal supporters. For goodness' sake, the Colonnas were members of the Council of Cardinals. They approved the abdication of Celestine and supported my decision to retrieve the privileges he gave out. Until they went bad. Now they use these things as evidence against me. Once, they were humble men of God. They supported me then. Now they're after my blood?'

'Don't let him kill you.'

'Sciarra is not here about Celestine at all. No. It's vengeance. I punished the Colonnas for their rebellion against the Church and against papal authority. I tell you, the whole family is execrable. It's nothing more than vengeance.'

Boniface shut his eyes and faced upwards as if to strain spiritual essence out of heaven. 'Mother Mary, I plead for your spirit to guide me in righteousness and to give me courage.' He gazed out toward the gathering storm. 'Cardinal Jacopo Colonna and his brothers used their power in the Church to steal property and positions unlawfully. I took it all away and I excommunicated them. They have cause to hate me.'

The old cripple shrugged sympathetically. 'Belligerent and evil men. We know that. Discussing their evils won't save you.'

'Frederico, I am old and likely to leave this world soon anyway. It worries me not what Colonna will do to me. Anagni is my birthplace and it is fitting that I die here if I must. More than my life, I am concerned for the Church. Philip plans to unite the Christian Church under him as King of France with the pope under his authority. You see, it's the Church I worry about.'

'Philip is arrogant.'

'I have excommunicated him. Deprived him of throne and crown. I demand adherence to the laws of the Church from kings and priests alike. No earthly man is above the Vicar of Christ. Kings once served me openly, with crowns on their heads, accepted my authority and declared to defend the Church against its enemies. Philip seeks to change that.'

The room became gloomy as dark clouds covered Anagni. Blinding flashes of lightning and loud crashes of thunder shook both men to silence. Heavy rain pounded the palace with deafening ferocity. The sudden storm hurtled its full might at Anagni.

Boniface shouted above the noise. 'That's God's power, Frederico. Power that both thrills me and fills me with fear. God is on my side. I'm under trial. I must stand firm for the sake of the Church.'

'*Vostra Santità*, for the sake of the church, you should leave.' His pleading eyes glistened with tears as he took hold of the pope's hand and kissed the ring upon it. 'We can't fight Sciarra. Go to Rome. You could be there in half a day.'

'Tell the guards at the city gates to resist Colonna's entry. Boniface wrapped an arm around his friend's hunched shoulders and walked him to the door. His voice quickened. 'Inform the cardinals what's happening. I'm staying in the palace. Frederico, I'm the fourth pope from this kind city and I am not going to be the first to abandon her. This is the Gaetani Palace, the home of my family. Besides, Rome is full of filth and epidemics. I am safer here in Anagni.'

Ops room, Rome, today

When Luisa's historical journey came to a natural pause, Sebastiani checked his watch. 'So, after just ten minutes we've got hot suspects. The Colonnas were nasty people. Now what do we do?'

'I realize we need to be careful. Not jump to conclusions.'

'Not do rash things. Like hauling in all of Italy's Colonnas and interrogating them. And all others whose ancestors hated Boniface.'

'Your irony's understandable. But in my research I've unearthed many long-standing vendettas. They're not so unusual. One thing I should tell you. Boniface retook vast amounts of land and property from them. That hurt the family. It's documented in Vatican archives.'

'The power of popes. Greater than kings. I had forgotten.'

'And don't forget, he excommunicated them. That meant he was denying them their heavenly hopes. Very serious matter at that time.'

'At that time.' He waggled a finger at the side of his 'got-you' face.

She paused and tightened her lips, making him believe he had indeed 'got' her.

'In the Roman Catholic Church it's still a serious matter,' she insisted.

'The excommunication. Is that also documented in Vatican archives?'

'Yes, Colonel. I told you, I researched the material a few years ago. But I still have my notes about it.'

Sebastiani pressed the palms of his hands together against his mouth so his middle fingers held the end of his nose and fell silent for moments staring at the floor. Then he said, 'Let me tell you what I think about this now.' He suddenly started thinking again about her beauty, about his older age compared with hers. Distracted, he lost his thread, umm-ed and ahh-ed and then, covering his eyes with his hands, retrieved it. 'If what you say is true, and I take your word for it, I accept that Boniface made serious enemies. As far as I can see, more than just the Colonna family. Right?'

'Yes, that's right.'

'Now, I have some problems. We, the Carabinieri, believe the attack on Rome was set up over a few years. For it to be aimed at Emilio Gaetano specifically, the attackers must have known before bombs were placed that Gaetano would become pope. What do you say to that?'

'True. But, you know, like Pope John Paul II, it was known for at least three years that the only likely successor to the throne, if he lived or didn't go mad, was Cardinal Emilio Gaetano. It was pretty much a certainty.'

'So, assuming this hypothesis is true, this was the exact moment in history the Colonnas had been waiting for.'

65

'Yes. I guess so.'

'Another question. If it was a vendetta against the Gaetani family, why didn't the attackers just kill Boniface? Why blow up the Vatican? Why kill so many?'

'It wouldn't be the first time in history an act of revenge has been far greater than the offence causing it.'

'True. But I don't know. I accept the family connection. The Boniface just killed being related to your earlier Boniface. That's remarkable, I agree, not just coincidence.' He felt himself being drawn into the story and liking it. 'And it is conceivable that members of the Colonna family are still around, still seething with anger over their treatment by Boniface. But to blow up the Vatican like that, these people would need not just hate but great power, influence in high places and vast amounts of money.'

'Yes, they would need all those things. There are thousands of disgustingly rich and loathsome people in the world with influence.'

'I know.' But then he wondered what he should do with this information. It seemed fanciful but had a ring of truth about it. 'Where do we go from here?'

'There's more. Let me finish. It might shed light.'

Enthusiastically, he said, 'Okay. Five minutes. Let's see what we get.'

Anagni, 7 September, 1303

As the sun burned off the last of the early morning mist from the fields around the tiny city of Anagni, a heavily armed corps of over a thousand mercenaries on horse and foot clattered its way to the city to arrest a heretic pope on behalf of Philip, the King of France. Coached by his *conseiler* Guillaume de Nogaret, Philip had fabricated a case against Boniface and ordered him to be brought to France to face trial.

But their leader, Sciarra Colonna, pursued a personal vengeance against the pope that had subjected his family to war, purgatory and humiliation, and dispersed its members to France and Sicily.

Sciarra led his column of troops up to the city gate. There, he stood tall in his stirrups and turned to face his men. His large proportions and rugged, hairy appearance commanded respect and attention. Raising his sword in the air he shouted, 'Long live the King of France! Long live the Colonnas!'

He bared his big teeth in an insane grin as his mercenaries cheered and clattered their swords and lances. The frightened horses under them neighed and bucked.

'In the name of righteousness and the King of France, open the gate! Open the gate!' he shouted.

From above the gate, a man's voice bellowed, 'We friends of France welcome you.' With no struggle the invaders took possession of the city.

Colonna leapt from his horse and slapped its hide. '*Monsieur* Nogaret, I want this ended as soon as possible. I want his head on a stake.'

A door on the south side of the palace council chamber opened with a creak that filled the capacious room. Jose Maria Lopez, the Spanish Cardinal of Santa Sabina, walked briskly up to the pope and bowed his head. '*Vostra Santità*, we've been attacked. A large army of mercenaries has entered Anagni.'

'Well, we knew they were coming. Are they being resisted? I hear no fighting.'

'There is no fighting. Our citizens have let them into the town. Your accuser, Guillaume de Nogaret, has delivered this document. It has King Philip's seal. It accuses you of terrible crimes.'

'Oh. What crimes?'

Lopez flushed, knowing the charges could not possibly be true. 'I'm so sorry.'

'Don't concern yourself, Jose. Just read what you see.'

As he read the charges, he shook his head sombrely. 'Gaining office illegally by deposing a legitimate pope in office, heresy, moral perversion and idolatry.'

Boniface responded dispassionately. 'Is that it?'

'No. It also demands you cancel your papal bulls against the Colonna family, restore its members to the Church and abdicate immediately from the papacy. Then you are to surrender to Sciarra Colonna.'

Boniface studied the anxiety in Lopez's face. 'You know I won't give in to evil.'

'If I don't return an answer by midday, they will attack the palace. They will kill you.'

'I am the spiritual head of mankind, answerable only to God. Not to any man. I'll not sully the sublime position of the papacy by releasing this evil family from excommunication. I will not return an answer.'

'Then we should prepare for an attack. We don't have much time.'

These words animated Boniface. 'Quickly. Discharge the servants. Gather all priests to the throne room. I'll join you there shortly.'

Darkness filled his heart. Proud Boniface, long imbued with the greatness of his familial papal predecessors, sensed the imminent end of his reign and the Gaetani line of popes.

Pope Boniface, in full pontifical vestments, entered the throne room to find only Cardinal Lopez waiting.

'Where are the others?'

'They've fled. Colonna has killed Frederico.'

A violent commotion filled the building and suddenly the huge doors burst open. Carrying his pastoral staff in his right hand, and the keys of St Peter in his left hand, Boniface slowly mounted the steps and sat on the throne as a gang of Colonna's men crashed into the room. On seeing the grandeur of the pope enthroned, their turbulence turned to silence and they knelt down and bowed their heads.

'Get up! Get up!' Sciarra screamed. 'What are you doing?' He stormed up to the throne and made as though to thrust his sword into Boniface's neck but held it a hair's breadth from his flesh. Spluttering as he ground his words into the pope's face he shouted, 'Benedetto Gaetano is filth.' In the silence that filled the throne room, everyone could hear Sciarra's vicious, grating undertone. 'Renounce the papacy now or I'll kill you.'

As he raised his sword to strike, the pope stood, raised his arms and head to heaven and prayed. Then he smiled triumphantly, chest heaving rapidly. 'Go ahead. Cut off my head. I have been betrayed like Christ. I am ready to die as his pope.'

Sciarra sneered. 'I'm going to kill you right now because you are evil. You persecuted and robbed my family. I curse you and your family for eternity. My king, Philip of France, has judged you. You are full of sin.'

He grabbed Boniface, thrust him to the stone floor and beat his face until he bled. He raised his sword again as Guillaume de Nogaret entered the room.

'Sciarra. No, no.' Nogaret strode to him shaking his head. 'We must take him to France. There he will be tried, found guilty and die.'

'Yes, he will die soon enough.' He turned to his men, 'Disrobe this vermin and parade him before his own people. Then throw him into the dungeon.'

They stripped Boniface of his papal vestments, dragged him out onto the streets, lifted him onto a horse to face its tail and paraded him through the town. In the dungeon of his plundered palace, Boniface suffered three days without cover and food. The town's people rose up against the invaders and ousted them from Anagni. They returned Boniface to Rome to be cared for but he died within a month.

Ops room, Rome, today

'Two important things here, Colonel. In the Colonna case, excommunication was never rescinded. It still holds.'

'Yes, I know. It's in the Vatican archives.'

'Yes,' she replied, with a tinge of exasperation.

'The other important thing?'

'The curse. Sciarra Colonna cursed Boniface and his family for eternity. A serious matter. If the curse were to be fulfilled, as was expected and believed, the Gaetani family would always suffer in some way.'

'And the Colonna offspring would do their damnedest to make sure of it. Umm.' He turned sightlessly to the activities of his men while drumming his lips with a finger.

'Look,' she said, 'the history is as I have told it. Verified by many different sources. But I'm not claiming those events definitely led to the bombing. You realize that already. What I am saying is that it's a reasonable hypothesis and deserves some investigation. Wouldn't you agree?'

'First, answer me this. I can see that, if the Church's excommunication ruling on the Colonnas was never rescinded, the Colonnas might want to destroy the power that made the ruling. The Church itself.'

'I think you're thinking like me.'

'Say your hypothesis is right, how in heaven's name is a feud like this perpetuated?'

Her open hands came up with her shoulders and her lips tightened in a smile. 'Good question. Carved in stone way back when, perhaps.'

Sebastiani showed the first sign that he had taken to her arguments. 'Your account mentioned the Colonnas had been dispersed.'

'You might not find any Colonnas today you could connect to the Colonnas of that time. You're right. The family was dispersed. And names have probably changed. But I could research for modern-day relatives. Just as the Gaetani have a very long and traceable family history, an old and powerful aristocratic family like the Colonnas probably has too. Let me try. If I find something, we examine it. If I don't, nothing's lost.'

'Very well. Nothing ventured, nothing gained. But your research must not cause problems for my investigation. Keep this between you and me. Report anything you find only to me.' Nothing should come to light that might embarrass him, that was his thinking. 'Okay. Let's give it a go.'

'Thank you.'

'What do I call you? Doctor Fabian? Professor Fabian?'

She smiled. 'Call me Luisa.'

'Good. I'm Fabio.' He felt as though he had been pleasantly drawn into a fresh and vibrant personal relationship.

'As beautiful as this place is, Luisa,' he said, for the first time showing any signs of recognizing the Master's work, 'I have to go. My bosses are waiting for my report.' He smiled whimsically and nodded. 'Interesting talk.'

She looked past his shoulder and smiled distantly. Her smile took on meaning when he turned to discover the object of it: the approaching Luca Ferri.

'Hello,' she said.

'Doctor Fabian.' Then turning with military snap to Sebastiani, Ferri said, 'All set up, sir.'

'Right, Major. Then I'll leave you to it. Ops meeting. Tomorrow morning, nine-thirty.'

'Sir, we have a meeting with the Vatican's master builder tomorrow morning at eleven.'

'Handle that alone. Before the meeting I'll be at Fiumicino. Enzo Martino's got something for me. Afterwards, I'll be with Doctor Franchi,' he said, dreading the thought that meeting with Franchi would be the usual waste of time.

'Will do, sir.'

'Better still, have Luisa with you in case you need her expertise to hand.'

71

'Yes sir.'

Before setting off, Sebastiani perused the ops room with an air of satisfaction. 'Yes, beautiful. Incidentally, Luisa, what foreign languages do you have?'

'Fluent French and English, written and spoken. Good Russian. I also have excellent Latin.'

'That should help.'

'I imagine you've called me to this crappy place because no one comes here so no one will hear our secrets. This is dreadful. Why not my club? Or Harry's Bar?'

'Ricardo, you're a snob,' said Sebastiani. 'It's a decent bar with a decent menu and it's near your office.'

Da Corte sneered. 'We all have different tastes, I suppose.'

'And I'm in a hurry. I learned a long time ago that spy lunches take very much longer than anti-terror sandwiches at the bar.'

'Bullshit!'

'Look at you. Those chubby cheeks and growing waistline. You're getting out of shape.'

Da Corte ballooned his cheeks and laughed. 'What this about? Can't be social at this time of day.'

Sebastiani and Ricardo Da Corte had both studied and shared wild times together at Rome University. They also joined Italy's secret service around the same time but Sebastiani moved on to mainline military police work over at the barracks.

Da Corte had made it good in intelligence and, now Rome's head of operations in the *Agenzia Informazioni e Sicurezza Interna*, reported directly to Italy's top internal security boss. His rank was above Sebastiani's and in both his service and private lives Da Corte was on first-name terms with military and political high-ups, a fact to which Sebastiani attributed his consistently polished appearance and upper-crust diction. Da Corte was always in civilian clothes and dapper. Dapper was how he found him for this luncheon meeting.

'I have a daughter,' said Sebastiani.

'A daughter? Well, credit to you, Fabio. You never give up, do you? Who's the lucky mother?'

'Wait a minute. It's not like that at all. It's something strange and I need you to help me with it.'

'Strange? We live in a strange world.'

Sebastiani laughed. 'We agree on something, at least. Anyway, let me tell you this. I got a call from a woman late in the evening on the day of the explosions. Completely out of the blue. She claimed to be my daughter. Very convincing, too. Said she worked for French intelligence. DGSE, in fact.'

'Military external intelligence.'

'Right. And it all made sense because she was on our encrypted line. I checked. The call was from the DGSE office in Paris. The thing is she said she was my daughter and that her mother was Bernadette Bruneau. Do you know the name?'

'Should I?'

'I knew a Bernadette Bruneau at university. You were around then. I'm sure you and yours were with us many times.'

'I don't recall the name.'

'It wasn't so much the names that interested you in those days, as I remember.'

Ricardo frowned. 'Careful, Fabio, careful.'

'Her name is Elaine Bruneau. Maiden name so I suppose she's not married. But you never know. Reckoning dates, I'd say she's about thirty-six.'

'And you're not certain about her. If she's bona fide. Is that it?'

'She's obviously French secret service but why would she make contact with me now? Right after the attack?'

'What's her job?'

'I don't know. She wouldn't tell me anything about her work. She's coming to Rome to see Conti. I asked her why but she wouldn't tell me that either. I suspect she's an agent.'

'Aah. Conti's got his fingers into something with French intelligence I don't know about. Interesting.'

'There's something international going on that I don't know about. I want to know. It seems to be nothing to do with the Rome bombing but I'd still like to know what she's up to.'

'She obviously had tabs on you before we were bombed, but I don't find that extraordinary. What makes you suspect her?'

'Hard to explain. Just a feeling. It seems to come together oddly. For me, at least. Conti is national anti-terror boss. Suddenly he has a catastrophe to handle here in Rome. Then I discover from Elaine Bruneau he was already deep into a serious crime he hasn't told me about. Actually, she said she was looking at a serious crime not connected to the Rome attack. But why would she be seeing Conti about it?'

'From what you say, we don't know what her meeting with Conti is about. But a one-on-one with him means she is high-level. My guess is she is an agent. Could be a director, of course. If she is up to something naughty, I would assume Conti is also.'

'No, Ricardo. I know Conti. I hadn't thought of it like that. She's probably okay. It's just curious and I can't drop it from my mind. But what if she's not clean? A double agent? I don't know.'

'Trying to find who else she might be working for and why would be tricky. Anyway, I take your point: she is probably clean but the timing of this contact is odd.'

'What's behind the Vatican attack that would interest foreign intelligence people? We both know. Plenty of things. And their spies are always active. But her concern for my well-being gave me the impression it was not the Vatican she was interested in.'

Da Corte stared at Sebastiani but remained silent.

Sebastiani asked, 'How are you with the DGSE?'

'I know people.'

'Will you check her out for me?'

Da Corte sat resting on his elbow just staring into Sebastiani's face. At last, he said, 'I will do this for you but only if you promise never to bring me into this dreadful place again.'

CHAPTER FOUR

Sebastiani received the phone call with controlled alarm.

'Who else knows this?' he asked the caller silently.

'Just me, sir.'

'And you routed the message to me. Why did you do that? Who gave you my name?' Had the guardroom *brigadiere* held this deadly information to himself?

'No one, sir. Urgent anti-terror call. Your name's top of the phone list.'

He removed the phone from his ear, stood silent for a moment and then said, 'Tell no one about this. I'm on my way now.'

Within two minutes, Sebastiani popped his head into the duty officer's room and said, 'I'm taking your man. Get a replacement for his watch.'

The abducted soldier looked on quizzically but followed Sebastiani without question to his car.

'Get in. You're with me for the rest of the day.'

'Sir,' he responded, in the manner expected of a long-service, military-wise veteran.

Fearing the ears of spies within his force, Sebastiani said no more until the car had exited the barracks and then only to say 'Don't talk' in case his car was bugged.

'Right, set the address in the sat nav.' His usual driver, Caso, knew Rome so well he had no use for it. But he could not be trusted today.

Twenty minutes later they had reached their destination, the entrance to the Ospedale Santa Lucia. Only after they had got out of the car and closed its doors did Sebastiani talk openly.

'What's your name?'

'Marsella, sir.'

'Okay, Marsella. The doctor who called you. His name?'

'Doctor Vettori, sir.'

'And how did he know his patient was an anti-terror subject?'

'Said he thought the man looked like one of the bombers shown in the newspapers.'

'Bomb suspects.'

'Yes, sir.'

'Did he say what state the patient was in?'

'No sir.'

'Very serious matter, Marsella. Tell no one about it. That's an order. No one.'

'Sir.'

'He's in pretty bad shape.' Doctor Vettori, a short, round man with an earnest face carried metal-rimmed pulpit spectacles on his nose-end. Although the day was hot he wore a pinstripe suit complete with waistcoat, into the tiny pockets of which he stuck his thumbs. He led Sebastiani through a door identified in bold lettering as Intensive Care and into a machined-filled care station where a nurse, sitting on a high stool, turned controls and checked dials.

Hasan Muhammad Al-Qali lay motionless upon a high bed. An array of coloured and transparent tubes connected him to complex medical equipment mounted on trolleys and in racks. Sebastiani studied the heavy bandaging around the head, torso and legs, and the plaster casts enclosing the full length of both arms.

'My God. Will he live?' He braced himself for an explanation of a wound that would rob him of an important witness.

Vettori dipped his head, stared over his glasses, spoke gravely and shook his head. 'I must be honest with you. He's in a very bad state. More than that I cannot say. We'll know more in a day or so.'

Other nurses entered intensive care talking loudly.

'Can we continue this somewhere more private?' asked Sebastiani.

The doctor put a hand lightly on the back of his arm and drew him away from the patient. 'I'll empty the staff room. We can talk there.'

'Thanks.'

'To answer your question. I can't say if he will live. He's in a critical condition.'

'Was he stabbed?'

'No. Why?'

'I can't answer that.'

'No. No stab wounds.'

'I have a desperate need to talk with him. How long…'

Vettori raised both hands against Sebastiani's question. 'I cannot say. He's in coma and there's no way of knowing when he'll come out of it, if at all. His other wounds? If he lives, they'll take a long time to heal.'

The doctor replaced his thumbs into his waistcoat pockets again and proceeded to explain the patient's condition in the manner of a professor. 'He was beaten all over very badly with a heavy object. Hit at least three times on the head. He has hairline fractures in his skull. We've scanned his head and there appears to be no damage to the brain, but it's too early to tell. He's probably still in shock. Broken bones in hands and arms, and several ribs. The ribs and arms are no real problem. They'll mend quite well. I repeat, if he lives. The breaks in the hands are more complicated and will probably require some restructuring. Vettori's expression turned grim. 'He's been badly tortured.'

Just like his brethren, thought Sebastiani.

'Something unusual.' For some reason, whoever did this chose not to damage his face. Would that be because of some religious taboo?'

The question threw him. He had to rethink. Was Ferri right after all? Were Hasan and his friends attacked by Italy-loyal Islamists and not Carabinieri operatives? 'I don't know. What I do know is that he's very important. There are people who would kill him if they knew he was still alive. Has he had visitors?'

'No. He has no identification so we've not been able to inform anyone.'

'How did he get here? Who brought him to the hospital?'

'The police called an ambulance. How they found him I don't know. I imagine they thought as I did at first, he was just another victim of the bombing. But he was found in an alley across from the Vatican museum. I don't know how he got there. You must talk to your colleagues. I'm surprised the police didn't recognize him.'

'I'm not,' snapped Sebastiani. 'How long after his admission did you phone the Carabinieri?'

'About two hours ago. I realized he was the bomber from the newspaper picture. For me the likeness was clear.'

'All I can tell you is he's a police suspect and in danger. Believe me, it would not help him or my investigation if he were to be identified.' Sebastiani lightly drummed the edge of the bed mattress with his fingers. 'He should go to a prison hospital. Can he be transported?'

'If you're certain he must, but you know, like many others in my hospital that have been injured in the Vatican explosions, he's not yet been identified. I'm the only one here who's made the bomber connection. For goodness sake, you saw his bandages. He can stay unidentified until he comes out of the coma. He shouldn't travel.'

'Then he can stay here. As soon as he shows any signs of waking, I need to be informed.'

'No problem. But remember, he's in a bad way.'

Just six hours of rough sleep in the last sixty hours of duty had dulled Sebastiani's eyes and greyed his cheeks. He had difficulty concentrating and expressing thoughts clearly. What's more, the sight of over 1500 coffins lined up neatly inside the huge hangar failed to stir him emotionally. His mind was flat: able to observe, rationalize, and explain – though none of these precisely – but absolutely not able to share in the anguish of the suffering, sobbing relatives. As though emotion had been excised from his being, he watched grieving relatives embrace each other or prostrate themselves over coffins, some mere caskets, and saw it as an act with no depth or meaning. He excused his lack of feeling as tired insensitivity; his conscience would chastise him later.

The coffins, each with attached clipboard, had been arranged into two large groups, to separate those killed at the bridges from those killed in the Basilica.

'What did you say, Enzo? Lost you for a moment.' He studied the clinically garbed specialists quietly opening coffins, pointing into them, and making notes, some with laptop computers recording data. His mind was misty, as though in a dream made eerie by the whispering backdrop of the hangar shell.

'It's okay Fabio. I'll say it again, this time without the face mask. There's a mixture of professionals here. Forensic pathologists like me, but also dentists and anthropologists, and so on. We've even got a couple of DMORT guys who worked at the World Trade Centre. They're very good at process. Led us through a neat way of dealing with the bodies. They're very helpful.'

'Sorry Enzo, what's DMORT?'

'I never remember. Let's see.' Doctor Martino produced a sheet of paper and read it out loud. 'Disaster Mortuary Operational Response Team. What a mouthful. Typical American.'

Martino had a long association with Sebastiani's murder cases. As resident pathologist at the Ospedale Santa Maria in Rome, he was the master of his lab domain, but here, just one of a large team of specialists drafted in from all over Italy to help identify the dead and formally certify deaths.

'Oh yes.' Sebastiani recalled the US had established a nationwide network of emergency teams to deal with mass fatalities. It appalled him that Italy had made no such provision, despite the demands of the Italy-wide association of anti-terror groups and local civil defence organizations. The Italian political stance: it is only necessary to protect Italy against attacks then we do not need dedicated emergency teams. He doubted these same politicians would have learned a lesson from this attack.

Martino, still explaining: 'We've done well to get all the bodies out of the Basilica in three days and retrieving them from the bridge. We had luck that this hangar was empty. Luck's the wrong word. Never completed. It's been empty for years. Like a lot of projects in Rome, eh Fabio?'

Martino returned to his notes. 'Facial identification is not so much a problem. In nearly all cases, the faces are complete and easy to compare with passports – where passports were carried. Most of the people killed were foreign nationals so it's going to take time to contact relatives to identify them. But we're running all possible checks on all the bodies: dental, DNA – the lot.'

Doctor Martino's explanation would normally have sparked Sebastiani's interest but today it irritated him. 'Why did you want me here, Enzo? Do you have something special for me?'

'Ah, you're thinking about Cardinal Ricci.'

'I'm not thinking about anybody. You called me.'

'Because there's a suspicion Ricci was killed after the bombing and the collapse of the roof, I've had his body taken to my lab at the hospital. I looked at him before coming here. The obvious thing I noticed was that his clothes were not as full of stone dust as other victims from the cathedral. But then I'm more interested in what's happened to their bodies. No, apart from this first observation, his head wounds are similar to many who died in the building.'

'Clean clothes suggest he was not in the Basilica when the roof collapsed.'

'I would say that.'

'I'd like to see Ricci today. With you, if possible.'

'Okay Fabio, I can take a break anytime and come back. I'll be here for most of the day anyway. Before we go, a couple of things you should know. Firstly, not all the human parts pulled out of the Basilica were from people killed in the terror attack. The collapsing roof broke open some of the sarcophagi and spread old bones and bits of embalmed human tissue about the place. We have to identify and register everything organic that's found. The Graffiti Wall, in case you're interested in the bones of St Peter, was left undamaged,' the pathologist seemed pleased to announce.

'I guess that's important to know.' Sebastiani struggled to show interest in Martino's long explanations and quickly lost patience with him. 'You had something special for me, you said.'

Martino pointed across the room. 'Come with me.' He tugged at Sebastiani's tunic sleeve and led him through the well-ordered coffins to one with a label that read 'To be identified'.

'Look at this. Put these on first.' Martino gave Sebastiani surgical gloves and then opened the lid of the coffin. 'My old teacher, Professor Rossi, Rome University Department of Pathology, found this curiosity. We don't know who this person is. No identification was found on the body. Look at the face. With that damage it would be difficult to say who this was. The curious thing is that the face has two identical deep wounds but slightly distanced from each other. Straight wounds and deep. Can you feel that?'

He took Sebastiani's hand and guided it over distinct ridges in the body's face.

'It's as though this person was struck twice in the same way with a heavy piece of sharp stone or something similar. It's possible this was done by falling masonry, something that bounced and struck again in the same way. But this is impossible in the circumstances. In other words, it looks like we have the body of someone else whose death is suspicious.'

81

'Oh Jesus. Another complication. Enzo, get this body taken to your lab too.'

'I've already arranged that. I've yet to examine Ricci and this man more fully. If there are no other signs of impact on the body, as one would expect from a roof collapse, then I would take it, off the record, so to speak...' He looked around, pressed a finger against his lips and raised his eyebrows, 'I'd say they were murdered.' He closed the coffin lid. 'Important but not suspicious. We've found five bodies that show no evidence of being hit by falling masonry at all. We have to look at these a little closer too but they were all old people and it appears they died from natural causes. Probably heart attacks brought on by the intense excitement.'

'Thank you, Enzo.' He wondered what could possibly be natural about being literally scared to death. 'As for Ricci and this guy, looks like someone among our rescuers at the cathedral was busy doing something very nasty to them. I appreciate your time, Enzo. By the way, what's going to happen to all these bodies?'

'Some government department is trying to find freezer space for all the corpses. They must be moved out today because the cooling system rigged up in here is just not enough.'

Sebastiani spread his arms to mark off the group of coffins among which he stood. 'Enzo, are all these bodies from the Basilica?'

'Yes.'

'Have any bodies been removed from here already?'

'No, except for Ricci, who's in my lab, they're all here.'

Putting his hands on Martino's shoulders he peered down at him and spoke as though cautioning his own son. 'Enzo, these bodies are not to be moved until I say so. I'm getting forensics people here. Fingerprints and photos.'

'What's on your mind?'

'If this man was murdered, his killer could be here. Here, in one of these coffins.' He plucked off his latex gloves and threw them into a bucket pointed at by Martino. 'We're analyzing everything from the ruin. Maybe we'll find something that matches the wounds.' He let out a weary sigh.

'You know, Fabio, you should get some sleep. You're beginning to look like some of my clients.'

'Smart ass. Come on Enzo, let's go to your lab.'

'Okay, pay attention.' Ferri silenced the chatter of the hundred-odd officers assembled in the ops room. 'You've been briefed already so you know what to do. Interview in pairs. You know the names of the people to interview, and the times. Does anyone not have this timetable?' He waved a single sheet of paper above his head.

'What's important to find out is why these priests were nowhere near the cathedral or in the procession when the bombs went off. I would have expected them to be part of the parade. I want to know where they were at that time, why they were somewhere else, and who they were with. In particular, don't forget to ask about Cardinal Ricci.'

He waved another sheet of paper. 'These people said they didn't know him, or didn't want to say they did. Make sure you get answers to these questions. It's important you crosscheck their answers on these points afterwards. Whatever else you can learn is up to you. And none of them leaves Rome until we let them go. Is that clear? Make that clear to them. All of you be here at six o'clock for a review of the interviews.'

Luca Ferri set off to collect Doctor Luisa Fabian from her office in a chauffeur-driven Carabinieri car. 'Best if I pick you up,' he had said, and his excuses for doing so stood to reason. 'Driving yourself to the Vatican today is not a good idea. You just might get confused driving around the diversions now the bridges are barricaded. I would. My driver knows the way.'

That's what he'd said to her. But in the style of any Italian male, he wanted to demonstrate his charm and elegant manners, not to mention his important, chauffeur-eligible status in the Italian

Carabinieri. And for reasons mainly to do with Italian masculinity and flair he chose to go without a jacket and present himself instead in his badge-filled Carabinieri officer's blue shirt.

'Okay, stop here.' His car pulled up at the courtyard entrance of the beautiful Palazzo della Sapienza, a classical baroque building in the Corso del Rinascimento.

Arriving ten minutes early for his appointment with Luisa Fabian, he busied himself reading notes in preparation for their meeting at the Vatican.

After only just starting to skim through the papers he was distracted by her animated waving. Stepping out of the air-conditioned cool of the car he walked toward her with a self-conscious gait and a weak smile. '*Buongiorno*, Doctor Fabian.'

'Hello.' She cocked her head to one side. 'We're working together. Call me Luisa.'

'Luisa, I'm Luca.'

'That's what I call a good beginning.'

'Good.'

'Come with me,' she said. 'I want to show you my office. You can't come to Palazzo della Sapienza without seeing my office. I'm very excited about it. First have a look inside the church, it's beautiful.'

'We don't have much time.'

'Oh, go on. Just a few minutes.' She took his hand and led him through the doorway.

Ferri sounded happy to be in the quiet coolness of solid seventeenth-century stonework. 'I've never been inside this church before. It's wonderful.'

When he turned to her, he flushed when he noticed her eyes roving over his face as though studying his features.

'Isn't it? Baroque,' she said, still looking at his face.

'I suppose it is.'

'Sorry. I'm not trying to be a know all.'

'Don't apologize.'

'I'm just enthusiastic about classical architecture.'

'Then I suppose you know who built it.'

'Francesco Borromini. Did you know that?'

He raised his eyelids and pressed his lips together in a smile.

'Well, he was the architect. In my opinion, his finest work. Look at the way he gives depth to the cupola from in here. Curved triangles rising up to the dome. This illusionary perspective featured in a lot of his work. A favourite technique, for sure.'

She guided him to the courtyard.

'And my office window, up there,' she said, turning and pointing to the upper levels of the adjoining palazzo while shielding her eyes from the glare of the sun, 'looks right out across the courtyard to the wonderful cupola on the top of the church. This all fits perfectly with my job. I'm very lucky. Come on. Come and see my office.'

Luca Ferri struggled to make conversation. 'Does all this make you feel religious?' Ill at ease talking about religion, especially with new acquaintances, he regretted bringing it up.

'Luca, I am religious. That's why I did my doctorate in the History of European Religion. I know, I know. You don't have to be religious to study religious history.' She led him up stairs, along corridors and then into her office. 'Just look at this.'

'Wow! I bet you know people in high places.'

'Isn't it beautiful? I was lucky. My office before this was in the main university building over at the Piazzale Aldo Moro. And that was fine. They asked me to move so they could knock down a wall in my office to make a larger office for my boss. I complained at first, until I found out where I was moving to. This is nicer than my boss' office.'

She led Luca to the window. 'The very first university in Rome stood in these grounds. One of Pope Boniface's few achievements.'

'Which one?'

'Sorry, Luca, what?'

'Which Pope Boniface?'

'Oh. The eighth. Your Colonel Sebastiani and I had a fascinating discussion about him.'

Ferri looked at his watch. 'I'm sorry, this is interesting but we need to go now if we're going to be there on time. Do you know where the office of the master builder is?'

'I get so carried away. This place does that to me. It's a wonder I get anything done. Yes, I had not forgotten our appointment today. And I do know where his office is. I know pretty much where everything is in the Vatican. I'm ready when you are.'

The beautiful, effervescent and friendly Luisa Fabian left more than a pleasing impression on Luca Ferri. He wondered if she was already attached.

Clicking footsteps on the well-trodden marble floor of the high-arched corridor echoed loud along the full length of its emptiness.

'Here it is,' said Luisa Fabian. 'Been here many times. And Toni's a nice man. He was my contact point when I had business to do with Vatican buildings. When I first came here, he spent two whole days showing me around.'

Ferri pressed the buzzer to the left of a door that identified its occupier as Doctor Antonio Vitale.

'*Entrare!*'

They entered a large white room with a high ceiling and, a meter down from the ceiling, a cornice of vine leaves and grapes. Ordered minds had attached floor plans, line drawings of building details and hundreds of photographs of various buildings within the Vatican City in neat rows and columns on all four walls. All these and the tidily stacked shelves of files and reference books bespoke the orderly nature of Toni Vitale and his workers.

Two large, traditional crystal chandeliers filled the room with intense brightness. An enormous oil painting of the front entrance aspect of the Vatican as it was three hundred years ago provided a backdrop to Vitale who sat in a short-sleeved shirt and tie at a heavyweight Italian desk that might once have been a dining table for twenty people. He got up and greeted them at the door.

'Hello Luisa. How are things at the university?'

They shook hands.

'Fine, Toni.'

'And you are Major Ferri.' Shaking his hand, he said, 'I hope I can be of help.' He pointed to the chairs on the other side of the table from his. 'Please.' He stood until his visitors had sat down.

Ferri opened his briefcase and set it on his lap. Luisa smiled benevolently at Vitale.

Although within the Vatican grounds, the building housing Vitale's office had escaped the explosions with severe scratching and great luck. Even the large glass windows that now looked out onto ruin some one hundred and fifty meters away had miraculously survived.

Ferri looked expectantly around the room. 'Just us three for the meeting?'

'*Si.* I'm the only one in the building. In the circumstances, I decided there was no point in anyone being at work. I assigned them all to sick leave until further notice.'

Ferri unpacked documents from his briefcase and glared across at Vitale. 'Your building records, *Signor* Vitale. Very interesting. The company that repaired the dome and the roof. Let's see.' He leafed through the papers on his lap. 'Yes. MMGT is no longer in business. They went out of business just two weeks ago. Very strange, don't you think?'

Vitale didn't answer but while Ferri perused his documents, he looked across at Luisa and shrugged.

Ferri leaned back and stared at him. 'What's even stranger, *Signor* Vitale, we're having trouble getting to the directors. Mancuso, Magnini, Graziano and Tamburo. MMGT. Is that correct?'

'Those are the names they gave on the contracts.'

Vitale leaned his sturdy arms on small piles of documents carefully ordered before him and looked at Luisa, his face pained and appealing.

Ferri placed his documents on the desk and bent forward, his forearms on his thighs. 'They've disappeared. Well, not all of them.

Rico Tamburo we found dead. Killed in uncertain circumstances. Did you know that, *Signor* Vitale?'

Luisa looked at Ferri askance with her mouth pinched and her eyes creased, and then turned to Vitale. 'What do you think, Toni?'

'I never met the man. I'm told he died on a building site. Accident. Hit by a mechanical shovel, I think. Building sites are dangerous.'

Ferri consulted his notes. 'You signed the contracts.'

'Yes. The repair work was put out to tender, as always. It's a Vatican rule.' He then sat back and relaxed his arms.

'And an Italian state rule.'

'Right.' Vitale continued unprompted. 'Naturally we asked for bids from companies with experience in Vatican work, and MMGT was one of those. The contracts were fixed price.' Suddenly raising a hand, he said, 'Wait. There is one thing. MMGT did not always have this name. But we knew the same people were involved under the new company name.'

'And the previous name?'

'I know it well. They did good work for us over many years. Tinas Alonso. As the master builder, I awarded and signed off the contracts.'

A hiatus was filled by Ferri looking through papers, Luisa glaring at him and Vitale looking anxiously at each of them in turn.

Then Vitale said, 'The *Guardia di Finanzia* took my records away. When do I get them back?'

'They're still checking them. That will take some time.' He looked across at Vitale without speaking for moments, wondering whether he would venture something useful. Nothing came; only the discomfort of another long silence.

'*Signor* Vitale, we believe workers of MMGT placed the explosives that brought the roof down on hundreds of innocent people. And they must have had inside help. Can you think of anything that now makes you suspicious?'

'No. I've tried to think about this. About how explosives could be brought into the Vatican. I assumed our police at the entrance would have detected weapons or explosives. Lots of building materials were brought in but they were all checked by...' Vitale dried up.

'Go on tell me. Vatican priests. That's right, isn't it?' He sat back in his chair and studied Vitale. Beads of sweat had now formed on his brow. 'And what were Cardinal Ricci's responsibilities?'

'He had religious oversight of the building work. That the work didn't offend any Roman Catholic rules. There are very few of those that affect repairs, but that was his job. He gave directions to people on site. He sometimes worked with Luisa. Right, Luisa?'

'That's right, Toni. Just occasionally, to make sure new pieces followed traditional design.'

Ferri slotted his documents into his briefcase and stood. 'What do you know about Cardinal Ricci?'

Vitale stood too. 'A good person. Kind. He was Roman and loved Rome and its people. They're crazy but good. That's what he used to say. He did charity work for the homeless and worked for an organization tracing missing children. That's all I know, really.' He looked at Luisa. 'I just cannot believe he could be involved in such a dreadful crime.'

Intentionally to rescue Vitale from Ferri's harshness, she asked him softly, 'Toni, how long will it take to rebuild the Basilica?'

'Let me see. When the roof came down it damaged most of the support columns in some way and severely damaged the walls. Except for the portico and a few odd attached buildings and rooms, the remains of the Basilica will have to be demolished and rebuilt from new. How long? My estimate,' his chin crinkled as he pouted momentarily, 'fifteen to twenty years. Montecassino took ten years to rebuild from rubble but rebuilding this Basilica is a far larger project.'

After closing the door on Vitale, Ferri said, 'He's as innocent as the day is long. He would not have stayed in Rome – or Italy even – if he had been paid as much as this job was worth.'

'I thought you gave him a hard time.'

CHAPTER FIVE

The dark stony stare on the face above the arched entrance to the exclusive Quartiere Coppedè mocked Sebastiani as he sat in his car on the Via Tagliamento waiting to turn right into the Piazza Mincio. Spies and fools in the Carabinieri have by now leaked the home address of the chief investigator of the Rome bombing to minor miscreants who have connections to major miscreants who just might have had a hand in the devastation.

Alone on the street he was at risk. In just such a situation, an ex-colleague who had been investigating Sicilian Mafia don Luigi Porrello was recently assassinated in Palermo, blown up as his car slowed at a junction. Sebastiani's mind became fully concentrated on that possibility for himself. From here onwards, his training told him, it could happen. Even at home now he wouldn't be safe.

Turning right into the Piazza Mincio, he false-footed the accelerator causing the tires to screech up blue smoke from the dry road. His eyes darted in all directions, into his car mirrors, around the Piazza and down the road he drove slowly along. Even though he saw no signs of new road works, he drove, as best he could, around anything not part of the original tarmac. In his left outer field of vision he sighted the green Bentley sports coupe that was always illegally parked on the road in front of the politician's house, one of Gino Coppedè's beautiful Art Nouveau buildings that filled the area around the Piazza Mincio and its famous Frog Fountain. As he passed the fountain, he saw a group of four men in casual clothes with business briefcases entering the Polish Embassy in the Via Brenta across the way. No other cars were parked in the Piazza and no other people were to be seen.

Down the road from the Polish Embassy, two heavy concrete columns, each with a large ornate lantern on top, formed a symbolic gateway from Coppedè's noble area to Sebastiani's more middle-class part of the Via Brenta. About to pass through the gate, he instinctively braked hard as his outer vision caught sight of a man carrying a long black object at his shoulder stepping quickly from behind the column to his right. Going for his gun, he sped forward twenty meters, screeched to a stop and then, half out of the car with gun in hand, he realized his assailant was the gardener and the object raised in his hands was an electric hedge trimmer. The lean, swarthy man, who Sebastiani had learned was Romanian, stood there stupefied, a hand clutching his long, black hair.

Peeking over the car, Sebastiani waved a hand. '*Buongiorno!*' he shouted.

With a bemused smile the gardener returned a shrug and went on his way.

He noticed only when he got back into the car and grasped the steering wheel that sweat covered his hands. 'Idiot, Sebastiani.'

Even so, he stopped well short of his garage door before pressing the Open button on the remote control.

Sebastiani spent most of his private time at the barracks where he had comfortable accommodation, cooked meals, access to his favourite sport, badminton, and the company of like-minded souls. And, in this pressured investigation, that's where he knew he should be. But only at home could he get uninterrupted sleep to clear his mind for analyzing the attack reports.

He wandered into the main bedroom, removed his tunic, threw it on the bed and flopped down beside it. The clean and ordered state of the apartment told him that his ever-reliable Polish *donna delle pulizie* came in and did her stuff once a month in his absence.

Soon, he got up and took the reports from the briefcase and laid them out like overlapping tiles on his desk. The same hand had written all the labels. Calligraphic and neat, he thought. But why hadn't they used a word processor?

Laying the pathology and bomb squad reports to one side, he opened the one marked Analysis of Photographic Material and flicked through its hundreds of photographs, many taken from cameras belonging to people now dead. The photographs bore marks highlighting details analysts considered relevant. He studied an enlarged video sequence.

'Cardinal Ricci.' The red-cloaked cardinal was walking away from the debris and (the notes assumed) toward the Sistine Chapel. He read the notes attached to the sequence:

> Person identified by Vatican Human Resources department as Cardinal Ricci. Photographic evidence he was alive after roof collapse. Found dead among other corpses near entrance of cathedral nave with deep fractures in his skull. Fractures caused by impacts to the head by roof masonry, identified by compatible particles found deep in the wound. Ricci was seen alive after the cathedral roof had totally collapsed and, therefore, could not have been killed from falling masonry. Assumed to have been killed some time after the explosions and roof collapse. See pathology report about the time of death.

He retrieved the pathology report and read its front cover, which was also a sign-off form for the various specialties and among its signatories Doctor Enzo Martino's scrawl appeared. He skimmed through the text until he found the time of death summary.

> Ricci TOD cannot be differentiated from the TOD of the other victims.

'Killed after the bombing but not long after,' he murmured.

Next, he paged through the Scene of Crime report for anything to do with Ricci and stopped at a photograph he recognized from the video sequence he'd already seen. 'He's walking away from the ruin. How the hell did he get back into the cathedral dead? Someone must have seen him being carried back.'

Sebastiani sat back in his chair, linked his hands behind his head and let his mind replay the mayhem in the cathedral on that day. The dust-covered and unrecognizable wounded frantically trying to extract themselves from the rubble and carnage, firemen and paramedics treating the wounded and removing the deceased.

'How could a body be brought back unseen? Two people with a stretcher?' He looked through the photographic material again and studied the detail in all the photographs that included stretcher bearers – most of those from the cathedral – but found nothing that fitted with how he imagined Ricci could be stretchered back into the chaos of the Basilica on the day.

He pulled his jacket off the back of the chair and dug out his mobile phone from its inside pocket. 'Ferri. Colonel Sebastiani here.'

'*Buona sera,* sir.'

He spun round to look at the wall clock. 'Where are you?'

'Headquarters.'

'I'm looking at the reports. Have you seen them?'

'Right in front of me.'

Good to know you're working late, Ferri, he thought. 'What do you think?'

'I've only studied the SOC report.'

'Comments?'

A pause filled by the rustle of papers and then Ferri's answer. 'Just one. It didn't say if anyone tried to find whatever broke Ricci's skull.'

'I haven't done all the reports yet but I thought the same. Looks like he was killed outside the cathedral. Lots of people inside so I don't think he was killed there.'

'Right.'

'Maybe the murder weapon was carried into the cathedral with his body and disposed of there.'

'The report doesn't mention any search for material clues outside the cathedral. It also doesn't say if he struggled. There'd be no evidence of a struggle if he wasn't expecting an assault. Even if

93

there was no blood in that outer area and no signs of assault, those facts should be mentioned.'

'Damned right. Finding Ricci's killers would be a big step for us. Make sure we take up the omissions with the report authors. We'll talk tomorrow. *Buona sera.*'

Sebastiani had no sooner entered his office and set his handwritten notes about the Rome attack reports on his desk when General Conti tramped in. He struck an indignant pose, with fingers resting on a nearby filing cabinet and the clenched knuckles of the other hand pressed into his waist.

'*Buongiorno*, sir.' Sebastiani removed his cap and hung it on a stand, then removed his tunic in the same casual way and hung it with the cap.

'Colonel, I don't know how you can be so relaxed. I want to know how things are going. Four days since the attack. Expected you to set up a regular status meeting with me by now.'

Conti flattened a hand on the desk and read the front sheet of Sebastiani's notes but apparently having gained nothing, barked at him. 'Well. Where are we?'

Conti's pushy entrance and odd countenance did not fit well with Sebastiani's tired start to the day.

'I want to be constantly informed all the right things are in place and operating well. I expect you to have our culprits identified soon. Early every morning. Status. That's what I need. You can arrange it through my secretary.'

'No sir. I cannot do that. This investigation is fully active and I don't have time to attend a meeting every day.'

'What? Damn you. I need to know what the hell's going on.'

The colonel could only agree. 'I can phone you status from wherever I am.'

'Okay, okay. Glad to know you've got the balls to stand up to me when I'm being stupid. Ferri can inform me where you are. I'll get to you somehow.'

'Yes sir.'

Conti sat down in a chair at right angles to the desk. 'Get him in here. You can both bring me up to date. And I want your understanding of the reports. I've studied them and they seem pretty comprehensive.'

Sebastiani pressed buttons on his desk telephone. 'Major, come to my office. Bring your report analysis and be prepared to give a status update.'

'How's he doing, Fabio?' Not listening to his response, Conti grasped the peak of his cap, drew it slowly backward off his head, smoothed down the hair on the back of his head and then laid his cap and white gloves on the desk. He stretched out his legs, crossed them and with left and right swings of his head, studied his shiny black shoes from every angle.

What a performance, thought Sebastiani. 'Generally, sir, or on this particular case?'

'Oh, generally. I'll find out in a few minutes how he's doing on this case.'

'Thirty years old. Still young. A good leader. Well thought of. Here in Italy and by other national anti-terror groups.'

On merit, Ferri would be Sebastiani's choice to replace Conti as Italy's national anti-terrorism boss – eventually. An unrealistic idea, he knew. Only members of influential families occupied that lofty position. Ferri's family, like his, was not influential.

'I've worked with him for over two years. His organization has a tremendous record. High success rate in tracking down and prosecuting. Good to work with. Very ambitious.'

'Fast tracked to major three years ago. Yes?'

'Yes.'

'I get the impression…'

Ferri entered the room. '*Buongiorno*, sir.' He carried a notebook and, according to the look on his face, a world of worry.

Sebastiani hand-signalled him to sit and said, 'We've discussed the reports. They're comprehensive but there are gaps. We raised the same concerns. We'll take them up with the report writers.'

'Gaps, such as?' Conti cast an expectant wide-eyed look at them.

Sebastiani answered. 'Cardinal Ricci we know was outside the Basilica after the explosions and was probably killed outside the Basilica itself, but no one has examined that area. At least, the SOC report doesn't say anything about it. Since then Ferri's team has been looking at the area around the Basilica.'

'And what have you found?' Conti tapped the desk. 'You, Ferri. What are the results of your search?'

Despite Conti's grouchiness, the major gave an unhurried, firm and clear response. 'Traces of blood. Lots. On the Basilica steps down toward the colonnade. These could only have been from the injured who got away in this direction. The dead and wounded were carried away on stretchers and the seriously wounded were treated and bandaged on the spot.'

'And these blood traces were not mentioned in the SOC report?' Conti thumped the desk. 'Who produced the damned thing?'

'State police SOC team,' said Ferri. 'Credit to them. The other reports were well done. In the Basilica, blood was all over the place and on the victims so I understand them missing this. But now we're looking at a possible murder. The SOC team didn't know that then.'

This explanation did nothing to remove Conti's angry scowl. 'And what now Colonel? Major?'

Although Sebastiani had no idea where the samples collected could be, he answered anyway. 'We're waiting for the results from the lab.'

'And what other items were missing from the SOC report?'

Ferri said, 'Those were the two main things. No mention of a search for evidence of where and how Ricci died. We suspect that was outside the Basilica. And no mention of the blood traces in that area. There were other things, minor things. Not significant.'

'Okay, that'll do. Status every day, as agreed. The world wants results. And so do I.'

'Yes sir.'

Conti stood and put on his cap. 'Have you read the papers today?' He studied his reflection in the glass of the military picture behind Sebastiani's desk and painstakingly adjusted his cap. 'The right-wing papers are still pushing that al-Qaeda crap. We've said enough times it's unlikely. Are you keeping in touch with that stuff, Fabio?'

'I am.'

'Some interesting theories from the left, too.'

Gladio again, thought Sebastiani. 'Yes. The CIA blew up the Vatican to generate worldwide anti-Islamic tension.'

Conti's smiled ambiguously. 'That's it for now. Don't forget, every day, status. Ferri, the colonel will tell you about it. Through my secretary. Just phone her early every morning and tell her where you are. I'll come to you.'

They stood to attention until Conti had left the room.

Sebastiani's telephone rang; he dismissed the major before picking it up.

'*Pronto.*'

'Fabio, hello. Enzo Martino.'

'Hello Enzo.'

'Have you read my autopsy reports? My pathology report?'

'I skimmed it. We're analyzing all the reports at the moment.'

'Okay, well, you have your priorities. There is no question that both bodies brought into my lab were murder victims. The cleric Ricci and the unidentified corpse I showed you in the hangar. Neither had the multiple scars nor bruising you'd expect after being hit by a roof. But there is something else. The scene of crime report places the unidentified body by the Graffiti Wall. Remember, St Peter's bones?'

'That was not in the path report I read.'

'Then you have not read the update.'

'Apparently not.'

'The important point is, this unidentified person was killed a significant time before the roof collapsed. I did a time-of-death

97

check on all those bodies assigned to me. He died about three hours earlier. About eight o'clock that morning. Fabio, do you hear me? Are you still there?'

No, he was not there. At least, his mind was not there. With this new information, it was back in the cathedral.

CHAPTER SIX

'Unbelievable. just look at that. Giulio Gagliano.'

Sebastiani knew the name well: Giulio Gagliano, freelance contract killer and, because his payers either threatened or bribed his judges, free to pursue his trade. Sebastiani peered at the large computer screen where Ferri's ballpoint pen pointed. 'Is this from the photographic report?'

'Yes.'

'Then I've already seen it and missed him. Not very clear though, is it? You sure?'

Ferri uncoiled from his stoop. 'We've had him in the courts several times. Plenty of photos. Lucchesi here has done image comparisons on the computer and the images from the Vatican fit with his general build and posture. His facial characteristics and head size also fit. In one he's looking at the camera. That was lucky.'

The Gagliano figure on the screen, an oldish man in clean white overalls, baseball cap and clean white trainers, despite the muck and dust all around, walked – head down, eyes concentrated on the crumbled stone, marble and concrete that lay before him – toward the rescue activities apparently just arriving to help.

Lucchesi zoomed the image and pointed to Gagliano's hands. 'He's wearing black leather gloves.'

Sebastiani stooped to the screen again. 'Not to keep his hands warm.'

'They're clean. He's just got there. Difficult to know when but we should be able to measure the shadows. Quite a while after the explosions for certain because the dust has settled.'

Sebastiani ran his eyes around the background of the rescue scene. 'Nothing that shows Gagliano and Ricci together?'

Lucchesi spun his office chair to face him. 'No, sir. We're going through it again. We'll look for that.'

'No blood on his overall?'

Ferri umm-ed and looked at Lucchesi, who answered.

'Some of these images are from cameras with poor resolution. Larger blotches would show, but small specks no. We've looked.'

'Well done. This will help.'

'We're doing mug shot comparisons on all photos, including those we rejected the first time round.'

'Are you sure that's Gagliano?' The colonel peered at the screen with eyes squeezed narrow. 'Doesn't look clear to me. What do you think, Ferri?'

'No doubt about it. He's the known killer on the scene and Ricci is found murdered. Why else would he be there?' He aimed his ballpoint pen at the screen again. 'In this second picture, I reckon he's dumped the body and heading out.'

'Where was it found? I don't remember getting that detail.'

'We don't know,' said Ferri. 'Dead and wounded were removed as fast as possible. Lots of the bodies were near the entrance. They were all running out into the piazza when the bombs exploded. So perhaps it was there.'

'Umm.'

'At the time, it wasn't important to know where bodies were. Ricci was just another one of the dead.'

'Right.' Sebastiani leaned his hands on the back of Lucchesi's chair and bent closer to the screen. 'Are there any pictures that show if he's with anyone? An accomplice? Someone carrying a stretcher?'

Lucchesi answered. 'No. We looked for an accomplice. Nothing.'

'Never mind. I'm convinced. Bring Gagliano in right away. Do we know where he is?'

'We're looking,' said Ferri.

'Good. What charge?'

'Suspicion of involvement in terrorist activities.'

'Stick with the terrorism charge. That's important.'

'Of course.' Ferri laid his pen on Lucchesi's computer desk and sat on the edge of a table. 'I arrested him twice before I joined your department, sir. He was never convicted though. Not a Mafia man. Do a job for anybody.'

'Go find him, Major. And while you are organizing that, get everybody to the ops room for eight o'clock this evening. I'll give an overview of how I see things. I want feedback from the troops. I'll be looking for a report on the interviews with the cardinals. Invite Luisa along.' He saluted and left.

About a hundred and fifty men milled around before him in the ops room, some in Carabinieri summer wear, the rest in civilian shirts, the great variety of which reflected the range of ages in his team.

He spotted Luisa Fabian and noticed she was the only woman in the room. He had never before thought of it as serious that no women detectives worked in Rome's anti-terror organization. He noted the fact as an omission to be dealt with.

'Right everyone. Sit down and be quiet.'

And while they did, his gaze settled on Luisa who stared at him earnestly. He looked away and continued.

'It's five days since the explosions. Identifying Gagliano was good but after five days, not much progress. If we don't find the bombers soon, they could strike again. So, where are we?'

He folded his arms and walked a couple of steps toward the window, from which point he could see the top of the still-standing portico of the Basilica. Then he turned to his flip chart list.

'So far, we know the attack was done by a well-coordinated organization. Huge amounts of Semtex brought into the Vatican and built into structures. The timing of the Basilica work shows the attack was set up over two years, at least. Now give me some good news. People identified. Arrests pending. Anything.'

Ferri, sitting at one end of the first row, raised a hand. 'Sir, an update from today. *Guardia di Finanzia* cleared all the Vatican work records. Contracts, transactions. All clean. Still investigating Tamburo's death.'

Sebastiani saw Conti enter the room and sit in the back row but ignored him. 'We still don't know if the attack was against Italy, against the Roman Catholic Church, against the papacy in general, or against the new pope. Islamic fundamentalists had threatened Italy but this is nothing like their work. They'd have no possibility to set things up in the Vatican over such a long time. And they've denied it anyway. An attack on Pope Boniface? That's also unlikely and I rule it out. They would have to have known from about two or three years ago that he was going to be pope.' Sebastiani paused and looked around his audience. 'Comments? Feel free to interrupt me.'

Luisa Fabian raised her arm.

'Doctor Fabian.'

'It was understood for a number of years Emilio Gaetano would become the next elected pope. He was the powerhouse behind his predecessor so it was assumed he'd succeed him.' She shifted on her seat. 'There were no other likely candidates, unless someone was elected on purely political grounds.'

'Thank you, Luisa. I know your thoughts on this. Still an unlikely reason for the attack, don't you think?'

She shrugged.

'Look at this.' Sebastiani switched on a projector and the Gagliano photographs he'd studied earlier appeared on the wall behind him. 'Overnight we arrested a suspect for Cardinal Ricci's murder. This man. Giulio Gagliano. By the way, where's he being held? Regina Coeli or at Mamertino? Ferri?'

'Terror suspect, sir. Mamertino.'

'Good, then for Christ's sake don't mention the name Ricci to Gagliano. Gagliano is a terrorist for the time being. And that's the way we talk to him.'

Sebastiani unfolded a handkerchief and brushed it across his forehead. 'Gagliano's not saying much, and he won't. But search his home and see what comes up. Forensics would be grateful to have this overall and the shoes he's wearing here. Look for them. Get to know where he's been in the last months, who he's been speaking to.'

He pointed at the next item on his flip chart. 'The mystery death in the cathedral. So far the body has not been identified but we know the man had his face battered in about three hours before the roof exploded. We still have six other unidentified corpses.'

Sebastiani thought of Doctor Vettori's patient. 'The fourth Milan bomber suspect. Update me somebody. Any news?'

An old hand shouted from the back, 'Still nothing, sir. Not a trace.'

The colonel suppressed a smirk. 'Keep at it. It's an important piece of work.' He sat down and rested the ankle of his right foot on his left knee. 'Right, someone tell me where we are with the cardinals. Are they guilty as hell or do we let them all go to France?' Sebastiani looked around. 'Major Ferri.'

'The interviews are complete. The forty-two priests from Via Rusticucci plus three who were here in Rome but not at that meeting.'

'Background details?'

'All we need to know. Alibis are all okay. One odd thing though. Many of them are French. Not all of them but a fair number. As far as we can tell they've told the truth and we can do nothing more. But it's possible they planned to be somewhere else when the bombing started. Maybe they knew beforehand it was going to happen. What do we do about it, sir?'

'We let them go to France, of course.' Conti's words caused a scraping of chairs as faces turned to the rear. 'That's what they plan to do. They're not expecting to be found as accomplices to this awful crime any more than I expect them to be. I've seen your document, Major. I don't think the number of French clerics is significant. Let the priests go. Anyway, in this modern world of policing, they're not out of our clutches just because they cross an EU national border.'

Sebastiani looked for further words from Conti but none came. 'That's it. This time tomorrow. Dismissed.'

He waited until the noise of the departing *carabinieri* subsided then turned to Conti, expecting to be tongue-lashed again.

'Hello Fabio. Over there?' Conti pointed to seats away from the remaining *carabinieri* and, as they sat, he said, 'This is a fabulous room. *Stanza dei Segreti*. Painted by Raphael and his apprentices. Did you know that?'

Sebastiani smiled. 'Doctor Fabian told me.'

Conti turned and scanned the whole room. 'Look at these frescoes. Amazing talent. You know, he actually did one or two himself. Good that we can see such things to remind us we're human.'

Experience had taught Sebastiani that soft words from a superior usually preceded an unpleasant disclosure. 'Doctor Fabian told me the paintings on the third floor are even more impressive. I've never seen them.'

'They are impressive and you must try to see them. Pope Julius the second occupied this room until he moved upstairs. Before we came here, it was always locked.' Conti paused. 'Fabio, I'm getting a lot of stick from upstairs. Your name comes in for a lot for criticism.'

'I hope you're defending me.'

'I am.'

'If they don't like what I'm doing, they can always move me out.'

Conti crossed one leg over the other in a slow, studied manner and brushed a fleck from his trousers. 'All I want to know is that reports, internal or in the press, do not in any way distract you.'

'Why would you ever think so?'

104

'It's all too immense and people in high places are watching us.' Conti stood and walked to the window, impelling the colonel to stand. For a few moments, Conti studied the activity around the mobile communications vehicle outside then returned.

'Fabio, I've known you a long time. I trust you.' He adjusted his cap and fingered the knot of his tie. 'Right, I'll leave you to it. You have things to attend to. Ciao!'

Sebastiani watched Conti leave and then phoned Luisa Fabian. 'Can you come back to the ops room?' He pulled at the flesh on the bridge of his nose. 'Good. See you in ten minutes.'

'Here I am.'

'Luisa. This won't take long. It's important.'

She tilted her head to look at his eyes. 'You look burned out. Are you all right?'

'I'm fine.'

As reaction to internal stirring brought on by her tenderness, Sebastiani stood behind a chair and gripped the tubular frame of its back. With elbows locked stiff he rocked it on its rear legs. 'Would you by any chance have a reason to go to France?'

She undid the buttons of her white linen jacket, sat on a chair and set the handbag hanging from her shoulder on her lap. 'I have no plans to go. Where in France were you thinking of? Somewhere particular? When? And why?'

He rubbed his temples. 'I want you to go to France as soon as possible. Avignon. Because that's where the leaders of the Roman Catholic Church are moving the Papacy to. The palace at Avignon.'

'I picked that up in the meeting and that was the first I'd heard about it. How did you find out?'

'Archbishop Collineau told the Italian military the day after the attack. For their safety. That's what he said. Can the pope just up and move like that?'

'He's not the pope. There isn't one. I'm surprised he's going to do that. They have to elect a pope sometime soon. A pope can theoretically move the Papacy where he wants to. Perhaps those still living are claiming authority to do this as a group.'

'I can tell you, they are. From the start, I've been suspicious about why they find it necessary to move to France, especially with all the administrative and legal offices here in Rome. Why would they move?'

She raised her chin, ran a fingertip down the front of her neck and looked beyond him. 'That's curious. It's the last thing I would have expected them to do.' Her mouth dropped a fraction as she returned her gaze to him. 'I find that amazing.'

'I want you to go France and try to discover what their real reasons for going are.'

Luisa crossed one leg over the other, momentarily exposing her thighs. Sebastiani looked down at his chair and rocked it on its back legs again.

'There's no pressure on you to go,' he said. 'You just say no, and that's fine.'

'I love France and I speak excellent French. Luca told me you do too.'

'Not excellent, I can tell you.'

Luisa frowned. 'What would you want me to do in France? What information would I look for?'

'Who are these French cardinals? What's so important in France that they have to be there? I don't believe it's just for their safety. There's no evidence they've been threatened. Nothing to implicate them in the bombing, either. I thought they could be involved but it was just one option among many. But I still want to know what they're up to. I know, I could ask the gendarmerie or even Interpol for information. But I don't trust them to get what I need. If you find something interesting, then I might have to call them in. You would do better. Besides, I don't want to stir up a hornet's nest.'

She stood, folded her arms and smiled. 'This is detective work.'

'No, Luisa, it's research. And you do not go alone. Do you have a friend who could go with you?'

106

'I do research all the time on my own. It's not a problem.'

'Okay. Will you do this for me?'

'Who pays?' She put her hands on her hips and put on a pixie smile.

'I'll cover all your expenses.'

'No question, I'll go. But you'll have to tell me what I should be looking for.'

'I will do that but this business is just between you and me. The clerics shouldn't know anyone from the Carabinieri is checking up on them. I don't want anyone in the team to know either. Not even Ferri. I have private reasons for saying that. You'll have to tell him you're taking a break.'

He looked at his watch. 'Damn, already late. I've got to clear up some things with Major Ferri. Look, I've got nothing prepared because this idea occurred to me only after our meeting this evening. Can you come to the ops room tomorrow? I'll be there most of the day. Okay?'

She nodded.

'Right, that's it. Can I give you a lift?'

'No thanks. I've got my car.' She grinned and kissed him on the cheek. 'France. Terrific!'

CHAPTER SEVEN

Ferri handed Sebastiani a folder and then closed the office door.

'Good work. It's classified confidential. Did the Vatican quibble?' The colonel pulled out the document and flicked through its dozen or so pages, which listed the names of all the clerics nominated to attend the first mass of the new Pope Boniface X.

'Not at all, sir.'

'We'd have got them anyway.'

'They identify all the priests. Their positions in the Church, their personal backgrounds. All we did was add what we know about them. Injured, uninjured, dying or dead. Only a few of the names have ceremony responsibilities against them. What they were assigned to do on the day.'

'Well done, Major. What about the mystery man with the beat-in face? Is he part of this list?'

'Still don't know. The only cleric not identified whose name is on this list is a Bishop Sinclair.' He pointed to the document. 'It's marked there. Bishop Francis Sinclair. But which one of the unidentified corpses he is, we still don't know.' He took the papers and flipped through to Sinclair's name. 'He's American. Resident administrator at a Roman Catholic seminary in France. A place called Barbentane. I've asked the French police to send us Sinclair's identification. I'm still waiting for that.'

Sebastiani turned to the map of Europe pinned to his office wall. 'Do you know where Barbentane is?'

'Yes sir. Here.' He jabbed a finger on a point below where the River Rhone bends to the west and joins with the Durance just south of Avignon.

'Near Avignon?' Sebastiani smiled wryly. 'That's interesting, don't you think? Like you said, curious so many of the priests are French. Now we have a dead American with French connection. Avignon, eh?'

'Could be a link between the French priests and the attack.'

'If Sinclair is our mystery man with the battered face, that would be interesting. But if he turns out to be just another killed by the falling roof then Archbishop Collineau would be right.'

'How so?'

'It would show the French did not know about the attack beforehand. Otherwise, Sinclair would not have been there. I assume.'

'Of course, sir.'

'Let's see what we get from the French police.'

Sebastiani heard Luisa's heels clicking on the marbled floor of the ops room. He turned from his discussion with team members at a computer, collected his briefcase and made his way toward her...and then just stopped and stared. As she glided along in front of the huge painting of Solomon, her light summer dress moved like gossamer over her, exposing her slim form, her unsupported breasts and shapely thighs.

'My God.' The words formed in his mouth but they were silent. A flush of warm blood filled his loins. He snapped open a clasp on his briefcase and moved a chair. 'Hi Luisa!'

'Am I too early?'

'Not at all. There's so much to see in this place it's difficult not to be distracted. Even for a Philistine like me.'

'I can't imagine you not appreciating art. But then I've only known you a short time. When this is over and you lot are out of here, I'm going to study this room. It was never opened before, not even to students. The only people allowed in here before you came were priests with dim eyes and saggy chins, and the cleaners. How long are you staying?'

'I'm just tying up a few ends. Then I'll go.' He moved closer and dipped his head to her. 'Look, I still have no plan for you. I want you to take a look at a place called Barbentane. Do you know it?'

'Barbentane? Why yes, I do.' She clasped her hands. 'St Alphonsus college for priests. Across the river from Avignon. I did a six-month course there as part of my religious French. I know it well. I guess there are still people in the seminary who know me. Is that a problem?'

'I don't think so. It's probably an advantage.'

'I have a free hand, don't I? I go about my research in the way I see best. Right?' She intoned her questions as demands.

Sebastiani felt relief that Luisa was willing to shoot off to France at his behest without pestering him for lots of details – itinerary, setting up meetings with target names, travel options, and so on – that he did not have the mind to deal with anyway. 'Certainly. You've done research before. That's what this is. I have a list of ten priests and as much detail about them as we've been able to collect. They're either French or have other connections to France. One of them is not French. But I'm fairly certain he's dead. Bishop Francis Sinclair, an American. Know the name?'

She shook her head. 'Before or after my time. I got to know one priest very well but only because he was Italian. Father Cantello.'

He wrote the detail in his notebook: Fr. Cantello, Barbentane.

'He was very old then so I suppose he's dead now.'

So he struck through the entry. 'Dead.'

'I said he could be.'

'Doesn't matter. Sinclair's the important one for me. The gendarmerie promised us information about him. We're still waiting. I've no idea when he was there.'

'I know the place well so that's a start.'

110

'Good. Just find out what you can.' He punctuated each item of the things she should look for with a barely perceptible side-to-side movement of his head. 'Who they mix with, what they do in France, about their families, family histories, and so on. In particular, I want information about Archbishop Collineau. I repeat, this is just research. Don't get side-tracked into anything dangerous.' He handed Luisa the briefcase. 'It's all here. There's three thousand euros in the case. That's travel, food and accommodation. Use it how you like. Go when it's convenient, but I would hope soon. Come back to Rome after two weeks, or earlier if the money runs out.'

Luisa took the briefcase and peered into it. 'That's a lot of money. I'll be careful.'

'Good.' Sebastiani combed through his hair with open fingers. 'Phone me as necessary. Don't forget. Keep in touch. I want to know you're safe.'

'I'll let you know how it's going. Don't worry.'

Ferri came into the room. '*Buongiorno* sir. Hello Luisa.'

She smiled generously. 'Hello Luca.'

'Major. Good that you're here. I'm trying to get out of this place as soon as I can. News on Bishop Sinclair?'

'Yes sir. He's not the murdered man.'

'Okay,' Sebastiani drew out while rubbing a visor of fingers back and forth over his eyebrows. 'What about Gagliano?'

'So far, no breakthrough. Apart from the photos, no hard evidence he was at the cathedral on the day or that links him with Ricci's murder. Whatever he was wearing then, he's got rid of. But we've got him and the photos. Computer comparisons are very reliable. It's him, no mistake.'

Sebastiani picked up his briefcase. 'I want to talk with him. Fix me up for eleven tomorrow. Right, I'm off. Anything else before I disappear?'

'Nothing.'

'I wonder if Gagliano has any friends in the French clergy.' Even to himself that sounded as though he might be too fixated on France and the French priests.

CHAPTER EIGHT

'Giulio Gagliano, good morning. I am Colonel Sebastiani, head of Rome anti-terror. I suspect you know me already.'

He held a document file for a fraction of a second before Gagliano's face and then slapped it on the bare table that stood against the wall of the interrogation room. There were two simple wooden chairs, one occupied by Gagliano watched over by a guard, the other taken by a police officer operating a recorder at a small table, and a large one-way mirror on the wall. Apart from these, the room was bare – and pleasantly cool on such a hot day.

'We know a lot about you, Giulio. You're a killer. My, you've had a bad time.' Resisting the urge to touch the bruise over Gagliano's brow, Sebastiani floated his hand just above it by way of inspection. 'And no sleep by the look of you.'

Giulio Gagliano was fifty-eight years old, thick-set and seedy with tousled dark hair remarkably devoid of grey. This graduate of Naples' worst slum gang sat motionless, slumped a fraction to one side, hands cuffed behind his back, feet chained together, his eyes fixed on the floor midway between himself and the colonel.

'I don't normally talk to low-life like you. But your crime against Italy is so immense I wanted to know personally what sort of person would do such a thing.' Sebastiani moved to the wall and leant against it. 'Gagliano, contract killer turned terrorist. I don't believe this is your usual territory, Giulio. Dangerous business, terrorism. As you'll find out, we give special treatment to terrorists. And we've only just started on you. Who paid you to do this?'

The prisoner closed his eyes, pressed his drooping lips together and winced as he lowered his head onto his chest.

'Giulio, do you know what the European Convention for the Prevention of Torture is?'

He shuffled a foot in response to the word 'torture' but otherwise remained motionless.

'The European Convention prevents us, the Italian Carabinieri, from beating the hell out of you, torturing or degrading you. So, you're in luck as far as rough treatment goes. But you have already degraded yourself. Terrorism, Giulio, terrorism. The big money guys have bought you out of trouble before, but they'll have nothing to do with you now. They'd be arrested for involvement in a crime against the nation. Organizing, participating in or supporting terrorist acts.'

He stood back and studied his prisoner. He'd seen him perform under interrogation before: always impassive and silent, no matter what the treatment. But he knew Gagliano absorbed his words.

'If we find you've been involved in any way, then cheerio Giulio. Italian law is very, very hard on terrorists. It's a new world and the law is tougher now. No remission for terror, Giulio. There's no real loyalty in your business. We'll soon have people talking about you. And you're on your own. If you go down now, you'll get life, and that's that. The oubliette. We throw you into a deep, dark cell and forget you even existed. Am I making myself clear? Life for acts of terrorism means just that. No remission. We have all the evidence we need to put you away forever. Unless you want to help yourself and us by naming names.'

Gagliano turned his head and looked to the floor at his side.

'I don't understand you Giulio.' Sebastiani moved away from the wall and brushed dust from his shoulder. 'A lot of people have picked up a whole lot of money for this job and they're all keeping snug and quiet. You had a big payday too. But you, Giulio, we've got you and you'll never use it.'

'I'm not a terrorist.'

114

'Sorry, I didn't hear you.' He moved closer to him. 'Say that again.'

Gagliano raised his bruised head and spoke wearily. 'I'm not a terrorist. And I was never at St Peter's Basilica. Never in my life.'

'I thought you might say that.' Sebastiani took a photo from the file. 'Look Giulio, we've got you on camera at the cathedral. How could you be so careless? We have solid evidence you were there on the day. And you were not there to help with the dead and injured. Don't forget the oubliette.'

Gagliano closed his eyes and moved his head to and fro. 'I'm not a terrorist. I was never at the cathedral.'

'Seems like you won't get the chance to convince me. You're being moved to Regina Coeli. They're not kind to prisoners there. I think they'll ignore the European Convention. Because you're a terrorist, you're still officially under my jurisdiction but those state police just like to do things their way. And you'll probably be there for at least twelve years before you get to court. The rules have changed since you were last with us.'

He watched Gagliano hustled out of the room, sat on the vacated chair and phoned Conti.

'*Buona sera*, Colonel Sebastiani. Do you have news for me?'

'Sir, I've been interrogating our prisoner Gagliano at Mamertino. Tomorrow, he's being transferred from here to Regina Coeli. The state police are helping us do the transfer. It's all set up. I don't want anything to happen to him on the way there or in Coeli. He's important. I would appreciate you talking to the Interior Minister to make sure he's kept safe while he's in police custody.'

'Do you have any reasons for thinking he might be murdered in custody, or let loose?'

'The media have reported that we've made arrests but haven't mentioned names. We've told no one we're holding him. But we can't keep that secret long. His clients will soon know he's with us and they'll be concerned about what he's going to say. Who knows what contacts they have in the military?'

'What do you suggest?'

'I want the word of the Interior Minister that Gagliano will not to be harmed in any way. I'll have him checked by a doctor before the transfer. If he's so much as scratched when he gets to Regina Coeli, someone will suffer.'

'Isn't this all going too far? My God. Okay, I'll see what I can do. Get back to me in an hour.'

Immediately after Sebastiani replaced the telephone receiver, it rang. '*Pronto.*'

'Major Ferri, sir. Are you still at Mamertino?'

'Just on my way to the barracks. What do you want?'

'Half an hour of your time, sir. It's important.'

'Certainly. My office?'

'I'll be there in ten minutes.'

'You look dreadful. You should give up the late-night parties. Have a seat before you collapse.'

'Parties? That'll be the day. Been all night talking with countries.'

'Ah now, good. Anything?'

'US counter-terrorism just sent this. Low-key stuff but with possible connection to the Rome attack. A right-wing religious group has been bombing Roman Catholic churches in the US. It's extreme right and all white.'

He handed Sebastiani a single sheet.

'White supremacists?'

'Didn't say.'

'Have I got this right? WASPs can also be Roman Catholic, right? Roman Catholicism is widely accepted in the US?'

'Yes sir. I checked. About sixty-million Roman Catholics in the US.'

'That's what I thought.' Sebastiani grasped his knees and sank his neck into his shoulders.

'But it's all been in America. Nobody's been killed. They bomb under cover of darkness. And they always leave a message after a

116

bombing that identifies them as the Holy Catholic Church of America. Their use of the term Catholic means 'universal', I'm told.'

'Why do people do these things? It's terrible. They have a cause?'

'They're against pagan Roman Catholicism. The Roman Catholic Church. The pope.'

Sebastiani raised his eyes to the ceiling. 'Pagan Roman Catholic. Umm. Are you religious, Major?'

The question threw Ferri and he shuffled awkwardly. 'Not really, sir.'

'It's disgusting that people's religions stir them to acts of violence.'

'Will never end, sir.'

'This is all taking place in America. Why is it a CIA matter? What does all this have to do with our investigation?'

'The church has started networks in other countries. Canada so far. But two of their people have visited Italy.'

'In Italy? How long has this been going on?'

'About three years.'

'Three years! Then why the fuck didn't we know about it before? Didn't the US guys know about this?'

'Yes. They didn't tell us till now because they thought we Italians would blow their operation.'

'That's baloney. If these people turn out to have been involved in the Rome attack, that would mean US counter-terrorism acted criminally. I just can't believe this.'

'This is what my US contact told me. I understand other countries were made aware but have also kept it to themselves.'

Sebastiani settled his elbows on his desk, closed his eyes and stroked his temples. 'I sometimes think we pay a heavy price for the stupid behaviour of some of our politicians when they're abroad. They tar all us Italians with the same brush. I'm sorry; you didn't hear me say that.' And as a mollifying afterthought, 'What I said about our politicians is probably not true. Even so, I think you

117

might consider leaking this little gem to one of your journalist friends. Go on, tell me what's going on here in Italy. What possible connection can this Holy Catholic whatever-it-is have with the attack on Rome? Just a minute.' He pressed a button on his telephone and lowered his head to it. 'Colonel here. Please, a pot of coffee right away.' He held the button pressed. 'You too?'

Ferri nodded.

'Make it for two.' He released the button and sat back. 'Are people from this church in Italy now? At this moment?'

'Positive. The two I mentioned. We have their IDs and we know they last came into the country in January this year. They booked into a hotel in the city for one week and then disappeared. They had tickets with American Airlines to return to the US in February but didn't use them. We don't know where they are. I've circulated their descriptions to all Carabinieri and state police units. And the media. That was before coming to see you.'

'My God. I find all this bloody ridiculous.'

'Luisa's gone to France. Research, apparently. Glad to be in the real world and away from the police. So she said.'

This statement made Sebastiani's stomach lurch. 'Research? That's interesting.' He changed the subject. 'Do you still have someone looking at the MMG...? What was the name of the building company?'

'MMGT.' Ferri took out his notebook. 'Mancuso, Magnini, Graziano and Tamburo. A couple of our men are on that. Tamburo was the one who was killed. There's no evidence he was murdered. The workers we spoke to wouldn't talk. Scared. Someone had got to them. But I'm investigating his death. It could have been an accident.'

'People get killed on building sites.' Sebastiani stood and picked up his cap. 'How many days is it now?'

'Seven.'

'Are we making progress?'

'General anti-terror work is good. In the last two days, three arrests, all for organizing terror campaigns. A new cell identified in

Rome is under surveillance. But none of this has anything to do with the Vatican attack.'

'Thanks.' Sebastiani adjusted his cap and yawned. 'I'm off to get some sleep. Call me any time you need me.'

CHAPTER NINE

Still half asleep, he propped himself up on one elbow and pressed the answer button on his cell phone. 'Luisa, hello.'

'*Buongiorno* Colonel. Did I wake you?'

'No, no,' he lied. 'Where are you calling from?'

'Paris. I'm in the Brasserie Bijou café next to my hotel having breakfast. Coffee and croissants.'

Sebastiani checked his watch: half-past seven in the morning and Luisa sounded as bubbly as at any other time. 'Paris?'

'I got here yesterday. I'm making my first report back to you. Well, nothing much to say yet, but I thought I'd let you know I've arrived in France.'

He slid his legs over the side of the bed and sat there a few seconds with his eyes closed in an effort to catch up with the exuberance on the other end of the phone. 'Paris? Not Avignon? Why Paris?'

'The national archives are here. A great starting point. Detailed info on all the clerics on your list.'

'Isn't that information in the Vatican archives?'

'No, it isn't. Only Italian clergy have detailed historical records in the Vatican. But it doesn't have the history for the French clerics on your list. That information is here.'

Anyway, he had given Luisa an open brief and he trusted her. 'Okay Luisa, fine. Good. Have you planned what you're going to do after Paris?'

'I've worked out an itinerary for the whole trip. Do you want to hear it now?'

Fearing his fuzzy brain would not take in the detail, he declined.

'Should you want to know, I'm staying at a nice little three-star hotel not far from the rue des Francs-Bourgeois where the archives are. This is like old times for me. It's great to be back in Paris. You sound distant. Where are you?'

'At home.' Still half asleep, he made for the kitchen and coffee. 'Look, you don't need to phone every day, just when you find anything important.'

'And if I can't get you, who should I contact? You told me not to tell Luca Ferri what I'm doing in France.'

He scratched an ear with the telephone hand and filled the electric kettle with the other. 'Yes. I said that. I didn't want him to know because he's bound to think I'm obsessed with this French thing. But if you come across anything interesting you can tell him. Just don't say you're there for me. Or just leave a message in my voice mail.'

'Okay, colonel. *Ciao!*'

Sebastiani took his coffee to a window that overlooked the Via Brenta and registered surprise when he saw his Carabinieri car already waiting for him, an hour earlier than planned. His trusted driver, *brigadiere* Dino Caso, sat on the front seat of the car with his legs stretched out of the open door, reading.

He sat at the table to finish his coffee and played the plan for Giulio Gagliano's transfer to Regina Coeli prison through his mind. The operation he worked out with Ferri was not complicated but state police could be careless. Better to see first-hand that it proceeded without surprises.

'Buongiorno, Caso. *Come sta?'*

The all-round big man Caso got out of the car and replied with a personable smile and a salute. The colonel liked this steady, reliable man whose excellent knowledge of Rome's highways had served him so well.

'Barracks, sir?'

'Yes please, Caso. What's that you're reading?'

'Musical score, sir.'

'You play in a band?'

'No sir, I sing. Classical tenor. I'm in an operatic company. Semi pro.'

'My God, that's a complete surprise. We've known each other ages, Caso, and I never knew that. What's your taste?'

'Singing, sir? Puccini. Tosca. La Bohème. I love it.'

He climbed into the car feeling sad and irritated. For over five years, Caso had driven him around Rome in all manner of circumstances and he hardly knew the man; only that he was married with three children. Christ, how tragically ignorant my life can be, he thought. 'How's your family?'

'Fine, sir, thank you.'

'Do all of them now go to school?'

'Two of them are at school. The baby is too young. Only three.'

'Congratulations. I have only one child. My son is nineteen. I sometimes wished we'd had more children.' Then he remembered Elaine Bruneau's phone call and flushed. I have a daughter too but all I know about her is that she is a French secret service agent who is in hush-hush business with Conti. But you, Caso, don't need to know that, he thought.

At the junction of Corso Trieste and the Tovelo cul-de-sac, a scooter suddenly appeared in front of the car. Caso braked hard and screamed, 'Get down!' He threw the gear change into reverse and stamped on the accelerator. Sebastiani pressed his hands on the seat in front of him as the car sped backward at high speed. Blue smoke from the spinning tires obscured his view out of the car. The loud bang from a gun and sudden whiteness of the shattered windscreen churned his senses. Caso lurched backward from the impact of the bullets that slammed into his chest and then slumped forward. The car spun and crashed backward into the raised garden strip that separated the two sides of the road.

Shaken and disorientated, Sebastiani couldn't pull his gun from his belt. He heard the thin scream of the scooter approaching and then saw its pillion rider, a youth in red sweater and black helmet, pointing a gun at him. The side window shattered and he shrieked as the bullet tore a chunk from the side of his thigh.

The rider, moving unsteadily on his pillion seat, then fired one more shot into the car. The bullet pounded into the back of the rear seat.

Sebastiani lay on his side trembling but aware. He pulled out his walkie-talkie. 'Emergency. Ambulance and murder squad to junction of Corso Trieste and Via Tovelo. Two suspects on a scooter between Tagliamento, Regina Margherita, and Nomentana. Red sweater and black crash helmet.'

He felt for the pulse in Caso's neck but his driver was dead.

'I'm sure you feel weak at the moment but you'll be walking in a few days.'

Doctor Tomasini, Director General of the Celio Military Hospital in Rome, stood tall and intimidating at the end of the bed with his arms folded. 'We'll get you exercising your leg. Don't want it going stiff. Your driver is dead, did you know?'

'Yes. Caso was a fine man. I'm so sad he died.' In his own ears, these words did not match the gravity of the event that had robbed a family of its provider.

'You were lucky.' He patted Sebastiani's good leg. 'I'll see you again this evening.'

He ignored the installed telephone at his bedside and called Luca Ferri on his mobile. 'Hello. Gagliano's move go okay?'

'No problems. How are you?'

'I'm fine. Caso was killed.'

'I know. Dreadful.'

'I just hope nothing happens to Gagliano in prison.'

'They know he's important. I've informed the media he has been arrested in connection with the attack on the Vatican.'

123

'Great. Now the birds will start singing. Good move.'

'I've got some news.'

'Go on.'

'We didn't find the two who shot you up but the bullets taken from your car and Caso's chest came from the same weapon. A 9 mm Glock 17.'

'Austrian police issue.'

'That's right. Many countries have them.'

Sebastiani lay back on his pillow and closed his eyes. 'Let's cut it there. Get my laptop here and those interactive CDs of the Vatican. One more thing. I want your investigation chronology and report to date. I can keep busy while I'm here.'

'*Pronto*. Vatican administration, *Signora* Alessia Piacenti speaking. What can I do for you?' Such a precise and complete introduction suggested a young woman new to the Vatican.

'Colonel Sebastiani, Rome Carabinieri. I need to speak to *Signor* Sabbi.'

'Ah, that's not Administration. I'll put you through.'

A sharp, querulous voice greeted him. 'Sabbi speaking. What do you want?'

Then he remembered the ferret face and mordant demeanour of the man who had signed back into Vatican custody all the religious objects retrieved from St Peter's Basilica by the police, the fire brigade and their helpers. 'I'm Colonel Sebastiani of Rome Carabinieri. I want access to all the articles and items placed on and around the Basilica altar for the mass on the day of the explosions. All of them. I also want any other objects normally used at the altar. Understood?'

'Can't do that without the authority of the pope.'

'We don't have a pope. *Signor* Sabbi, if you don't do as I say, I'll have you arrested for obstructing the police and thrown into prison. Just collect those objects together and make them available to my investigating officers. Then you stay where you are. They'll be with you within two hours. Do I make myself clear?'

Sebastiani replaced the telephone and lay back against his pillow. 'Little shit,' he blurted out, and then winced as pain shot through his wound.

'Thanks for coming, major. Won't keep you long. It's difficult on the phone.'

Sebastiani lifted his laptop computer onto his good leg.

'See this,' he said, half-turning the computer toward Ferri. 'This is what I meant on the phone.' He pointed at a list displayed on the computer screen. 'Clergy responsibilities on the day of the explosions. Look, Bishop Francis Sinclair, deceased. Duties at the high altar preparing the mass. Do you see that?' He pointed to the details against Sinclair's name.

'You're on the Internet.'

'Vatican web site.'

'Up to date, then.'

'Bloody concentrate, will you? Preparations for an important mass like this can take hours. This could mean Sinclair was there from early on. Organizing something. I don't know what. People and music, apparently. He could have been around when our man was murdered. About eight in the morning.'

'Do you think Sinclair killed this man?'

The colonel scratched the back of his neck. 'I don't know. I don't think so. But he's a suspect.'

'The wounds were odd.'

'Two deep depressions in his face.'

'Yes. I'm thinking about the weapon. What's there at the altar?'

'Watch this. The CD.'

'Latest version?'

'Updated for the celebration. Says so on the label. It's comprehensive too. I've learned a lot about the Vatican in my hours alone in this damned room.' He sped through a series of links to a high frontal view of the papal altar under Bernini's bronze *baldacchino*. 'Here's the altar.'

Ferri stood suddenly and pointed to the computer screen. 'There it is!'

'What are you talking about?'

'Two of them. The altar candlesticks.'

'Christ. Yes.' Sebastiani zoomed further until a brass altar candlestick filled the screen. 'And heavy. Too heavy to swing at someone? What do you think?'

'No. They're heaved about all the time by priests.'

'You're right.' A stabbing pain jerked him back on his pillow where he rested for minutes with closed eyes. 'Phew.'

'You okay?'

He opened his eyes and nodded. 'Well done. That's a good bet.'

'I need the candlesticks used on the day.'

'Send some of your men over to the Vatican. A little man by the name of Sabbi should be sitting, shit scared, by his precious altar bits and pieces. Impound them. Get forensics to run some tests. Maybe find something that matches our mystery man. And fingerprinting. We have the fingerprints of everyone killed in the Basilica. Sinclair's too. See what you can dig up.'

Ferri sat, dug his fingers into the dark stubble on his chin and peered at the computer. 'I don't know. Something odd about this. Pity we don't know where this man was found. If a body was lying around in the cathedral for three hours, someone must have seen it.'

'Unless it was covered. Look at this.' Sebastiani clicked on an icon and from the virtual tour index, selected an image of a red-curtained railing half-enclosing stairways leading down to crypts. 'According to the CD, this area is closed off during a mass. It looks like there's a large recess here. Enough to stash a body? Don't know. Send forensics to take a look.' He grimaced and drew air through his clenched teeth.

'Painful, eh?'

'Now and then. Major, what time did Sinclair start work? Was he there when the man was killed?'

'So far, nothing on that. And I don't know who to ask.'

'Contact Luisa, she'd know who to ask.'

'I'll find out somehow. But now, I have to go.'

The colonel rested back on his pillow and smiled. 'If Sabbi is not there waiting for you, arrest him and put him in a cell overnight.'

Sebastiani's mobile phone rang.

'Fabio, hello. Ricardo Da Corte. I'm in reception. Are you able to walk? Or hobble? The garden is wonderful. Nice place for a chat.'

Ten minutes later Sebastiani and his crutch sat with Ricardo Da Corte in a white gazebo and a cooling breeze.

'How are you?'

'It's not so bad. I'll be out of here fairly soon.'

'Don't rush it. That's always a mistake.'

'Do you have news of Elaine Bruneau?'

'I do, although I can't tell you much. I would but our inter-agency agreement with the French forbids me to. Sorry.'

'I understand.'

'Elaine Bruneau is most certainly your daughter. That's something to please you.'

'That's the confirmation I hoped to hear. Thanks.'

'I'll tell you this, too. She is very senior level and good.'

'A director? Intelligence agent?'

'Intelligence agent.'

They sat quietly looking out to the trees for the time it took a couple of bandaged *carabinieri* to walk past the gazebo.

The colonel idly spun his crutch on its rubber end. 'What about Conti? Why is she going to see him?'

'I know now what that's about and why he's talking to French intelligence but I can't tell you about it. Although there was no reason to have kept that secret from the Italian intelligence community. Could be he had private reasons. But that is a strange one.'

CHAPTER TEN

'Mail, sir.' The ward orderly placed the letter on Sebastiani's bedside cabinet. No stamp so obviously delivered personally to the hospital. He didn't recognize the style of the hand that had written the address, *Colonel Fabio Sebastiani, Celio Military Hospital*. First holding the envelope up to the light and then turning it around and feeling its contents, he held it at arm's length and stared at it.

He could see it contained a folded sheet – no wires or lumpy objects. But who knew he was in the hospital? The military had not released his name to the media in connection with the incident, so somebody had leaked the information. He peeled back the envelope flap, withdrew the page and unfolded it; the short message it contained shocked him into an involuntary movement that shot a pain through his injured leg.

I didn't kill you this time, bastard, but I soon will.

He laid the sheet on his cabinet and pressed the nurse-call button.

Hands waving the air, the male nurse floated in, walked to the foot of the bed and stood there with arms akimbo. 'Yes sir, what can I do for you on this lovely morning?'

'Get me a sterilized, clear plastic bag. I want to put this in it,' he said pointing to the letter. 'And tweezers.'

'Yes, sir. I'll be right back.'

He had learned in just one day that every movement of the body employs the muscles in the legs in some way and, for him in this injured condition, painfully.

A knock at the door prepared Sebastiani for the plastic bag and tweezers. 'Come in.'

General Conti peeked round the door. 'Ah. You're here. Hello Fabio.'

'*Buongiorno*, General.'

Sweeping his arm in a slow-motion *bocce* ball throw, he scooped up a chair from its place against the wall and set it by the bed. As he sat he shook Sebastiani's hand. The gentle softness of the Conti's handshake surprised him: too delicate for a man of his stature but, he assumed, sympathetic to his weakened state. Conti had perfectly manicured and soft hands, which induced Sebastiani surreptitiously to contemplate his own. The general's hands bore no scars from labour. But why would they? He was a favoured son of the Italian upper class, evidenced by his fine, back-of-the-throat eloquence, which rang as pretentious in Sebastiani's ears. His rare outbursts of excitement contained expletives but Sebastiani read this as out of character and an attempt at being a normal soldier. Despite these characteristics and his favoured progression to superior military rank, he held him in high regard. Conti protected him from the Gods and supported him technically. And he had a long and reputable service in the military.

'Sorry to see you in this condition, Fabio. How are you?'

'I'm okay.' He affected a brave-boy smirk.

'Some new terrorist group has tried to kill you, I hear.'

Sebastiani pointed to the letter. 'I've just received confirmation of that fact.'

Conti raised himself on the arms of his visitor's chair and leaned over to look at it. 'Ah. What does it say?'

'It's a threat letter. Someone plans to kill me. Soon, apparently.'

'That is worrying. Let me see it. I'd better not touch it.'

'I'm waiting for tweezers and a plastic bag.'

Conti glared into the distance. 'You know, anyone could have guessed you came here. Even so, I'll take the letter with me. Forensics can run an eye over it. I'll set a man working on the leak. If it's from inside the force, that's not good news.'

The door opened without warning and the male nurse bounded in again and laid the requested items on the bed. 'Here we are sir, one plastic bag, sterilized, and tweezers.' He stood there looking as though anticipating reward for services rendered.

'That'll be all for now.'

'Very well, sir.' Holding his head proudly, he pranced to the door and took one last look back over his shoulder before disappearing.

'I thought you were going to give him a tip,' said Conti.

'Not today.' He took up the tweezers and grimaced.

'Just a minute, let me.' Using the tweezers, the general re-folded the letter and put it into the plastic bag. 'I'll get this to the lab.'

'Thanks.'

Conti slouched back in his chair. 'Something you should know.'

'Sir?'

'The cardinals. They're meeting the prime minister.' He glanced at his watch. 'Today, I think. Yes, today. They're moving to Avignon. Some are leaving Rome tomorrow. It's causing a panic. Behind-the-scenes diplomatic argy-bargy. Unusual situation.'

'The papers say they go with the Prime Minister's blessing. That will make him the most important person in the country.' Another injudicious political statement and he regretted it. Where did Conti stand on the political spectrum? He didn't know but assumed right of center, around the same point as the Prime Minister's.

'I've read such articles. I hope you're not taking them seriously, Fabio. The important thing is you've got all the information you want before these people go.'

'I'm confident we have. Anyway, they're not out of reach just because they're in another country. Said so yourself.' Sebastiani shifted his body weight onto his hands and shuffled to gain comfort, which strained his voice as he spoke. 'I suppose they'll elect the pope in France. In the meantime, Catholicism is without a leader. I wonder what they'll do with the Basilica.'

'I've heard no mention of a plan. As a ruin, St Peters is attracting hoards of visitors. I've never seen so many people in the Via Della Conciliazione. Funny how people like to see devastation.' Conti lowered his voice. 'What's more, on instructions from the Minister of the Interior we're to keep that area as open as possible to attract sightseers. Anything for a buck, eh?'

'How do you see things now, sir? The investigation.'

'In your absence, Ferri has been reporting progress. Not all bad, I'm glad to say. But all the success we've had so far has nothing to do with the Rome attack. We've rounded up terrorists, known and suspected. That's good. But we still have no idea who bombed us or why. Not good enough, is it?'

'We've got Gagliano.'

'I know.' The general smiled cynically and threw his gloves into his upturned cap. 'Pretty small fry.'

'I disagree. He was definitely involved. He's not broken yet but I'm confident he will. An important witness once he does.'

'Colonel, our only one.'

'True.'

'The only thing he's said till now is that he wants his lawyer. His lawyer? Christ!'

'When he realizes we can hold him forever without giving him a lawyer he'll talk.'

'I hope so.'

'His only bit of the action was killing Ricci. If we can get him to admit that, we'll get the rest. He'll confess to Ricci's murder if he understands the alternative is twelve years in prison without trial, and life if convicted.'

'A scenario for doing a deal.'

132

'It is.'

'Lot of pressure from above, Fabio. We need a big fish soon.' Conti retrieved his cap and gloves. 'I'm sorry. I know there's not much you can do from here.'

'I have control from here. I have up-to-date status information and I know who's doing what.'

Conti stretched his neck to peer at the laptop on Sebastiani's side cabinet. 'You're up with all this computer stuff, are you?'

'Enough to get by, sir.'

'I'm happy I do not have to use them. Anyway, I'm too old to get started now.' He donned and adjusted his cap. 'Time to go.'

Conti departed, leaving him alone with his computer and his thoughts. The computer had gone to sleep and he had no intention of waking it up. He lay back with his hands behind his head and stared at the white ceiling, trying to fathom a connection between Giulio Gagliano, a definite party to the bombing, and the French priests, whom he suspected of involvement.

There should be no connection but I feel there must be, he thought. Who has employed Gagliano to commit murder that would mix it with French clergy? It's a ridiculous idea.

But Luisa's clever reasoning about the Gaetani family and the Colonna vengeance sworn against it had him hooked. Somewhere, somehow, Gagliano fitted into that vengeance. And perhaps also, the youth on the scooter who shot him.

Sebastiani swept an excited smile around his empty room. Ferri's telephoned news had suddenly lifted him above boredom.

'I've got the forensics report with me.' Finding the Holy Grail – apparently – caused Ferri to talk loudly. 'We were right. He was murdered with an altar candlestick.'

'I'm looking at it on my computer.' He sat up in bed with his laptop computer wobbling on his uninjured leg. 'There's a large center crucifix and a candlestick either side of it.'

'It's one of those at the side.'

Sebastiani paused and stared at the object he displayed. 'It doesn't look so big after all. Wouldn't need to be strong to kill somebody with that. Is it hollow?'

'It's hollow but heavy. The one identified as the weapon was damaged by falling masonry, but not badly. There are good fingerprints all over the shaft. And traces of blood on the base. Doc Martino confirmed the face wounds fit with the shape of the candlestick base. And the blood is from this man.'

'Fingerprints? Did forensics identify who they belong to?'

'The murdered man, Sinclair and the second unidentified body.'

Sebastiani slumped back and closed his eyes. 'Two unidentified corpses had their hands on that candlestick. The bodies, how were they dressed? Priestly garb?'

'I don't know. I saw them at the mortuary, naked. But I know that no identifying objects were found that matched these two people. Why wouldn't they be carrying money or credit cards? I can't imagine anybody targeting these two particular people to rob them.' A pause and then, 'Christ!'

'What is it?'

'You're right. Only two bodies remained unidentified. That's why they were at the mortuary. It's strange both left traces on the candlestick.'

'What are you thinking?'

'The two missing Americans. I'll take another look at the clothing.'

'You should.'

'We had no reason to think those two would be among the dead. If they're the Americans we've been searching for, it could tie Sinclair to them.'

'What time did Sinclair arrive?'

'We have a witness that he was there a little after eight-thirty. The man was murdered about around eight.'

'But that's close. You know, I think the mists are beginning to clear.'

'We should investigate the French priests.'

Sebastiani smiled. Ferri seemed to be moving to his view. The leading lights of the Church involved in the devastation of St Peters and the murder of Pope Boniface X? The possibility was solidifying.

'I believe you're on the right track. If you haven't already, look at Sinclair's accommodation here in Rome. Get your French contacts to check him out in whatever that place is called.'

'Barbentane?'

'Barbentane. That's it.'

'Till now, we had nothing on Sinclair. What we know now ties him to a murder. Wasn't in that category until this call.'

'Right.' He sat back surprised he had spoken so long without feeling tired. 'Useful call. Thanks.'

'I'll check what we've got on the American Catholic Church. Anything I can do for you?'

'Well, the doc said if I could arrange transport, I could leave the hospital right away. I guess the quietness gives me a chance to study the data. But I can't do that all the time. I'm bored out of my mind. I'd feel better at the barracks. Any chance of you organizing transport for me?'

'Of course. Does that mean you're not taking sick leave?'

'No, Ferri. It bloody doesn't. I can choose where I want to be on sick leave. Even at the barracks. If you could do that as soon as possible, I'd be grateful.'

'No problem.'

'I can hobble around now. It's painful but the doctor encouraged me to move about.'

'Will you be taking charge, sir?'

'No. Conti was clear about this. I'll be available for consultation only. And you, boss, will take the blame for anything that goes wrong. And lots will go wrong, believe me.'

Later that day, Ferri stood at Sebastiani's door accompanied by one of his investigating team. 'Tirelli's got intelligence on Bishop Sinclair. I think you should know about it right away.'

'Tell me about it, Tirelli. Something interesting is it?'

'Yes sir. Bishop Sinclair was staying in Rome at the Hotel Santa Cristina in Trastevere and was booked in for another four weeks. I checked the register. Someone checked him out just one day after he was killed at the cathedral. All his belongings had been taken away. I checked with Vatican administration. They made the booking in the first place and said his things had been collected. When I asked to see them, I was told it was not possible. They had been incinerated. Wouldn't normally be a problem. But now he's suspected of being involved in a crime. I tried contacting the person who burnt the things. It was a French priest and he's already returned to Barbentane.'

Sebastiani's forehead creased into deep furrows. 'Did you ask why this was done?'

'I did. They said it's the usual way where the deceased has no relatives. And Sinclair had no known relatives.'

The colonel set his chin on a balled fist. 'I would say someone in the clergy has something to hide. Don't you think? And what do your friends in France say about his apartment there? Surprise me, Tirelli.' He rocked gently backward and forward in his chair.

'I had a phone call from the gendarmerie in Barbentane. Sinclair's accommodation has already been occupied by another priest and his possessions have been destroyed.'

'Don't waste time in the Church, do they? Someone is covering up something very serious. Don't you think?'

'Yes sir, I do.'

'And what do you think we should to do about it?'

'We and the French police should be working on it together.'

'Well done, Tirelli. I agree with you totally.'

CHAPTER ELEVEN

Luisa pulled the flight tickets from her travel bag and checked the details. An hour's wait before boarding, take off at two forty-five; should be there by four this afternoon. Hire a car and then find a hotel somewhere in Nimes. Next day travel to Chateau la Duc, the country house of *Madame* Yvette Collineau and arrive anytime during the morning between nine and eleven-thirty, as arranged.

Sat at a shaky desk in her hotel room she reviewed her notes about each of the cardinals. A summary sheet headed *Cardinals' Return to France: Why?* set focus on the purpose of her France assignment, and pages for the listed priests gave their religious and personal details.

She had not asked Sebastiani why he had selected these particular cardinals in case it prejudiced her research. But what made them so special?

Except for two, none of the cardinals seemed remarkable. They had all contributed to the establishment of places of learning or care but the history of Roman Catholic priests is full of such works.

Archbishop Collineau, the most senior priest to escape the Rome attack was now the assumed head of the Roman Catholic Church, so he's special. But Luisa set her mind on learning yet more about him from his mother, Yvette Collineau, the very next day.

She dragged her finger to the name Bishop Francis Sinclair. He'd worked near Avignon and likely had a close relationship with Archbishop Collineau. So, even though there was no Sinclair in her memory of Barbentane, Luisa had him marked for research.

Something all these priests had in common gave her cause for suspicion: not one of them bore the marks of the conservatively Roman Catholic and secretive Opus Dei. Although there were no particular identifying characteristics, her trained eye could spot clues in biographical data, teaching activities and associations with known members. In her reading of the signs, none of those listed practiced the severe dogma of Opus Dei. So, might these priests oppose adherence to strict doctrine enough to do harm to the Church? An idea not provable and not worth chasing, she thought.

Luisa's appointment with Yvette Collineau was made on the pretext of historical religious research, which always gave her admission to castles, cathedrals and other buildings of religious importance. And it required only telephoned confirmation of her credentials at the university in Rome for the Chateau la Duc visit to go ahead.

The asphalt drive meandered through great oaks and then opened up into an expanse of trees, lawns and flower gardens. Luisa slowed her car at the sight of the beautiful baroque architecture of the Chateau and then parked next to a red Ferrari on an open area of white gravel in front of the house.

An elderly woman stood at the door with her hands clasped across her stomach and head tilted to one side.

'*Bonjour Madame*, I'm Luisa Fabian.'

'And I am Yvette Collineau. Welcome to Chateau la Duc. You are Italian, and so was my family. That made it easy for me to decide I would like to meet you.' Her hand swept to the door. 'We can talk comfortably inside the house.'

The old lady led Luisa through a large rococo hall of grey marble and tall bevelled mirrors.

She noticed her awe. 'A little too much?' Drawing her further into the house, she explained, 'It's all my husband's doing. I would have settled for something less grand. But it's always been more or less like this since it was built. So we have to blame Marcel

138

Collineau, my late husband's ancestor.' She raised a hand over regally upholstered chairs. 'Take a seat. Eduardo is organizing coffee. Now, please tell me again the purpose of your visit.'

Luisa sat forward in her chair. 'I'm researching the influence the French clergy have had on the current teachings on the Roman Catholic Church. There have been many French popes and many high-ranking French cardinals. But I want to know about the contribution your own family has made. After all, the Collineau family has produced many cardinals.'

The old woman sat stiff and silent for a moment as though struck dumb by the words. 'I suppose you're right. Come with me, I want to show you something.' She walked Luisa to another extravagant baroque room and to a finely inlaid glass-topped display case. 'This room is filled with the spirit of amazing history and all because of this.'

Together, they peered through the glass at a fragile-looking document that had turned sepia with age and on which a curious French text had been written with an educated but unsteady hand.

'This is the family covenant. Read it then I will tell you all about it.'

The cruel axe will send Collineau to his God in the Kingdom of heaven. Yet Rome and its demon king Gaetano, the false Pope of burning hate remains. Raise the sword of righteousness and strike the head from his body, cursed now and forever unto his last generation. Slay also his accursed, satanic harlot, the nemesis of our family and of mankind.

Signed by myself, Cardinal Jean Collineau in this Year of our Lord 1628, the fifteenth day of October.

Luisa read it and recognized the telltale words that placed the document around the 17th century. Then her expression of interest suddenly froze into incredulity as the meaning of the text became clear. She shuddered. She scanned the ceiling and then returned her gaze to the document. A glint of a memory showed through and her mind wrestled to recall an event from many years before, but it all faded as Yvette Collineau called for attention.

'Look at these paintings.' They depicted men in various modes of dress covering hundreds of years. 'These are my husband's ancestors. These start with Cardinal Jean Collineau in the early sixteen hundreds. That's him. Right at the end. Actually, it's the beginning. But I must tell you, Colonna was the original name of this family in France.'

Luisa's mind whirled back to Sciarra Colonna and his ousting of Pope Boniface VIII. 'Wasn't Cardinal Jean celibate?'

'Good question, my dear. Let me explain. At various times the Collineaus changed the family name. This was a trick used in reclaiming lands confiscated by the Roman Catholic Church.' She shrugged as though to be relieved of the detail. 'Despite the name changes, they're all Collineau family. Some faces are brothers and sons of other faces but I don't know their names. And you are right, many of them entered the church. The priests have no documented offspring, of course – celibacy and such. Fourteen pictures, in chronological order.' Her pointing finger swept from left to right. 'From there…to there.'

'And this last one. Who's he?'

'My late husband. Maurice. Archbishop Roger Collineau's father.'

'No women?'

'My dear, you might believe from this the family has been male dominated. And you would be right. These men have a place in this room because they have carried this family covenant down through the centuries. Each one in turn has passed it on to his successor. Can you believe this? I find it all childish. We women are excluded from secrets. That's a man's thing. The secret society, the
140

Freemasons, the lodge. All that stuff,' she cast away with a backward fling of her head. 'And we wives find out about such things because we play games with our men in bed. Apparently, it has an ending but with whom, what and when, I have no idea.'

'What about all the Collineau priests?'

'There have been a number of those in the family. And some were cardinals. My son, of course. As far as I know this family has never produced a pope.'

'Do you think your son will become pope?'

She sighed deeply. 'I'm not sure. I'm told he will be. If you had come tomorrow you would have met him. He's coming here before taking up office in Avignon.'

'You must be very excited.'

'Oh, I am.'

Eduardo appeared. '*Madame*, I put coffee in the sitting room half an hour ago. Shall I make some more and bring it here?' He spoke in French but with an Italian accent.

'Please, Eduardo.'

Then she looked around the room. 'Jean Collineau's spirit is here. Let us sit and share his company.'

And so they sat and contemplated the portraits in silence.

Yvette Collineau rested her elbows on the padded arms of her chair and pressed her fingertips together in front of her face. 'I guess the best place to start is with this first picture, Cardinal Jean Collineau. He didn't get on well with the Roman Catholic hierarchy even though he held high office within it.'

Paris, Cardinal Richelieu's Palace, 1628

The warm glow from the open fire fought bravely against the sunless, cold October daylight breaking into the room from the large windows along one side of the cheerless palace chamber. The man in scarlet warming himself at the fireplace, Amand-Jean du Plessis, Duc de Richelieu, one-time favourite of the queen mother, Marie de

Medici, was now, after isolation, restored to favour and the highest office in the government of King Louis XIII.

Cardinal Richelieu's fortunes, skills and ruthless politicking had led him to the highest seat of the Roman Catholic Church in France, and the appointment by King Louis to the position of Secretary of State, making him the clerical and secular master of all France.

Standing with one hand on the mantle above the fireplace and a foot on the fender, he studied the small bursts of gas erupting from the heart of the fire and igniting into a confusion of purple, blue, red and yellow jets, shooting out in various directions and replacing each other in a colourful pyrotechnic display.

The door at the far end of the room from Richelieu opened to admit his obsequious secretary and personal adviser, De Fancan, who bowed low and solemnly announced the visitor. '*Éminence*, the Bishop of Orleans, to discuss the legal matter of estates.'

'Ah, Cardinal Jean Collineau. It is such a long time since we last met.' Richelieu's words, shouted as the visitor approached, reverberated in the large room in the tone of a long, lost friend but the meeting had no friendly purpose. Stroking his beard, he said, 'I am informed you live in Paris.'

Collineau rubbed his hands together. He had travelled a long way in a horse-drawn carriage that did little to protect him from the cold, damp day. 'That is true. At the moment. Yes.'

'Have the goodness to tell me if you still have that same grand estate outside Paris?'

They had first met in Paris when both had sought to enroll as officers in the French military academy. Both had changed their minds and had taken unlikely opportunities to join the Roman Catholic priesthood.

Jean Collineau entered the Church at the age of twenty-three knowing he would gain immediate high status and great wealth. He had grabbed this opportunity undeterred by the need to join a seminary and learn theology and was consecrated as Bishop of Orleans, the vacant See his father had purchased for him.

Richelieu became Bishop of Luçon when the erstwhile occupier of that See, his brother, died. His great zeal on behalf of the church and his support of the French monarchy won him favour and high influence. His ruthless policies and actions in support of church and state also brought him powerful enemies. Where he could root them out he conspired for their assassinations.

Jean responded unenthusiastically. 'Yes, I still have a home in Paris. But I'm mostly away.'

'Ah. That is why I've seen nothing of you.'

'We last met in Rome, many years ago. Pope Paul the fifth, you might recall.' Collineau turned his back on the Master of France and uninvited to do so, laid his old and crumpled leather document case on the huge table. Without removing his heavy black cape, he sat on one of the twenty ornamentally-carved, high-backed oak chairs arranged along its two long sides. 'You were a mere priest then, of course.'

The Master sneered and sniffed. Thrusting his hands into the folds of his long red cassock, he strode briskly round the table to face Collineau but remained standing, a power position he consciously adopted for seated adversaries. 'Do you not understand the situation you are in? I suspect you might soon regret your disrespect for the chief minister of France.' He slapped his hand on the table. 'Are those the property contracts and title deeds I have asked to see?'

Collineau withdrew from the leather case a collection of documents neatly bound by a purple ribbon. '*Éminence*…or do I call you honourable Secretary of State? So difficult to know.' He untied the ribbons. 'Lawyers produced these documents and they have held them secure. They have not been doctored in any way. Why should you need to examine them?'

His accuser gripped the edge of the table and leaned over to peer at the papers. 'Are these for all your properties in France? So few for so many estates? Surely these are not all.' His words reflected his rapid and challenging movements.

'My properties are few but large and extensive. These are what you have asked for. It would not be possible for me to bring all the supplements for ancillaries. There are many hundreds.'

Richelieu stared at the papers, placed a clenched fist against his mouth and blew audibly into it. 'I see.' Shoving his leather-bound notebook across the table, he said, 'Give me the names of your lawyers. I require to have those supplements examined.'

'These properties belong to me. This is ridiculous.'

'You are entitled to your view on the matter. And I understand your anger.' He then walked so quickly to the main door of the room that his long, white side locks swung upwards against his red cap like a dove's wings. He opened the door, glared back at Collineau and shouted, 'Come in gentlemen.'

De Fancan led three stern-faced men into the room, all dressed heavily against the cold and damp October weather. One, a corpulent well-groomed man of about fifty years, whose dark townsman's robe fell over his ample midriff to the heels of his boots, coughed and ventured 'Good evening.'

The other two men, of greatly differing heights and bundled up in mean, heavy woollen cloaks, stood silent and gaunt. They played nervously with the shabby woollen hats they held in their hands.

Richelieu barked at the men, 'This meeting will take only minutes.'

Collineau remained seated, stiff-lipped and silent, playing absentmindedly with the chain of the silver crucifix hanging from his neck.

'These gentlemen are officials of the state. *Monsieur* De Beaufort is a land transaction professional who is employed by the government. That is, he is employed by me. He is to take your papers away and peruse them. Without question, he will expose your illegal acquisition of vast areas of France.'

The Master of France sat down opposite the defendant, cold smugness filling his narrow face.

Collineau looked to each end of the long table then scratched at an eyebrow. '*Éminence.* I know what you are doing. Whoever examines these documents will see all of my father's property was transferred to me legally. But no one will have chance to say so. My father did all things perfectly legally.'

'My dear fellow cardinal, the pope has informed me your father was not an honest man. He illegally acquired property belonging to the Roman Catholic Church and you knew about this when you signed ownership so you are as immoral as your father. Your family has been land-grabbing for centuries. How was that possible?'

Collineau looked around to remove himself from Richelieu's fixed stare. 'I do not know why the pope should be interested in property that has been in my family for more than three hundred years. King Philip gave these lands to my family. My ancestors defended and supported him. They fought for his kingdom with their private armies. They sacrificed their lives. I am simply in the line of inheritance.'

'The Church has had problems with your family for many years. Rebellions, false teachings and such things. Pope Urban calls you all the brood of the devil.'

'Outrageous nonsense.'

Richelieu raised a finger. 'And our beloved pope commands we remove the demons from you and your kin before sending you off to heaven. I must obey. For this reason, I have sent your sister and brother to the Bastille.'

Collineau's hands shot to his cheeks. 'What! You are condemning us to death? I protest. They have committed no crimes. This is barbaric and unjustified.'

'Whatever it is, until this matter is cleared up, you are going to the Bastille to join them.' He held out an arm toward the grey ghosts and wiggled his fingers. '*Lettre de cachet.*' As he took it, he said, 'This is a warrant for your arrest and imprisonment.' He fingered the red, wax disk attached to it. 'The seal of His Majesty, King Louis. This is a serious matter.'

Collineau stood and squared himself to his prosecutor. 'What you are doing is immoral and illegal. And you know it. I pray God will protect my family from you.'

'You should pray for the mercy of the judge. You will be facing him soon enough.' He flicked his hand toward the door. 'Take him away,' he said disdainfully.

Without further protest, Jean Collineau walked from the room trailed by the two grey ghosts.

Richelieu then turned his attention to the other silent witnesses of his summary inquisition.

'*Monsieur* De Fancan, go now and ensure the prisoner sees but does not speak to his sister or brother in the Bastille.'

'*Éminence.*' De Fancan bowed and left the room.

The Master laid a flat hand on the documents. 'Now, *Monsieur* De Beaufort. I command you to employ your fine knowledge, skill and diligence to make sure these lands are returned to the Roman Catholic Church. With one exception. You are to consider now how I can best accept ownership of the estate and house in Paris. Do you understand?'

La Calmette, today

Yvette Collineau's long account of her ancestor's dispute with Richelieu and his imprisonment seemed at first to tire her. Her eyes closed and her head fell slowly onto her chest. Then, as though her tiredness had been pretence, she returned to full alertness. 'There's more to this, of course. But some other time, I think. I'll ask Eduardo to bring some more coffee.' She looked at her watch. 'Oh, perhaps not. It's lunchtime. Luisa, you are welcome to stay for lunch.'

'Thank you, no. I've taken enough of your time. And I have to drive to Avignon today. You've told me what happened to only one of these men. To tell me about them all would take a long time.'

'Not so my dear.' Yvette waggled a correcting finger. 'No, no. Jean was special. His parents were already dead, he had no offspring – he was celibate – and his brother and sister had no offspring. By getting rid of these three, Pope Urban believed he would rid the world of a rebellious family and take back their lands for the Roman Church. Can you imagine? Ten days of torture and then beheaded; all of them.' She threw her hands apart in completion of the act. 'For Richelieu and the pope that was the end of the Collineaus, who had no other legal relatives.'

'No more relatives? Then how could the line continue?'

'Not so fast. I didn't say that. Legally, there were none. But Jean had another brother, and that's him.' She pointed to the second picture.

The women stood and, for several silent moments, studied the bony, insipid face of the first inheritor of the covenant.

'Claude. I can see the name plate on the frame,' said Luisa.

'Right, Claude the bastard.'

'Jean Collineau must have written the Covenant.'

Yvette crossed her arms tightly under her breasts and heaved them up in drawing a deep breath. 'I believe so. Although I am now wondering how that could be if he was in the Bastille. I'll have to ask my son.'

'I'd better go.'

'But you don't have to.

'You're very kind but I must go.'

Madame Collineau took her hand and patted it. 'I'd love to see you again. You must come back.'

'Of course, I want to complete my research on your family.'

She looped her arm in Luisa's as they walked together to the large front terrace.

'Who drives the Ferrari?'

The old woman laughed and clapped her hands together. 'My dear, that's me. I like to drive Eduardo around the countryside.'

147

CHAPTER TWELVE

Sebastiani stood at the full-length mirror longer than usual, bent his head this way and that, turned round and looked over his shoulder, then manipulated a hand mirror in combination to peruse the back of his head.

He'd been in hospital eating less than a man's measure and, naturally, he'd lost weight. Maybe slimmer and healthier than before but his overwhelming belief was that his clothes didn't fit as they once did.

'*Merda!*'

The light-grey linen suit he now had on, guaranteed spotless courtesy of the dry cleaners, and the other two suits he'd already tried on just didn't fit as they did a few weeks ago. He pulled at the sides of his trousers and the front of his jacket. 'Too big.' Then he stared hopelessly at the other suits that lay on his officer's single bed, and scowled. 'They're all too big.'

A flush of worry swept through his chest. He checked yet again the date and the time by his watch and shuffled out to his car. Would his newly found daughter care how he looked? No, certainly not. Would she be impressed with his rank of colonel? Also, no. Would his being Rome's anti-terror chief mean anything to her? Yes it would; she was secret service. But what would she say about his being shot?

These and similar vanities busied his mind while waiting for Elaine Bruneau to appear in the hotel lobby. He laid his walking stick on a chair and flicked through her photographs again, checking the details written on the back of each. One and a half years old: a chubby, in his view, overweight baby. Twenty-three years old, graduation ceremony at *Université d'Angers:* good university, he knew that. Thirty-five, last year's date and similar to how he would see her today. It irritated him that she'd sent no photos of her mother, Bernadette.

'Colonel Sebastiani?'

The hotel receptionist stood near him.

'*Si?*'

'*Buongiorno*, sir. A lady is waiting for you in the private lounge. I'll take you there.'

And there she was, framed by the scarlet brocade curtains hanging in sweeps at the windows behind her.

She stood in front of one of the four easy chairs placed around a low inlaid coffee table, shaking hands with and saying goodbye in French to a tall, slim man of – he guessed – middle eastern extract, while intermittently half-smiling in Sebastiani's direction. The man left without acknowledging him.

He looked for Bernadette in her but saw no resemblance to the image in his memory. Taller than her mother, Elaine had an overall dark aura heightened by her short black hair and graphite grey costume. She wore a skirt cut just above her knees, an unimaginable choice for her mother way back then. But he acknowledged her formal elegance as appropriate for her current role in life.

Supported by his walking stick, he hobbled toward her.

A warm, olive-skinned smile greeted him as they shook hands.

'*Madame* Bruneau?'

'Yes. Italian, if you wish.'

'French is okay.'

'Good. I think we should relax, don't you…Colonel? You should call me Elaine.'

'Elaine. Hello.' He glanced at his stick. 'I did warn you about the injury.'

'Yes. You were shot. I know. Are you in pain?' Her tone carried an officious quality.

'It's just a bit awkward.'

'Let's sit down.'

149

Sebastiani used the arms of the chair and many silent grimaces to sit. Only then did he notice the briefcase and green document folder on the table in front of him.

Shaking his head in a short awkward silence, he looked at her askance. 'You need to convince me. The timing's right, but that is not enough.'

'I know. That's why I'm here. It is one reason but not the main reason. I'll explain later.'

She spoke more crisply that he recalled on the phone but in his ears, still pleasantly paced and modulated.

'They've left me a pot of coffee.'

'No thank you.' He wondered if she had picked up his affected withdrawn and suspicious response.

'This is a funny situation. I had ideas about what to say but now they don't seem right.'

'First, show me some proof.'

She removed a wad of documents from the green folder, all the time searching his face. 'These are copies of everything I have. You can keep them all.'

'Copies?'

'I have originals of the most important documents.'

His eyebrows rose as he tried to peek into the green folder. 'Let's see what you've got.'

She handed him a dog-eared black and white photograph. 'This is original.'

His eyes lit up. '*Mama mia*! Bernadette. I remember her. This photograph. We were at Via Brenta. I remember this very moment.' *Fabio, I love you and I want you to love me forever.*

'This is me with mother three years later. You can tell that's me. Can't you?'

He studied her face and sighed. 'The likeness is unmistakable.' He recognized Bernadette's handwriting in the words *Little Elaine and me in the desert.* 'Your mother's hair was reddish. Yours is jet black.'

'Because I have an Italian father.' She looked keenly for his response; he smiled vacuously.

150

'Fill in the years. What happened to her? Did she return to France?' He sat forward in his chair to get the reply and secretively to compare her features against his memory of Bernadette.

'After Rome, she went to Lyon and lived with her parents. That's where she had me. Then to Tunisia.'

'Tunisia?'

'She packed me and a suitcase and went off to Tunisia with a prince.'

He laughed. 'You're joking.'

'No joke.'

'Amazing.'

'But it's true. A real prince. Mother's father, my grandfather, was a diplomat. Middle East postings. Granddad knew his father. We lived there in luxury for about fifteen years. I still don't know why but we went back to Lyon.'

'Did she ever tell you why she left Rome?'

'I knew you'd want to know that. It was very simple. She was pregnant and wanted me born French. Mother never wanted to marry and believed you, being Italian and Catholic, would insist on it.'

'I'm not sure I would have. But it's all in the past.'

She handed him another document. 'My birth certificate. Careful. It's as old as I am.'

He acknowledged the wit with a smile and then read the words aloud. 'Father: Fabio Alberto Sebastiani. City of Rome, Italy.' Apparently out of his control, his lips massaged each other while he rested his head on a finger. He took a deep breath to release an answer to the question she had not yet posed. 'You have a brother. Stepbrother, I suppose.'

'I know. Roberto. Padua University.'

'You know so much.'

'It's easy.' She passed over her ID card. 'I'm secret service. You had forgotten?'

Her confidence reminded him of Luisa Fabian and he assumed, for the first time, this must be the nature of modern professional women.

151

'Forgotten? No. But this is unbelievable.' Wrestling his injured leg and sudden uneasiness, he sunk back in his chair. 'That's the other reason you're here. It's something to do with the Rome bombing. You'd better tell me.'

'I'm part of a team investigating a terrible crime. It has nothing to do with the Rome bombing but more than that I cannot say. I can only tell you this.' She placed a hand on the briefcase. 'General Conti must have these documents today. I'm asking you to take me to him.'

'No problem. I'll get you there.'

'Thanks. It's very important.'

'How long are you staying in Rome?'

'Today, briefing with Conti. Soon as possible, I fly away.'

'Where to?'

'I can't say.'

'Who was the man who left when I came in?'

'No more questions.'

'Tell me this. Does Conti know I'm your father?'

'Of course. I informed our Paris HR people as soon as I knew some four years ago. Now I have an assignment with Italian anti-terror. General Conti would need to know. No more questions, Colonel.'

'Please, don't call me colonel.'

'Fabio?'

'That's better.'

She kissed her fingers, reached over and pressed them on his cheek. 'You know, it was on the cards I would come to Rome sometime but I wasn't sure about meeting you. The bombing. That's what made me sure. I realized then what I could have missed.'

'I'm glad you changed your mind.' A first touch of emotion peeped through.

'I am too. You're nice. I just had to phone that night to make sure you weren't killed.'

'You said you had a father.'

'Henri Ferrant. Fell out of heaven and into my arms, mother used to say.'

152

'Sounds good.'

'He is.' She smiled delicately. 'Are you sad?'

'What about?'

'I shouldn't have asked you that. I'm sorry.'

'Not a problem. Sad? Not at the moment.'

'Do you have time for me today?'

'Naturally.'

'Look through this stuff first. I think it'll answer a few questions for you. Then we can go through the whole story. Take me to lunch. A good Italian restaurant. Put on your uniform. I want to see you as a colonel.'

As they left, her arm wrapped in his, he moved to one side the Private Meeting sign someone had placed by the door.

'*Bonjour, Madame* Bruneau.' Conti shook Elaine's hand and continued to hold it while his other hand directed her into the room. Lead crystal drinking glasses and bubbling mineral water in bottles glistened on a tray in the middle of the long, glossy conference table. He closed the door, walked her to one of the fifty chairs placed around it, held it while she sat and then took a seat opposite her. 'I trust Italy is treating you hospitably.'

'Everything is fine, thank you.'

She opened her briefcase and took from it two bound documents, which she laid in front of her.

'I hope together we can eradicate this dreadful business,' said Conti. 'Is it only Africa in this case?'

'As far as I know, yes. And it's all coming through Tunisia.' She slid the documents across to him. 'This is what I have for you: the names of terror suspects in Tunisia who are linked to the transportation of children to Europe. Just a few names and background information that might be useful for your interrogation of suspects in Italy. I expect to learn more in Tunisia.'

Conti leafed through the documents. 'Terrorist groups employ children in their armies but rounding them up and shipping them out for immoral purposes is new to me. Is this a TCG activity?'

'No. This is not an Islamic terrorist organization, as such. And it does not have the Islamic objectives of the TCG. It is new and growing and it targets the current Tunisian government only, as far as we know. My feeling is it will get absorbed into the TCG.'

This made him sit up. 'How do you mean, absorbed? The TCG is totally fragmented.'

'You are right. I meant as far as aims are concerned. But at the moment, they operate independently and they transport children to fund their campaign, buy weapons and such. And it is very easy for them. The uprisings in North Africa have left many children orphaned. For religious Islam, children drifting on the streets are a dishonour and a stain on their society. They are treated brutally. Someone has seen an opportunity for making money out of this situation. Unfortunately for the waifs and strays, that someone is a terrorist and the market for this trade is ripe in Europe. The people who organize the collection and transportation of the children are powerful. Our secret service has identified politicians and police, in Tunisia and the receiving countries.'

'Have you named suspects in France?'

'Yes. No arrests yet. We have been doing surveillance on suspects for some time, to see who they contact. We now believe some of those contacts are Italians living in Italy. We need you to investigate the Italian connection.'

'Terrorism and transporting children. An odd combination of activities, wouldn't you say?'

'My intelligence tells me that it pays.'

'Why are you going to Tunis?'

'I have a contact there, a low-level politician with information about suspects in Tunisia. He wants a lot of money for the information. I'm going there to check him out.'

'And to learn the names of the European dealers.'

154

'Not from this man. For that information, I have a trusted local who has infiltrated the terrorist group itself. As I said, we have already identified suspects in France.'

Conti stroked his chin. 'Colonel Sebastiani would not be involved in this investigation. You should know that.'

'Nor would I expect him to be.'

'He should not know what's going on here. Have you told him anything?'

'No. I have told him nothing about my reasons for being here or about Tunisia.'

'How did he take the news about you being his daughter?'

She smiled broadly. 'At first, he was sceptical. And that's understandable. It must have seemed strange me phoning him immediately after the bombing but I just had to find out if he was okay.'

'And why not? He's your father.'

'We met for the first time, earlier today. He seems a very nice man.'

'I've worked with Colonel Sebastiani for many years and I can tell you he is.'

'Well, I think that is it, General. You have as much information about Tunisia as is available at this time.'

He tapped his finger tips on the documents. 'Right. I'll provide resources to look into the Italy side of this immediately.'

She stood, took a bottle of mineral water, poured a little into a glass and drank it. 'I will debrief you on my Tunis trip when I return.'

'Fine. When do you leave for Tunis?'

'Tomorrow morning.'

'I trust it works out well. We have to crack this one quickly.'

They shook hands.

'Good luck, *Madame* Bruneau. Have a safe journey.'

Conti walked her to the door and as soon as she had left the room, his face turned sour. He walked quickly to his private office and picked up his encrypted phone.

Stiffly uniformed, Sebastiani made his way along the downward sloping path to his waiting car and driver.

He stopped and stared at the car. I'm going to miss you, Caso, he thought. Ever-dependable *Brigadiere* Dino Caso, the kindly husband and father with a nature not fitting the stereotypical *carabiniere,* gone forever.

Sebastiani last visited Rome's Campo Verano cemetery to bury his mother fifteen years previously on a cold and rainy December day, a day ever vivid in his memory because of the large number of mourners that attended.

Today's July sunshine provided glowing warmth that failed to lend itself to the sad departure of an old colleague. He had honoured Maria Caso's request for a small military presence at her husband's funeral service by being the sole representative from the Carabinieri.

Sebastiani hobbled through the ancient Vassaletti portico of the Basilica San Lorenzo Fuori le Mura, past the guarding lions of stone, occasionally resting his free hand on one of the relief-decorated sarcophagi for support. He looked around at the frescoes depicting events in the life of St Lawrence and his friend St Stephen, and their martyrdom and wondered about the name of the basilica: St Lawrence Outside the Walls. Outside what walls? Rome's walls he guessed. He'd never enquired. After entering the nave, he remained standing at the rear of the congregation to avoid the embarrassment and pain that would accompany any efforts to sit.

His mind drifted away from the service and became fixed instead on what he could remember as open issues of the case. Rico Tamburo's death, a suspicious killing that was certain to become a murder inquiry. Would Cardinal Ricci's suspected killer, Giulio Gagliano, reveal the prime culprits of the explosions? He doubted it. Then there's the American Holy Catholic Church connection, if any. The man likely murdered with a brass candlestick was still unidentified. And now Caso's murder, not directly related to the Rome attack, as far as was yet known.

Luisa Fabian still researched in France but whether in Paris or Avignon he had no idea. No phone call so far so she had discovered nothing that might tie the French clerics with criminal activity.

The gentle sweep of violins stirred Puccini's *Che gelida manina* from somewhere in the church and swept Sebastiani's mind to a performance of his favorite opera long ago. Love, hope and castles in the air, he remembered. He closed his eyes and smiled at seeing the statuesque Dino Caso in his pauper's garret, singing of love to his beautiful Maria. His eyes drifted to her, sitting in the front row, her face buried in a handkerchief. Poor Maria, he thought, bereft of her strength and shield.

Sebastiani leaned on his walking stick with both hands, head sunk onto his chest, apparently praying – but he never prayed. Dino Caso was dead. He'd never heard him sing and now he never would.

While coffin bearers carried Caso to his final resting place in the Campo Verano, Sebastiani walked back to his car.

'Sir!'

Ferri's call from his car parked under the trees on the other side of the Piazzale San Lorenzo removed Sebastiani's concentration from the painful business of walking. He stopped, motioned his own car to drive off and for the major to come to him.

'*Buongiorno*, Colonel.'

'What are you up to?'

'We've arrested the man who shot you and Caso.'

'What have you got?'

'Tip-off to an address in Piazza Cina. Ammunition and explosives. And we found a 9 mm Glock 17 pistol. The signature on the bullets fits you and Caso.'

'Anybody we know?'

'No. The man's an anarchist who hates the police. You happened to be in the wrong place at the wrong time. Could have been anybody in uniform. But we've got him and some of his friends.'

157

'Good.' Sebastiani reeled unsteadily and grabbed Ferri's arm. 'Well done.'

'Gagliano wants to speak to you. I can take you directly to Regina Coeli.'

'Let's do that. But for goodness sake, get me to your car. Ooh God, I've just got to sit down.' The colonel took off his cap and wiped a handkerchief across his forehead. 'It's getting better, you know.'

From the car, he watched Caso's mourners trickle from the church across the road. 'Wait a minute, Luca.'

The major dropped his hands into his lap and stared at his boss. 'Sir?'

'What do you do in your spare time? Do you sing or act in a theatre, or something?'

He looked suspiciously at the colonel. 'I don't sing or act. I like sports. Tennis, judo, karate. And I ride motocross.'

'Motocross? That's riding a noisy motorbike up and down hills through the mud.'

'My girlfriend got me into it. She does it too.'

A girlfriend! 'Isn't that odd for a woman?'

'She's better than me.'

'Interesting. Good to know what your colleagues get up to.'

Sebastiani hated Regina Coeli prison and avoided contact with it as much as possible. But today this dark and forbidding place offered a glimmer of hope in providing a breakthrough in his investigation. He sat on a chair in the center of a grim interrogation room and manoeuvred himself to the least painful position for his leg. 'Right Ferri, bring him in.'

Two guards walked the shackled Gagliano into the room and then stood as silent sentinels at his side. Major Ferri stood in a corner, arms folded.

The colonel wagged a finger at one of the guards. 'Bring him a chair.' He looked the prisoner over. 'Your bruises have healed, Giulio. They must be treating you well here.'

158

Gagliano's voice quavered. 'I've been tortured. That's why you sent me here. To be tortured.' He rocked and tried to grab the back of the chair that had been put near him.

'Something wrong with your legs Giulio?'

'See for yourself.'

Sebastiani looked at a guard. 'Help him sit down.'

'I've been tortured.'

'I warned you about it. What else have you got to say?'

Gagliano muttered, 'I want a lawyer.'

'What? Speak up for God's sake.'

'I want a lawyer.'

'Ah, a lawyer. The games have started, have they? Christ.' It set him off readjusting his position on the chair. His shout startled everyone in the room. 'Haven't I already told you, Gagliano? You're not entitled to a fucking lawyer! Help me out of this fucking place.'

'No, wait. I want to tell you about Ricci.'

'Changed your mind, have you? Then be quick. Tell me.'

'I want a deal. Without me, you're dead, you know that.'

'Don't try that on me, you filthy scum. Tell me what you know about Ricci. You killed him. You bastard. I just need a confession. Then we can talk about getting you a lawyer. Not before.'

'I'll tell you when you get my lawyer.'

'Your lawyer? You have a lawyer?'

Gagliano nodded weakly.

Sebastiani closed his eyes, fidgeted and manhandled his injured leg into a new position. He fell silent for moments and then asked, 'What's his name? Her name? Your lawyer. What's the name?'

'Paolo Olivera.'

Sebastiani grabbed his thigh in two hands and groaned while he manipulated his leg into yet another position. 'Fuck it.' He shuffled his cap around and then glared at the prisoner. Gagliano was right. Without him, the case was stuck in a hole.

'Major, get his lawyer. Tell him to come and see me at the barracks today. I'll be there all afternoon.' He said to Gagliano, 'Major Ferri here will see you later today. You can tell him everything.'

159

Gagliano sensed a victory and smiled as the guards led him out of the room.

'Not too bad, Major. At least, we'll get a confession for Ricci's murder.'

'We'll have to wait and see. Looks okay.'

Grunting and straining, Sebastiani tried to raise himself off the chair. 'For goodness sake, help me up.' He stood a while, panting. 'Contact me at the barracks then you can bring me up to date over lunch. How are your reviews with Conti going?'

The major forced a half smile. 'On this case, not good. No progress to report.'

'Then we'll force the Gagliano confession today. Fuck lunch. Get his lawyer.'

Fifty minutes later, Sebastiani, the lone observer on one side of the one-way mirror, studied Paolo Olivera as he entered the interrogation room on the other side. His youthful appearance surprised him and he wondered if he was old enough to be representing one of Italy's most hardened criminals. But he recognized in Olivera that aloof confidence established lawyers display in the presence of the police, in his case accentuated by his oily black hair brushed back tight to his head, his high chin, upright stature, and his pinstripe suit. Against Ferri, already sitting at the interrogation table, he looked a mere boy. Sebastiani checked his loudspeaker and sat back, injured leg up on a chair, and watched.

The lawyer sat and then spoke fiercely. 'My client and I have had just fifteen minutes to discuss his situation in this prison. I believe I understand his position. Clearly, he is being illegally held as a terrorist. There's nothing that ties *Signor* Gagliano to any acts of terror.'

'Gagliano will be brought here in a moment,' said Ferri. 'We will talk formally when he's here and not before. This will be a recorded interrogation and the information recorded can be used in a court hearing.'

Olivera stood momentarily as guards marched the prisoner into the room. This time he walked freely but with hands cuffed in front of him. The two exchanged glances but did not speak.

'The interrogating officer is Major Ferri. The others present are the prisoner Giulio Gagliano, his lawyer *Signor* Paolo Olivera, and a recording officer.' He looked at each in turn as he identified them. 'Two prison guards are to stand outside the interrogation room by the door.' He gestured with his head and the guards left the room.

'Aren't you going to give the date and time?'

'*Signor* Olivera, you should know that time and date are automatically recorded. You know what I mean?'

The lawyer's face flushed.

'That's it, put the turd in his place,' said Sebastiani aloud. Noisy rumblings in his stomach reminded him it was a long time since he'd last eaten.

Ferri folded his arms on the table. 'Giulio Gagliano, you've been held in prison because we have evidence you participated in terrorist activities and that you worked with others to plan and execute them.'

The young man burst onto his feet. 'My client absolutely denies this. He's been kicked in the legs and testicles, beaten about the ears, and deprived of sleep, food and drink. Torture is against the European Convention.'

Ferri silently waited for him to sit and then turned to Gagliano. 'Giulio, you have indicated you want to change your account of why you were in St Peter's Basilica on the day of the explosions. I'm simply after the truth so all you need to do is answer truthfully. Do you still deny you were there at that time?'

The lawyer shot to his feet again. 'Don't answer that.'

The major clenched his teeth and looked at one of the guards. '*Signor* Olivera. Listen to me. This is your client's only chance of getting out of here. If you keep interrupting, I will end this interrogation. He would then return to the terrorist quarter of this prison and lose all rights to have you represent him. We're here because *Signor* Gagliano wants to change his story.' He turned to the gangster. 'Right?'

'Right.'

'Then let's get on. Giulio Gagliano, what were you doing at St Peter's Basilica after it was destroyed by explosions?'

'I was there to kill Ricci.'

'Cardinal Ricci. And did you kill him?'

'Yes.'

Olivera pulled in his chin sharply and glared wide-eyed at his client.

Then Ferri asked, 'How did you kill him?'

'I smashed his skull.'

'So, you admit to killing him. But that had something to do with bombing the cathedral. Did your bosses tell you why Cardinal Ricci had to die?'

'My job was to kill Ricci. I don't know anything else.'

'You don't know why he had to be killed?'

'No idea.'

'Who were you working for? Who gave you the contract?'

'I don't know. Someone posted the job through my door.'

'What do you mean, posted? By mail?'

'No. Just dropped in the mailbox.'

The major clasped his hands together under his nose and stared across the table. 'Listen, I don't believe any of this. You're in a bad situation. If you want to get out of it, you've got to give me more. I want names.'

'Why do you think *Signor* Gagliano is not telling you the truth? He's already confessed to Ricci's killing.'

The young lawyer seemed to be speaking only for the sake of appearing to represent his client but Gagliano did not to hear him.

'I want a deal. I know names and who's running what. I want a deal.'

Ferri threw his hands in the air. 'We're giving you the chance to get a fair trial. It'll get you out of the terrorist cell you're in. That's a good deal.'

'I'll give you names if I get released to a safe house. You need this information. Torture didn't get it out of me and you won't unless I get a deal. Like I said, you need it.'

'Tell me why Ricci had to die. What was his part in all this?'

Gagliano looked contemplatively into the middle distance. Then he said, 'Ricci was a weak link in a big operation. Lots of people involved. That's all I'll say. Up to you now to give me what I want. I want to disappear to safety. I want witness protection.'

The major looked for telling signs in his response to his next question: 'Rico Tamburo. Do you know him?'

Gagliano looked up, surprised, and shook his head. 'No.'

'He was murdered. We think his death had something to do with the attack on Rome. Perhaps you killed him.'

'I don't know him.'

From the darkness of the observation room Sebastiani remained unexcited despite Gagliano's offer, which is what he expected. His mind wandered through a labyrinth of arguments. The French cardinals; what of them? Till now they had been an itch on his back his fingers couldn't quite reach. Now he saw a different picture. Whatever they were up to, if anything at all, it likely had nothing to do with the Rome bombing, and probably nothing to do with Italy.

The Mafia? Not in their line of business. They perpetrate terror in other ways. Anyway, Gagliano shunned the Mafia. But he was definitely in the plan and had been prearranged, so who paid him to kill Ricci and why? Archbishop Collineau could in no way be connected to this crook. Sebastiani could now dispense with fruitless efforts involving the French clergy and concentrate on getting the most out of his prisoner.

The scraping noises of moving chairs signalled the end of the interrogation. Ferri opened the door and ordered the two guards into the interrogation room. 'Stay with him. I'm arranging relocation.'

The major introduced Sebastiani to Olivera.

Regaining his confident self, the lawyer said, 'Ah, then it was probably you who ordered *Signor* Gagliano's torture.'

Sebastiani looked to one side, fighting off an inner urge to commit a violent act. '*Signor* Olivera, I need to know how you came to be representing Gagliano. How did you get this piece of work?'

'That's private information.'

'I am head of the Rome anti-terrorism organization. I know his crime had some connection to the explosions in Rome. I'm trying to discover what that connection is so if I ask you a question I do so in the interest of national security. I'm telling you to answer my question. If you refuse...' He raised his eyebrows and smiled. 'Let's say you would regret it.'

Olivera fiddled with the handle of his briefcase. 'I was phoned the job this afternoon and I came to the prison right away. I'd had no previous contact with *Signor* Gagliano.'

Sebastiani moved his leg and set his wound on fire. Grimacing, he asked, 'The name of your law firm, what is it?'

'Studio Legale Francesi. My expertise is criminal law. Colonel Sebastiani, I now expect the police to bring a formal charge against my client and get proper legal proceedings under way. Do you understand?'

'Then, *Signor*, you have failed to grasp what took place in the interrogation room. Goodbye, sir. I don't expect we'll meet again.'

He watched the young man disappear from view, turned to Ferri and smiled. 'There you go, an idiot with a lucrative future in prospect. For God's sake, check him out and his law firm.'

'I'll do that. Let's eat first. I'm starving.'

Her plane touched down at Tunis-Carthage International Airport at twelve-twenty but Elaine Bruneau was still in the airplane thirty minutes later. She moved slowly, travel bag in hand, toward the only exit door that had been opened. Other passengers had started to complain but she and her companion, Alan Bintloff, remained composed and silent. When she stepped through the plane's exit door and into Tunisia's fierce midday sun, she saw the reason for the delay in disembarking. Five men in suits at the bottom of the boarding steps checked passports and, as the border was officially in the main building, she knew something unusual was going on. She turned to Bintloff and smiled.

At the bottom of the steps she set her professional countenance and handed over her passport to a sharp-featured, unsmiling man.

He looked at the passport, waved it at his colleagues and then put a gun to her head. In swift action, others snatched away her travel bag and handcuffed her.

'What are you doing?'

The unsmiling man lifted a plastic packet out of her bag. 'Heroin.'

'A setup, is it?'

'Get her out of here.'

She caught a glimpse of Bintloff in handcuffs before she was hustled into the back of a white van and driven away.

Major Ferri handed Lucchesi a mortuary photograph. 'Is this the same man?'

Since the photo analyst's success in identifying Gagliano, he had become the assumed expert in the business and the major had requisitioned his expertise to determine the names of those corpses from the Basilica still to be identified.

Comparing the photograph with the image on the monitor marked Clifford T. Simms, he said, 'No question, Major. This is the same man. I can do facial measurements in the computer to confirm it but these two images are the same person.'

'Great. I think so too. At least that body is no longer a mystery. What about this one?' He passed Lucchesi a second mortuary photograph.

'What a mess. What did that?'

'A heavy, brass candlestick and a bit of muscle. This man was hit a couple of times in the face with an altar candlestick. Did a lot of damage. What do you think? Does this face belong to Edward C. Barnes?'

'Not so clear.' Lucchesi spent several minutes comparing the mortuary photograph with the image on the screen. 'It doesn't look too much like the CIA image. And our corpse has much less hair. That's from an old photograph. Let's get it all into the computer and do some measurements.'

'Okay. Get the results to me as soon as you can.'

'Simms and Barnes. Good. No more unidentified corpses lying around.' Sebastiani lifted his injured leg up onto his desk. 'Aaaa! That feels so good.' He pointed to the papers in Ferri's hand. 'What do we know about them?'

'Only what's in the CIA report. Family information. Not much but it does say they were members of the American Holy Catholic Church.'

'What were they doing in the cathedral on the day of the big bang with no identification?'

'They wouldn't have been there if they knew it was about to be bombed.'

'Well, it's left us with a couple of bodies. Are we doing anything about it?'

'The American Consulate is taking them over. They're in touch with the relatives.'

'I reckon this is a good time to get the team together and run down through these questions. Maybe they've got some new intelligence. Get them in the ops room for a six o'clock start. I need an update. Sorry, Major. You're in charge. I'll be in civilian clothes and limping just as badly as I can. And I'll keep quiet, I promise.'

'Fine by me. It's about time the men saw you again.' Ferri drew up a chair and sat down by Sebastiani. 'Before I go I've got something I want to talk to you about. Rico Tamburo. The death certificate said he died from an accidental blow to the head during work on a construction site. Hit by a mechanical shovel. That's strange. I've watched how these machines are operated. They're dangerous. But Tamburo was a boss. What would he be doing near a mechanical shovel? Examining the work? I don't think so. These things make a hell of a noise. You'd have to be deaf not to hear it.'

Sebastiani rubbed a hand over the stubble on his chin. 'As I remember, the police report said Rico Tamburo's skull was shattered and the wound fitted the type of impact. What are you getting at?'

'I want to have a look at Tamburo's body.'

'And what good would that do?'

'I did another round of interviews with Tamburo's workers. Those I could find. One of them told me that's not how it happened. No mechanical shovel was operated on the day.'

'Oh? Then I agree. Get Tamburo exhumed and examined. Doc Martino should look at the body. And the doctor who signed off the death certificate, who is he?'

'I'll bring you the file this afternoon.' Ferri stood to leave but turned back. 'When is Doctor Fabian coming back from France?'

Shocked by the suddenness of the question, the colonel wriggled uneasily in his seat and winced at the pain this movement caused. He'd had no contact with Luisa Fabian since the day he was shot and, given the paucity of clues collected so far, his mind had drifted from the French clergy anyway. 'I'm not sure. I understood she was coming back at the weekend.'

Sebastiani got out of his car in Via Monte Cenci.

'I'll be back in about an hour,' he said to his driver.

'Sir.'

The poorly maintained cobbled street tested his efforts to walk normally but it pleased him that he could get along without a stick. Making his way slowly along gave him a chance to ponder the state of the apartment blocks in Doctor Bonni's district. The city's elders had seen fit to leave this area to natural disintegration. On most houses, much of the rendering had either cracked or broken away completely.

Many of the shutters hung from their hinges perilously close to falling altogether.

Doctor Bonni's fortunes had waned, apparently.

He talked himself along the house numbers. '130, then nothing, across the gap, and 136. Where are 132 and 134?'

A narrow side street bordering number 130 led him to the back of the building. Oleander shrubs, now in full bloom, had found their way into this shadowed and cool back yard. His eyes scanned to the top of the house over three narrow balconies each draped with washing.

Number 132 turned out to be the dirty blue door at the top of a metal staircase of twenty painful steps and before ringing the doorbell, he paused with one hand against the wall and read the words *Dottore* A. Bonni inscribed on a polished brass plate.

Sebastiani pressed the bell and listened for any sounds from within but he heard none until the door opened.

'Ah, *Polizia.* Do you have identification?' said the small, round-shouldered old man in a sagging grey pullover and slippers.

'*Buongiorno,* sir. I am Colonel Sebastiani.' He flashed his identification card. 'Are you Doctor Bonni?'

'Yes.'

'I need to talk with you. May I come in?'

Doctor Bonni said nothing but stood to one side. Sebastiani removed his cap and walked through a dark passage and into a large living room furnished in a traditional Italian style with lots of dark wood that smelled of polish. Cardinal red curtains gave warmth to the room. He sensed Bonni lived comfortably here.

'Do you live alone?'

'Since my wife died, ten years ago.' Bonni looked toward a photograph standing on the large dresser. 'That's Emilia's picture there.' Emilia held his gaze until he released it with a melancholy drop of his head. Then he seemed suddenly to remember Sebastiani was with him. 'Are you here about the Tamburo death?'

That Bonni immediately assumed he was calling about Rico Tamburo surprised him. 'Yes, I am.'

'I thought you'd come and get me before now. I did something very silly.'

CHAPTER THIRTEEN

'Ferri, I've been wrong all along.'

'Sir?'

'Gagliano's confession, Tamburo's murder. These two men have nothing to do with Roman Catholic priests. And how many Cardinals want to blow up the Vatican? It's got to be a private organization.'

'I think you're right, sir.'

'So forget the inside job theory. And for God's sake slow down.' Sebastiani stopped, huffed and bent over and held onto his knees. 'We'll get there soon enough.'

But setting off again at a slower pace did not remove the bared-teeth pain-strain on his face.

The major said, 'I'll reassign the Sinclair detectives.'

'Okay. Where does this leave the two dead Americans, Barnes and…and…'

'Simms.'

'These two made me believe it could be a religious thing. Even so, I'll bet they were up to no good in Italy.'

'Barnes was murdered three hours before the devastation, killer unknown, and Simms was killed in the explosions. They wouldn't have bombed themselves.'

'No, Ferri. Nor would Sinclair.'

'He was a priest so he was probably busy at something religious.'

'You should recheck that at the meeting.'

'Right, sir.'

'The two Americans could have been in the cathedral for any number of reasons. But it's possible someone wanted them dead.'

In the silence that followed, and having excluded fanatically religious Americans, Sebastiani's mind conjured up pictures of possible villains, either a powerful wealthy organization with a vendetta against the church, or a political group acting for economic or grandiose power reasons. Although he had no idea who instigated the attack, he could not get the possible involvement of the Mafia out of his mind, even though they had never touched the church. Now, Mafia don Luigi Porrello has friends and victims in high places. Oh, for God's sake, stop clutching at damn straws.

After a hiatus of several minutes, Sebastiani continued as though there had been no pause. 'The state police can deal with the Americans.'

His mobile telephone buzzed. '*Pronto*. Sebastiani.'

'Hello Colonel. Doctor Vettori.'

'Excuse me, Major. Private call.' He moved away. '*Buongiorno* Doctor. Is our patient walking?'

'No. I'm afraid he's not. Do you know what lobar pneumonia is?'

'No, but will he make it?'

'It's not looking good. I'd say the odds are against him.'

Thank God for Gagliano, he thought.

Of the huge investigation team, only about thirty were in the ops room for Ferri's update, the highlights of which – Gagliano's interrogation and possible deal, Tamburo's exhumation and Doctor Bonni's arrest – gave Sebastiani little or no cause for cheer. The major closed the meeting and sat down next to him. 'Evening sir.'

'You're looking tired.'

'I'm losing sleep over Gagliano.'

Sebastiani put his hands in his trouser pockets and stretched out his legs. He had distinctly less pain now.

'What are you doing with him?'

171

'I'm putting him in our safe house in Giulianova. He'll be under guard until we get what we agreed.'

'Giulianova is not safe. Half the bloody Carabinieri know our safe houses.'

'The Mafia doesn't.'

'Do you believe the Mafia are the only people who want his mouth shut permanently? Anyway, by now they know as many of our safe houses as you or I. We have other enemies. Even in the Carabinieri.'

'If we can't trust our own then there's danger all the way.'

'He's our only witness. I want him out of harm's way until we've made arrests, so forget Giulianova.' Sebastiani put a hand on the back of his neck, looked up at the ceiling and shook his head. 'Fuck it: I'm taking control of this.'

'Ah. Okay. What do you want me to do?'

'I don't want any foul-ups. We've got to get that bloody murderer out of Regina Coeli and to a place of safety before somebody takes him out.'

'Then leave it to me. I can do it.'

'No. I'm taking control. You Ferri and a few notable exceptions I trust, but very few others, especially those state police at Regina Coeli. It's going to be a fast job, into Coeli out with Gagliano and away.'

'General Conti?'

'Better to keep him out it. I'll deal with him when we have Gagliano out of here.'

Ferri stood back, doubt taking over control of his face. 'What's your plan?'

'Plan? I've got no plan, Major, but I know someone who can pull this off. My old friend Colonel di Angelis.'

'*Stormo Incursori?*'

'Right. Give him and his commandoes a bit of excitement. He's at Furbara, come on, let's go.'

They tracked down Mario Di Angelis in an old concrete building on the edge of the Furbara airfield. He was dressed in aircrew overalls and flying boots. Hand guns, assault rifles and hand grenades lay casually on a table under a coat rack on which his combat gear hung.

'Major Ferri, meet Colonel Di Angelis. Mario, it's good to see you. It's been a long time.'

'Not long enough, you old shit, Fabio. What the hell do you want?'

Sebastiani turned to Ferri with a smile. 'The colonel is angry. Did you just chuck a woman out of his bed?'

The major remained stiff-faced and silent but shook his hand.

'How are things, Mario?'

'Fine, fine. Want a drink?'

'No.'

Di Angelis poured himself a whiskey. 'Urgent, you said. What do you want? Something to do with that fucking Vatican catastrophe? I'd sure like to get the bastards behind that fucking liberty.'

'You might just get your chance my friend. Major Ferri here has made a deal with my only witness, a killer named Gagliano. Witness protection program. I want him moved out of Regina Coeli to a safe house.'

'Christ. Can't you do that yourself? I don't want my men doing kids work.'

'This is not kids work. I believe there are people in the Carabinieri who want my prisoner dead – and possibly me now. He knows names and it's possible some are people we know. You're one of the only few I can trust.'

'Trust me? Ha! Okay, let's talk. This Gagliano needs to be moved from Regina Coeli to a safe house, the name of which you are going to tell me when I need to know.'

'Right.'

'Okay let's do it!' Mario held his chin. 'An emergency medical evacuation from the barracks, with helicopters. That'll do it.'

'What?'

173

'An emergency night exercise. We do enough of the fucking things. One more ain't gonna be noticed. You put the order in, Fabio. God knows we need all the fucking experience we can get after this Vatican shit.'

'Helicopters?'

'Can't get them into Regina Coeli so we fly him out of the barracks. Three choppers, three prisoners and diversionary moves.'

Sebastiani nodded. 'I see.'

'Not yet you don't. I'll tell you how it's all going to go. My people move them out of Coeli in armoured prisoner transporters, three of them, each a Gagliano, no names no pack drill. They take separate roads to the barracks, Nobody but us three here is to know my destination is your barracks. Nobody, is that fucking clear?'

'As a bell. And you, Major?'

'Clear.'

'You two are not as dumb as I thought. Now listen. Emergency medical action so the ambulance choppers will come from Viterbo and I'll clear that with the commandant there. Your man Ferri here can sort out the details with him. Right, Major?'

'Yes, sir.'

'As far as the prison is concerned Fabio, you call them when I give you the word, as we're knocking on their door. Tell the governor we are taking them away now for military questioning to do with the Vatican bombings, top secret and all that shit. My team move in and as soon as the doors open and we take control. Peaceful control, all above board, keys and everything, no threats, nothing. Just everybody behaves; this is an official operation with no prejudice. I will keep it cool. We are just doing our jobs and it's coming from the top. You getting the picture gentlemen?'

Sebastiani and Ferri took a long look at each other.

'You, colonel, control the parade ground movements. This is a piece of piss and it's so safe that you can pretend to be boss and wear the smart tunic.'

'Sarcastic bastard; you never change.'

'Shut up and don't distract me. When the prisoners get there, they don't get out of the transporters until you give the word. I personally will be handcuffed to the real Gagliano all the way to the safe house, which incidentally Fabio, is known to only you and me. You will not tell me that until I arrive at the barracks with the goods intact. My men will stay with him there until you get what you want, sound good?'

'Fine. Our prisoner move starts at 02:00 tomorrow night.'

Sebastiani's watch read 02:36. His heart raced as the prisoner transporters and troop trucks entered through the main gates of the barracks and headed toward him.

Soldiers in combat gear poured out of the trucks and took up positions. The armored vehicles reversed onto the parade ground and parked side by side. Lights and heads appeared in some of the windows of the surrounding buildings.

The colonel's mind swung between relief and disgust that Gagliano, his great hope for the investigation, would soon be on his way to freedom with all his rotten character stains removed in a new identity. Ricci would be the sacrifice for bringing mass murderers to justice.

On his headset he listened to Ferri shouting orders to his men.

'Sebastiani here, Major. Show me you're ready.'

Ferri raised a lighted baton and responded, 'Ready sir.'

Silence filled the area as Sebastiani scanned the night sky. Against the lights everywhere around the barracks square, only a few stars sparkled directly above. He pressed the headset microphone to his mouth. 'Bloodman One, Two and Three. Joker here. Commence medical evacuation.'

Distant, noiseless lights blinking in the black sky suddenly changed to brilliant flashing as three air-thumping army helicopters with large red crosses hovered over the barracks and settled in a line along the center of the parade ground.

More lights came on in the buildings.

The ear-splitting noise raised Sebastiani's excitement. 'Joker here. Wagon three, unload.'

The back doors of a prisoner transporter opened. Commandoes sprung out with their blanket-covered prisoner and ran to the farthest helicopter. Then the colonel ordered redirection. The group hesitated, changed direction and piled into the middle one. He played out this deception until the final group had clambered aboard the last machine. 'Bloodman One, Two and Three. Joker here. Clear to go, clear to go.'

They lifted off together and turned eastwards.

Suddenly Bloodman Two exploded into a searing, white-hot ball of fire and crashed back down onto the parade ground. Its flailing rotor blades chopped lumps and sparks out of the asphalt as it also sliced through a group of soldiers that had failed to get clear. Its thin rear end separated from the main body and swung around as if trying frantically to free itself from control wires that held it to the screaming, lurching inferno. Bloodman One, hit by the blast, crash-landed and its occupants scrambled out and fled. Bloodman Three disappeared over the rooftops.

Pandemonium erupted as sirens wailed and men scattered in all directions.

Sebastiani hurried to a doorway to shelter from the burning debris still falling from the sky while Ferri stood staring at the blazing wreckage, uselessly trying to hold back the heat with his arm.

The major screamed into his microphone, 'Guard alert. Outer guard, arrest anyone trying to leave.'

The colonel hobbled to him. 'If Gagliano's in that, it's investigation dead stop.'

'I don't know where he is. Either dead in the blaze or up there in that chopper.' Ferri pointed in the direction taken by Bloodman Three.

'And Di Angelis is with him. Call Viterbo. Get somebody after it.'

'Done that. No radar so it's now on the ground.'

176

'This is not Mafia, it's the military.' He sunk his face into his hands. 'Those poor bloody soldiers.' He then stood with his arms hanging impotently to his sides, a silent, shimmering silhouette.

Within ten minutes, ambulance crews dashed in and out of the flashing blue lights to the dead and injured while fire crews fought the blaze.

Sebastiani withdrew to the silence of a building and tapped a number into his mobile phone.

A quiet voice answered. 'Da Corte.'

'Sebastiani. Sorry to wake you.'

'You didn't. I've heard about the sabotage. Do you want to come to my office?'

'Soon as possible.'

'I'm still at the Via Lanza bureau. Eight-thirty, okay?'

'Thanks.'

He looked stone-faced at the tragic scene as large halogen lamps poured light onto the wreckage and the activities of troops around it. A crane hoisted the deformed engine and heavier sections of the helicopter onto a flatbed truck to directions shouted from the glare. In the background, stooping and crouching indistinct human forms collected the myriad smaller pieces of debris.

Marco Fontana, bomb squad chief, handed Sebastiani a small, charred mechanism. 'Part of a barometric switch.'

The colonel glanced at the object then glowered in the direction of the wreckage. 'We were overheard all the way, from the moment we first spoke to Di Angelis. Fuck it.'

Fontana looked sideways at him as if not to understand, but continued. 'Anyway, this,' he said, pointing to the object, 'detonated the explosive at a height set into it. Obviously it was meant to make sure Gagliano was killed.'

'Any chance of fingerprints in all this?'

'Highly unlikely. To be honest, the burn-up was complete. Whatever got blasted out has the best chance of showing clues.

177

Everything to do with the explosive, which is where any prints might be, was just burned up. It'll take a while to identify the bodies.'

Sebastiani gazed unseeing into the flickering flames and blue lights, contemplating the human cost. The many injured from hot pieces of metal and burning fuel blasted out in all directions by the explosion would survive. The dead would be mourned, perhaps even Gagliano whose crime led to the deaths of those innocents involved in his departure. He would need to come to terms with the fact that these men died because he had turned to a reckless old... No, Mario's plan was foolproof, so what went wrong?

'Marco, when you've done, let me know the type of explosive used.'

'I already know what it was.'

But Sebastiani didn't hear him.

CHAPTER FOURTEEN

The sight of Conti coming out of the morning darkness distracted Sebastiani and he knew now that shit would hit the fan. The general stood for a while looking around at the activities then beckoned him over.

On approaching Conti, he expected a typical brass hat response: removal from the case, demotion, an assignment out of harm's way, or all of the above.

'General.'

'*Che casino*, Sebastiani. *Che casino*.' He clasped his hands behind his back and scanned the scene. 'Tell me about it.' His voice carried an acerbic edge.

'Couldn't be worse. Gagliano's either dead in that mess or he's been flown off somewhere. If he's alive he could be with friends or enemies.'

'Either way, it's bad news.'

'I know. It also means our communications systems are not secure.'

'Or someone guessed your moves. All a bit too obvious, in my view.'

'I disagree. Our security was comprehensive.'

'Your security, Colonel Sebastiani, was *flawed*.'

'When traitors in our own service can listen in we don't stand a chance. I've warned you about this before, sir. Traitors in the Carabinieri.'

'What makes you say that?'

'Viterbo found the pilot of the helicopter that disappeared. Throat cut. It's hard to see on the barracks surveillance system but there were others in the Gagliano chopper ready to take over. My plan was overheard from the beginning. I've been bugged the whole time.'

'Paranoia, Colonel. Traitors? Ha! Anyway, you should have considered that and provided for the possibility.'

'Gagliano was tracked from his cell right into the helicopter. I can't believe it. It was a good security operation.'

'Evidently, security was not the best possible. From what I understand, nothing more than a circus performance. Three armored trucks, three helicopters. That's the shell game, isn't it? Would have done better if you'd put Gagliano on a corporation bus.'

Sebastiani grunted.

'You should have discussed it with me beforehand, colonel. I would have talked you out of this approach. A calamity. An avoidable calamity.'

'We've lost any hope of making any arrests soon. I take full responsibility.'

'That's how I see it so I'm taking you off this case.'

'That's a bad move.'

'Careful how you speak to me, Sebastiani. I'm replacing you, got it?'

'Your decision…sir.'

'I still want you in the team, to act as consultant to the new investigation commander.'

'Who will take over?'

'I will let you know.' Conti scanned the activities. 'What a mess.'

The flashing blue light from a stationary *Polizia* car in the distance guided Ferri and his convoy of troops along the winding road to the cliff tops three kilometres southeast of Stella Polare. Out to sea, the first thin crack of morning light outlined the horizon arc in the still-dark night. He got out of his truck and walked toward the only soul in sight, a state police officer standing at the car.

'Found me then, sir.'

'How did you find out about this?'

'A ship reported the fire to Rome *commissariato* and they relayed the message to Stella Polare station.'

'I'm surprised you're alone.'

'I'm not, sir.' He pointed to trees on the land side of the road. 'My *assistente* is over there.'

'Is he searching for something?'

'No.'

The *assistente* appeared, coming out of the bushes zipping up his trousers. The officer pulled a clown's face and looked out to sea.

'You've called the fire brigade, I suppose.'

'They're on their way.'

'Then it's not all bad. Stay here. I can see where it is. Have you searched the area?'

'What for, sir?'

'Never mind.'

Bloodman Three stood with its wheels in the shallow water of a stony inlet burning furiously. Its cabin had been blasted apart.

Ferri turned to his men. 'Seal off this area a hundred meters around me. Six of you get down there and see what you can do. The rest, search the cliff tops.'

He pulled out his walkie-talkie. 'Sir, Major Ferri here. We're down near Stella Polare. Bloodman Three is on fire in a small bay below the cliff tops. It looks as though it's been flown there and exploded. No sign of life or bodies so far. My troops are on their way down to it.'

Conti examined Sebastiani's face. 'News, Colonel?'

'Nothing concrete, sir.'

'That means you haven't found Gagliano.'

'Correct.'

'I take it this has something to do with the Vatican attack.'

Seeing his boss as a black and formless shadow in the bright halogen light that blazed behind him, he moved to where he could interpret his body language. 'Gagliano was the target so it has everything to do with the Vatican attack.'

'This is a big setback. How are we going to progress from here? What do I tell my boss? My God, what do we tell the Minister of Defence? The Prime Minister?'

'I don't know. If we don't find Gagliano alive then we're back at the beginning.'

'There's a mass of media people outside the main gate. I'll see to them.' Conti half turned his body as though about to depart. 'I want to speak to the whole team. Arrange that for nine o'clock this morning. You do not attend.'

'Where do you want the meeting?'

'Not here. The operations room. I want to announce the change in team leadership. I can argue mitigating circumstances here. The traitors in our midst. That's why I am recommending you keep your rank. While I'm shuffling leadership, I want you out of it. Take two week's leave from now, and this time, unless I request your presence here, stay away from the barracks.'

'Oh God.'

'Fabio, you're the scapegoat. There has to be one in a situation like this. *Buona notte*, colonel.' He looked up at the brightening sky. 'No. *Buongiorno*.'

His walkie-talkie buzzed. 'Sebastiani.'

'Ferri, sir. We've found four bodies close by. Gagliano, Colonel Di Angelis and his men. All shot in the head.'

The colonel closed his eyes and bit on his knuckles. 'They must have shot them as soon as they stepped inside the chopper, right here where all the noise was.'

'IDs have gone.'

182

'Okay Major. Listen, General Conti ordered me out of the way. He wants a meeting of the team in the ops room at nine o'clock this morning. You see to that. Phone my apartment if you need me.'

At seven o'clock, after just two hours sleep, Sebastiani phoned for a taxi and then, in quick order, completed his ablutions, donned a tack suit, baseball cap and sunglasses, and grabbed a drink of tomato juice from the fridge. Outside, he stood for a while in the cool morning air and deep-breathed.

At seven-fifty, the taxi arrived. The driver's greeting as he got in surprised him. '*Buongiorno*, Colonel.' The Romanian gardener.

So much for the camouflage, he thought. '*Buongiorno*. Since when have you been driving taxis?'

The driver, his mind apparently more occupied by their previous encounter, missed his question and its unintended accusing tone. He guffawed. 'I thought you shoot me to death.'

Sebastiani drew in a long breath, which crinkled the flesh around his eyes. 'Cavour metro station.'

The man laughed again. 'Yes, sir.'

After about thirty minutes, Sebastiani stepped out of the taxi and, with his back to Cavour station, looked across the Via Giovanni Lanza to the familiar red building that housed the internal security agency. Its open and unguarded large, brown double door belied its function as a high-security bureau in which spies operated for the State.

A dusty hall led him directly up a staircase to a landing and a guard. He showed his Carabinieri ID and the guard gave it a perfunctory half-glance and nodded his head toward an unlocked door, which opened to Ricardo Da Corte and his outstretched hand.

'Hello, Fabio.'

'Thanks for giving me time.'

He looked Sebastiani over. 'Bit sporty today.'

'It's my camouflage. I discovered this morning it doesn't work.'

'Why do you need camouflage?'

'There are people I no longer trust and I don't want them to know what I'm up to.'

183

'I'll accept that. Come with me.'

He led the colonel along a passage filled nearly to the ceiling with large cardboard boxes and crates.

'Moving?'

'We're growing, Fabio. Internal terror's got bigger and cleverer. You know that. We're changing to come to grips with it. We're moving to plush new premises with lots of powerful computers so that our enlarged army of clever and young shiny-faced officers can keep their eyes on an increasingly dangerous world. A lot of the guys you and I worked with for years have either gone or are on their way out.'

'I didn't know this was happening.'

'Why should you? We don't tell anybody anything. Anyway, it's all recent.'

'I enjoyed working here. Internal security had a different name then.'

'Different ethos, too.'

Da Corte led him into his bright open-plan office with a few plain-clothes night workers still at it in amongst the boxes, and then to his large office in the corner, littered with cardboard boxes in the process of being packed with electronic surveillance equipment.

Sebastiani went to the window and looked down at the street below, now filling with impatient early morning drivers on their way to work. 'The traffic noise is dreadful. How do you put up with it?'

'It was the same when you were here, Fabio. You have become used to silence.' Da Corte picked up his desk phone. 'Coffee?'

'No. I want to get back quickly.'

He returned the phone to its cradle. 'Calamity at the barracks. That's why you're here, right?'

'I've lost the investigation.'

'I know.'

'Good to know intelligence is still flowing well.'

'You want me to look at these people you no longer trust?'

Sebastiani took a sheet of paper from his shoulder bag and handed it to him. 'Two names, Ricardo. I want you to look at them. Surveillance job. The first of these two knew I was transporting

184

Gagliano so could have organized the sabotage. The second should not have known beforehand so if he did I want to know how.'

The spy glanced at the paper and placed it under a paperweight on his desk. 'No problem.'

'I want you to do me a favor? Check all correspondence from and to the barracks? Post, telephone calls, e-mails, everything and everybody. See what you can find.'

'We're pretty stretched but I'll try and set something up. But it's no longer your case so who should have this information?'

'Just me.'

'Fine.' Da Corte sat on a corner of his desk and played with the paperweight. 'The helicopter sabotage. Sicily?'

'Definitely not. It was a commando-style operation with military communications. Killed the target man and scampered. They hijacked a chopper to do it. So either someone's got into Viterbo who shouldn't or there's an organized group of military personnel in Viterbo in the pay of someone big that wanted Gagliano's mouth shut. I believe the latter and it's definitely to do with the Vatican bombing.'

'You've got to hand it to them, it was slick.'

'I'd like your men to debug me. At the barracks and my home. Major Ferri too.'

'Leave that with me.' He shook Sebastiani's hand. 'You know, Fabio, if you get yourself decently dressed, we could meet for lunch.'

Sebastiani collected on a plate anything he could find in his apartment kitchen for a late breakfast and set it on the table with his coffee. The telephone in the hall rang. He cursed and went to it with knife and fork in one hand. '*Pronto.*'

'Ferri here, sir.'

'*Buongiorno.* What is it?'

'At this morning's meeting, General Conti handed the Vatican investigation to me. I thought you should know.'

'Thanks. It's what I expected.' Nevertheless, Sebastiani harboured a silent question about Conti's judgment in handing over the case to the young and relatively inexperienced – although astute and resourceful – Luca Ferri. 'That's good news. Well done.'

'I'd rather be working with you on this one, sir.'

'This case will do your career a lot of good. You're clever. You'll get these bastards. Any news on the helicopters?'

'No. Marco was at the meeting. Nothing in the wreckages, forensics will have a report in a week.'

'Fine. I'll look for it on the system.'

'Conti told me you'd be available as consultant.'

'Yes. I'll be working for you.'

'I've let you down, sir. Sorry.'

'Total rubbish, Ferri. You've nothing to apologize for. I'm paid to think ahead and I should have seen holes in our security.'

'Someone's got you under surveillance, sir.'

'You too. We are going to be debugged. I've organized that.'

'Thanks. How should we operate, colonel? You and me.'

'Anyway you say, I suppose. Do you have any ideas?'

'You could do your own thing and just report important things to me. When you need manpower, just ask.'

'That's a good arrangement. I'll try not to tread on anyone's toes. The database will show me who's doing what. It's not a problem.'

'What will you do now?'

The smell of coffee pulled Sebastiani and his telephone back into the kitchen. 'Conti ordered me to stay away from the barracks for two weeks. I'll walk as much as I can to get my leg back into shape. It's much better now.'

'Got to go now, sir. A meeting with General Conti.'

'Ah. Good luck, keep in touch.'

Sebastiani, sat at the kitchen table staring at his untouched breakfast, drifted into melancholy. It had fallen to him on several occasions to explain to distraught parents how and why their sons had perished while on duty.

This time though it would be especially difficult. His operation for Gagliano's flight to freedom had failed and unnecessarily sent young men to their deaths. Some just a little older than his son, Roberto, they had great life expectations. In his sombre mood, he wondered how he would explain this tragedy to their parents.

CHAPTER FIFTEEN

Luisa Fabian, sounding concerned and excited, spoke loudly into the telephone. 'Fabio, will you please tell me what the devil's going on? This is dreadful. What happened?'

'Hello Luisa. Are you're talking about the helicopter crash?'

'Of course I am. What else? Crash? I read it was an explosion.'

'Sabotage. It's very complicated. I'll explain everything when you return to Rome. You should come home right away; there's nothing more to do in France.'

'What on earth are you saying? I don't agree. I believe there are things going on here you would find relevant to Rome. Come and see for yourself. Though I guess, for the time being, you're tied up with this latest tragedy.'

Sebastiani sat in an easy chair, balanced a notebook on his thigh. 'There's more to it than that. A lot has happened, the helicopter sabotage, the bombing, the Vatican, everything. They are not the people you're looking at. I can't talk about it over the phone.'

'Okay. Then I'll come back to Rome.'

Sex with the naked Luisa popping in and out of his mind made him unaware of the shapes he drew in his notebook. 'What did you say? Oh, yes. You're coming back this weekend anyway, aren't you?'

'If you no longer want me here, I can fly back to Rome today. There's an afternoon flight from Avignon to Ciampino.'

'We'll talk about it then. Tell me what time and I'll come and pick you up. Ciampino you say. When you know, send me a text message.'

'Will you have time to come and get me?'

'I'll have time.'

Sebastiani fumbled the telephone off its cradle. '*Pronto.*'

'Ah, Colonel. Doctor Vettori.'

He stiffened and pressed the phone hard to his ear. His telephone connected to a system that clicked in and alerted all stations when it detected recorded names and 'Hasan Muhammad Al-Qali' or any part of that name would do it. 'How is our unidentified patient?'

The doctor had prepared himself. 'Still unidentified. He's been out of intensive care for a week but today, for the first time, he regained consciousness. He can't speak yet but he's out of danger.'

'As soon as he becomes in any sense mobile, I must get him to a secure place.'

'That's your business and I understand. I'm sure he will be able to speak before he can move. As soon as he can whisper, I'll contact you again.'

The news summary on the front page of his *Corriere della Sera* hit Sebastiani like a brick.

French financiers arrested in Tunisian Republic

Tunis, Wed. (World News)

Two independent French finance specialists, Elaine Bruneau and Alan Bintloff were arrested today at Tunis Carthage International Airport and charged with spying.

In the Tunisian Republic, spying carries the death penalty. Full story page 4.

The telephone in Sebastiani's Via Brenta hallway rang and drew him in extreme agitation away from Page 4. 'Hello!'

189

'*Buongiorno*, Sebastiani. General Conti.'

'*Buongiorno*, sir.'

'I've sent a car round for you. It's probably waiting outside your house as we speak. Come to my office at the barracks right away.'

Conti's man saluted Sebastiani as he got out of the car and then walked him along to the small conference room attached to Conti's barracks office.

'*Buongiorno*, sir.'

'*Buongiorno*, colonel. It's about your daughter, Elaine Bruneau. Have you seen the papers?'

'The media obviously got the information before us.'

'I found out yesterday evening.'

'Arrested with a colleague, the papers say. Spying for the Americans. Were they?'

Conti sat back and pointed to a chair. 'Americans? Of course not.'

'Then why were they there?'

'Bintloff was there on legitimate finance consulting business. He's what the papers are saying. Works for the Paris headquarters of the Redland Mining Company and had a valid reason to meet with their finance people in Tunis. Elaine was with him ostensibly as a representative of a French government trade mission. But she was spying.'

'I don't understand. What's Italy's involvement? Why was she here to see you?'

'She told you nothing then. About her trip?'

'Of course not. Why would she?'

'She *is* good.'

'Why was she in Tunisia?'

'The details are not clear. Apparently, a low-order local politician has busied himself with a French diplomat in the capital and claims to know people who transport African children through Tunisia to Europe. He wants a lot of money for more information but doesn't want his government to know. Elaine was there to check on his claims with local contacts.'

'Why a French diplomat?'

'I don't know. Because he speaks French, I suppose. Who knows? The Tunisian claims an organization is routing African kids into a European Mediterranean country that could be France or Italy. From there, they are traded throughout Europe for big money through a single source. Word has it that businessmen and politicians on both sides – whatever both sides are – assist the operation.'

'Then it's a Mafia job.'

'No. Absolutely ruled out.'

'Police have got to be smoothing the way.'

'Nothing on the police so far, but not ruled out. There are bound to be people in official places who know about this.'

'Elaine was the only one sent for this job?'

'And I see why. Absolutely perfect for it. An experienced high-level secret-service agent. She speaks native French, widely spoken in Tunisia, and Arabic, including vernacular Tunisian. How about that? Excellent English and Italian. Made for the job, wouldn't you say?'

'There's a lot about my daughter I don't know.'

'The Tunisian secret service has evidence she was spying. They say.'

'Have they?'

'Let's say their intelligence services appear to have made some fairly accurate guesses.'

'Guesses? Or she's been betrayed.'

'Possibly.'

'What are you doing to get them released?'

'You know the rules, colonel. For now it's for the French only and there's nothing I can do. And I realize it's your only daughter we're talking about here.'

'Can't we talk to our politicians and work this through diplomatic channels?'

'Franchi has tried already. The government wants to know the exposure from our side and if there is a big enough exposure, they might act.'

'Christ.'

'Bear this in mind, Fabio, arbitrary arrests in Tunisia are commonplace so they might just release the two of them without charge. This happens often, apparently.'

'And they might not. Tunisian police ignore the law and they use vile torture methods in their rotten prisons, especially on spies.'

'I understand how you feel but I can only promise to do everything possible. Everything I can.'

Sebastiani had known Conti a long time and was confident he would pull out all the stops to help Elaine. Nevertheless, an uncanny agitation now tinged his trust in him.

'Your Carabinieri colleagues don't need to know any details,' said Conti. 'No one else does.'

As Sebastiani and Luisa entered the ops room, its only occupants, a couple of officers at computers and a group of relaxed lower ranks arguing animatedly about football all stared toward them.

Luisa put her travelling case on a chair and walked from him to re-examine Raphael's Solomon. Her voice echoed. 'Fabio, I love this painting. I can't get over the fact I didn't know about it before the room was opened up for you and your men.'

As she returned to him, he stared at her as though seeing her eroticism afresh after a long absence and he could not turn from it. 'I'll wait for you. Are you going to be here long?'

'I need just a few minutes with administration about working with you. The university wants to know how I've been spending my time. I don't want them taking these last two weeks out of my leave.'

She studied his walk. 'You seem to be walking normally.'

'I'm fine now, thanks.'

'It's unbelievable about the helicopter sabotage. Do you know who did it?'

'I wish I knew. It's beginning to look as though a renegade commando group is trying to shield whoever bombed Rome but I really don't know.'

'Does the helicopter thing mean you're off the case?'

'Not totally. I'm now a consultant to Major Ferri. It's his investigation now.'

'How does all this affect me?'

'You must ask him but I guess he'll stop our French investigation.'

'Look Fabio, I know it would be hard to change your mind about this, but I think you should hear me out on the French side of things. Just too many things about the Collineau family are more than coincidences. I've discovered something that ties most of the other cardinals to Collineau.' She put a hand on his shoulder and smiled tenderly. 'Trust me.'

'Tell me if you wish but Major Ferri's the one you have to convince.'

'If I can convince you, you can help me with Luca.'

'Now is as good a time as any other. Or is this not a good place to talk?'

'I'm hungry.'

'I know a good vegetarian restaurant. You're vegetarian, right?'

'I think I'd rather go home and cook something. I've been travelling and I need a shower. If you come with me I can tell you my theory.' She looked at her watch. 'There's still time for me to get to administration, but I need a lift home so don't forget to wait for me. And my other bags are still in your car.'

'I'll be here.'

'Well, Fabio, this is where I live. My apartment is on the first floor and it has a wonderful view across the city. I love it.' And Luisa's home, Via Calandrelli 16 was a fine address to be had in a much sought-after part of Rome. 'When I bought it, the agent told me it had the best of classical architectural styles. Nonsense. He didn't know he was talking to an expert. Come on, have a look.'

They got out of the car and stood together on the pavement eyeing the decorated ledges and cornices that ran the full breadth of the building and separated the floors.

'Nice,' said Sebastiani.

'Nice? Fabio, it's wonderful.'

She wrapped her arm in his arm and led him along a path lined with date palms and tall pines to a large front entrance half hidden under clematis and wisteria.

As he pulled the door open for her, she said, 'I've got a whole lot of Collineau history to tell you.'

They passed through a stark white marble hall, up a carpeted staircase and then into her large modern apartment.

She pointed to a sofa. 'Stretch out on that and give me a few minutes to freshen up.'

He immediately fell asleep and when he woke she was sat at a table in a white bathrobe reading a newspaper.

'Welcome to the world,' she said, placing a chair by him. 'You must have been very tired, you've slept for over an hour. I've made some coffee...'

Sebastiani sat up. 'Please.'

'I've got a lot to tell you, can you take it right now?'

'I'm fine. Go ahead.'

'Before I start, tell me why you chose the particular ten cardinals for me to research.'

'Very simple. We already had details of all the cardinals who attended the celebrations, their jobs on the day, that type of thing, but the Vatican personnel people gave me more on these priests and they are surprisingly similar. They're all French for a start. Well, Sinclair was not French but he tied in with them enough to be included – except he was the only one killed. It was strange that so many French cardinals survived the attack. Those on my list all had positions in or near Avignon and they'd all been involved with homes for destitute children in that area and in a big way. The clergy do this work, you told me, but all of them doing this work in that one area made me suspicious. It occurred to me that they might be involved in a crime, something to do with children.'

Her face turned sour. 'For goodness sake, if you knew all this why did you send me to France?'

'Good question. It now seems a waste of your time.'

'But I really believe it was worthwhile. Listen, Fabio, I was at Archbishop Collineau's preliminary installation address as the new leader of the Catholic Church, and I was Rome University's official representative.'

'You're amazing.'

'This was an internal ceremony, a formality so that he can officially sign papers. A coronation is in plan for Paris in nine months.'

'Then he'll be pope of the Roman Catholic Church.'

'No, his announcement was clear on this, not Roman Catholic at all but pope of the Holy Catholic Church, cleansed of the paganism bound into the history of Rome, was how he put it.'

'Another schism. Isn't that what this is?'

'I think so.' She looked intently at him. 'The problem is that since the Rome attack, there are very few people in power in the church to contest any of this. There's now a strong French power base and they can do almost anything they like, and there's no need to clear any of this with earthly governments.'

Her radiance distracted him. 'What did you say?'

She bent over and kissed his cheek. 'You lost concentration. Shall I stop?'

'No. The French power base. What will Roman Catholics throughout the world say about this?'

'It'll be a hard sell to those who are interested in power: you know, the Europeans and Americans. The vast majority are poor third-world countries and I think they will accept whatever the pope says. He can say it is necessary for the continuation of the church. This has been planned for some time.'

'Before the Rome attack? In which case, a takeover could be the prime reason behind it.'

Now that Sebastiani had taken the bait, her intensity disappeared. 'Exactly what I thought, but I don't believe that's the prime objective.'

'For goodness sake, what could be more prime than that?'

She leaned across to a side table for her notebook, causing her bathrobe to fall open and expose her nakedness to him. Unconcerned, she slowly pulled the robe together and retied the belt. 'There's the work these clerics do for children, which is exceptional and could be seen as good works. I don't know.'

'I had people working with the French on that but I suspect Ferri will withdraw them.'

She raised her eyebrows, pulled her shoulders forward and flicked her hands outwards in a gesture of acceptance. 'What interests me is motive. What could be in the mind of someone to make them devastate Rome? I am not, and don't want to be a detective, but listen. I see a history that might show why it was done. I want to run it past you in case I'm a million light years away from the truth.'

'Run it past me and we'll see.'

'Let me tell you about the Collineau family. This is not the original name. They were once the Colonnas and they were not French but an aristocratic Italian family and very Roman Catholic. They produced some powerful cardinals who used their positions to do a bit of land-grabbing from the Church in Italy. Then along came Pope Boniface the eighth who disputed their ownership of the stolen properties, so they rebelled against him. In the end, he confiscated the land and excommunicated them. The Colonnas fled to France, got friendly with King Philip who hated Pope Boniface and used the Colonnas to get rid of him.'

'Ah, you told me,' said Sebastiani. 'He repaid them with land belonging to the Roman Catholic Church.'

'Right, so by royal decree, it belonged to the Colonnas legally. That's where all this started.'

'Yes, I remember this and I still say seven hundred years is a long time to hold a grudge.'

'But, Mr Detective, I have proof that the persecution continued.'

Whereupon Luisa explained how imprisonment, torture and execution of Colonna family members at the behest of popes forced them to change their name to Collineau and retrieve the properties through legal means.

'But Rome identified the Collineaus as the old Colonnas and the persecution started all over again.'

Sebastiani sniffed.

She laid her notebook on a table and folded her arms. 'What I could not find in documents I got from Archbishop Collineau's mother, Yvette Collineau.'

'And what evidence did you pick up from her?'

'Evidence? Typical detective. She explained Jean Collineau's execution in Cardinal Richelieu's time. That gave me a lead to check historical documents again and I discovered she was right: the pope had commissioned Richelieu to punish the Collineaus once and for all time.'

'Confirming the persecution of the family by the Roman popes.'

'At least, partly.'

'She must be old. What's she like, this *Madame* Collineau?'

'You should meet her. She's a very interesting woman and has a beautiful home in La Calmette.' Luisa laughed and slapped Sebastiani's knee. 'I think she's up to something sexual with her young Italian factotum.'

He chucked his head back and laughed.

'Well, what about my hypothesis?'

'I think your motive theory is never likely to be fact. I'm sure you're finding the links but you span centuries to make them. I don't doubt the history is right but you are asking me to accept so much.'

Luisa knelt on the sofa and laid her hands on his chest. 'Perhaps you're right. Remind me I have to talk to you about the Collineau family covenant.'

He stood. 'It's getting late. I'd better go.'

She stood too, and faced him. 'Oh no, please don't go. Stay with me tonight?'

He closed his eyes and raised his head to heaven.

197

'Perhaps I should not have asked you.'

He put his hands on his hips and shook his head slowly.

'I know it's wrong and I should not have asked. But I think a lot about you.'

'Oh?'

'Fabio, we're human and we have needs. Why not stay with me tonight?'

In the subdued light her dark, dilated pupils sparkled.

The cell door opened and Elaine Bruneau closed her eyes against the stark light that suddenly fell over her. A group of guards grabbed at her arms and manhandled her out of her stinking solitary confinement and along the corridor to the room filled with implements of torture, just as they had done on the previous three days. And there he was again, the six-foot-six monster with his baton under his arm and anger in his round, puffy face.

'I want a lawyer, please,' she said.

He laughed. 'In Tunisia, we don't allow women to show disrespect to men,' he said in Arabic.

He had said the same yesterday so she dropped her head and waited. She didn't feel the punches that churned her brain to swirling numbness, only the sharp electric pain as her knees hit the concrete floor. The guards threw her back into her dark cell leaving her wondering why he had not stubbed out his cigarette on her body as he had done before.

In a perverse sense of reasoning she understood his anger. On her first day in the prison, he had ripped open her blouse and fondled her. She had grabbed his fingers and brought him to his knees, humiliating him in front of other men. This made it clear that this cultured Parisian woman was a practitioner of the martial arts. She was now paying for that impulsive act.

Elaine sat alone in a cell on a concrete bench, her head throbbing, fingers pressed against her ears to shut out the screaming of suffering souls in the nearby torture chamber.

'They were there waiting for me,' she whispered. 'Somebody I know betrayed me.' Bintloff knew nothing about my real reasons for coming to Tunisia, she thought. Discount him. Simon Moulard and his team knew why I came but they're my friends and not one of them would turn me into the Tunis authorities to be locked away and tortured. The French ambassador to Tunisia started the whole business so he has to be trusted. Discount him, too. General Conti knew? But Sebastiani, had spoken of him in such glowing terms, she remembered.

She fell asleep but within what seemed like minutes of the last beating, the door crashed open. Men burst in, pummelled Elaine with their fists and hauled her like a dead carcass along the corridor to the torture chamber. There she was strapped spread-eagled onto a table of horrors, under a hot light that burned at the edges of her broken flesh.

'Today, you are going to hang. It would be a terrible waste if I didn't put you to good use first.' He spoke French.

Elaine fought against the searing pains and her whirling brain to identify the man, a young well-groomed officer whose presence seemed incongruous in this room of terror.

'I had to make a choice. At first I thought I should give my men your last moments alive for their pleasure. But, you know, our good behaviour prisoners have not seen women for years.'

He nodded at the guards and then left the room. They stripped her naked and stood back as a group of men in prison clothes entered the chamber. Elaine gritted her teeth and stared at the ceiling.

After a seeming eternity of vile sexual abuse she stood on a trap door, terrified and now dressed in a *hijab*, hands bound and a noose around her neck. Another officer came onto the scaffold and whispered in her ear.

CHAPTER SIXTEEN

The officer removed the noose from around Elaine Bruneau's neck and untied her wrists. 'You are to come with me, please,' he said politely.

Holding her elbow, he walked her slowly from the hanging chamber, out into the scorching sunlight to a black limousine parked with a door held open by a surly prison guard.

She stood for a while considering how to get into the car without setting fire to the wounds that filled her body.

'Let me help you,' he said.

'Where are we going?' she asked weakly.

'We are going to the interior ministry where your sentence is to be reviewed.'

With teeth clenched, hands gripped across her stomach and assistance from the officer, she managed the agonizing manoeuvre onto the back seat. She sat quietly, head slumped and eyes closed, cherishing the softness of the car seat and its support of her pained back. Elaine did not see the long straight road stretching to the distant outline of Tunis where they were heading to.

Then after just a few minutes, it seemed to her, the officer's voice drifted into her hearing.

'*Madame* Bruneau. We have arrived.'

Elaine sat up startled and strained her eyes open to read the Avenue Habib Bourguiba street sign close by. She recognized the office of the interior ministry from photographs in her Tunisian assignment file now locked away in Paris.

Under the watchful eyes of the officer, two young women in police uniforms helped her out of the car and into a wheelchair.

'I'll take it from here,' he told them.

He pushed her into the building and along corridors guarded by armed soldiers and then through the open door of a large, grandly appointed office. An elegantly dressed man of about forty turned from a window, walked quickly to her and dismissed the officer, leaving them alone in the room.

'*Bonjour*, *Madame* Bruneau. My name is Ahmed Ayed, I am the assistant to the minister of the interior.'

'I wish to speak with the French consul, please,' she said expecting to be beaten for her impudence.

'All in good time. I have reviewed your case and you are to be freed so you have no need to fear.' He took her passport from his jacket pocket and handed it to her. 'You have had unbelievable good fortune, *Madame*. Papers of your imprisonment and sentence were passed to my desk for review and I recognized the name, Elaine Bruneau.'

She slowly raised her dejected face to him. 'You know me?'

'We have never met but I already knew your name and that you were French secret service. You and I have collaborated on a case, a Tunisian terror group in France four years ago.'

And now you are a minister's aide, she thought. Although bruised, her mind put up the shield that kept her alive in the torture chamber. 'I don't know you.'

'It doesn't matter. The ministry is concerned to discover the intended activities of the French secret service in Tunisia but… Well, your government has apologized and given assurances about future cooperation.'

'Who betrayed me?'

'I can only say that a high-ranking Italian informed the Tunisian authorities that you were spying for the Americans in an operation that could compromise Tunisia's security. It's no wonder you were sentenced to hang. This person also alerted us about your arrival at Tunis airport.'

201

'Who is this person?'

'I cannot tell you. But since then, I've discovered that it's nothing to do with the Americans. You were here to investigate a city politician about the transportation of African children to Europe.'

'And how do you know that?'

'Our authorities received information about it and arrested a man for withholding information about the crime. This man told us everything about it and we are investigating.'

Elaine sat quietly for moments smiling faintly. 'The Italian who informed on me must be involved in it.'

'No comment to that, *Madame* Bruneau.'

The army officer who brought her entered and took the handles of her wheelchair.

Ahmed Ayed said, 'The car that brought you here will take you directly to the airport and place you on a diplomatic flight to Paris. I want you out of the country as soon as possible.'

As the officer wheeled her toward the door, she called back to Ayed. 'You know who betrayed me. Who was it?'

'Wait! Bring her back to me.'

Sebastiani leaned against the large polished sink unit and looked on in silent amusement. He could not see why it was necessary for Doctor Enzo Martino to flit around so busily in what looked to him an empty autopsy laboratory.

Except for the partially covered, partially decomposed body on the dissecting table, the place was empty of everything that was not part of the stainless steel accoutrements of the laboratory itself. He was as animated as a hungry ferret: opening small stainless-steel drawers, fingering documents and closing them again, washing his hands at the stainless steel dissecting sink, checking through his cutting tools, adjusting the height and position of his stool, adjusting the height of the dissecting table, manipulating the lights above the dissecting table several times, opening a large drawer to check for the availability of cadaver bags, tapping the pocket of his green autopsy lab coat.

Sebastiani wondered whether Martino was nervous about explaining Tamburo's autopsy to an officer dressed in jeans and blue check shirt and, carrying a plastic shopping bag, looked as though he was just off to the supermarket.

No, Sebastiani convinced himself. It was just nine o'clock so this must be his normal start of day procedure.

The colonel peered at the beige label tied to the big toe of the body and read aloud, 'Rico Tamburo.'

Martino drew back the cover to expose his cutting work on the cadaver. 'Cause of death,' he said at last, 'two blows to the back of the head with a hammer-like object.'

'A-ha!' Sebastiani strode to Martino and looked over his shoulder at the report from which the forensic pathologist read.

'Right kidney severely damaged by two blows from a blunt object, marks consistent with hammer blows. But unlikely to have caused death.' Martino looked directly into his face. 'For your information, the person who did this was probably left-handed and made a strike from the front. Both injuries to this kidney show marks made by the shaft close to the hammerhead, which indicate the direction of the blows. He was also struck just once by a larger object.' He ran his fingers over the head wound. 'Square-sectioned, sharp-edged metal bar perhaps. Mechanical shovel is nonsense. But much later. After death. This blow caused a deep cut in the head but no blood flow. *Signor* Tamburo was a regular user of heroin. Lungs and stomach show evidence of that. Puncture marks on his arms. I've examined his other organs and they're in reasonably good shape, given the time he's been in the ground.'

Sebastiani stretched to look closer at the report. 'No doubt about it then, he's been murdered. What else have you got?'

'Patience, Fabio, I'll get there.' The doctor read down the page. 'Injuries to the soft tissue inside the mouth and lips as if some hard object had been thrust into his mouth. Any suggestions?'

'Gun?'

'Could be, but that's not something to speculate about in my autopsy report. Amazingly, no damage to his teeth.' He pulled open Tamburo's lips. 'Look, they're in good shape.' Citing again from his report, he said, 'Multiple skin bruising around the mouth and other parts of the body suggesting he was roughly manhandled but he put up a fight. Look at the knuckles and wrists.'

Martino posed no question about why Tamburo was taken to a building site to be killed but Sebastiani suggested a reason just the same. 'Just burying him would have aroused suspicions and the police would have got involved. An accident is easier to deal with when you can pay off the attending doctor.'

'What are you doing about the doctor?'

'Doctor Bonni? He's admitted the crime and has been charged but he denies knowing who paid him the money. If you could see this man, Enzo, you'd know he's telling the truth. He's frail and lives alone in a shabby area of town.'

Martino drew the cover back over the body. 'Unusual for an Italian physician to fall on hard times financially, but it happens.'

'I guess so. How did they know he'd be into taking a bribe. He's not a criminal. That's what can happen when you're broke. He was told Tamburo was a crook and was dead already. So what?'

'You seem to be sorry for this Bonni character. He's a criminal.'

'Sorry for him, yes, and you're right, he's a criminal but crime was never his livelihood. As soon as he saw me he owned up and gave me the packet of money right away. Hadn't even opened it. Anyway, since discovering what Bonni did, we've been investigating Tamburo's death as a murder. I think his death is related to the Rome attack. The problem we have is the construction company no longer exists and the bosses have disappeared. The men who worked for the company know nothing, of course.'

'Bonni's packet of money. No clues?'

'Forensics need a few more days with it, but I'm not hopeful.'

Martino swung round on his stool to face him. 'How's the investigation going?'

'There's been a major setback. Did you know Ferri is now leading the investigation?'

'Two of his men came here this morning and took Tamburo's fingerprints. They told me about the change.'

'Did you give them the report?'

'No, I thought it best to give it to you first.'

'I'll make sure Ferri gets it.' Sebastiani tapped Martino's arm. 'I must go now. Take care of yourself. *Ciao!*'

Luca Ferri, grinning from ear to ear, walked toward the main door of the ops room to meet Sebastiani who was entering.

'You look as though you've got some news, Ferri.'

The major motioned the colonel to sit and straddled the seat in front of him. 'CIA intelligence about the two American Church members, Simms and Barnes. Surprised they didn't pick this up earlier. Barnes especially. Long-serving pyrotechnics officer in the US Marine Corps. After that, he worked as consultant to government agencies and companies in counter-terrorism and security. He was an FBI certified bomb expert.'

The colonel rocked back in his seat. 'That's a good find. What about the other man?'

'Simms had a history of violent behaviour and spent long spells in a prison mental hospital. According to his record, he was psychopathic. Even so, he was released on condition he attended a day center, until he disappeared. Psychopathic; he could be Barnes' murderer.'

'Do you have anything on their movements in Rome?'

'They both stayed at the same hotel. Now this is suspicious. The same hotel as Sinclair.'

Sebastiani's eyebrows arched. 'Oh, yes.'

'It's a small hotel run by nuns. They saw the two Americans together often but never with Sinclair. They never checked out but never returned. The hotel staff cleaned out their rooms and gave their passports and property to the *questura* in Via Nazionale. The idiots there held onto them expecting the owners to pick them up. I've got the passports with me.'

'What bloody fools.' His frustration with the incompetence of the Rome state police knew no bounds.

'One of the nuns speaks English and she says she often heard them arguing.'

'Did she say what about?'

'A Mister Callon. On the statement, it's Callon.'

'Was she hearing the name Colonna? Or Collineau?'

'Exactly. The FBI already had the name. The big man at the top of Holy Catholic Church of America is Robert Colonna.'

'Christ alive!' Sebastiani's face lit up. 'I don't believe it. That's incredible.'

'Colonna is filthy rich. Oil, freight, shipping. Owns a supermarket chain. I'm running a trace. Maybe he connects to the Collineaus in France. He could be related to Archbishop Collineau.'

Luisa's history lesson is coming alive again, he thought. 'If we make the link, what then?'

'You've been right all along. The French clergy.'

'With Colonna's money.' Sebastiani sat for moments playing with the corner of his mouth. 'We know he's something to do with Simms and Barnes and they are suspects. We're on to something here with this Colonna find.'

'It's too early to talk to him in the US.'

'I agree. It could screw up what your friends in the CIA are doing. Just keep in touch with them. If we prove Simms and Barnes planted explosives here, extradition would be on the cards. For me, France is a major concern – again.'

Ferri studied Sebastiani's face. 'This is where you could help. Chase up the French side of things. You've got the background so you know what we're looking for.'

'Yes, I'll do it, of course.' He looked toward a man in casual civilian clothes sitting alone near the door, a security badge clipped

206

to his open-necked shirt. 'Okay major. Good,' he said without looking back. 'I believe I know where to start.' He hesitated and then said, 'Come with me.'

As they made their way through rows of chairs toward him, the man got up and walked out of the ops room, letting the door close behind him. They followed him into the open-air ruin of St Peter's Basilica, now cleaned of all debris and patrolled by state police and members of the Swiss Guard. Several organized groups of visitors, all that was permitted now, followed their guides around various parts of the ruin and listened in silence to their explanations of the devastation.

The man stopped at the base of the demolished altar, where they joined him. '*Buongiorno* sir.' he said, addressing Sebastiani. 'The whole team is safe and back in Rome.'

'I'm relieved to know that, Pico. Too many people have been killed on this case already.' The colonel made the introductions. 'Major Ferri, this is Lieutenant Alessandro Pico of special operations.'

The lieutenant's presence, deriving from his powerful build and easy, confident manner, projected a certain disregard for the higher ranks standing before him and he looked disparagingly at Ferri. 'Sir?'

'The major is now running the investigation so there's no need to report to me on this anymore. After the helicopter sabotage mine was the head that rolled. But I sent you so I want to hear what you've done.'

Pico leaned back against a remnant of one of the high altar canopy supports, now just a spiral stub lying at the base of the pedestal on which it once stood. 'Sicily's clean. They had nothing to do with this,' he said, sweeping his hand around the ruin. 'Don Porrello called a truce and put together a meeting of the family heads. They all deny it.'

Sebastiani sat down on one of the altar steps and looked around the ruin. 'Firm, is it?'

'You can forget the Mafia. If there was anyone of them involved in this they would deal with it themselves, and there are no moves so far.'

'Good, then you can wind up your operation.' Sebastiani smiled, stood and shook Pico's hand. 'Thanks. I'm nothing more to do with your end of the business. Clear everything with the major.'

Pico fished a mobile out of his pocket and handed it to Ferri. 'You'd better have this.'

Ferri recognized the type of telephone. 'Encrypted.'

'It's for calling me. Only me. Got that? Only me.'

The lieutenant had dug the knife of insolence into senior officers for as long as Sebastiani could remember and was convinced the military had paid him back – by forgetting to promote him. Because he missed out on promotions, he continued to offend.

'Only you,' Ferri assured him.

Sebastiani sat at his alfresco café table in the Piazza Navona twiddling the stem of his empty wine glass, waiting for Luisa. Since they made love, she constantly intruded on his thoughts and at the sight of her approaching, his heart leapt. He stood awkwardly and waved. 'Hello, Luisa!'

'Hi, Fabio.' She kissed his cheek.

He picked up his empty glass. 'I had Barbaresco. It was good.'

'Then, I'll have the same.'

'It looks like we'll be working together again.' Sebastiani leaned back while the waiter set the glasses on the table then said to her, 'You know, I was all for dropping the France investigation but you've convinced me not to do that. Now Ferri's discovered some possible connection between French priests and a man with a lot of money.'

'I can help you, yes?'

'Certainly.'

'Good. I'll be pleased to be working on this still. It interests me.'

'Just remember you're a researcher, not a detective.'

'Remind me when I get out of hand. Where do we start?'

'Let's take up from where we left off: the Vatican vendetta against the Collineaus.'

'Okay. So far, I have only found records that show church property was retrieved from them. There's a long way to go on this bit of research.'

'I can wait. The Collineau covenant, what's that?'

'Yvette Collineau showed it to me. It's a document in her house at La Calmette. I have a photograph but I forgot to bring it. Sorry.'

'Tell me what it's about?'

'It's a long story. The covenant has been handed down from generation to generation and commands its inheritor to destroy Pope Gaetano and his harlot. The wording is strange and symbolic. I assume the harlot is Rome or the Roman Catholic Church but it seems to assume there will be a future Gaetani pope.'

'And there was until a few weeks ago.'

'I had the strangest feeling I'd seen the text before and shiver now to think of it. Like an evil presence breathing onto the back of my neck.'

Sebastiani smiled.

She poked his shoulder with her finger. 'I know what you're thinking. Believe me, I'd never been to her house before but as I read it, I knew beforehand what it said.'

'Perhaps it's something you've read in a book.'

'I have a feeling that what I'd seen before was not in French and not in a book.'

'In a graveyard, perhaps. There are cults who have symbolic wording engraved on their headstones.'

'It's no good, I just don't remember.'

'Who wrote the French version?'

'Yvette Collineau said it was written by her husband's ancestor, Cardinal Jean Collineau. Cardinal Richelieu threw him into the Bastille – on the orders of the pope, I hasten to remind you.'

'Beheaded. Sister and brother too.'

'You've got a good memory.' She placed a hand against the side of his chin and blew him a kiss. 'That's good because I've lots to tell you.' Then she bent forward and patted the edge of the table with her fingers, 'I've got a riddle for you.'

'Go on.'

'Yvette said Jean Collineau was the author of the covenant. But if he'd been arrested and denied access to others, how could that be? How could he possibly pass on the document if he was never seen alive again? She was not able to explain that.'

'What do you think?'

'What do I think? I can see how it might have been done.'

Paris, The Bastille, 1628

Cardinal Jean Collineau walked slowly down the fifty stone steps leading to the dungeon in the bowels of the Bastille that would be his last place living and breathing on earth. His two guards had not fettered him for they knew this man to be physically weak and he would not attempt to run. How could he? They followed him down at his pace.

A single flickering torch on the glistening, cold, damp wall made shadows dance a devil's caprice under the low, vaulted ceiling, which held the acrid air in deathly, stinking stillness.

One of the guards took the torch from the wall and led Collineau to the iron bars of a cell. 'Take a look, *Éminence.*'

The surrounding gloom made it difficult for Collineau to distinguish the two human forms pressed against the far wall. 'Poor souls.'

'Hey, you! Wake up! Wake up. No sleeping here.'

The guard's shout shocked Collineau.

'Look, *Éminence*, look.'

210

Collineau peered at the murmuring shapes in the shadows. Sudden horrific screaming, crying and gurgling sounds like puking drunks filled the darkness. He lurched back as hands grabbed at him through the bars. 'Aahg, aahg.' No words; only fearful sounds. The torchlight illuminated the terrible figures behind the bars: a young woman and a youth, bedraggled and howling.

The guard pushed Collineau closer to the bars. 'Look, don't you see?'

But he did not recognize them. 'Who are these poor people? What are you saying?'

'*Éminence*, take a good look. They know you. They're your brother and sister.'

'You're lying! You dreadful fool. I don't recognize these people.'

'Your brother and sister are trying to speak to you.'

Gradually, out of the grim and grimy, distorted sight before him, Collineau began to see the tender facial lines of his sister. Intense horror gripped him. 'No! No!'

He attempted to put his arms through the bars to touch his beloved kin but the guard pulled him back and pushed him to the floor.

'Orders from above. You're not allowed to talk to each other. So I cut out their tongues.' The guard hit Collineau hard over the head with a bar, knocking him unconscious. 'And now you, *Éminence*.'

Collineau, his sister Emiline and their younger brother Christian did their best to communicate with hand and face signals across the cells that separated them. They understood the smiles and the weeping, which contained love, encouragement, sympathy and hope. After ten days since his tongue was cut out, the burning pains in Collineau's mouth and throat had subsided but he was physically weak from his diet of foul water and water-soaked pieces of bread. He was resolved to die and prayed for the day of release to come

211

quickly, for him and his brother and sister. He also resolved he would meet that day in the soundest possible state of mind and to that end he would try to eat whatever food was put into his cell.

The door at the top of the stone steps creaked open and then slammed shut but the noises stirred no one below. Nor did the sound of descending footsteps promise any improvement in the situation of the incarcerated. Death was the only possible outcome.

'Jean. Jean Collineau.' The voice from outside Collineau's cell was hushed as though in deference to the plight of its inmate.

The familiar voice brought the captive to his feet. Giddy from weakness, he fell heavily against the wall and put a hand against it to steady himself. He waved at his old friend, Deacon Alain Daubert, and patted the lips of his voiceless mouth.

The priest laid papers on the watchman's table and peered through the dim light toward the cell. At the sight of Collineau he shut his eyes and wrapped his hands over his face. 'Oh dear, oh dear, oh dear.' He reached through the bars and grabbed Collineau's shoulders to steady him as he struggled to stay on his feet. 'Jean, my dear friend. I don't know what to say.' Daubert turned to the guard and ordered him to stand at a distance.

Collineau's face lit up with a tender smile as he took his visitor's wrist and shook it fiercely.

'Jean, I've been appointed to give prayers for you and your family at your executions.' He paused and held Collineau's grimy fingers. 'This is not wholly true. I asked for that privilege. I don't know what's behind all this. I know only that Rome ordered your deaths. You are all going to die in just a short time.' The poor flickering light sparkled on the tears filling his eyes as he looked around the dungeon. 'It's to be done right here. I'm staying with you until it's over. I must talk to Emiline and Christian. I'll have time to bid you farewell.'

Collineau smiled and nodded.

'I've brought writing materials for you. You might want to leave some words that I could pass on.'

Daubert shouted to the guard. 'Help the Cardinal to the desk. Bring a light.'

Collineau sat at the table and stared for minutes at the writing paper, pen and ink before him, minutes in which an image of Jacopo Colonna's Latin text and its meaning gradually filled his mind. Then, with a smile of release, he mustered the remaining strength of his last living moments and took up the pen.

After completing his task, he signed his name, laid the pen on the table and stared down at the text, then turned and slowly nodded his head. His tears conveyed the importance of what he'd written.

The deacon read the page, looked around the dungeon, up its steps and into the dark corners and then bent to his friend's ear. 'It is for Claude. Yes?'

Collineau's scrawny hand grasped his arm and with tearful eyes, he nodded for the last time.

Daubert rolled the document into a scroll and concealed it inside his inner garment. As the priest moved away, the condemned cardinal sighted the executioner standing before the block, shoulders and covered head pulled back in a posture of strength, his axe held across his chest.

Jean Collineau smiled.

Rome, Piazza Navona, today

'And there you are, Fabio.' Luisa finished the last of her wine and then twisted and tilted the glass. Its prismatic stem dispersed the sunlight and sprayed a rainbow over her bare silky arm. 'Two things the history books tell us. Daubert was a close friend of the Collineaus and he was at their execution. I can find nothing that hints at exchanges between them. But, for me, this is the only possible way the covenant could have been passed on.'

'I don't know the history.'

'If you look at this from the beginning, Boniface the eighth, then you can see why a feud between the Church and this family developed. Boniface was severe in confiscating their properties and excommunicating them, but they had provoked him. Their properties were hard won and they wanted them back. This was at a time when Boniface was struggling to uphold the authority of the pope against belligerent kings. Some scholars defend his actions. When you read all this stuff, Fabio, it's clear that at different times there have been angels and devils on both sides of this feud.'

Sebastiani motioned to the waiter then asked Luisa, 'What did you get from France that was not here, or on the Internet?'

'*Madame* Collineau was a big break. And Jean Collineau's covenant is not on the Internet. But, I tell you, reading the Covenant made me shiver. I'm certain I've read the text before. In Latin perhaps? But I don't know where.' She looked somberly at her glass.

'Anyway, you've convinced me your trip was worthwhile.'

'I've no doubts at all. Just her describing the history of the Collineaus gave me a point from which I was able to trace back to the Colonnas and forward to the Collineaus again.'

'All in one visit?'

'No, three, and in these I collected a lot of detail about the family from Jean Collineau to Archbishop Roger Collineau, and the Internet does not make these connections. Going back the further three hundred years to the Colonnas was not easy because the information was scarce and not so detailed. The family lived in the same area for hundreds of years, so that was helpful. The entries in records offices and churches make big jumps but the information is valid. Searching the Vatican archives would take a long time and we want quick results, don't we?'

'Yes. How soon can you go to France?'

Her eyes lit up. 'Do you mean it?'

'Of course. With me.'

She leaned toward him and put her hand on his. 'That would be nice.'

'No problem with the university?'

'They know I'm still assigned to the Carabinieri so it's not a problem. I can go anytime you want, but when, where and why?'

214

'When? Saturday. Where and why? Avignon and Collineau. I think that's clear, don't you?'

Grinning, she raised her glass. '*Salut.*'

Tycoon and fundamentalist Christian, Robert Colonna, leader of the right wing Holy Catholic Church of America, sagged back in his easy chair. He linked his hands on the top of his head and pensively gazed out from his penthouse to some distant point beyond Lake Michigan, of which he had an uninterrupted view and the comforting sense of dominion.

He was agitated, his mind wrestling with a dilemma. Should his visit to Europe be only to visit Yvette Collineau, sight the family Collineau Covenant and take a walk in the Vatican ruin? Would it be unseemly to pursue also an obvious religious business opportunity?

The answer rested on his view that the hope of everlasting life for Europeans would not be worth a candle until the pure Bible-based, evangelical Christianity of America supplanted Roman Catholicism world-wide. Why not broadcast the real truth in Europe? Use the airwaves to proclaim Christ as the head of the Holy Catholic Church, not some poor virgin girl. Get the politicians and corporation bosses to understand the benefits of symbiotic relationships with our religion, just as in the USA.

Colonna suddenly realized that he'd drifted from his conversation with Gordon Shepherd standing nearby, holding documents. 'What did you say?'

'Only that the meeting went well. The corporation's in good shape and the shareholders have gone away happy.'

'Big deal.'

'What do you mean?'

'I don't know, Gordon, maybe it's all the modern technology that's taking the joy out of business for me. Slick new software tools for strategies, tools for decision making and all driven by very skilled and good managers. I only have to breathe an idea and it changes the

215

world within five minutes. All well and good, some say, but I don't know.'

'You give a lot of input to strategic decisions and make a big contribution to the corporation's good health.' Mississippian, Gordon Shepherd, like his boss, a product of extreme right Republican ideology and evangelical Christianity, looked worried. 'That's got to be your main concern.'

The tall Texan pulled himself out of his chair. His six-foot-two was exaggerated against Shepherd's slight frame.

'You are wrong, my friend. The matter that most concerns me is my heavenly inheritance, being there with Jesus Christ after I pass through that golden veil. And I would not have known a thing about heaven's door being shut on my family had the Right Reverend Francis Sinclair not awakened me to that diabolical excommunication hovering over us like the sword of Damocles.'

'Sinclair was a bishop.'

'Whatever he was, he was the one who convinced me of the rightness of our venture. Tell me, Gordon, what makes our Christianity so wonderful?'

Shepherd frowned and pondered for a moment and then said, 'Well, it binds millions of souls in the hope of eternal life in heaven.'

'It does that – and more. Go on, think about it from an earthly view.'

'Umm. I know that your own Christian-based corporation and its influence on politics have contributed to the good of the America people.'

'Well said. Mine and other corporations have made America the most powerful country on earth. Our religion, our political system and business combine in a fine way and our people understand that and benefit. We are right to break the Roman Catholic system that just gets richer and richer while its people starve. Our victory over the Vatican is the greatest coup in history.'

'You are making me think you have another reason for going to Europe I don't know about.'

216

'We will stay in Europe for few months and meet with our contacts with a view to buying up media companies. Employ people who see things our way. Pick up a few right-minded Italian, French and what have you, commentators and preachers.'

'Evangelical preaching to the masses?'

'You've got it. Get a few stirring messages across to them. Like the fear we have of the scourge of communism reasserting itself again in western Europe if they don't resist it with a strong, American-supported Bible-based Christianity. It will be a start in converting Europe to righteous American conservatism, make it part of the American coalition. I've had this ambition since I first understood the truth.'

'That's a big undertaking.'

'It'll take time for sure but with our faith, it can be done.'

'Do we continue targeting Roman Catholic churches here?' asked Shepherd referring to Colonna's bombing campaign on American soil. This had been the start of his righteous war against Satan and his Harlot who had spread her 'defiling pagan Roman ideas' around the world.

'That's no longer a concern now that the Vatican job has been accomplished. I'll leave you to put a stop to that.'

'No problem.'

Colonna seemed to drift off again. 'Bishop Francis Sinclair.'

'What about him?'

'I will never understand why he stayed around in the cathedral to get killed.'

'I wonder about that too. He must have known what was happening. Yes, the timing was out but he had constant contact with Barnes and Simms, if what we're told is true.'

'It's gone well so far and I feel positive,' said Colonna, 'if a bit tired.'

'You're fine. Maybe the crusade is wearing you down.'

'I don't think so. I supply the money and others do the bombing, so that's no stress for me.'

'Don't you think sometimes the whole thing has gone far enough?'

'Don't go weak on me now, Gordon. The worst is over. I know what you're thinking because you are a fine Christian man. Yes, more people died in Italy than was intended but that's the sorry consequence of using a psychopath to do a delicate job. Whoever chose Simms for the Vatican? Not me.'

'He was the only Church member with the experience.'

'And we didn't know about his madness. Anyway, it's done and my family is free of that terrible and unjust excommunication that would deny us Colonnas a place in God's heaven, that's the important thing. I not only have a heavenly hope but also a chance of getting back the family fortune stolen over centuries by those thieving Roman popes.'

'On that matter, I can report a breakthrough. The pope in prospect, your nephew Archbishop Roger Collineau, has instructed the Vatican council to meet with officers of the Holy Catholic Church in France to determine who should now control the Vatican's world-wide assets. We'll get a report while we're in Europe.'

The Texan smiled. 'The coffers of God forever filled with the loving kindness of faith. Is Roger directly involved?'

'For his signature only. Your finance experts will be on hand.'

'Good. He wouldn't understand any of this so best to keep him out of business discussions. There's billions at stake.'

'Estimates vary between ten and forty.'

'That's enough.'

'We're visiting Yvette Collineau so we will see the Covenant, right?'

Colonna lurched back. 'See it! I'm bringing the damn thing back with me. It's the Holy Grail of my cause.'

'Sinclair insisted Roger Collineau was next in line to receive it.'

'Sinclair's dead and has no say in the matter. Anyway, so what? Roger can be pope but I'll be the power ever standing at his shoulder.' He peered slit-eyed across Lake Michigan. 'What's that fancy line?'

'*Éminence grise*. Power behind the throne. Is that what you mean?'

'That's what I mean.'

'How will you explain that to Yvette?'

'That point does not need to be raised with Roger Collineau or his mother. Ah, we'll see how it goes.'

'Okay, boss.'

Colonna rubbed his hands together. 'Right, are we ready to go?'

'Have you packed your Lithium?'

'Gordon, I enjoy my manic states. But I know they can be extreme. Rest easy, I've packed the tablets. So, are we ready to go?'

'Chopper's on the pad and running. Your business jet is cleared to fly us out of O'Hare in an hour.'

'And then France.' A dubious adventure, he thought as he gazed out to the lake. 'God help us.'

CHAPTER SEVENTEEN

The sight of a cluster of officers at the coffee machine stopped Sebastiani in his tracks. 'Marco, grab me a coffee and come to the terrace.'

'Macchiato?'

'Macchiato's fine.'

Italians in a group exchange chatter in high volume and all contending against each other. The ability to converse despite this quirk is built into Italians at birth.

Fontana broke into a smile. 'Sounds like the starlings at Termini station. Typical Italian.'

The colonel humpf-ed and turned his head away. 'I'm Italian and I can't talk in shouting matches.'

'I do it all the time. It's a big-family thing. You're an only child, right?'

'Yes.'

Fontana chuckled. 'I'm from a big family. If I hadn't shouted, I would have said nothing and got nothing to eat.'

'That's why you speak so loudly all the time.'

Sebastiani made his way to a shaded table with a couple of chairs, musing over the depth of Fontana's husky voice.

Marco returned with two coffees in plastic cups and disappointment on his face. 'Sorry, colonel, the coffee's cold.'

'Doesn't matter. Just tell me about the explosion.'

'The burn-up was total. The explosive was dynamite, Group B, but there's not much that connects to anyone.'

'Not much? Does that mean you found something?'

'Like I said, not much.' Fontana drained his coffee and threw the plastic cup into a waste bin.

'Come on, Marco. What?'

'It's unusual. Our dogs found no trace of explosive here at the barracks and we looked everywhere. If the stuff had been packed here, they would have pointed to where it was done.'

'Regina Coeli.'

'Right. It wouldn't take much dynamite to cause an explosion like that.'

Sebastiani dragged a nearby chair into position and rested his injured leg on it. 'As soon as it got under way, everyone knew it was an emergency exercise. But who knew Gagliano was going? Suddenly and by helicopter?'

Fontana dug a sheet of paper out of his pocket. 'Ferri gave me this list of people who knew and when they knew. Until about an hour and a half before the helicopters landed, you, Colonel Di Angelis and he were the only ones who knew the night exercise was set to get Gagliano out alive. Di Angelis was with the prisoner escorts all the time until they got into the armoured transports so it's unlikely any of them blabbed.'

Sebastiani laid the side of his neck in his hand and gazed out over the terracotta rooftops. 'Ferri told me others milled around when the prisoners got into the transporters.'

'Yes, he told me. You know, someone had already prepared the explosive.'

'And it had a barometric switch so it was intended for an aircraft. Do you know which one of the escorts carried the explosive on board?'

'No idea.'

'Gagliano knew names so whoever took him knew he could make a deal with us. They discovered he'd said nothing and shot him to make sure he couldn't. It's a conspiracy and some of our *carabinieri* are part of it.'

'At Regina Coeli, they'd know which prisoner was Gagliano.'

221

Sebastiani closed his eyes and suppressed a yawn with his hand. 'Without knowing a good while beforehand that would not have been an advantage.'

'Of course.'

'I kept the three teams pretty much separated as they boarded so it looks as though someone passed over the explosive at Regina Coeli.'

'And some poor soul took it on board.'

'It was a professional job, Marco, so we may never find out how it was done.'

After spending much of the time squinting against the brightness reflecting from the white marble of the terrace, Fontana put on sunglasses. 'I discussed the sabotage with Ferri and Conti this morning and they had no ideas.'

'Did they mention the guy who shot me?'

'Conti had a negative forensics report on the letter you got in the hospital. No prints from the man we arrested.'

'Thanks.'

Fontana stood, said 'I'm off' and shook Sebastiani's hand. 'If anything new comes up, I'll let you know.' He went to walk away but came back. 'I don't know how to say this, Fabio. You've known Conti a lifetime.'

'Yep. True.'

'Did you know he's gay?'

Sebastiani sat back and pulled in his chin. 'What?'

'Ah. You didn't. Sorry.'

'Are you sure? How do you know that?'

'It's what some of the men say about him. But, you know, at our meeting today… He has those mannerisms.'

'I find that hard to believe.' Sebastiani's mind raced down through the past and he recalled his own suspicions about this side of Conti and how he'd thought of his traits as a characteristic of his high breeding.

'I just wondered if you knew. Nothing wrong with it, of course.'

'No, no. It's okay. You're right.' Then he thought there could be something wrong with it if it gave other *carabinieri* – of whatever ranks – power over him.

In Avignon, Sebastiani and Luisa Fabian had both booked into the Hotel de l'Horloge but in separate rooms. His act of propriety, not hers, although he would claim he arranged it this way out of professionalism.

Before coming to France, he had made arrangements to present his suspicions about the French clergy to gendarmerie chief, *Commissaire* Moreuil and waited on Moreuil's man to collect him.

Luisa, with her comprehensive knowledge of Avignon's Catholic community to facilitate his access to information sources and to continue her Sebastiani-assigned research, sat with him.

Together, they sipped coffee in an open-air café in the Place de l'Horloge at a table shaded by a colourful parasol. A light breeze made the temperature pleasant, unlike hot and humid Rome at this time.

She put on her sunglasses, looked up and bathed her face in the late July sunshine. 'Collineau intends to keep the Catholic Church here in France for all time. That's what I believe. And he's using his family name with the Pope title. That's new. No, I think he's fulfilling a personal wish to break Rome's hold on the Catholic religion.' She took off her sunglasses and bent toward him, her incredulity fixed in a scowl. 'Fabio, he's not coming to Rome for Pope Boniface's burial service. People will wonder about that.'

'People will generally believe what their newspapers tell them. Some of the media will be outraged, some will hardly mention it. That's usual.'

'When are you expecting your gendarme?'

'Renaud d'Anjou.' He looked at his watch. 'In about fifteen minutes.'

'I'm going to be doing more police work than religious research. It won't be easy for you to get a private audience with Archbishop

Collineau. Your best chance is meeting him at his home in La Calmette.'

'I just want to find out what he has to do with the Barbentane seminary. I might not have to meet him.'

The square vibrated with mini-theatres, acrobats, musicians and a mass of sauntering tourists. Sebastiani wondered if gendarme d'Anjou would find him amongst it all. 'I can't investigate Barbentane without the French police but I hope they don't expect to follow me everywhere.'

But the scene distracted her. 'Isn't this super. It's like a holiday. Thanks.'

'Colonel Sebastiani?' The policeman removed his cap and bowed his head. '*Capitaine* Renaud d'Anjou.'

Sebastiani stood and held out his hand. 'Colonel Sebastiani. This is *Madame* Fabian, University of Rome.'

'*Madame.*' Renaud d'Anjou dipped his head courteously toward Luisa and then, with a frown, turned to Sebastiani. 'Colonel, you are to come with me, please.'

'I should come too, yes?'

'*Non, Madame*. Please enjoy your coffee and relax.'

The policeman's manner dispelled Sebastiani's intention to explain Luisa's research mission for her university. He followed d'Anjou but when they reached his car, the gendarme held up his hand. 'Please do not get into the car.'

'Aren't you taking me to *Commissaire* Moreuil? I have an appointment.'

'He does not wish to meet you, Colonel.'

'Just a minute. I've come from Rome to see him.'

'No, sir. I am to tell you. You may do as you please with regard to your project and you will not be hindered in any way. If you discover criminal activities in France, you are to report them from Rome for us to investigate here.' D'Anjou saluted, got into the car and drove off.

As he returned to the table, Luisa asked, 'What was that all about?'

Sebastiani slumped into his chair and glanced back to where the car had been parked. 'That's odd. What's that you're drinking?

'Ice coffee. I'll get you one. What did he say?'

'I don't believe it.'

Luisa screwed her face. 'You look disappointed. What did he say?'

'The gendarmerie agreed to give me support in my investigation. Now that I'm here, they've changed their minds. Why would they turn down a formal request from the Italian Carabinieri for help in investigating a crime?'

'Does that mean we have to leave?' She folded her arms and stared at him tight lipped.

He did not hear her. The rejection of a perfectly normal cross-border police request and what might lie behind it filled his mind with unease. 'That's strange.'

'Fabio, I'm not following you. Answer my question. Does that mean we have to leave Avignon?'

'No. You and I are going to work on this as best we can without the gendarmerie knowing what we're up to. Think you can do that?'

She slapped the flat of her hand against her bosom. 'Fabio, you scared me for a minute. Of course I can.'

'Good. Then we'd better make a move.'

'We could start right now.'

'You're right. Let's go through what you have on the cardinals. Concentrate on those who definitely have links to Avignon or Barbentane. Ignore the rest.' He pulled out his notebook.

'I can tell you those without looking at my notes. The important ones are Sinclair, Roland Giuliani, Jean-Paul Martin and Michel Blanche. The others had nothing to do with Collineau or Avignon. Or Barbentane. Or Sinclair.'

'Tell me what you know about them.'

'Sinclair worked specifically at Barbentane. The other three have Sees in the archdiocese of Avignon. Collineau's archdiocese. I know they've held meetings with him. Sometimes together, sometimes separately.'

That surprised him. 'How do you know that?'

225

'I researched the information on my last visit. I showed my Rome University ID around the secretaries and they let me see daybook appointments and records. Mostly the topics covered administration matters. Some dealt with homes for destitute children and the Catholic schools in the archdiocese.' She narrowed her eyes. 'These are the sorts of things one would expect.'

'How do we speak to them without arousing suspicion?'

'Why would you want to speak to them? If they discovered you're a policeman that would kill everything.'

'In France, I'm not a policeman so I can't just go poking around like one.'

She raised her coffee cup toward her lips but stopped in mid-action. 'A suggestion?'

'Yes.'

'It wouldn't be difficult for me to get appointments with Giuliani, Martin and Blanche. We simply do a round trip of the dioceses. Ask how they're involved in the care and education of children. It might be obvious if something isn't right.'

'And then we go to Barbentane? Check out Sinclair.'

'Yes, and then Barbentane. We could do the whole thing tomorrow.'

In the walk back to the Hotel de l'Horloge, they avoided the topic that most filled their minds: the possibilities given they lodged in the same hotel. Instead, they consolidated their plan for the next day with more detail than they could hope to fulfill. The conversation got lighter after they had collected their separate room keys.

'There's a message for you *Monsieur* Sebastiani.'

He took the note and sat in one of the period chairs at a small, half-round wall table across from the reception desk to read it.

> *Colonel Sebastiani. Go to Marseille immediately. Contact Inspector Simon Moulard at the Marseille police headquarters. After Marseille, return to Rome and arrange meeting with Gen. Conti. Mag. Luca Ferri.*

'Marseille?'

Luisa joined Sebastiani at the table. 'What is it? Did you say Marseille?'

'I have to go right away. Look.' He passed her the note. 'If Ferri's telling me to go now, it must be important.'

'Just a minute. If you go to Marseille, what do I do? And Rome? Will you be coming back?'

'I'll be coming back. We go together to Barbentane. Don't go there without me. You can try the other three cardinals. Giuliani is the only name I remember.'

'Because it's Italian.'

'See what you can find out. What's the time? Five fifteen. I think Marseille's about 70 or 80 kilometres from here. I can be there between seven and eight if I go now. Can you organize a car for me?'

'For goodness sake Fabio, go by train. I've done the trip many times. You go to Saint Charles railway station, right in the town. Now go on, get your things together and I'll get the information together.'

Sebastiani read the telegraphic note that Luisa had pressed into his hand.

> *New Hotel Select, 4, alées Léon Gambetta, near Saint Charles train station. Taxi to Police Headquarters, rue du Commissaire Antoine Becker.*

With her quick action plus good luck with train times, he waited only ten minutes before leaving Avignon TGV railway station for Marseille Saint Charles.

The four-star-rated New Hotel Select. Sebastiani showered, donned his navy blue suit and tie and took a taxi to Marseille police headquarters, arriving at six-thirty five.

The desk officer strained over Sebastiani's name. 'You are Colonel who? Would you say that again sir, slowly?'

'Sebastiani.'

'Forgive me Colonel. I will see your ID. Ah! Sebastiani.' His face beamed as his finger picked out the entry in the appointments book. 'Go to room 202 on the second floor.'

He knocked and opened the door and was greeted by the foul stench of ash trays, walls yellowed by nicotine, and the drawn thin face of a bald-headed small man sitting behind a desk strewn with a mass of unordered papers.

'Inspector Moulard?'

The man held on to the worried look that greeted Sebastiani's first sight of him. 'Yes. What do you want? I'm busy.'

He flashed his ID. 'Colonel Sebastiani, Rome anti-terror. I've been told to contact you.'

Moulard wasted no time on pleasantries. 'I phoned your Major Ferri about one of our arrests. Name of Eric Reynaud. Says he knows who bombed Rome.' He lit a cigarette and immediately broke into a lung-wrenching cough. 'It's about Rome so you should speak with him.'

'Has he given any names?'

'No.'

'Is he telling the truth?'

'That's for you to find out. He says he's got information about Rome and pedos in the church.'

'Why is he in prison?'

'Reynaud said he had pictures of the pedos so our super bright Inspector Babin threw him in the cells for possessing illegal pornographic images. Babin says he must be part of it but he's a shit head.' Moulard stood and sat himself on the front edge of his desk and poured acrid breath over the colonel. 'Babin interrogated him overnight. The man stuck with his story so I think he's telling the truth. I'm overall in charge but he's Babin's prisoner.'

'Does Reynaud have a criminal record?'

'No. He's the caretaker at the St Alphonsus seminary in Barbentane.'

Barbentane connection! 'When can I talk to him?'

'When Babin's finished with him.' Moulard returned to his chair and rested his feet on the desk. 'We've got our own investigation to complete. Then you can do what you like.'

Sebastiani looked at the grimy chairs on his side of the desk but remained standing. 'When will you complete your interrogation?'

'I'll speak with Babin. Probably tomorrow.'

'Where's Reynaud? Here?'

'Yes. That's it then. See yourself out. Tell the officer at the desk where we can reach you. I'll give you a call.'

Sebastiani had got up early, breakfasted leisurely then packed his bags in readiness to leave for Rome after his interrogation of the prisoner Eric Reynaud in Marseille police headquarters. He slung a case onto the bed and snatched up the telephone as it started to ring. '*Pronto!*'

'*Pronto?* This is France, *Monsieur* Sebastiani.' A crackle of laughter broke into the voice at the other end. 'Moulard here.'

'*Bonjour*, inspector.'

'A disappointment, Colonel. Can't tell you on the phone. You'd better come to the station. I'll be in reception.'

A long, black vehicle swooshed to a stop in the parking space ahead of Sebastiani's taxi, coming close to ripping off the door he had just opened. He sat back in the car and watched two men in black suits and caps jump out of the vehicle, swing up its back door and pull out a grey plastic coffin. They hastened through the main entrance of the Marseille police headquarters and he followed, composing in his mind a picture of one Eric Reynaud lying dead in his cell.

'Stay here. I won't be too long,' he said to the driver.

In the reception area, he pushed through a tangle of people throwing their arms about in a heated argument. In a chair by the wall, a crying woman in her fifties sat alone and unattended.

'Colonel!' Moulard appeared from the hubbub with his cigarette-stained hand outstretched to greet Sebastiani. 'Bad news, I'm afraid.'

'Reynaud?'

'Dead. About two hours ago. Heart attack.'

A heart attack while in your custody, *Monsieur* Moulard? '*Merda.*'

'Bang goes your interrogation.' He sounded happy.

'That's bad.'

'You'll be heading back to Rome, I suppose.'

In Sebastiani's ears, the chirpy rise at the end of this statement made it sound like a brush-off. 'I've no reason to stay in Marseille.'

The noise in the reception area dropped to a murmur and a pathway opened up through the milling bodies as the two black suits reappeared with the coffin stretched between them. The crying woman stood, touched the passing coffin and then wrapped her hands over her face.

'Thank you, Inspector. I'll be in touch.'

'Yes, Colonel. Do that.'

Sebastiani stood at the door of his taxi and watched the woman walk down the road and stand at a nearby bus stop with a hand over her mouth. He approached her showing his Carabinieri badge. '*Excusez-moi.* You are *Madame* Reynaud?'

'*Oui.*'

Seeing her use a sodden tissue to wipe her tears he gave her his handkerchief. 'I saw you at the police station. I'm an Italian police officer. I came from Rome to speak with your husband.'

'They murdered him.'

If the prisoner Reynaud did have information about the Rome attack as he had claimed, then he held it as likely that she was right. 'You live in Barbentane, yes?'

'Yes.'

'I'm going to Avignon. I can give you a lift.'

She said nothing but got into the taxi and sat staring forward with the handkerchief pressed against her mouth.

'I'm sorry about your husband, *Madame.*'

She lifted her watery eyes and red nose out of the handkerchief. In a breaking voice she said. 'Why should that concern you?'

'I came from Rome especially to speak to him.'

'Oh?'

'It is very important I talk to you. What is your name?

'Alice. Alice Reynaud.'

The Reynaud cottage sat in the corner of a large well-tended vegetable and fruit garden in a narrow pot-holed cul-de-sac. The house itself though cried out for attention. Its roof tiles looked as if any moment they would clatter to the ground, taking the drooping rusty gutters with them. The front door and windows frames had last seen fresh paint many years ago. This view of the house and its garden gave Sebastiani to believe the Reynauds were poor but good people. Alice led him along a rough stone path to the door, unlocked it and pushed it open. It creaked.

She now looked to be more mid-forties than the fifty plus he had given her in the police headquarters. She wore black skirt and grey pullover, apparently already to mourn her dead husband.

While wiping the handkerchief over her eyes and mouth, she led him along a dark, narrow passage to a bright but small living room overcrowded with furniture. Between sniffing and sobbing, she asked, 'Coffee, *Monsieur*?'

'Thank you, no.'

She reminded him of Dino Caso's wife Mary in the church the day of Caso's funeral: alone, vulnerable without her man and on the verge of breaking out in tears at the slightest careless word. He told himself to proceed slowly, draw out information gradually. He cast his eyes along the titles of the books that filled an old bookcase against a wall.

'They're my husband's. He was very religious.'

She sat in an easy chair and showed him an open hand to the chair opposite hers but he walked to photographs hung on the wall and took one down. 'Is this your husband?'

'Yes. That's Eric.'

He looked along the bookcase again and then around the walls and at the lamp hanging in the middle of the ceiling. 'Alice, you've a lovely garden. Show it to me.'

'Why?'

He put a finger to his lips. She led him out of the house through the back door, which creaked open like the front door, and they settled in the middle of the garden.

'*Madame*, your husband had information about the bombing in Rome. Did he tell you about it?'

'Rome? Yes.'

'And he gave you that information. Yes?'

'Eric told me it was dangerous. *Monsieur*, no one will find it. And as long as I have it, I am alive.'

'You should give it to the police.'

'The police?' His naiveté made her laugh. 'I don't trust them. My husband was an honest, God-fearing man and they had no right to put him in prison. He went there to tell them what he'd found. I told him not to.'

'What had he found?'

'Pornographic pictures.'

'Where? In Barbentane?'

'Up the road. In the seminary. That's where he worked.'

'Just pornographic pictures? Nothing else?' And if there's nothing else, then I have no further interest in Eric Reynaud, he thought.

'No,' she said. 'There's more information.'

'Can I see it?'

'No.'

'Then can you tell me who it belonged to?'

'A priest. A dead priest. Eric found it in his room when he cleared it out.'

'Who was it, Alice? What was the name of the priest?'

'An American. I've forgotten his name.'

'Alice, I've come all the way from Rome especially to speak with your husband. I need that information for the Italian investigation into the Vatican bombing. I'll tell the police I've got it then you'll be safe.'

'You can tell them, if anything happens to me the diaries will be published.'

'Diaries?'

She closed her eyes and put her hand over her mouth.

'Give them to me. I'll make sure you are protected.'

'I don't know what to do.' The corners of her mouth dropped and her red-rimmed eyes glistened.

'Alice. The seminary where your husband worked. Is it far?'

'You can see it from here.' She pointed to a building just visible through trees. 'He was the caretaker. Maintenance and repairs. But only the seminary. He was not responsible for the children's home. He upset the priests. They didn't like him. Especially that bishop. Eric called him a pervert to his face.'

'Bishop? What bishop?'

'That dreadful American. I told you. The dead priest. It was all his.'

'The diaries?'

She hesitated and then let her hands fall. 'Yes. The diaries. And the filth.'

'The American. Do you remember his name?'

'Sinclair. Horrible man.'

'I need to know what's in the diaries. Alice, you've got to trust me. Give me the diaries then you won't be in danger.'

She frowned and shook her head. 'I don't know.' Then, emphatically, 'No. No, I will not.'

'Do the diaries mention any names? A single name would help.'

'I've never read them. Eric said they did. I don't know.' She looked around the garden and then at the house. 'After Eric died the gendarmerie came here. *Commissaire* Moreuil himself. They searched the house and the garden. They seemed to be in a terrible hurry. They left a big mess. Then they searched my mother's home and his church. They didn't find anything.'

'Have you destroyed them?'

'No. And that's why I'm still alive. I know where they are and I'm not telling anyone. I'm afraid.'

'You got to trust me. Then, if I tell the police I have them you'll be safe. Don't you see?'

She bit on her fingernails. 'No. And don't try to follow me because I don't intend getting them.'

Exasperation needled him. 'I have to go to Rome but I'm coming back. I'll come and see you.'

Sebastiani left the Reynaud's garden both irritated over Alice's foolishness and anxious for her safety. Dangerous people have by now concluded she held incriminating information.

He phoned Moulard. 'Hello Inspector. Sebastiani here.'

'Colonel, hello. What can I do for you?'

'Reynaud's wife. What are you doing about her?'

'What about her?'

'Her husband had information identifying criminals. She's in danger.'

'I can't see how. She's not the one who had the information.'

Sebastiani wondered if Moulard was stupid or just considered Alice's security to be of no importance. 'Someone will find an excuse for believing she has it. She could be a target.'

'Okay, Fabio. Leave it with me.'

His taxi had moved from where it had dropped them in the cul-de-sac, and now stood on the other side of the road facing in the direction of Avignon. Looking round for it had given him sight of another car, a blue saloon that was not there when he went into the Reynaud house. When he walked on past his taxi the other car started up and moved along the road slowly after him. As it came near, he walked into the road causing the car to brake. It then drove off around him but Sebastiani would not forget that startled face or the car's registration number for that matter, even though probably false.

His flight back to Rome was booked for tomorrow evening and he had one more night booked in at Avignon's Hotel de l'Horloge. He showered the hot day off his body and read the French newspaper that had been put on the bedside table when the room was made up during the morning.

His mind tangled with the obvious questions. Why would an honest, God-fearing man die in police custody if it were not to keep his mouth shut about what he had found? It seemed senseless to him that Reynaud's captors had silenced him before discovering how he had come by the incriminating information and where he had secreted it? Why would a super bright Inspector Babin not want to do that? He'd made a panic move to shield himself and others from culpability in a serious crime? 'Of course,' he murmured. 'Moulard would see it that way too, so what's his take on Babin?'

Sebastiani lay on his bed, rested his head on his hands and dozed off. Minutes later he sat up with a start. He checked his watch and realized he had time to return to the Reynaud's house with Luisa.

Dressed light for the hot day, he went down the corridor and tapped on her door but got no response. He took the stairs down to the lobby and spoke to the receptionist. '*Madame* Fabian. She is still booked in the hotel, no?'

'Yes, sir. She went out about three hours ago.'

He sat in an easy chair and started to flick through a magazine from a nearby table when she walked into the lobby.

'Luisa.'

'Hello Fabio. Phew, I'm hot. I must go to my room.'

'I need your help.'

'I've been doing work for you, checking out the Collineaus here in Avignon.'

'Did you find anything?'

'I'm hot. Let's go to my room and I'll tell you about it.'

They took the lift.

'Luisa, something urgent. I want you to come with me, today.'

'Where?'

'Barbentane.'

She slotted in the key card and pushed open the door to her room. 'Barbentane? The seminary?'

235

'Do you know an Alice Reynaud from your time here?'

'Reynaud? From the seminary?' She threw her briefcase onto the bed and stared at him. 'I know the name Reynaud but not Alice. Reynaud was the name of the caretaker at St Alphonsus when I was studying there. I remember him because he helped me with my luggage when I came and when I left.'

'That's the man. His wife is Alice. Was. He's dead.'

'A-ha.'

'He died in police custody yesterday. In Marseille.'

'This is leading somewhere, yes? Let's talk after I've cooled off. I'm going to take a shower.'

'Shall I wash your back?'

She smiled. 'I'll shower alone, thank you. Before I go, here's something for your notebook. Jean Collineau spent some parts of his life in Avignon, which could be significant. Give me ten minutes.'

'Ten minutes.'

And after fifteen minutes she came out of the bathroom in a white bathrobe, her black hair still wet, glossy and combed right back from her forehead. 'In the shower I remembered that I used to go to a little house in Barbentane to buy fruit. Except that the lady never took money. A little house all by itself just down the road from St Alphonsus.'

'The Reynaud house is just down the road from St Alphonsus.'

'And you want me to come with you. If it's the person I remember, she was good to me and it would be nice to see her again. Why do I need to come?'

'Well, dear Alice has stashed away information that her husband claimed gave the names the people who bombed Rome. She told me the gendarmerie ransacked her house trying to find it so now she fears for her life. I need you to convince her that she'd be safe if she gave it to me. You'd handle that better than I could, especially if she remembers you.'

'Of course, I'll try.' She shoved him gently toward the door. 'I'll meet you in reception in ten minutes.'

Ten minutes again? 'Bring your briefcase.'

The taxi dropped them at the Reynaud's gate.

As they walked along the path to the door Sebastiani's eyes caught the movement of the net curtains, which opened a fraction for an instant. Before he could knock, the front door creaked open.

'*Bonjour*, Inspector. I know you, *Madame*.'

'And I know you. I used to come here for your fruit during my time at St Alphonsus. I knew your husband. You're Alice.'

In a moment of surreal silence, and while Luisa still held her hand, Alice crumbled to the floor, blood pouring out of her right temple. Luisa's hands flew to her face and she shrieked. Sebastiani dragged her stumbling into the hall over Alice's body, kicked the door shut and ran to the window but got no sight of the powerful motorcycle he heard racing off into the distance.

He led her shaking and crying into the living room, then grabbed a blanket from the bedroom and draped it over Alice's body. After telephoning the emergency services and Moulard, Sebastiani set off around the rooms with great urgency looking and looking although not knowing what he was searching for.

He riffled through Eric Reynaud's religious books but found nothing, then looked at photographs on the sideboard, on shelves and in frames hung on the wall but again nothing. Gazing out to the garden, his eyebrows arched, 'Yes!' Hastening back to the living room he stared at several framed photographs of Eric Reynaud on the wall and took one down. Reynaud standing proud among growing vegetables with a foot resting on the shoulder of a gardening fork, in the background a garden hut and, beyond that, a building with a cupola and a cross.

'Are you okay, Luisa?'

'No, I feel dreadful. I'm shocked.'

'I'm sorry.' He wrapped his arms around her and she held onto him.

'Poor Alice. It's our fault. I feel so guilty.'

'That's not true. She was a target long before we got here.' He kissed her forehead.

'Just the same, I feel dreadful.'

'There's something we must do right away. Take a look at this.' He showed her the photograph.

She recognized the man immediately. '*Monsieur* Reynaud.'

'Right. What's the building? Is it a church?'

'That's St Alphonsus.'

'The seminary?'

'Yes, why?'

'Diaries. Quick. Before the police get here.'

'Diaries?'

'Come on.'

They scurried out of the house, down the path and onto the unmade-up road leading to St Alphonsus seminary. He took her hand and hurried along with her, all the time scanning around for spying eyes.

Hedgerows lining the road blocked out views left and right until they came to a barred gate, which gave them entry to a field of rented gardens, totally absent of gardeners. Each of the fifty of so garden plots had a tool shed at one corner and all the sheds looked alike.

'Oh my God. Which one is it?' he asked.

She handed him the briefcase. 'Give me the photograph.' She walked around the well-worn grassy paths enclosing the gardens, her head nodding as she compared her position relative to St Alphonsus with Eric Reynaud's position in the photograph. She stopped and looked back at him. 'This looks like it.'

Sebastiani checked. 'I think you're right.' He shook the padlock. 'Who'd want to steal anything from here?' Then he tried kicking down on the padlock with the heel of his shoe.

'Here, try this.' She handed him a key.

'Where did you get that?'

She pointed to a house brick. 'Under that.'

'Let's get these things out of here.' They threw out spades, garden forks, lawnmower, sickle and a scythe, the lot, but found nothing. 'Sorry. I was wrong.'

She stepped into the shed and pressed her weight up and down on the floorboards, which squeaked. 'This is a false floor.'

Using a rake, he levered the floor planks loose and retrieved an oilcloth from which he took three large, black, leather-bound desk diaries, one for the current year and, two for the previous two years and a buff folder containing photographs. You're fantastic.' He skimmed through pages before putting them in the briefcase. 'Call a taxi, quick.'

'Aren't we going to put the tools back?'

For the first time, he yelled at her. 'For goodness sake call a taxi.' He threw the tools back into the shed and latched the door shut. 'You take these to the hotel. I'll go back to the house.'

Sebastiani opened the gate only to find Inspector Moulard standing to the side with a gun in his hand.

'Colonel, hello.'

'Simon Moulard. Are you going to arrest us?'

'No. Introduce me to the lady.'

'Luisa, Inspector Moulard, Marseille police. Professor Luisa Fabian, Rome University.'

'*Mon dieu*. Professor? So you are not a detective?'

'No.'

'Then, what are you doing here?'

'Researching.'

'I am sure you are. What is in the valise?'

Luisa looked at Sebastiani.

'What's on your mind, Simon?'

'I've been standing here for a little while. Watching your backs in case danger should come along. I think you should share with me what you've found. Pay me back. That's Eric Reynaud's evidence. Yes?'

'Yes,' said Sebastiani.

'Please give it to me.'

With gun in hand, Moulard placed the briefcase between his ankles and pulled out the folder with the other hand. 'This is dreadful. Have you seen it?'

'No.'

'Pedos. Unbelievable.' He dug his hand into the briefcase again. 'Diaries?'

'I understand they contain the names of people who bombed Rome. I haven't looked at them yet so I'm not sure. I believe they're more interesting for me than you.'

'This should not go back to the Reynaud house. Moreuil, the Avignon boss, is there, making an asshole of himself. Don't want him getting his hands on this.'

Luisa's taxi drove up.

'Come on, Simon, what are we going to do?'

'I'll take the briefcase with me,' said Moulard.

'Wait a minute. I need to know what's in those diaries.'

'Sure you do. I'll call you first thing tomorrow. Then we can go through them together. You go. Neither of you were at the house when Alice Reynaud was shot. I got a call from an anonymous bystander. I'll come to your hotel. I don't trust you canny Italians.'

'Trust me on this. The killer is a professional sniper with a perfect shot from distance and he was on a big, powerful motorcycle. Simon, I told you to look after Alice Reynaud.'

Luisa lay face down on her hotel bed and sobbed. 'I just can't get over that poor woman.'

'You're trembling.' Sebastiani took off her shoes and rested his hand on her back. Charmed by her body warmth and the delicate fragrance of her perfume, he kissed her shoulder.

She turned to face him. 'I'm scared. Stay with me, please. Hold me.'

'You don't need to be scared. Alice's killer doesn't know you or me. Don't worry, I'll stay with you.' He embraced her and kissed her.

'That poor woman.'

He pulled aside the folds of her gauzy wrap-over skirt and laid a hand on her taught stomach.

Dressed in shirt and trousers, Sebastiani sat on her bed, rested his back against the headboard and studied her standing at the window. He watched for every movement of her curves beneath her loose-fitting, satin pyjamas.

She let the net curtain fall and sat next to him 'There's a market in the square today. Quite a lot of people about.'

'Well, it is eleven o'clock. What are you thinking?'

'I don't know what to think.'

She wrapped her arms around his body and laid her head on his chest.

'Still frightened?'

'That poor Alice.'

'Moulard should have called by now. What's he up to?'

She sat up and faced him. 'You shouldn't have trusted him.'

'He had a gun.'

'He wouldn't have used it on us, would he?'

'Who knows? I don't know what he'd do. We're in France. He had every right to take the diaries. He wouldn't trust anybody else with them anymore than I would. I just hope he doesn't have of a reason to destroy them.'

His mobile telephone rang. 'Moulard?'

'Colonel Sebastiani?'

The Italian voice surprised him. 'Speaking.'

'Sir, it's Major Ferri.'

'Hello, Major.' Sebastiani raised his eyebrows at Luisa and tapped his pursed lips with the side of a finger.

'You're coming back to Rome today, is that right?'

'You sound anxious.'

'I am.'

'What' about?'

'Not on the phone, sir.'

'I've got a flight booked for this evening. Could have done with a couple of more days here but if it's urgent, I'll come.'

'It is. I'll be at the barracks tomorrow morning.'

'I'll be there.' He threw the phone onto the bed. 'Damn.'

'What is it?'

'Ferri wants me back in Rome.'

Luisa sat sideways on the edge of the bed. 'Must I go too?'

'Only if you want to. If you're feeling okay then you can stay. You've got unfinished research to do, for me.'

'I feel fine. I'll stay.'

'Something's wrong. Moulard should have called by now.'

He telephoned Moulard's number at the Marseille police headquarters but got routed through to his anti-terror colleague, Amand Tassin.

Tassin was polite but his news was unhelpful. 'Sorry Colonel. Inspector Moulard will be away for at two weeks.'

'Okay Inspector. It's not a problem. Many thanks. *Ciao*.'

Luisa stood at the foot of the bed in a light summery dress with her head erect. 'I'm ready for you to take me to lunch.'

'Then, let's go.'

'While you're in Rome, I can research Barbentane.'

'Don't do that, it's too risky. You'll be okay on your own in Avignon but don't go to Barbentane without me. I'll be back in a couple of days so wait. I don't want you getting hurt.'

CHAPTER EIGHTEEN

On the way to the barracks, Luca Ferri stopped his car at the southern entrance of the Villa Borghese Park. 'A walk, sir? I reckon you should exercise that leg of yours.'

'A walk?' Sebastiani shifted in his seat and glared at him. 'You want me to go for a walk? Here, in the park?'

'Serious and confidential.'

'I can see that in your miserable face.'

Ferri smiled.

'Okay, Major.' Sebastiani grunted as he manoeuvred himself out of the car. 'Nice to know you have concern for my health. I've been on the go for weeks and I can now walk without a limp or a stick.'

'Good. Let's go.'

The two men set off down the tree-lined Viale del Museo Borghese toward the onetime home of the Borghese popes, now the Galleria Borghese and home to Bernini's breathtaking sculptures, and paintings by Titian and Raphael.

'It's years since I visited the Museum,' said Sebastiani. 'Have you seen the Bernini sculptures?'

'Never been inside the building.'

'How he achieves the appearance of soft flesh in marble is an unbelievable talent. But then you haven't brought me back from France to discuss either my health or famous Italian art. What is it Ferri?'

'You said someone in the force is working against us.'

'And I still believe that.'

'So do I.'

'Got somebody in mind?'

'Conti.'

'Conti! Conti? Are you out of your mind? What on earth are you talking about?' He chuckled cynically. 'Come off it. I just don't believe that.'

'I think you'd better listen to what I've got to say.'

'No, no. You're making a big mistake. Conti's an old soldier and a good one. Fantastic record of service to Italy and the Carabinieri. Known him for years and years. Let's get to the barracks, I don't want to hear this.'

'For God's sake, hear me out!'

That stopped Sebastiani in his tracks. Balls at last, he thought. 'I'm listening.'

'Your old secret service friend Ricardo Da Corte told me this.'

'Oh yes. What?'

'On the evening of the sabotage, General Conti and someone at Viterbo exchanged encrypted telephone calls.'

'Deciphered?'

'Partially. They spoke in code.'

'Ricardo's certain it was Conti?'

'Yes.'

'Partially deciphered. Nothing clear, then. Nothing incriminating.'

'No.'

'That's no good then, is it?'

'Who knew the helicopters were coming?'

'Only you and me. Yes. Just you and me. At first.'

'I thought so too. No one else was to know. It was an impromptu night exercise. But someone was alerted that Gagliano was about to be moved out.'

'Di Angelis and the prisoner escorts stayed with you all the time until just before take-off.'

'Yes. But only Di Angelis knew what was happening. Think about this. I arranged for the three medical helicopters from the army to be on standby in case of emergencies. That's what I told the Viterbo base commander. I personally gave him the request and told him it was an exercise to test readiness and that no one else should know. It was your show so I couldn't tell him the details. And I didn't. And he couldn't tell anyone something he didn't know, so he didn't tell Conti about the Gagliano transfer. But he did tell him to expect the helicopters at the barracks, requested by me. It would take a dummy not to make the connection.'

Sebastiani stared at the Borghese museum, sparkling white against the luscious green of the park in the bright afternoon sun. 'How do you know he told Conti?'

'I asked the base commander if anyone had been informed about my request. Only General Conti, he told me. Conti was at the barracks the whole day and stayed until the wreckage was removed.'

'You're making me nervous.'

'There's more.'

'Oh?'

'I checked with forensics about the letter you gave Conti. He never passed it on to them.'

'Are you sure?'

'Positive. No record of it ever reaching the lab.'

'Just a minute, Fontana told me Conti received a report about it.' Sebastiani bit on a knuckle for several moments. 'Think he lied to Fontana?'

Ferri shrugged. 'Don't know. He could have.'

'There's got to be an explanation. What are you going to do?'

'Confront him?'

'Christ. Don't do that.'

'At first, that's what I thought I'd do. I know, it's too risky.'

'Good you thought twice.'

'So, what should I do?'

'Look, I've seen how these things work out. Don't do anything yet. Leave it with me.' Sebastiani took off his cap and ran his fingers around its inside rim. 'Given this, and assuming ill intent on Conti's part, he could be screwing our investigation. But I've known him for years; I just cannot see it.'

245

'We've got to suspect the worst. We've got to suspect Conti is a traitor.'

'That's putting it strong. I don't know. Okay, he phoned Viterbo but that could have been for any number of reasons.'

'Encrypted?'

'Umm.'

Ferri motioned to walk back to the car. 'What do we do?'

'The only thing that can be proved is that Conti did not deliver the letter for forensic analysis. As it turned out, that wouldn't have been much use. We arrested the guy who shot me. It could have been useful to confirm he wrote the letter but it wasn't so important.'

'Bomb squad and forensics found nothing from the helicopter wreckage. And the search in the barracks, also nothing.'

He sensed Ferri's agitation now that he had declared his suspicions. 'Are you worried you've told me this?'

At the car, the major opened the passenger door.

'I don't like accusing General Conti. On the other hand, I think we need to be open about what we know.' Ferri's next words confirmed his nervousness. 'I trust you, sir.'

Sebastiani patted his shoulder. 'Likewise Major, likewise.' He looked at his watch. 'I have to go. Would you believe it? I have a meeting with Conti at two. He wants to know if my trip to France had any value.' Sebastiani slapped his cap onto his head and adjusted it. 'I'm saying nothing to anyone about what you've told me.'

'When are you going back to Avignon?'

'In two days. Luisa's still there.'

'I guessed she was. I've had no contact with her for the last week. But then I've had no reason to.'

'Get me back to the barracks.'

Conti looked disturbed. 'Listen Fabio, I'm not interested in your escapades with the French clergy. I'm not convinced we have anything to go on there that will help this investigation. It's just drifting on and it aggravates me bloody intensely.'

Sebastiani listened to and understood Conti's arguments while at the same time weighing them in an untrusting light.

'It's a waste of time.'

He could feel the mistrust gaining the upper hand. 'This is a valid line of enquiry.'

'I'm not convinced. You're misusing an important resource. I'm talking about your own participation.'

A personal agenda? Sebastiani set himself against being swayed without evidence. Conti had been his colleague of many years.

'That's it,' Conti continued. 'I accept I could be wrong. If that's what Ferri wants, I won't countermand it. If it turns out I'm right, he will pay severely.'

'He's following my advice. I'm responsible for the France inquiry. I know the French police have information that I'm certain will open up the Rome investigation. You should continue to support me.'

Conti acquiesced and softened his tone. 'Okay, Fabio. I trust you. This withdrawal of gendarmerie support. Does that prevent you from operating effectively? If necessary, I can get our Ministry of Defence involved.'

'No thanks. It's better the way things are. I don't want the French on my back telling me what I can and can't do.'

Grimacing, Conti massaged his right elbow and lower arm. 'I play tennis because it keeps me in reasonable shape but the pain is dreadful. It's becoming too much. I'll just have to give it up and stick with the flying club. What happened in Marseille was disgusting. I received a report this morning. They've suspended the interrogating officers.'

'Reynaud? The Marseille police have a reputation. Death in police custody. Happens often there apparently, so the media tell us. And no one's ever been charged so I suspect they'll get away with it this time too.'

'Prisoners have died in custody here too. Rules can't stop the natural cruelty in some people. Unfortunately, such people seem abundant in the police forces of this world. So, someone believed

247

he had names to name and killed him because Rome wanted to interrogate him. Right?'

'I'm certain.'

'There you go. Now I'm giving you a reason to be in France.'

Sebastiani drew in his chin. 'Then you support our France inquiries?'

'Yes. Yes I do.'

'Good.' Thinking the discussion was closing, Sebastiani stood and moved to the door. 'I'll do whatever I can to make it worthwhile.'

'What's your first move?'

'I have contacts in the Marseille anti-terrorist group. I'll try and get to Reynaud's interrogating officers. Moulard is one of them. I'll start with him. Moulard. My God.' He shook his head fiercely. 'A dreadful little man.'

'See what you can do. I don't want anybody else here to know you're doing this. I'm serious. There's a traitor in the team.'

In Sebastiani's ears, Conti's words did not betray a man attempting to deflect suspicion from himself.

'Your daughter. Elaine Bruneau.'

'Yes, sir?'

'She's being sentenced today.'

These words wrenched him stiff. 'I know. Tunisia hasn't executed for years. I expect she'll get life.'

'That's what I hear. I'm sorry.' Conti smoothed back his hair. 'Franchi and I are discussing the matter. I'll do what I can. Are you able to telephone her?'

'I try often but I've spoken with her only once. It's very difficult but I'll keep trying.'

'Sorry, Fabio.'

'That's the way it is. What about Bintloff?'

'Released without charge.'

'Good.'

Conti stood and folded his arms. 'Well, duty presses. Five thousand troops required for the weekend demonstrations against

248

the Church's move to Avignon. The Rome demonstration will be huge. Milan and Bologna are the other hot points this weekend. Curiously, nothing in Palermo. Does that tell you anything?'

Sebastiani shrugged his shoulders. 'I'm sure they would protest too if their Mafia overlords didn't have good reasons to stop them.'

Sebastiani had often questioned why the Carabinieri had located the Rome forensics unit over at the Ministry of Defence building in the Piazza della Marina and not at the barracks where it would be more convenient for everyday access. Today, though, he found its remoteness advantageous. He did not want to be spotted by Conti checking on his 'negative' report on the terrorist threat letter he'd received in hospital or by Ferri who had claimed Conti had not delivered it for forensic examination.

'The letter was in a clear plastic grip-seal bag. Does that help?'

'A plastic grip-seal bag? General Conti, you say. Wait a minute. I'll go through the log and see what was booked in recently.' Doctor Luciano Nardelli disappeared into his office and returned after half a minute with what looked to be the plastic covered letter that Conti had taken from Sebastiani in the hospital, holding it between finger and thumb of an outstretched arm as though it gave off an offensive smell. 'Here it is.'

'That's it.' Sebastiani peeled the bag open. 'Can I handle the letter?'

'Yes. I've finished with it.'

He unfolded it. 'I'm told you found nothing to identify the writer?'

Nardelli pouted. 'Who told you that? Here's the report. The analyst found fibers from a sweater. The sweater to which the fibers correspond is also here, taken from the home of the assailant. Sorry, should have brought that along.'

Nardelli disappeared again and returned with the sweater.

'So, why wasn't this item recorded in your log?'

'I'm sure it was. Everything brought in here is logged immediately. Come with me, we'll check on the computer. Conti's the name?'

'Yes.'

Nardelli entered a Find on the name Conti and then peered at the screen. 'There it is. One day after the assault on Colonel Sebastiani. Ah. That's you Colonel. Sorry, I didn't realize.'

Sebastiani sat in his car and stared out of the windscreen, perplexed. Ferri would surely realize he'd check on Conti's failure to deliver a piece of evidence to the lab? Such a simple, sloppy error not worthy of him, the star policeman noted for his precise work. Unless he had phoned for the information and the forensics people couldn't find it. Why wouldn't they? Nardelli had found the entry so easily.

Then he thought about the helicopter sabotage. What was Conti doing that day? I saw him first about four in the morning. He'd taken the base commander's call about the helicopter exercise certainly but that doesn't tell me from where. Conti could have taken the call at his *grande suite* in the Via Nazionale. A call to him is automatically switched through to whichever one of his phones he sticks his code card into. But he could have an accomplice at the barracks.

The visit to forensics had shattered Sebastiani's trust in the two people he most believed in. Either Ferri had lied or Conti acted out a sham. Any one of these possibilities could put the investigation in jeopardy. On the other hand, the major could have been misinformed.

The chirpy sound of his mobile phone dispelled the mental picture.

'*Pronto!*'

'Colonel Sebastiani?'

'Speaking.'

'Our unidentified patient has started whispering,' informed the covered voice of his amateur spy at the Ospedale Santa Lucia.

Sebastiani grinned and banged the steering wheel with his open hands. 'Yes!' The resurrection of his first witness had beamed a light along the dark road ahead, dim but a light none the less.

Now to France to retrieve the Sinclair diaries.

CHAPTER NINETEEN

Sebastiani arrived back in France with clear objectives. The first, a visit to Moulard's replacement in the anti-terror group in Marseille out of respect for international cooperation, would probably be a waste of time, he believed.

'The anti-terrorist group is on the second floor. Inspector Tassin's room is 206. If you should need it, the gentlemen's toilet is down the corridor to the right. The coffee machine is over there. But don't drink the coffee. It's dreadful.' The desk sergeant laughed out loud and returned to studying his day's list of visitors.

Amand Tassin presented a stark contrast to Moulard: mid-forties, smartly dressed and polite. He had set aside half an hour from his day especially for Sebastiani. '*Buongiorno*, Colonel,' he said with his best-effort Italian accent. 'Have a seat.'

'*Bonjour*, Inspector. I need just a little of your time.'

'Coffee? I'll get the kitchen to send some up.'

'No coffee, thanks.'

'What can I do for you?'

'Inspector Moulard invited me to talk to the prisoner, Eric Reynaud, and I came to Marseille especially to do that. You probably know, he died before I could meet him.'

Tassin nodded.

'I'd like to have a clear understanding about his death. A formal statement from you so that I can explain the matter to my bosses in Rome.'

'Inspector Moulard was the senior interrogating officer but he's been suspended pending an inquiry.'

'Yes, I heard.'

'That's the usual thing in cases like this.'

'The report says a heart attack and I have no reason to doubt that. But given the information Reynaud claimed to have, I can see there might be people anxious that he didn't go public with it.'

Tassin looked at him slit-eyed and played with his chin but then his eyes widened. 'Ah. I know what you're getting at. That has happened here but I don't think so in this case.'

'Moulard was the senior interrogating officer. Did he interrogate Reynaud?'

'No. Only officer Babin was present when he died. The police medical officer examined the body and wrote the death certificate. I'm sure everything was done correctly.'

'I'm sure.'

Tassin laid his elbows on his arm rests and frowned askance at Sebastiani. 'Are you staying in Marseille long?'

'I leave for Avignon this evening.'

'I'll do what I can to get the report. Give me half an hour. I'll have something prepared for you.'

He read Tassin's demeanour as pleasant in a formal way but not welcoming.

At the duty desk, Sebastiani accepted a large brown envelope from the sergeant that Tassin had left for him; he opened it immediately. It contained just one sheet, a copy of the death certificate, which stated what he already knew: cause of death, heart attack. It said nothing about the conditions under which Reynaud died. He assumed Tassin had not put himself out to dig for that information and Sebastiani left it at that.

He turned the visitor's book round to sign out.

'Are you here with the other Italian officer, Major Ferri?' the desk sergeant asked.

He looked aghast at him and scanned the open page for Ferri's name. 'Yes. Has he left?'

'I saw him yesterday, sir.'

'Who was he visiting?'

The sergeant turned the page. 'Inspector Moulard.'

'Ah, right.' Sebastiani walked out of the building biting on his lower lip.

Luisa dug into her handbag, checked for her notebook and digital camera and then left the hotel. She made a beeline across the vibrant, tourist-filled Place de l'Horloge, with the plan of filling out the Avignon history of the Collineau family over the last four hundred years. Her experience had taught her the best place to start would be with the historical records in the Cathedral's archive library. Coming from the direction of the hotel, she reached the Cathedral itself before getting to the library.

She glanced up at the golden Virgin Mary on the cathedral tower and then went inside, curious to see if the final resting place of the Avignon popes had changed since she studied at Barbentane. Nothing had changed, only the Cathedral timetable and events notices pinned to the board at the entrance.

The timetable of Church events took her eye. 'I don't believe it.' She got closer to read the item, a forthcoming seminar at St Alphonsus seminary to be introduced by the new Leader of the Holy Catholic Church, Archbishop Roger Collineau with the keynote item to be given by Cardinal Roland Giuliani. She leaned her back against the wall, pulled out her notebook and began talking under her breath. 'Roland Giuliani. It's him. Yes. It's him.' Her eyes continued down her list to Michel Blanche and Jean-Paul Martin. 'I wonder.'

She bit on the cap of her pen and read the date and time of the event given in bold black letters at the bottom of the sheet. 'Today at two o'clock. Three hours.'

Back at the Hotel de l'Horloge she left a note in reception for Sebastiani and took a taxi to Barbentane, then walked the familiar kilometre of country road to St Alphonsus seminary. Once inside the grounds she ran to catch up with the only person in sight, a cardinal walking ahead of her toward the double doors of the main entrance.

She called to him. 'Can you help me?'

'The information office is at the gate.'

'I know. I tried. There's no one there. I want to speak with Cardinal Roland Giuliani. How can I get to him?'

The cleric puffed out his cheeks. 'That would be difficult today. He's tied up with a seminar.'

'I know. I hoped to attend.'

'Who do you represent?'

'Rome University, Religious Studies.'

He smiled and narrowed his eyes. '*Madame*, your French is excellent.' He winked an eye. 'Although I did detect a trace of accent. If you have some identification, it shouldn't be a problem.'

She showed her ID card.

He read it and, in Italian, said, 'Welcome to Barbentane and St Alphonsus, Luisa Fabian.'

She inclined her head and smiled. 'Thank you. Perfect Italian.'

'That's because I am Italian.'

And so she continued in Italian. 'Now, can you help me? I am trying to contact Cardinal Michel Blanche and Cardinal Jean-Paul Martin. Are they attending the seminar?'

His face stiffened and his voice soured. 'I'm afraid I cannot help you.' He turned and hastened to the entrance door, his change in attitude leaving her confounded.

Gathering clouds darkened the sky and it started to rain. She ran to the still-unoccupied gate office and stood under its porch, which gave little shelter.

'Damn.'

She tried the door handle but the door was locked, so she decided to return to Avignon. She had already heard Collineau's induction address and convinced herself there would be little new to learn from the seminar anyway. Then she remembered her totally vain efforts in those earlier days to lure a taxi to St Alphonsus during the tourist season. If the Barbentane-Avignon bus came at all, it did so infrequently so she phoned for a rental car.

Two Avignon Car Rental cars arrived and a man got out of one of them shielding mobile order and payment equipment under his raincoat. '*Bonjour, Madame.*'

After entering details into the device, he handed her documents and keys for the car standing at least ten metres from her in the pouring rain.

'Hey!' she shouted. 'For goodness sake, don't leave it there.'

But he scurried off with his raincoat over his head to his partner's car, which then raced off.

Luisa stood under the porch looking for a break in the clouds but gave up when the clouds became even darker and the rain more intense. Handbag over her head, she splashed through the slush to the car. She sank into the driver's seat drenched through but cheered by the thought of her hotel shower, just a half an hour away.

She started the engine and looked back at the main building and saw the Italian cardinal standing at a window and staring icily at her. She shuddered and drove off.

Five minutes after leaving the seminary, a gendarme standing by his police car with a cape over his shoulders signalled her to stop.

Lowering the window, she asked, 'What is it officer?'

The gendarme stooped as though to speak to her but then stood upright and shouted something she did not understand. Suddenly, the passenger-side door was wrenched open and her face smothered with a chloroform-soaked cloth. She shook her head violently and thrashed out with her fists but within seconds she slumped forward into her safety belt with her hands lifeless in her lap.

'Get her into the back of my car. When you've done that, one of you take her car back to the rental company. Don't forget to drop the keys in the box.'

Gradually she regained consciousness in darkness on a cold stone floor, wet through, her arms and legs bound, nausea wrenching her stomach. She was unable to focus on the two male voices echoing weirdly distant in French. Then suddenly her mind cleared.

'She's awake,' said one.

'Say something to her,' said the other.

The first one took up again. 'Luisa Fabian, you are an Italian Carabinieri officer.'

'No.'

'I've got your ID here. Look.' He pushed her pass for the Rome operations room close to her face.

'You stupid fool. I don't know what you're doing. I can't see.'

'You were snooping around in Barbentane. Why?'

'Please untie my hands and legs.'

'We can't do that. What were you up to?'

'I'm wet and cold. Will you please untie me?'

He slapped her face. 'You don't understand, *Madame*. If you don't answer my question I will kick your face.'

'I was in Barbentane to attend the seminar at St Alphonsus.'

'You are Italian police. What are you doing poking around St Alphonsus for? Asking about priests.'

'Ah. Then I know who sent you after me.'

'You know *Monsieur* Giuliani?'

The face at the window with the icy stare, she thought. 'I know him well.'

'He said you were up to no good.'

'Please untie me. My hands and legs are hurting.'

Interrogator number two broke in. 'I reckon we ought to use the needle. Juice her. Loosen her up.'

'What have you got?'

'I don't know.' He fished in his pockets.

In the unsteadily scanning flash-lamp light, Luisa got her first glimpses of her prison, a small cell built from black, stone blocks that let in no warmth. Her jailers had blacked out the barred window above her head. The heavy, barred door opposite made her realize this was a prison cell, a very old one. In her former days in Barbentane she had never seen a prison so she had no idea where she could be.

A crackling noise added to the theatre as the man flashing the torch about took a cellophane package from his jacket that claimed the

257

hypodermic syringe it contained to be sterile, and a small phial from his trouser pocket. 'HiTripomix.'

'HiTripomix? Never heard of it. Is that a truth drug?'

'I don't think so. It's all I've got. I can't see the small print.'

Luisa looked at their faces in the flashing light but could not make out their features.

'It's got several chemical names. Amphetamine is one of them.'

'Then we'll try it.'

'You're crazy,' she said. 'Amphetamine is not a truth drug.'

He slapped her face again. 'Keep silent or I will kill you now. Get on with it, Rene.'

'Don't call me Rene.'

'Oh. Right. No names. Sorry, Rene.'

'Idiot.'

'You're both idiots. Let me go.'

While Rene prepared the injection, the other interrogator sat astride her, increasing the pain in her hands.

'Ready?'

In the poor light, Rene had understandable difficulties. 'I can't see. Hold the torch. Keep her arm still.'

'Oo.' Luisa groaned and slipped into unconsciousness.

An eerie expectant silence fell on the scene.

'Is she dead, Georges?'

'Don't say my name.'

'She can't hear if she's dead.'

'Christ!' Georges sprang to his feet. 'Dead?'

'She's either dead or faking it.'

Georges put his head near her mouth. 'She's breathing. She's not dead.'

'I see the center of your evil mind and it is beautiful in its mystery.' Luisa's voice became quieter and resonated deeper now than the voice with which she had chided them previously and it told them in Russian that her God had lifted her on high.

'What's she saying?'

'I don't know.'

258

'She's possessed.'

'Let's get out of here.'

'Shall we untie her?'

'Come on. Let's go.'

They left her bound and incarcerated in a locked cell but they had set her mind free to travel the mystical worlds of hallucinations and dreams.

She looked down at the face of a young blond-haired girl in a coloured dress who had taken her hand. They embraced on a patch of grass under a willow tree by a river and then the young girl led her through murky and threatening shadows, but she felt no fear, only excitement.

She passed alone through a door leading to a church crypt that she recognized but in a place she knew she could never have been. Large golden Latin words and numerals embossed in the worn stone floor that lay before her glinted in the altar's candlelight. The golden words, though individually clear, made no sense. A rapidly metamorphosing object flashed myriad colors around the crypt and filled her with lightness and happiness. An inner voice enticed her over the Latin characters and through the column-supported arches to the altar. Large lanterns of jewel-laced golden crowns hanging low from the ceiling vanished in the sudden blackness that engulfed her.

A white mist loomed in the darkness and the young girl now dressed in a white, flowing communion dress, emerged from a glow in its midst. With her head drooped forward, she seemed to be praying. Luisa knew that the young girl must move forward over the golden words that have no meaning and recite a Latin text by heart before the altar. Luisa felt it: an evil being hiding in the dark places and she feared it, not for herself but because she anticipated it would devour the girl before she could fulfill her task that would reveal the mystery that Luisa must learn. Her eyes fixed on a stone sarcophagus that lay against a wall. A large dark outline leapt out of it with its companion, a slobbering, monstrous beast, which drew back its lips and snapped at the child's face. But the child walked unconcerned and unafraid to the altar and spoke clearly. Luisa read the Latin text engraved on a stone at the altar as the girl recited it:

> Our dear Sciarra has sent Gaetano, the vile king of Rome, to hell. But the false Pope of burning hate who has heaped curses on our family will come again in later days. Raise the sword of righteousness and strike the crown from Gaetano, cursed now and forever unto his last generation. Pour ruin on his accursed, satanic harlot, the nemesis of our family and of mankind.

> These are the words of Jacopo Colonna in this Year of our Lord 1303, the thirteenth day of November.

Luisa suddenly awoke, hands and feet still bound, feeling nauseous and wanting to pee. Her left arm had numbed through laying on it for over an hour. She levered herself to a sitting position with her elbows, pushed herself back with her feet and rested against the wall. Her mind had been made crystal clear by whatever her captors had given her and her thoughts ran wild. She had seen the Latin text. The young girl had spoken it faultlessly, just as written on the stone. 'I know it. I see it clearly now. The Latin text is engraved on a stone in a dark place. I can see it. But where is it? Where, where?'

Sebastiani had not realized his train had reached Avignon TGV station until the final braking jerk pulled his mind from the puzzle that had occupied it the whole journey: that Ferri had met with the Marseille police without telling him, even though the major had given over the French part of the investigation to him. Why would he meet with Moulard? And why didn't Moulard mention it? A memory slip? Nonsense. It must be something sinister, but what?

He reached hotel reception in a daze. '*Bonjour*. My name's Sebastiani.'

'Welcome back sir.' The male receptionist placed the key on the desk.

While taking the key, he noticed a letter in his mail slot. 'Is that a letter for me?'

'Ah! Yes, it is, sir.'

A note from Luisa. Very neat and in her usual telegraphic style.

Hello Fabio. Diocese schools all okay. Giuliani not available. Gone to Barbentane. Opportunity came up. Will explain. Call you Saturday afternoon around 4 o'clock.

Sebastiani gritted his teeth and snatched his travel bag from the floor. 'Barbentane? Silly bloody woman.' He checked his watch. Seven ten, Saturday. He turned to the receptionist. 'Has anyone phoned for me?'

'Sir, I've been at the desk since two. Since then, no one has phoned for you. Before that, I don't know. There are no other messages.'

Until now, Luisa had always been punctual and reliable. That she hadn't phoned the previous day as she had planned caused Sebastiani a sleepless night. The coffee at breakfast tasted good and strong but it had not raised him above ragged tiredness. At least the overcast sky gave his cotton-wool-numb brain relief from the usual glare of morning sunshine.

No phone call, no message in his post slot. No messages in her post slot either. He stood on the pavement wondering whether he should phone Ferri. If she'd had an emergency to deal with she might have phoned him about it. But he now held Ferri as uncertain territory. No, he thought. I'll give her time.

A dirty black Peugeot screeched to a halt in front of him and its right, front door sprang open to block his way on the narrow pavement. 'Sebastiani, get in.'

'Moulard.' He got into the front passenger seat.

The Frenchman said nothing, looked straight ahead and accelerated away from the hotel.

'Thought you'd gone forever,' said Sebastiani.

'It's worse than I thought. Where's your professor friend?'

'I wish I knew. Where're we going?'

'Not far.' Moulard took the Tarascon exit from the city ring road, drove through Rognonas and, after about ten kilometers, took a left turn into a single-track country road that zigzagged gradually upwards through thick woods to a small redbrick house.

'Where are we?'

No answer.

On arrival in France, Sebastiani had studied his map of the area and concluded they were near Châteaurenard.

Moulard got out and set off toward the house.

Glad to have extracted himself from Moulard's stinking Peugeot, Sebastiani stood for a while to get some idea of the location. Looking north through gaps in the woods he could see that the house stood high relative to the countryside from east to the west. He identified Avignon by its distinctive palace situated roughly to the northeast. Looking in the opposite direction and upwards, he could see an old sandstone building that he took to be the abbey of Saint Michel de Frigolet. Then we're not near Châteaurenard, he realized.

As soon as he stepped into the house the cigarette smoke made him cough.

Moulard attempted an introduction and, with the back of his hand over his mouth, he coughed his way through it. 'Colonel...Sebastiani, Rome...anti-terrorist group.'

In the natural gloom of the small room and the cigarette smoke that filled it, he failed to see clearly any of the faces but they all appeared to be in their mid-thirties or early forties and in casual clothes. Two of them sat side-by-side in low chairs, in the murkiness, a matched pair of gargoyles complete with pained and petrified stares. '*Bonjour*, gentlemen.'

'Colonel, you might know some of these people.' Moulard followed his pointing finger round the group with their names. 'Bertrand Parran.' Parran, two meters tall and proportionally built, shoved himself away from the wall with his backside and shook hands with Sebastiani.

'Bertrand,' said Sebastiani.

Moulard's finger moved on to a totally bald man in jeans and a tight-fitting, white T-shirt that outlined his powerful build. 'This is Jean-Paul Bonnet.'

Moulard then pointed to the gargoyles. 'And these two gentlemen are Pierre Didier and Henry Poret.'

He bent to shake their hands.

'Pierre has news that will interest you.'

Sebastiani expected another powerful being but when Pierre hauled himself from his deep seat and on to his feet, he was short and stocky.

Pierre said, 'It is about your daughter, Colonel.'

'Oh?'

'Elaine Bruneau has been released. She returned to France a few days ago and is now in a private clinic in Paris.'

Sebastiani fought back the crazy urge to hug the stranger for this precious revelation. 'Thank you, Pierre. That's fantastic news. How is she?'

'She was tortured. But she is okay.'

'Your daughter,' said Moulard. 'Elaine Bruneau. Yes, Colonel?'

'You know her?'

'Of course I know her. She is one of our Paris team. Sit yourself.' Moulard stubbed out his cigarette against the wall and lit another immediately.

Sebastiani scanned the seating options but remained standing.

Moulard sank himself into a grubby leatherette armchair. 'Reynaud's diaries are a bit of a mystery for me but interesting for you, perhaps.'

'I want them.'

'They're here.' Moulard pointed to a rickety credenza. 'Bertrand.'

Bertrand Parran dug out the three large diaries and the buff folder and handed it to Sebastiani. 'I know what this is. Pedophile photographs. That's a French police matter. I want the diaries.'

'They're all in English, Italian and Latin. Except for the name Sinclair, they mean nothing to me. These are the originals. Keep them.'

It was a defining moment: he would soon know the names of the conspirators.

'Take your time, Fabio,' said Moulard. 'There's a bench seat in the garden. Sit in the fresh air and read them.'

To get a sense of the development of Sinclair's activities up to the time of the Rome attack, Sebastiani started with the oldest of the diaries. Every page contained details of meetings planned, reports and reminders of personal engagements. Halfway through the first, he started to see clues in Sinclair's use of peoples' initials and their connection to tasks, requests for funding, manpower and commitment to the "Covenant cause".

The pattern of entries became familiar and he could now scan the pages and spot the entries that tied to an action in Rome. He rested back and squinted at the horizon. 'No wonder Sinclair had to die.'

'What's that, Fabio?'

Sebastiani gathered the diaries and Moulard took their place on the bench.

'There was a briefcase with this stuff.'

'It's around here somewhere. What do you make of them?'

He looked into the distance. Moulard had let him down already by not securing Alice Reynaud. What would he do with what I tell him? There's no option but to trust him. 'They're evidence of the plot to bomb the Vatican. That's all I can say at the moment. Except that now that I've got them I need protection.'

'I'll make sure you get back to Rome.'

'Look, Simon, I am worried about Luisa Fabian.'

'The professor, why is something wrong?'

'She should have phoned me yesterday but she didn't. That's not like her.'

'You think she's gone missing?'

'Yes. She's been reliable till now.'

'Any ideas where she might be?'

'She left me a note a couple of days ago saying she's going to the Barbentane seminary. But she can't still be there. She'd have told me if she was.'

'Then she's a missing person. Got a photograph?'

'No.'

'Never mind, I'll get the station to organize a missing person operation.'

'Why the men from Paris?'

'Some of our Marseille men are spending more than they get paid.'

'Do you know who's paying them?'

'No. But this looks like big stuff. Paris has been watching Marseille. Didier and Poret are French secret service assigned to me because I'm trusted. That's how I know about your daughter. She's part of the team.'

'My God.'

Moulard growled, stood and stretched his arms upwards. As he let his arms fall, one shoulder of his jacket sagged down an arm to make the other shoulder fit. This man did not become an inspector because of his dress sense.

'I'm doing a raid today and you are with me.'

'To keep me safe?'

'You might need this.' Moulard handed him a handgun. 'It is the best and latest, Sig Sauer SP 2022.'

'I hope I don't have to use it.'

'Safety precaution.' Moulard got up, walked to his car and then shouted back to him. 'Come over here and look.'

He handed binoculars to Sebastiani, who leaned on the roof of the car and focused them on the village across the valley to which the inspector pointed.

'That's Barbentane,' said Moulard.

The small town overlooked the rich agricultural land that lay at the confluence of the Rhône and Durance rivers. It sat high and missed the raging floodwaters that occasionally swept down the

Rhône valley in the winter months. During this early August time, the vast orchards were filled with red, green and yellow jewels, fruits that emblazoned the landscape.

'Can you see it? Got a town hall with a clock tower.'

'I see it.'

'The monastery is to the right.'

The colonel swept the binoculars three kilometres east from Barbentane to the cupola with a cross just visible in the distant trees.

St Alphonsus had functioned to transform novice priests into workers of the Vatican. Now they would learn to be workers for the pope in Avignon. The pope in prospect, Archbishop Collineau, had declared it: the Roman Catholic Church had its feet in pagan idolatry and must die.

For Sebastiani, it was the establishment of yet another schism but for Inspector Moulard, this was all religious confusion that didn't interest him one little bit. He had casually read about the Church's move to Avignon but could not see that the move would make any difference to its nature.

Moulard pulled at Sebastiani's sleeve. 'Can you see the monastery?'

'I'm looking at it.'

'Now look a little to the right. Do you see the other building?'

Sebastiani nodded.

'That's the Safe Home for Young Refugees.'

The home stood within easy walking distance for the St Alphonsus priests who came to care for the children. The seminary leaders had also given their generous friends from other professions – politicians, businessmen and women, police, entertainers, and so on, all of them anxious to give their individual attention to young boys and girls – access to the home.

Moulard parked his car outside St Alphonsus' main gate.

Sebastiani got out and immediately realized that the rough road continued on from where he stood to the Reynaud house. He walked a

266

few meters and could see the roof of the only house in the road, just above the hedgerow. He walked farther and saw the gate and outside, the same blue saloon car that appeared there on his first visit.

Moulard waited and watched until he returned. 'Looking for the Reynaud house?'

'There's a blue car down there.'

'So what?'

'It was there before. The day Alice Reynaud was shot.'

'I see.'

'Carry on without me, Simon. I've got something to do. But please get your men to look around the place for Luisa Fabian. This is where she was headed.'

An arrowed sign led Moulard to a little gate house set away from the wall on a grassy mound with a border filled with colourful flowers. The house had the small proportions of, and generally resembled, the colourful tiny house in a child's storybook, where the white bearded Policeman Thierry lived with his wife Claire-Marie.

'Hello, hello. Hello!' He bawled into the open window and tried without success to catch the attention of the porter, who was clearly deaf – and watching television at full volume to boot. Moulard banged the window with no effect, gave up, walked into the office and tapped the man on the shoulder. 'Hey, you.'

The old porter turned to him, his face frozen in fear and his scrawny hands shaking uncontrollably.

'Can you hear me?' Moulard turned down the volume.

The old man's trembling arms flailed the air and his mouth contorted as if hit by a sudden toothache. Then he settled and spat out words. 'Got an appointment?'

Moulard looked directly into his face and shouted with exaggerated lip movements. '*Monsignor* Geleve. I want *Monsignor* Geleve.'

'Why?'

Moulard showed him his police badge and the old man trembled again.

The inspector shouted. 'Get *Monsignor* Geleve here now.'

The old man picked up his telephone, a relic of the 1970s, and dialled a number. He pressed the telephone to one ear and dug a finger into the other, and waited. 'Ah! *Monsignor* Geleve. Inspec...'

Moulard grabbed the phone and introduced himself.

'*Bonjour*, Inspector. An unexpected visit from the police.' Geleve spoke softly. 'That's a rarity here. I'll collect you from the gate.'

Moulard dropped the telephone onto its cradle and turned to see the old man sitting in a corner staring at him with his face pinched.

'*Merci*,' he mouthed to the old man.

He drifted outside and waited by the gardens that filled the front approach to the seminary building. A few grey-clad and silent priests snipped, clipped and hoed in dreamy serenity. He felt agitated in this slow-paced and peaceful antimatter contrast to his own frantic world.

The man approaching smiled a smile of graceful peace and already from the distance, raised both hands in the way one does when about to embrace a long absent loved one. Moulard feared an embrace and raised his police badge in defence.

'What is it, inspector?' Geleve continued his lavish smile.

Moulard put a cigarette into his mouth and, without removing it, asked, 'May I smoke.'

'Many of the brothers smoke. It's deprecated but tolerated. Now, tell me what this is about.'

'I'm here to warn you of terrorist threats against Roman Catholic institutions in France.'

'But we have had official warnings about this from within the Church.'

'But I'm talking about an immediate threat in this area.'

'Oh dear, oh dear. Please come with me.'

Geleve led him into his office just off the entrance hall, a large room with white walls, vaulted ceilings and clean air smelling of wax floor polish. A white, alabaster figure of Mary on a plinth in the corner made supplication to her God somewhere above her. Geleve sat down at his French antique desk and invited Moulard to sit in a matching *fauteuil* in front of it. Then he took a heavy cut-glass ashtray from a drawer, inspected the green baize on its base and placed it in the corner of the table at Moulard's right hand.

Geleve replaced his smile with a frown. 'You gave us no warning of your visit.'

'We received the threat today so I came as quickly as possible.'

The *monsignor* appeared to show more attention to the ash growing at the end of the cigarette in Moulard's hand as it travelled over his precious desk than to the topic of terrorists. 'I see. Yes, I see. Dreadful. And you think it will happen here? To St Alphonsus?'

'Certainly. Our intelligence shows it's a distinct possibility. I'm here to instruct your staff about what to do.'

'Of course. Now?'

Moulard withdrew the cigarette from his mouth, ran his top teeth over the tiny piece of tobacco that remained on his lower lip, manoeuvred it onto the front of his tongue and then spat it to the floor. 'Now's the best time.'

'I'll gather them together in the assembly hall. But what about all our students, our novices?'

'Just the staff. The staff can pass the information down.'

Geleve moved to reach for the telephone on his desk and then stopped. 'Just one thing. We have an emergency procedure. When the alarm sounds, everybody gathers outside the walls.'

The inspector strained to contain his irritation with this man. 'No, that's too much. Do you have a loudspeaker system?'

'Yes.'

'Then use that to call the staff together.'

'We'll use the assembly hall.'

'Good. Do it right away.'

269

Moulard's planned raid on the St Alphonsus seminary, an operation sponsored by Paris gendarmerie, held only passing interest for Sebastiani so he withdrew to pursue a Rome-related operation of his own. He crouched his way along a grassy track the other side of the hedgerow from the road and stopped when he had a good view of the Reynaud house. There it was, the same blue car with the same registration.

The front door of the house opened and two men hastened into the garden in animated argument, one pointing in the direction of the rented gardens. They returned to the house but appeared again shortly after discussing what Sebastiani took to be a photograph. They hurried down the path and up the road, pushed open the barred gate to the gardens and disappeared from his view. They had been slow but they had worked out the location of the Sinclair diaries just as he had so he gave them credit for that.

He crawled through the hedge, placed a tracking bug under the car and then returned to the seminary.

Back at the seminary, Moulard stood at Geleve's side on the stage and watched the priests drifting in singly, in pairs, in groups, but all exhibiting the same slow-moving, peaceful quality.

The inspector looked for familiar faces. 'Because of the responsibility of staff members to instruct the students, we must make sure no staff members are missing. Are they all here?'

'Two tutors are in Paris but nobody else is missing, as far as I'm aware.' Geleve looked down into the seats of the auditorium and mutely counted heads. 'I think everyone's here.' And then he spoke loudly toward the seated staff members. 'Cassidy and Miller are in Paris. Is anybody else away today?'

Turning heads and murmurs disturbed the serenity. No one spoke but the message came back that only these two were absent.

He smiled. 'We're all here, inspector.'

Moulard put his radio telephone to his head, turned from Geleve and said quietly, 'Bertrand. I'm ready.'

He had to fill in the three minutes it would take Bertrand Parran's team to take control of the grounds and assembly hall. His loud cough as he turned to the audience invoked silence and attention.

'*Bonjour*. I am Inspector Moulard of the French anti-terrorist organization in Marseille. You know as well as I do that we live in a dangerous world. Many groups of people commit acts of terror. My organization has learned that such people are threatening to strike at the Roman Catholic Church in France.'

That's as far as he got when Parran and fifteen or so plainclothes police bearing handguns came into the hall and took up positions around the auditorium.

Sebastiani walked in after them and stood in the doorway.

The movement around the hall unsettled the audience. A few stood and made to leave.

'Stay seated all of you,' Moulard shouted. 'This is a police raid.'

Geleve stumbled backward and screamed, 'What are you doing?'

'Just stay where you are and keep quiet.'

'Inspector, this is an evil charade.'

Moulard rounded on Geleve. 'You are about to find out what's evil. And you let it happen here in your own house.'

Parran leapt up onto the stage and handed his boss the pornographic photographs retrieved by Eric Reynaud.

In the hush that filled the hall, Moulard's low tones resonated. 'Most of you here are as pure as the driven snow. You have nothing to fear. Some of you are not and those people I will take into custody to help with our inquiries.' He let the muffled stir in the audience settle then turned to Geleve. 'Tell me if the two men in Paris are in any of these pictures.'

The priest recoiled at his first glimpse of the photographs. 'My God. My God.'

'Get on and identify the people.'

Geleve leafed through the photographs, occasionally screwing his eyes shut and shaking his head. 'No Inspector, Cassidy and Miller are in none of these photographs.'

'Now, tell me if you see any of these men here in this hall.'

Without looking down into the auditorium, he whispered. 'Yes, inspector, they're all here.'

'Ah, good.' Moulard stood silent for a full two minutes peering down at his audience, just occasionally adjusting his shoulders within his oversize jacket. 'The following names please come to the front. Stand here in front of the stage.' He motioned to Geleve to call their names.

'Hector Gagnard.'

Gagnard's name appeared on Moulard's list. Under his name, the details: *Relocated from Montreal by the Church. Sought by Canadian police for questioning in connection with accusations of child molesting.* Gagnard remained seated, frozen by the sudden focus on him but Parran grabbed his arm and led him to the front.

Geleve called the name of the next face he recognized in the photographs. 'Cedric DeBellevue.'

Moulard found DeBellevue's name and scanned his details. *Arrested in Chicago. Disappeared after being released on bail. Suspected to have been moved out of harm's way by his superiors in the Church.*

DeBellevue wrapped his hands over his face, stood momentarily and then crashed to the floor in a faint, scattering chairs around him.

Moulard jabbed his hands into his hips and raised his closed eyes to the ceiling. 'Oh my God. Go on then, help him somebody.'

Pierre Didier strode to Moulard who inclined his head to him. 'Staff dorms secure. Children's home secure. The children are on their way to the emergency housing in Valence. Just forty-seven children. I've arrested the caretaker and his wife.'

A priest in a grey suit stood up and shouted. 'Would somebody please tell us what's happening?'

Moulard answered. 'I told you. This is a police raid. Sit down and be quiet.' He indicated to Geleve to continue.

'Tristan Menardi.'

Moulard read the details against Menardi's name. *Long history of accusations of child abuse. Never brought to justice. Church cover-up.*

Menardi stumbled to the front.

'Nicolas Demelly.'

Demelly stood up and screamed. 'Why? What's it all about? Tell me what it's all about.'

The inspector screamed at him. 'You know very well what it's about. Next.'

'There are no more,' said Geleve.

Moulard snatched the photographs and checked again the number of faces in them. 'Who are these others? These you've not called? You said there were all here.'

Geleve drew his lips in between his teeth. Teetering on the brink of a faint he held on to Moulard's arm. 'Those others are not in the church.' He pointed at the photographs in Moulard's hand. 'I recognize two of them.'

'And who are they?'

'A local businessman. Bernabe Riché. He's well known to us. He's been very kind. Gave us money for the renovation of our seminary and our home for refugees.'

Moulard looked at him sourly. 'Refugee children.'

Geleve looked around for a chair. 'May I sit?'

Moulard ignored the request and called to Parran. Sweeping his hand over the four collected at the front, he said, 'Bertrand, arrest these people. Handcuffs.' Then he turned to the astonished faces of those still seated. 'Stay in your seats. Don't try to leave the hall.'

He looked over Geleve's shoulder. 'And the other one? Who's that?'

'I'm surprised you don't recognize him, inspector. That's *Commissaire* Moreuil of the Avignon police.'

A smile lit up Moulard's face. 'Well, well, well. I didn't recognize him without his clothes on. *Monsignor* Geleve, I'm arresting you on suspicion of maintaining a house for the abuse of children.' He waved a paper in front of his face. 'A search warrant issued through the Paris

273

police authorities. My men are now searching all the staff sleeping quarters, including yours.'

'What do you think, Fabio?'

'A good operation. Well done.'

Sebastiani stood with Moulard and two of his Marseille team around a collection of identified cardboard boxes filled with DVDs, books and photographs that had been unearthed in private staff rooms.

Moulard sucked the last possible draw out of a cigarette, discarded it and lit another. 'I'll bet they're still wondering what this has got to do with terrorism.'

'I think we're pretty close to knowing that.'

Moulard launched into husky laughter punctuated by violent coughing. 'Moreuil. My God. When he finds out about our raid he'll shit himself.'

'No sign of Luisa, then?'

'Sorry, Fabio. No. The station radioed me. She's posted as a missing person. Police are making inquiries.'

'Thanks.'

'What were you doing down the road?'

He showed him the mobile telephone photographs he had just taken at the Reynaud house. 'Do you recognize this car?'

'No. Should I?'

Sebastiani showed the next photograph. 'What about these two men?'

'I know them.'

'They were looking for the Sinclair diaries.'

'A-ha! Now, why would these two crooks be looking for the diaries? That's strange.'

'But Simon, if they were working for *Commissaire* Moreuil it wouldn't be strange.'

Moulard burst out laughing and coughing again.

CHAPTER TWENTY

Moulard drove and Sebastiani read the GPS tracker display.

'They're 300 metres ahead now. Turning right into a forest lane. Don't drive into the lane yet, we'll be seen.'

Moulard pulled over just before coming to the lane. 'We can wait here. GPS won't lose them.'

'They're slowing. The lane ends. The car's gone onto a track that leads to a house. It's stopped. The house is about a kilometre from here.'

'Is there a location name? A house name or something?'

'Earth coordinates, but you don't want those.'

'Well, what do we do now?'

'Nothing until you get a few of your men here.'

Moulard got out of the car. 'Come on, Fabio. We're Italians and we're lost. And we want whoever comes out of the house to help us with directions.'

'But they know you.'

'I know them. They don't know me.'

They set off down the lane together. The house turned out to be large, old and dilapidated with several out houses around it in the same state of decay. The blue car was not to be seen.

Moulard stopped at the gate of the drive. 'It's a mansion.'

'Was.'

The Frenchman shouted. 'Hello, hello! Anybody there?' His barking frightened birds that scattered but he got no other response.

'We're supposed to be Italians and that's not Italian.' And so the colonel tried. '*C'è qualcuno?*'

'Not loud enough, Colonel.'

'Look.' Sebastiani pointed to an old tabby cat going to a dish that had been placed by the front door. 'It's fresh so someone's about.'

'Come on, this lost Italians game is ridiculous.'

They made their way back to the car.

'The garden all around the house is overgrown,' said the colonel. 'We can get up real close without being seen.'

'Stealth? You were right first time. I'm getting back up here in large numbers.'

Sebastiani got in the car and peered at the display. 'It's gone.'

'What's gone?'

'The blue car. It's gone.'

'Or they've found the bug.'

Even before Moulard's car reached the drive they could see thick, grey smoke rising up through the trees ahead. They leapt out of the car.

'Do what you can, Fabio. I'll get everyone here.'

But he could do nothing. Roaring fire had already engulfed the thick, tangled scrub and a complete wing of the house. 'They've cleared out,' he shouted.

Moulard rummaged in the shrubbery surrounding the weed-strewn forecourt. 'There's got to be another way out of here,' he shouted.

'There's a road on the other side of the house.'

Sebastiani ran off alone through the trees to the back of the house and into an overgrown garden. He stopped, pulled out the pistol Moulard had given him, checked its safety catch and held it ready. An explosion drew his eyes to the blue car, now a roaring and crackling skeleton half-buried in the bushes.

The fire had worked its way along the house but he reckoned he had time to look into the back rooms on the ground floor before it reached them. He raced through the open doors of the conservatory and into a large kitchen where water dripped from a tap and a pot boiled on a gas cooker. Smoke had already reached this part of the house.

An open door to his left led him down steps and into blackness. An escape route, he thought. Gradually, his eyes adjusted to the surroundings, a wide underground chamber.

A noise from the other end of the chamber startled him. Someone was calling for help.

'*Mamma mia*!' He groped forward until his hands reached a door locked by a slide bar. 'I'll get you out.'

'*Aiuto*!'

Only when he started to draw the bar free did he realize the captive had cried out in Italian. He threw the door open.

'Luisa?'

'My God, Fabio.'

She lay the other side of a locked prison cell door – and smoke had started to come along the chamber.

He kicked franticly at the lock but the old mechanism held fast. 'Move away from the door.'

'I can't,' she screamed.

'Go on. Roll yourself away from the door.'

Sebastiani shot at the lock several times until the door sprang free then kicked it open. He grabbed her up in his arms and turned toward the house where burning timber crashing to the floor blasted sparks into the chamber. The flickering light from the stairs lit up the plate on the wall. *Famille Beauchamp - repose en paix.*

'It's a mausoleum.'

Luisa buried her head into his chest. 'We're going to die.'

The smoke drifting along the chamber ceiling toward them was suddenly whisked off to the side. 'There's a way out.'

'Untie my legs.'

'It's too dark.'

'Put me down and try.'

'No.' He followed the smoke into a short corridor and could see the feathery traces ventilating into a thin crack of light. 'Close your eyes.'

277

He crashed his shoulder against the small door. It moaned angrily and swung completely open, throwing light onto decayed wooden benches on both sides of the littered fusty World War II air-raid shelter.

They came out in woodland overgrown with scrub. He looked for the house through the trees but could see only the smoke rising from it. He let her down and untied her bonds.

She wrapped her arms around him and turned her head from him. 'Don't look at me; I'm in a terrible state.'

'You're fine.'

'I saw it. They drugged me and I saw it.'

'What are you talking about?'

'I'm very hungry and thirsty.'

'Who drugged you?'

'I don't know.'

'Let's get back to the hotel.' He picked her up again and kissed her.

While waiting for Luisa to join him for breakfast in the street café attached to the Hotel de l'Horloge, Sebastiani studied the man sitting on the far side of the café. He'd sighted him several times before going to Marseille, and he was there yesterday. At first, Sebastiani took him to be a regular at the café, just grabbing a breakfast before work but he could see the man was spying.

'Fabio, hello, *bonjour*.'

Sebastiani heard Luisa but continued to look at the man, who moved slightly to look at her, got up and went to his car, a large, silver Citroen and still looking at her, put his mobile telephone to his ear.

'Fabio, don't be rude. I said hello.'

'Wait, Luisa. Sit down.'

'A little brusque this morning.' She looked round for a waiter and then sat down.

'Time to end our French adventure.'

'What? Oh no. I suppose it's because I fouled up on the Barbentane thing. The stone. I must find it, Fabio. I hallucinated and saw it. It's got to be here in Avignon.'

He took her hand. 'We don't need it for the investigation.'

'I think we do.'

'Tell me about it on the plane. It's too dangerous to stay here any longer. We've got to leave now. Come on, let's go pack our things and get back to Rome.'

'What? Can't I have a coffee first?'

'No. Now come on, please get your things together.'

Walking through to reception, he looked back until he could see the car without looking directly at it and then walked Luisa to her room. 'Be as quick as you can. I'll be outside your room in five minutes.'

As the taxi pulled away, Sebastiani could see the silver Citroen in the wing mirror follow on behind them.

'Ooh, I could do with a coffee,' Luisa groaned.

'The airport's fifteen minutes away. We'll get breakfast there.'

He watched for the road names. Once on the Avenue Pierre Sèmard they would soon meet the A7 motorway to the airport. But the taxi drove slowly through the small streets within Avignon's old city walls and the silver Citroen was close behind them.

The taxi driver suddenly braked to avoid the car that had swung across its front, then screeching brakes, flashing lights, gunshots and loud shouts filled the tiny street.

Sebastiani pulled Luisa's head down while screaming at her. 'Get down!'

Then more shouts from the road. 'Lie down. Get down on your stomach.'

Sebastiani peeked to see men in plain clothes throwing other men in plain clothes to the ground and kicking their legs apart.

The passenger door of the taxi opened. 'Come on you two, get out of there.' Moulard's light-heartedness wafted in with it his distinct smell of nicotine. 'It's all over.'

279

Sebastiani stood at the door of his taxi and looked at the scene. Unmarked police cars scattered in confusion effectively enclosed the stalking Citroen and the two Jaguars behind it.

Plainclothes gendarmes bellowed and screamed at the six men they had dragged out of the cars.

Luisa held her cheeks. 'My God. Now I know what you meant at the café.'

Moulard tucked his pistol inside his jacket. 'You're a keen-eyed copper Fabio.' He walked Sebastiani along the road as policemen handcuffed the men lying face down on the ground and marshaled onlookers away from the area. 'We let them tail you until we could see just how many cars they had.' He put his hand on Luisa's shoulder. 'They were determined to get you, *Madame*.'

As the gendarmes pulled the handcuffed men to their feet, Sebastiani scanned their faces and recognized just one. He'd seen him first in the blue saloon car at the Reynaud house and later, with another man, looking for the Sinclair diaries. 'Simon. You should question this one about the kidnapping and unlawful imprisonment of Luisa Fabian.'

'I think I can plant more than that on them. We know these people. And we know their friends in the Avignon police. They're low life trying to make it big.' Moulard looked round at Luisa. 'You taking her to Rome?'

'Yes.'

'She'll be okay there?'

'I think so.' He shook Moulard's hand, slapped his shoulder and then joined Luisa in the taxi.

'Are you okay?'

'Still shaking.'

He hugged her. 'You're safe now.'

Sebastiani was back in Rome, back at the barracks, back in uniform and back in the military. France had started to make him feel like a private detective, with Luisa Fabian as his assistant.

He skipped through his phone messages and stopped only when he heard the voice of Doctor Nardelli at the forensics lab.

'Colonel Sebastiani here. You tried to call me. What is it?'

'This is very bad and I owe you an apology. About the log entry for the letter General Conti brought here. The details were entered correctly but late. In fact, the entry was made the next day. I didn't notice it when you came here. About six entries before it have later times. Do you understand what I mean?'

'Yes, I do.'

'I apologize.'

If Ferri checked with forensics against the date Conti took the letter to the lab it wouldn't have appeared. It had indeed been delivered but logged in a day later. One of the two marks of suspicion against Conti and Ferri that could be struck through.

'Excuse me?'

'Nothing Doctor Nardelli. Nothing. That's fine. Thanks.'

CHAPTER TWENTY-ONE

Sebastiani leaned against a windowsill on the Via Brenta side of his apartment catching the warmth of the early morning sun on his back while reading his philosophy dissertation – with certain satisfaction. It had helped him achieve a higher-level Master's degree and offers of university teaching positions. He now tried to recall all the arguments he gave at the time for joining the Carabinieri instead. At least, the Carabinieri had given him adventure, which he doubted academia would have.

Even expecting Luca Ferri's visit, his stomach lurched when the door buzzer beeped.

'*Buongiorno*, sir.' Ferri, a young, middle-ranking officer in full uniform with a variety of badges, cap clamped under his arm, looked strong and impressive. He smiled confidently and shook Sebastiani's hand.

'*Buongiorno*, Major. Let's go into the living room. Coffee?'

'No, thanks.' The major placed his cap on a side table, sat and laid a square of paper on the arm of his chair.

'Tell me about Colonna,' said Sebastiani.

'He's coming to Europe. He's lodged a flight plan with O'Hare for Marseille and then later to Rome Fiumicino. The FBI's on to his bombing campaign in the US but they don't have enough on Colonna to stop him making the trip. For me, that's fine because we have enough evidence to make an arrest. Whatever happens, I'll seize him and his people when they land in Rome.'

'Good, good,' which were Sebastiani's fill-in words to end that discussion and start a new one. 'You asked to meet here. What's on your mind? Something secret?'

'Colonna's trip to Europe is part of it. I need you as a witness – to keep me in the clear with the Carabinieri.'

'My God. Serious. Tell me about it.'

'An FBI mole infiltrated Colonna's church some while ago. Recently, the mole put it about that I helped Barnes and Simms get the explosives into the Vatican.'

'That's very good of the FBI. Pity they didn't think to ask you first. FBI? Not CIA?'

'On this case, they co-operate.'

'I think you're going to tell me something I won't like.'

'I can tell you now, you won't like it. Colonna wants me on his team. He thinks I organized the helicopter sabotage. I don't know how he got that idea but that's what he thinks.'

'Christ alive.'

'They've already paid me for the job.'

'Money?'

'Lots of it. They opened a Swiss bank account in my name and poured money into it. Colonna pays me. I'm hooked.'

Sebastiani automatically looked around the room for spies. 'What the hell are you up to? It's ridiculous. Get out of it soon as you can. It's too dangerous.'

'Colonna's arranged a meeting with his European workers in France and I'm invited.'

Sebastiani slumped back in his easy chair and sat silent for several minutes, fingering his lips, grunting and shifting about. 'If they know who downed the chopper, they'll kill you. And I would bet they know who did it. They might just be toying with you. These people are fanatics.'

'We've got to find out who the traitors in Rome are. And France. This is a good chance.'

'Oh yes?' Sebastiani sat upright and gripped the armrests. 'Traitors in France?'

'Corrupt police in Marseille are on Colonna's payroll. They push everything through. Illegal drugs and child trafficking and Marseille's a clearing house.'

'I know some of this. Who did you see in Marseille police headquarters?'

Ferri fidgeted and flushed as though he'd been caught fondling the secretary. 'No secrets here, then.'

'And nor should there be. The visitors' book said you met with Moulard. Come on, who did you see?'

'Tassin. Crooked as hell.'

'I met him. Didn't know he was bent.'

'You met Tassin?'

'You asked me to do France so I got around.'

'He'll be at the Colonna meeting. Tassin and his sidekick, Babin. Babin's an idiot. They're both dangerous.'

'They know you're military police; what's their take on you?'

'They believe I'm in it for the money, just as they are, and it is big money. This is the reason I've come to see you, in case you have to clear my name. Whatever money I get I'll pass over to the Carabinieri.'

He stared at Ferri wondering if bravado had overwhelmed his sense of reason. 'Listen, I don't want you to do the spying. It's high risk. Just drop it and we'll say no more about it.'

'My CIA contacts would say something. They'd say I've wasted their time and a great chance. Those weak-kneed Italians. Anyway, I've been working it for three weeks and I don't intend to let it go. And the FBI mole is committed.'

'It's your decision. Do you need support?'

'I don't want others around; they would only get in the way.'

'When's your meeting with these people?'

'Tomorrow, near Marseille. It's a great chance and I have to do it.'

Sebastiani considered the likely outcome of the major's daring and he was not at all optimistic about his future.

'Your French inquiries are finished,' said Ferri. 'What are you going to do now?'

'Officially finished. There's still Archbishop Collineau but we don't have a case against him. So, yes, finished. You're the boss so tell me.'

'Come and see me when I get back from France.'

'Okay.'

Ferri looked again at his square of paper, put into his shirt pocket and stood to leave but Sebastiani placed himself strategically to bar his move to the door. 'Before you go, can we talk about the helicopter and Conti? Just a few minutes. Clear the air.'

'Okay. What about it?'

'On paper, I would be right to suspect either you or Conti of involvement.'

'And do you?'

'No, I don't.'

'I could suspect you,' said Ferri. 'And what's more, I should do.'

'Do you?'

'No. Someone apart from us knew the helicopters were coming. God knows how. Who knew we were shipping Gagliano out?'

'We don't know...yet. But we're listening and we'll know sooner or later.'

'Listening?'

'Our spies have been for some time. We're all playing games, Ferri. Unless Conti did it himself, he must be harboring suspicions about you. He could have had you arrested and I'm thinking it's strange that he hasn't at least had you in for questioning. And he's left you in charge. That's beyond me to understand. I don't understand Conti's game, if he has one. Good you declared the meeting in France.'

'The explosive was packaged a long time before the sabotage but I still think it was intended for Gagliano.'

'Yes. Desperate to get Gagliano one way or the other so it could always have been for him. Military trained foresight.' Distracted by a motor's roar, Sebastiani ambled to the window and gazed out. He watched his neighbor, the *principessa*, drive off in her champagne Lamborghini then turned to Ferri. 'If you suspect Conti, sometime you

285

must act on that suspicion. He might even be wondering why you haven't. Since we spoke in the park, I've not thought of any easy way to go about this. There's just the risk he had no part in it. Why not talk to Franchi about it?'

'That's not easy. This is a new situation for me. Sometimes I think I don't have the experience for this job. And I don't have the rank to deal with Franchi.'

'That's bullshit. Listen to me. There's something to be said for being indispensable in the eyes of top brass, and that's how they see you. When this is over, I'll get you to spend a few weeks with that bloody hooligan Pico.'

A treacherous thought had been hiding in Sebastiani's brain since the moment Conti side-lined him after the helicopter sabotage. Only his belief in Conti's integrity had held it at bay but at this very moment it struggled to surface. Why had Conti chosen the clever but inexperienced Ferri to replace him? A risky decision untypical of Conti. An important case like this. Instead, he could have brought in one or two experienced officers. Many good men were available. The investigation could fall apart. Is that what Conti wanted? His heart fought back: no, Conti's a good and honorable man who has made a professional mistake.

CHAPTER TWENTY-TWO

Robert Colonna rested back in the lounge of his personal Boeing 787 Dreamliner jet, *Wings of Faith*, comforted in the knowledge that his faithful followers had devastated St Peter's Basilica and scattered the Vatican priesthood, so Rome could never again rise as the leader of the Catholic world.

Now he was on route to Europe to see the results of his handiwork and build on that change and sow the seeds of the only true religion, the Bible-based Christianity of his Holy Catholic Church of America. He contemplated the words of this name and how right it was to drop 'America' but retain 'Catholic'. This clever trick would make the Holy Catholic Church acceptable world-wide as a natural successor to the now defunct Roman Catholic.

Wings of Faith boasted luxury, including an en suite bedroom with double bed and state of the art bathroom facilities.

The all-American crew of pilot and co-pilot, each with backup, and six young, female cabin attendants, had been hand-picked by Colonna. Also on board were his personal assistant of many years Gordon Shepherd, secretary Jermain Booth (Jerry to most but whom the tycoon alone called Jerra) and four bodyguards.

Colonna had established rules of informality in his empire and one was that everyone called him Bob.

Even his pilots.

'Bob, we land in Marseille in ten minutes. All passengers please fasten your seat belts. Crew, take positions for landing.'

This announcement sent skinny Jermain Booth into a tizzy. Her agitated body movements, tight black skirt and white blouse and clipped but timorous New York accent all bore witness to her starchiness.

She hastily tidied away documents in readiness for landing and ran Colonna through the arrangements. 'We're in France for just two nights, one night at a hotel and one with *Madame* Collineau at La Calmette, then we go across to Rome. The crew stays in Marseille. We go to Aix en Provence for our first meeting.'

'That's fine. Now just try to relax.'

'Okay, Bob, whatever you say.'

He glared at her and shook his head.

But she continued regardless. 'The limousine will come alongside, take us through customs. You won't need to get out. Aix en Provence is about ten miles out of Marseille. The Chateau De La Pioline is a small but high-class hotel. You'll like it.'

'Jerra, I'll tell you if I like it after I've stayed there.'

'Anyway, our first meeting is at two this afternoon.'

Jerry unlatched a cabinet to the side of Colonna's office desk, riffled through the documents then pulled out a sheet. 'As far as I know, just five people this afternoon: Inspector...'

'Just gimme their names.'

Then she read the list. 'Amand Tassin, Andre Babin, Patrick Moreuil. Moreuil owns the house. These are French cops. They've been looking after our interests in Marseille, Avignon and so on. Keeping Roger Collineau safe from inquiries. The Italian cop is Luca Ferri.'

Colonna twisted his body and head to look up at her. 'Ferri. He did a spectacular job in Rome. He impressed me. Does he speak English?'

'They all do. Babin's English is poor but we don't need interpreters.'

'I'm talking about Ferri. He's got class. I want him in the US.'

288

'Well, we'll have to see what we can do. The meeting with Yvette Collineau is whatever time we can get to La Calmette tomorrow. No rush.'

Commissaire Moreuil's house, an isolated, large property perched on a wooded hill at the end of a winding country track barely wide enough for one car, lent itself perfectly to secret meetings. As *Commissaire* of Police for Avignon, Moreuil commanded a regular house guard of two armed gendarmes whose only function on this day was to direct the visitors' cars to parking spaces.

Ferri, in full Carabinieri uniform studied the other meeting members as they took their places at the large oval table.

Robert Colonna, in double-breasted dark-grey suit, eased himself into the only high-backed ornate chair at the table, which gave him explicit headship over the proceedings. Jerry, now sporting a pinstriped grey trouser suit and surly attentive face stood immediately behind him to give moral and memory support should the need arise.

Colonna coughed into his fist. The light chatter stopped and all faces turned to him. 'If we're ready Gordon, get this under way.'

Shepherd, the typical American businessman in traditional dark-blue suit, stood to introduce the meeting. His slim physique and lean face gave the impression he ate healthily and trained regularly. He spoke with exaggerated pronunciation. 'Good afternoon gentlemen. I understand all of you speak English. Stop me if I say something you don't understand.' He looked at each face in turn. 'We've come a long way in fulfilling God's prophecies. The hold of pagan Rome on Christianity has now gone forever.' He paused and frowned as the Europeans shot bewildered looks at each other and fidgeted.

None of them had carried any thoughts about fulfilling prophecies. They had no spiritual common ground with the Americans and the only force binding them together was Colonna's money.

Shepherd raised his eyebrows and continued. 'Robert's organization has paid money into your Swiss accounts for your achievements so far but there is more to do and that is why we have called this meeting.'

Ferri tapped his knuckles on the table. 'One moment. I've completed my contract. I'm surprised you've called me to France. I got Gagliano out of harm's way. What more do you want?'

Tassin shuffled about in his chair. 'The same with me. Reynaud's dead. I'm finished.'

The totally bald and weasel-faced *Commissaire* Patrick Moreuil set his head back stiffly but remained silent. Andre Babin looked about awkwardly while pulling at the lapels of his slept-in suit and mumbled incomprehensibly.

Robert Colonna, picking up from Ferri, tapped the table. 'Gentlemen, please. It's risky but it will pay well. I look after my people.'

'I'd rather not be thought of as one of your people,' said *Commissaire* Moreuil testily.

Colonna flushed. 'Oh, I see.'

Tassin asked, 'What's the job?'

'Well, I have a big problem that you can help me solve. Police groups in Italy and France are snooping at my door. I feel very uncomfortable about this and I want you to take action to cut them out. Get rid of the main players in these organizations.'

Now is the moment to discover the Carabinieri traitors, thought Luca. 'Wait a minute. There is no way I'll do any more jobs in Italy if you don't tell me who your other people in the Rome Carabinieri are.'

The meeting froze. Ferri's probe had hit a nerve. Robert Colonna shifted around and stared at Shepherd who turned wide-eyed toward Moreuil who dropped his gaze to his entwined bony hands resting on the table. Tassin and Babin looked at each other and then at the other faces around the table.

'Well?' asked the major.

Babin stood and shouted, 'Would someone tell me what is happening?'

'Calm down, Andre,' said Tassin. 'We're coming to that.'

Shepherd sat calmly and placed his papers on the table. 'Mister Ferri, that's not something we need to discuss at this meeting. Let me make this clear. We don't want anyone disrupting our objectives. So far, it's gone well.'

'So tell me. Who do we have to get rid of?'

Shepherd left his seat and approached Jerry with his arm already outstretched to receive the document she offered. He read from it as any English speaker untrained in French would. 'In France, Simon Moulard, Paul Bonnet...'

Andre Babin interrupted in French. 'Is that Jean-Paul Bonnet?'

The American looked nonplussed.

'Here, let me read it.' Tassin took the document. 'Simon Moulard, that's my colleague. Jean-Paul Bonnet and Bertrand Parran. Resp.' Tassin looked at Shepherd. 'Resp?'

'Responsibility.'

'Ah, *responsabilité*. Okay. Responsibility Tassin and Babin. Mister Luca Ferri to handle the principal players in Rome's anti-terror organization.'

Ferri banged hard on the table causing Jerry to screech loudly. 'Stop this shit. I want no part of it.' He grabbed the document from Tassin, crumpled it and threw it to the floor. 'I've woken up to the real danger you are, to Italy and Europe.'

Colonna glared but spoke calmly. 'I have important business to attend to with these gentlemen. I don't like your aggressive nature, Mister Ferri. I think it's time you left.'

The major looked at his watch. 'I have a plane to catch. Ask him why he let his people die in the cathedral. For me, it's no longer important.'

Ferri's drive down the winding track and the concentration that required had not calmed him. Colonna and his band espoused a peculiar brand of Christianity whose philosophy, as far as it had been described to him, possessed a violent approach to change he could not grasp and his attempted intelligence-gathering act had given him no clearer understanding of them.

He wondered if losing control had been a mistake. With any luck, the others will have seen the display of anger as just an artifice. What had he gained from the enormous risk he had taken? Their mute reactions to his disruptions confirmed that a spy or spies operated in the Rome Carabinieri. They had not taken the bait so he had failed to learn names.

It struck him more clearly now than at the meeting that his behavior had put him at serious risk from the American side. The FBI mole's ploy had worked and he had been accepted into the Colonna arena on the understanding that it was he who had handed over the explosive to the Gagliano helicopter. But what if the saboteur was still at large? He wondered why he had not been betrayed.

Ferri stopped the car to report the meeting to Sebastiani on his mobile and study his map. 'Fuck it.'

The telephone gave a message about the battery and switched itself off. He dug down into his shoulder bag for the encrypted mobile for use only with Pico, looked at it, bit on his lips and then put it back in the bag.

Setting off again, he silently talked himself through another way back to Rome. 'Leave the Marseille flight booked as it is. Take the A8 and A10 to Genoa. I'm on that side of Marseille anyway. Leave the rental car in Genoa airport and take an internal flight to Rome.'

He reduced speed to take the curve in the track just before it widened out and joined the N7, his route to the A8 motorway. Looking to his right he saw a farm trailer and gauged there was just enough room to get through without driving onto the steep down slope at the left side.

A rounded hunched shape in the back of the trailer suddenly became a standing man aiming a Kalashnikov at him. In an instant stretched into slow motion by his accelerated thinking, an instant in which he felt no excitement or pain, he saw his own blood splash out of his left arm. Instinctively, he jammed his foot on the accelerator and steered the car left, away from the shooting, which continued after

292

he'd passed the trailer. The car grazed a tree, flipped onto its roof and skidded down the slope, coming to rest in shrubbery. The man jumped down from the trailer and continued firing at the rear of the car until it burst into flames and exploded.

Getting to the large baroque study in the La Calmette mansion took at least ten minutes after Robert Colonna had introduced Yvette Collineau to Shepherd and Booth at the entrance where he had hugged, kissed and flattered the *Madame*. He left his travelling companions in the hands of a servant to be shown to their rooms with the promise of a guided tour of the house later.

'This is incredible, Robert. After so many years.' She held her breath and clasped her hands together.

'Twenty-five years ago and in Chicago. We didn't know then that we would make such daring moves.'

'We didn't know Francis Sinclair then.'

'Our crusade has shown the power of the true Christian religion.'

'Not to mention the power of your money, Robert. Our plans have worked out well but there are still things to do before my son is enthroned. People things, making sure that further progress is not hindered by officialdom.'

'I believe we have those things covered. You have already done the most difficult part by convincing your son of the greatness of our Christian aims. His support was vital.'

'It was not easy and it needed the resolute Bishop Sinclair to convince Roger that his family's heavenly hope was barred by a terrible papal condemnation. Sinclair knew the history and visited Roger and I here many times to explain it. As he did for you, Robert.'

'Yes, and Glory be. Yvette, I'm anxious to see the Covenant.'

'I've sent someone to fetch it.'

Shepherd and Booth entered followed by Eduardo carrying the Covenant display case, which he placed in the center of the room.

'Please, everyone,' said Colonna. 'This is a spiritual moment.' When he dropped his head to pray, Jermain and Gordon did the same.

Yvette Collineau ran her eyes around the three and, with a smile crinkling her mouth, waited until they raised their heads and then said, 'Can't you just feel the spirit of Jean Collineau in this room.'

Jerry pressed her hands to her mouth. 'I feel it. It's eerie.'

The Texan stared down at Jean Collineau's last handwritten words. 'The Holy Grail of our cause.'

'Fulfilled totally,' said Shepherd.

Colonna turned to *Madame* Collineau. 'Yvette, my lovely dear, we must celebrate.'

She looked across to her servant, Eduardo, and without a word he left the room.

'I must take it back to America with me.'

Everyone's eyes fixed on Robert Colonna, all with the same puzzled look.

'Take what back to America?' asked Yvette.

'The oath of the Covenant has been achieved. You don't need it here any longer.'

'I suppose that's true but it's been in France for centuries.'

'I think it should always be with me, the leader of this wonderful crusade.'

'Perhaps you are right. I believe you have earned it.'

Colonna's eyes glistened. He put his hands together as though to pray but instead, made a pronouncement. 'My dear friends. We've driven our chariot of fire into the heart of the Roman Catholic empire and poured out the vengeance of the Horsemen of the Apocalypse onto the pagan throne. We've won a great victory, for our family and our Lord. Rome's attack started with Boniface, it's ended with Boniface. The Collineau Covenant is fulfilled.' He took Yvette Collineau's hand. 'This is a new beginning. Yvette, I'm going to raise your son on high. A new earthly Christian king with the power of Robert Colonna by his side. Next stop is Rome to see the dead harlot. Prophecy fulfilled and history in the making.'

Gordon and Jerry clapped.

'Yvette, I take it you'll join us on the trip.'

'The idea is wonderful but I have a son to look after. Next time, Robert, next time.'

Eduardo returned with the champagne and as the celebrators celebrated, like a road sign in a busy street he merged into the background, unseen by those he served.

Through force of habit, Andre Babin always parked his Renault Laguna in the same place. He came early every day to make sure he was able to. But everyone at police headquarters had come to understand the unwritten rule that the corner slot near the building was his. The car park was large so it wasn't an irritation to anyone that he had this quirk.

As he pulled on the handbrake he heard a tap on his side window. Moulard stood there, smiling. Getting out, Babin pushed back his mop of unkempt hair, dragged the knot of his tie from one untidy position to another that crumpled the collar of his grubby denim shirt and greeted him. '*Bonjour* Simon, *comment va-tu?*'

'*Ca va*. Andre, a word in your ear. Something important.'

He led Babin to Jean-Paul Bonnet's old Espace two parking spaces away. 'I've got some friends with me I'd like you to meet.'

The cabin door of Bonnet's car slid open as they approached it. '*Bonjour* Andre,' called Bertrand Parran from inside.

'Hello Bertrand. Simon, your whole team's here.'

'Get in Andre.' Moulard pushed Babin from behind while those inside grabbed at his clothes and pulled him in. Moulard clambered in after him.

As Bonnet accelerated out of the car park, Babin was forced to the floor and held firm.

'What are you doing?'

Parran clubbed him unconscious before he could say another word.

Andre Babin woke up and fought to gain awareness of his situation but a searing head pain forced his eyes shut and his body motionless. He knew only that he lay on his side with his wrists and ankles bound.

'Welcome to the world.'

Babin identified Moulard from the sound of his voice and the nicotine stink that accompanied it.

'Andre. Andre, are you with us?' asked Moulard.

Babin gradually opened his eyes.

'Your friends are here. Jean-Paul and Bertrand. Got a couple of guys from Paris anti-terror with me too. Say hello to Pierre and Henry.'

Babin raised his head to look at the faces but slumped back and closed his eyes. 'Where am I?'

'Our little hideout in the country so no one will hear your screams.'

Moulard kicked Babin in the ribs. He stiffened and groaned, then slumped again.

Jean-Paul took over. 'Your new Porsche looks great. Turbo Cabriolet. Getting fed up with your old wagon?'

'You're a crap head, Andre.' Moulard kicked him again. 'Shouldn't have bought the car. You can't afford a motor like that. And those high-class floozies. I don't know, Andre. You just hang onto your dick and let it lead you into bad places. Where'd you get the money?' He blew cigarette smoke into Babin's face.

'What do you want?'

'You're in it up to your ugly neck. You've got two options. Tell us what we want to know and you go safely to prison. Don't cooperate and die a painful death here and now.'

Andre spoke to the floor. 'What do you want to know?'

'You were at a meeting yesterday, *Commissaire* Moreuil's house. Tassin was with you. Who were the others? Was it a police meeting?'

'Yes.'

Moulard kicked Babin's head. 'Don't be so dumb. Tassin and Moreuil. Who were the others? What did you talk about?'

'Religious fanatics. Americans. They want us to kill people.'

'Who?'

'You. They know you've been watching them. They want you and your team dead. And the Italian.'

'So they've killed the Italian. Is that what you're saying? Speak to me Andre.'

Babin spoke to the floor again. 'I thought Ferri wouldn't do it.'

Moulard and his colleagues looked at each other.

'Andre, it's me, Simon. I know you're not bright at the best of times but you've rattled me. What Italian are you talking about?'

'Sebastian somebody or other.'

'Sebastiani?'

'That's it.'

'Got some news for you Andre. Someone shot Ferri after your little meeting. Who did it? Who set him up?'

'I don't know.'

Moulard put his hands on his hips and stretched back his head and shoulders. 'I'm getting a stiff neck. Sit him in a chair.'

Pierre Didier set off to the kitchen. 'Coffee anyone?'

Moulard continued the interrogation. 'Listen, Andre. The track from Moreuil's house leads into three small roads that all feed into the N7. Ferri was shot at the end of one of them. There was a gunman at the end of each road. Is that right?'

'I don't know.'

'No, you wouldn't. Did anyone make a telephone call immediately after Ferri left?'

'Yes.'

Sebastiani heard his telephone ringing and he ran up the inclined path to his office.

'*Pronto.*'

'Colonel Sebastiani?'

'Yes.'

'Moulard, Marseille.'

297

Grating cough, nicotine stink and oversize jacket: Sebastiani's memory completed the picture. 'Hello, Simon.'

'Has your officer friend, Ferri, made contact with you?'

'Not for a few days. Why?'

'I believe he's been killed.'

The information stunned Sebastiani into a pause in which he considered life without Ferri. A mist of disbelief gradually enclosed him. 'You're not sure…are you?'

'All I've got is second hand. Ferri was at a meeting with a group of Americans and a couple of our men.'

'Your men?'

'Corrupt Marseille police.'

'Ah.'

'I talked to Babin. He was one of them. You know him.'

'The name.'

'Babin said they talked about killing Ferri and I think they did. I've got the remains of the car that he rented. Bullet-riddled and burnt out. No body but traces of blood at the scene. Our forensics people are talking to your guys about DNA. I would not expect to find him alive.'

'You could be right.'

'Babin and Tassin have been arrested for killing Reynaud.'

'Tassin?'

'You trusted him.'

'But I know about him now. We learn, Simon.'

'Babin put a plastic bag over Reynaud's head. Simple, eh? He's weak so we'll get a confession. It's pretty certain *Commissaire* Moreuil and the Americans organized it. Watch out Fabio, they want you dead.'

'Not unusual in the anti-terror business.' Sebastiani took out his notebook and flicked through it. 'Simon, do me a favor. I've got the name of a Barbentane priest here. Cantello. Know it?'

'Cantello? Priest. Barbentane. I know the name. I'm sure we arrested him.'

'Have a word with him. Could be he knows something about Rome.'

298

'Okay, colonel.'

'I'm meeting the big chief of the Italian military tomorrow. Shall I pass on your regards?'

'Just say, 'up yours' from Inspector Moulard.'

CHAPTER TWENTY-THREE

'You're a difficult man to get hold of these days, Sebastiani. You spend more time in France than in Italy on this thing.'

Commandant General Franchi walked around his grand office in the *Ministero della Difesa* and around Colonel Sebastiani, parading his illustriousness and importance like his hero, Napoleon; *Emperor* Napoleon. Head erect to counter his inherited shortness of stature, he spoke into the air rather than toward his seated visitor, thus avoiding the eye contact he perceived would threaten him, make him feel less than he was, the top man of the Italian Carabinieri.

Taking matters into his own hands, he'd side-lined Conti to shorten the reporting line in the Rome bombing investigation and to accelerate the information route from the action men in the field up to the office of the Minister of Defense. This was how it would be understood in the upper reaches of the Carabinieri. Lower down the officer chain, though, it was generally believed Conti's failure to identify the helicopter saboteur forced the move.

Franchi stared down at Sebastiani, whom he had reinstated as lead person in the terror investigation, in this first of his regular action meetings with him. Ferri's disappearance – presumed assassination – and the fact that no other person could possibly be brought up to speed in time to make a difference had made him the obvious if not the only choice.

Sebastiani shook his head even before Franchi had finished. 'I have evidence that the attack on Rome was planned in France. Ferri discovered this. Corrupt French police are in criminal business with

300

local hoods working for Robert Colonna. He asked me to investigate that side of things in France and that's where I unearthed documentary evidence implicating them and Colonna.'

The sound of voices in a neighboring room filled Franchi's silent pause as he struck a pose and stared at Sebastiani. 'Ferri is dead,' he said, not finding words to close the previous topic.

'He could be. I'm not certain.'

'No one in the military is indispensable. What's your plan?'

'Arrest Colonna. Interrogate him.'

Franchi stopped at his desk, lifted the pen out of the elaborate black and gold marble desk set – yet another cachet of office, another little show of prestige kept strategically and prominently placed on his desk to be seen by anyone sat on the other side – made as though to write something, didn't, replaced the pen and then continued on his march around Sebastiani. 'Conti was very negative about France. Did you know that?'

'He did say he needed to be convinced. But my report should have done that.'

'No. He remained skeptical. Trying to join things together that didn't match. That's how he described it.'

Sebastiani stood and planted himself in the constantly mobile Franchi's track. 'The raid on the Barbentane seminary confirmed a link between the transportation of children through Marseille to a pedophile ring in western Europe and Bishop Sinclair, who looks to have been instrumental in the Rome bombing. That you know.'

'How would I know that? No one has informed me about such a thing.'

'Sir, how can that be? This was a major operation by our French counterparts. It dovetails with our investigation. I reported it all to General Conti two days ago.'

Franchi narrowed his eyes, stood thinking for ten seconds and then turned sharply and strutted to his desk. As punctuation to an over-dramatic sweep of his arm, he pressed a button and then looked silently in anticipation at his office door.

A young officer stepped briskly into the room, stood to attention, and shouted from the distance, 'Sir?'

In an undisguised gesture of superiority over the young man, Franchi ordered him to locate General Conti right away. 'I want him to phone me immediately. If you cannot find him get somebody to go and search. Now!'

'Yes, sir.' And he was gone.

Sebastiani smiled into his hand.

Franchi leaned on his desk with one hand while digging the other hand into his hip. 'There's something seriously wrong with Ferdinando Conti. He should have told me what's going on.'

The colonel nodded agreement but said nothing.

'Two days ago, you say?'

'Yes, sir.'

'I'll speak to him. I just don't know a thing about this raid.' Franchi's words diminished gradually into a barely audible murmur as he sat down at his desk. 'This is bad. This is very bad.'

'Two Marseille anti-terror police have been arrested for killing a possible witness and for assisting the transportation of children by criminals. The gendarmerie hold photographs of priests and others, including the police commissioner for Avignon, sexually abusing children.'

'What! And Conti didn't tell me? That's reprehensible Fabio, reprehensible. Who are these children? Where do they come from?'

'Imported from North Africa. They're shipped to Marseille and then routed from there northwards.'

'Bad stuff. But what's that to do with Rome?'

'Sinclair who organized that was instrumental in the Rome attack. I have evidence of that. Paid by an American to set up and execute the attack.'

Franchi pulled at the center of his top lip. 'Where's your evidence?'

'Documented evidence in a set of diaries. I have them here, with me.'

Franchi again stared narrow-eyed at him. 'Then you should present that evidence to the Operation Vatican Attack Committee.' He picked up his phone.

'Please come with me, colonel. They're waiting for you in the conference room.'

Sebastiani recognized the full-bosomed woman who had accompanied Franchi over the rubble in St Peter's Square on that first tragic day. She displayed her wholesome build as before but in an even deeper décolleté. This convinced him that Franchi dictated her mode of dress. She smiled but showed no sign of recognizing him. How could she? On their first encounter, he looked like a bloodied coalminer. She led him into the conference room and then withdrew to leave the ten available members of the Operation Vatican Attack Committee, Franchi and Sebastiani alone with their secrets.

Glaring tight-lipped at the prattling committee members, the Minister of Defence banged his knuckles on the table and then turned to Sebastiani. 'Colonel, I understand you and your team have made a breakthrough in your investigation.'

'Yes, minister.'

'Let us see this evidence.'

Sebastiani looked on as the evidence custodian entered the details of the three Sinclair diaries into a register and then into a computer. Conti would go to prison, perhaps for the rest of his life, on the evidence in these diaries. A man of courage and principle brought to grief by a wicked world. The colonel walked out of the Ministry of Defense and into the sunshine. He had placated the politicians and that little shit Franchi, and now wished them all to hell and off his back. To settle his nerves, he waved his driver away and set off walking down the road.

A motocross motorbike roared to a stop right by him. He pulled back and went for his gun as the rider pulled off his helmet.

'Want a lift?'

303

'Ferri! I thought you were dead.'

'Nearly, sir. Nearly.'

'How are you? What's been happening to you?'

'I'm okay. My arm was wounded. Grazed. It's bandaged. Got my ass roasted too but that's not bandaged so I have to be careful how I sit.'

'Why didn't you call me?'

'Didn't trust you.'

'Major... Fuck off. Pico's been turning your head.'

Ferri laughed. 'I learned it all from you.' He took a helmet from a saddlebag and offered it to Sebastiani. 'Come on, sir. Get on.'

'On that thing?'

Ferri wheeled the motorbike backward and forward under him. 'Beautiful day for a ride.'

Sebastiani took the helmet.

The luxury cabin of Robert Colonna's personal jet, Wings of Faith, was an airborne oasis of serenity where his bodyguards played cards and the female cabin crew chatted. But Colonna sat with his eyes closed and head against the back of his seat, sensing exultation. He was on his way to see first-hand his erstwhile archenemy's ruined seat of power in Rome, St Peter's Basilica, and to kick-start his evangelizing activities in the spirit of American evangelical Christianity – first amongst Italy's corporate bosses and their political friends.

'Come on then, Jerra, let's see it.'

'You must take your tablets, Bob, you've missed a couple of days.'

'And I'm fine so another day won't matter. Get the Covenant out for me.'

'Okay, one moment.'

She took a leather document folder from a cabinet and laid it open on his desk to display the roughly eight-inch square of fragile 17th century paper. 'It's your very own Covenant now.'

He leaned forward to stare at the document and floated his index finger over the faded text.

'A man's last words.'

Booth pressed her clenched hands over her mouth. 'It's frightening.'

Colonna felt her hands fall on his shoulders and assumed this act put her in contact with the wonder that filled him.

'This simple text has motivated me to remove the curse of evil laid upon my family and to build a righteous army in a struggle for Christian purity.'

The Texan got up, moved to a window and for some minutes studied the white clouds down below him. 'God will honor our courage.' His soft tone disappeared into silence.

The pilot poked his head into the lounge. 'Bob, we'll be landing in Fiumicino in twenty minutes. Please strap yourselves in.'

The captain then busied himself with directing Wings of Faith to Rome's Fiumicino Airport. 'Fiumicino Tower. 787 Whiskey Oscar Foxtrot. Request instructions for instrument landing. ILS established.'

A leisurely, Italian-accented English response: 'Good day, Whiskey Oscar Foxtrot. Sunny and calm here. Very light northerly wind. Clear to land 1-6-Lima.'

'1-6-Lima. Roger, Fiumicino. Passed outer marker.'

'Whiskey Oscar Foxtrot. On landing, exit runway 1-6-Lima at gate Alpha 6 and follow runway marshal's vehicle.'

'Roger.'

Suddenly, a change came from the control tower. 'Whiskey Oscar Foxtrot, new instructions. Discontinue approach. Turn right and climb to 3000 feet. Standard hold southwest of Ostia VOR. Await instructions for landing at Ciampino.'

The pilots raised eyebrows at each other.

The captain responded. 'Fiumicino, why the change?'

After a whole minute, a nervous voice informed him. 'Security alert. Whiskey Oscar Foxtrot, wait for instructions.'

The captain switched off voice communications long enough to tell his co-pilot, 'We've got trouble. Other aircraft are not affected.' Then he said, 'Fiumicino tower, Whiskey Oscar Foxtrot. Standard hold. Awaiting instructions.'

'Bob.' The captain spoke over the lounge loudspeaker. 'We're being redirected to Ciampino. We're not landing at Fiumicino.'

This news and the sweep upwards of the jet from the gentle three-degree glide path unsettled the passengers.

Then the anticipated boom in the captain's headphones, 'Captain! What's going on? Why are we climbing?'

'Security alert on the ground.'

'What the fuck for?'

His profanity froze Jermain Booth rigid. It was a sign that Colonna had gone manic, usually sparked by an adverse event outside his control after long periods of his refusing to take his lithium medication. She turned her alarmed face to Gordon Shepherd who was already glaring at her.

'Are you hearing me, captain? I asked you what the fuck for?'

But Fiumicino control tower switching in spared the captain's ears the rest of Colonna's obscene flow. 'Whiskey Oscar Foxtrot. At 3000 feet, take landing instructions from Ciampino tower.'

'Fiumicino tower. Whiskey Oscar Foxtrot. What's going on?'

But Fiumicino control tower cut out and Ciampino cut in. 'Whiskey Oscar Foxtrot. Visual descent and landing. Military escort to ground.'

The captain looked out of the left and right windows for military aircraft. 'Christ alive. Something is very wrong.'

This 'something' had also disturbed the lush confines of the lounge, where the angry good Christian Robert Colonna rampaged up and down, wreaking havoc and creating serious safety concerns. The aroused Bob naturally wanted to be informed but his intermittently bursting open the door to the flight compartment and pouring loud vocal abuse at the pilots was not working.

'Look, a fighter aircraft.' Shepherd spotted it first. 'What's going on?'

'That's what I want to fucking know,' Bob growled while taking his handgun from a wall cabinet.

Shepherd checked the other side of the aircraft. 'I think we're being arrested.'

This dreadful possibility silenced Colonna who sat slumped in his seat staring at Shepherd as though expecting from him a nifty resolution to the situation.

Loudspeakers confirmed Shepherd's news. 'Bob, captain speaking. We're being arrested. *Aeronautica Militare Italiana* fighter jets are escorting us down to ground.'

'Why's the bloody pilot speaking Italian?'

Gordon sat next to his boss believing the worst of Bob's wrath was yet to come. 'He only told us what we already know. Italian military jets are escorting us. We're being arrested.'

At 1000 feet, the fighter jets peeled off and did a round to land behind Colonna's plane.

A long questioning silence filled the lounge broken at last by an excited flight attendant. 'Look out the window. Look at all those flashing blue lights down there.'

'Fuck 'em!' Colonna sprang from his seat and peered out of each lounge window.

'Strap yourself into your seat, Bob. We're landing,' said Shepherd.

'Oh no we're not, Gordon, my friend.' He ripped open the door of the flight compartment and bawled in. 'Put your foot on the gas and get the fuck out of here.'

The captain and his co-pilot, entering the last phase of the landing procedure, broke into controlled uneasiness.

Without turning his head, the captain shouted, 'Get back to your seat and strap yourself in. We're landing.'

'Do as I say and get this plane out of here.'

'We'll be shot down.'

Colonna raised his gun to the pilot's head. 'Get us back up there, moron.'

'We're under arrest. We'll be shot down.'

307

Colonna shot the co-pilot in the head then pointed the gun at the captain. 'Am I being serious? Fly up into that clear, blue sky.'

The captain pulled on the joystick and headed skywards, pressing an excited body of people back into their seats.

As soon as the plane aborted the escorted landing procedure without warning, air traffic control activated emergency procedures on the ground, part of which was to obtain high-level government authority for any last resort actions.

As Colonna's plane leveled out and flew out over Rome and toward the sea the military jets appeared on each side again.

'Whiskey Oscar Foxtrot. Ciampino tower. Follow Air Force escort to Ciampino. Acknowledge. Whiskey Oscar Foxtrot, acknowledge.'

But Whiskey Oscar Foxtrot was too distracted to respond.

Colonna put the gun against the captain's head. 'Now get out of here and leave this to me.'

The pilot maneuvered himself out of his seat straps and the flight compartment and, with his countenance pleading for understanding, faced the alarm in the lounge cabin.

Jerry beat everyone to the flight compartment door but it was locked. 'Bob, open the door.'

A bodyguard threw her to the floor and shot at the door handle but the door stayed securely shut.

Jerry lay curled up on the floor just where she had been thrown, biting her knuckles and glaring into eternity.

The bodyguards alternately shot at the door and wrestled in vain with its handle.

The female cabin crew behaved as trained and did their best to care for those in distress – everyone.

The pilots (the captain and the two spares) strapped themselves into cabin seats. One put a mobile telephone to his ear, another wrote a hasty note and put it into his wallet, the other just sat back with his eyes closed and waited.

In the flight compartment, an exultant Robert Colonna had broken into Glory, glory Hallelujah. 'Come on, girl. We're on our way to heaven.' His rudimentary knowledge of flying had taught him enough to make the climb there: throttles fully forward, joystick back and held firm.

The sudden nose-up threw all those not strapped in or holding on to fixtures to the rear of the lounge. Shepherd crashed, hit his head on a table and then lay unconscious on the floor, blood pouring from his nose. Flight attendants joined in the screaming and shouting while the bodyguards, now on their knees, uselessly fired yet more bullets at the flight compartment door. Jerry remained in rigid shock, still curled up in a ball but, incredibly, now stuck in the toilet doorway.

But Robert Colonna had no fear. 'Hear me, Jesus. My earthly work is done. I'm coming, I'm coming. I see you. Lordy, I see you.' He slapped his dead companion on the shoulder. 'Come on boy, sing.'

Colonna fell silent when the aircraft suddenly acted against his will. As it reached the top of its parabolic climb, the joystick shook violently of its own accord and an alarm sounded. He pulled the joystick hard back but that made no difference to the aircraft's attitude. Then it started to descend and the tail drooped. The pilots knew immediately what was happening.

'That religious maniac has put us into a stall,' one screamed.

'We're going down fast. There's fuck all we can do now,' shouted another.

Then a calm voice from one of the fighter jet escorts. 'Whiskey Oscar Foxtrot. Air Force leader. Follow escort to landing. Whiskey Oscar Foxtrot, acknowledge.'

'Fuck off!' screamed Colonna at the controls.

The escort leader heard that as a hostile response and informed those on the ground. 'Ciampino tower, Air Force leader. Whiskey Oscar Foxtrot not complying. Assume hijack.'

Five minutes later. 'Air Force leader, Ciampino tower. Executive order from Ministry of Defence. Use all means to make situation safe.'

'Roger.' The fighter jets swept upwards and out of sight.

'Air Force leader to Whiskey Oscar Foxtrot. I have authority to shoot you down if you do not comply with the escorted landing. Acknowledge understanding.'

Wings of Faith gave no response.

Robert Colonna bellowed into his microphone, 'One of you pilots come in here and sort this shit out.'

The flight compartment door opened and Colonna stood there with a crazy look on his face. A bodyguard pulled the Texan into the cabin, held him briefly in a stranglehold then let him drop to the floor, dead.

The captain scrambled into the seat next to his lifeless co-pilot and fought to regain control of the plane. He forced the nose down, regained speed in the descent and returned to level flight. Then he turned toward Rome. Before he had time to inform the military escort jets that he was back in control, their cannon fire ripped through the windows spattering shredded flesh around the flight compartment.

A missile blasted off the tail and set Wings of Faith on fire.

The cabin filled with screaming horror as the plane spiraled downwards and plunged into the sea a hundred miles west of Rome.

The military escort lead pilot reported back, 'Ciampino tower, Air Force leader. Whiskey Oscar Foxtrot shot down at sea. Stand by for crash site coordinates. Out.'

Arguments between politicians and human rights groups about the legality and morality of shooting down the passenger airplane in questionable circumstances continued to draw world-wide media interest. Many had questioned the efficiency of the search team that managed to find the bodies of all those registered on the flight, including one with a bullet hole in his head, excepting that of well-known evangelist American tycoon, Robert Colonna, despite extensive searches. Tongue in cheek, one reporter suggested he might have been raised bodily to heaven and his God.

CHAPTER TWENTY-FOUR

'My stealth cleaning personnel installed bugs in all officers' telephones.' Ricardo Da Corte passed to Sebastiani what looked like a coat button. 'Neat, eh? They transmit to a permanently manned, multi-channel listening station here in this building.'

'All officers' telephones?'

'All fifty-six. Yours too, Fabio.' He patted Sebastiani's arm. 'It's okay, your secrets are safe with me.'

Sebastiani smiled, his demeanor ostensibly unaffected by this news but his mind racing through all his calls to Luisa Fabian. And if Da Corte's men had listened in, so what?

'It took a while but eventually our harvesting came good. We found Conti had made calls to Tunis. Encrypted but we deciphered. He was angry that the job had not been completed. We don't know what job.'

'Did my daughter's name come up?'

'Elaine Bruneau. Clear as a bell.'

'And this was before her release?'

'Yes. Just before her release.'

'Could have been angry about her not being released.'

'It had nothing to do with that. More to do with punishment, my spies tell me. I'd say he was angry she wasn't dead. *Signor* Conti has something to hide.'

'Umm.'

'How is Elaine?'

'Not sure. I've called her clinic but they won't give details over the phone. When I suggest a visit that tell me now would not be a good time.'

Da Corte just nodded. 'She was betrayed, that's certain. Whether Conti betrayed her, I don't know. What I can tell you is that he is a bad egg. Look at this. Something I got from his service provider. It's a list of telephone calls he made on the night the helicopter was blown up. They're all to *Tenente* Domenico Grizafi. Indeed, many telephone calls were recorded between Grizafi and General Conti in the last months.'

'That only tells us they communicated. What's wrong with that?'

'Nothing. Until you read the text messages they exchanged that night.'

Sebastiani read mutely from the printout Da Corte gave him.

> FC: *Dom. Three Viterbo med helicopters on standby. Seb's order.*
> DG: *Dealing with it. Gagliano no problem. Pilot fixed.*
> FC: *You are brave. Angelo too. I love you, Dom.*
> DG: *I love you too, Ferdi.*

Sebastiani suddenly braced himself, hands on the arms of the chair and leaning forward as though about to spring out of it – but he only cursed himself. 'I was right and then I discounted it. FC is Ferdinando Conti.'

'Sinclair diaries?'

'Yes.'

Da Corte picked up the text-message printout, sat back in his chair and studied it. 'Did you know he's homosexual?'

'I'd heard.'

'He's gone. Conti's gone and we've lost him.'

'We'll get him. But the Grizafis, I'll pull them in right away.'

'You don't have to.' Da Corte opened his desk drawer, pulled out a printed page and handed it to Sebastiani. 'As soon as any names came up in these exchanges, I arrested them.'

Sebastiani scanned the list of *carabinieri* names, the Grizafis and six others, some of them Sebastiani recognized as in his charge. Details against the names showed dates and times of contacts with each other and the nature of contact.

'Angelo Grizafi was interesting,' said Da Corte. 'Conti had given him a special assignment, which gave him a free run, apparently. He was absent from the barracks for long periods. I don't know why or where. He's an ace sharpshooter. Did you know that?'

'Then I'm pretty sure he was in France and very close to me at some time.'

'Something for you to investigate, Fabio. Right now, he's in the cells with the others. Our surveillance harvest was rather good, don't you think?'

Why always the change in the southern Italian weather on the 1st of September? The blistering hot and cloudless days of August had sweated out the bodily fluids of those natives of Rome who had dared to resist the annual exodus to the mountains for cooler, breathable air. Then, suddenly, the 1st of September. Heavy clouds, a lively wind and drizzling rain lent their gloom to Sebastiani's early morning mood. He stared sternly out of the window at the chunky 4x4 camouflaged ambulance and an accompanying armored vehicle pulling up outside.

The doors of the armored vehicle burst open and a dozen armed *carabinieri* in combat dress took up positions around the ambulance. Sebastiani had had poor experiences with important witnesses and now took no chances. In slower time, medics opened the rear doors of the ambulance and operated the patient lift to lower a wheelchair with patient to the ground. The patient wore an orange prison overall and a transparent cape, the sort that tourists buy from street peddlers for a couple of euros, as cover against the rain. He was handcuffed.

A large pulse of cool air that lasted the period the door was open assisted the entry of the patient into the prison reception area.

Sebastiani acknowledged the man in the wheelchair with a dip of his head and followed on as a male nurse pushed the wheelchair through barred and guarded security gates deeper into the building and into a suspect-identification room.

The instant the lights came on to show the identity line-up of eight men in Carabinieri uniform on the other side of the window, the patient became agitated and cried out, 'That's him! That's him, I tell you. Murderer!'

'Calm yourself, *Signor* Al-Qali,' Sebastiani demanded sharply. 'Calm yourself.'

'That man killed my friends.'

Sebastiani grasped the two arms of the wheelchair and glared into Al-Qali's eyes. 'Listen to me carefully.' He spoke slowly. 'These men are all *carabinieri*. Only one of them is a suspect in the killing of your accomplices and the assault on you. I want you to identify that suspect. Look at them carefully and then tell me which one you believe murdered your friends.'

Although Hasan Muhammad Al-Qali had claimed he could not recall the beating that had put him in a coma, his injuries had evidently not erased the memory of the brutal torture and murder of his friends by the man in the line-up with the boy's face and blue eyes. 'Number three. Third from the left.'

That is Angelo Grizafi, thought Sebastiani. 'I want you to look again.'

'I don't need to. That's him. He should hang. There were two.'

Sebastiani turned and nodded to a controller at the rear of the room and a blind closed to obscure the line-up room. Moments later, it opened again showing a new line-up of eight *carabinieri*.

Sebastiani bent to Al-Qali and whispered. 'You were right, *Signor* Al-Qali, there were two assailants and the other is in the line-up. Take your time.'

Al-Qali saw his assailant immediately. 'That's him. Number seven.'

Yes, that's him, thought Sebastiani, Domenico Grizafi. 'That'll do,' he shouted to the controller and the blind closed.

Tears filled Al-Qali's eyes. 'They tortured them. They're psychotic. They're murderers.'

'But that's what you wanted to be, *Signor* Al-Qali.'

'Mine is a righteous war.'

'You'll be in prison a long time. I hope it teaches you that slaughter of innocents is murder.'

Al-Qali whimpered and dropped his face into his hands. In sympathetic slow motion, his long, black hair flowed down around his head to conceal his distress.

Domenico Grizafi, handcuffed, stood to attention between two guards, head erect, his hollow-cheeked, athletic face rigid and his eyes glaring at some point above the heads of the interrogating officers.

The camp commandant started the proceedings by citing from the front page of a document he held. 'This is a preliminary inquiry. Its purpose is to determine the names of those involved in the sabotage of the helicopters here in the barracks. This inquiry has evidence that you, *Tenente* Domenico Grizafi...' He looked up at him. 'That you were involved in that crime and we now give you the opportunity to make a statement about your involvement and the names of others you know were involved. This inquiry is aware that you have already been charged with the murder of Italian nationals. If you have committed other crimes, you should declare these to be taken into consideration now. Whereas aiding this inquiry with good information about the sabotage might lessen your punishment, not declaring such crimes that are later discovered will be dealt with severely. Do you understand?'

In better days, Grizafi had placed such bargaining options to suspects. He nodded.

'It is the belief of this enquiry that you participated in the sabotage of the helicopter here at the barracks, which killed all its occupants and men on the ground.' The aged commandant's head swept from side to side as he read from the page again. 'Participation is given here to mean hands-on involvement, organizing, or providing personnel, or any combination in enacting the crime.' He returned his glare to Domenico. 'Did you participate in this crime?'

'No sir.'

'But you know who sabotaged the helicopter.'

'No sir.'

'Were any your brothers involved? Angelo Grizafi, for example.'

'No sir.'

'Tell me how you know that.'

'He couldn't. He wasn't anywhere near the barracks.'

Exasperated by the commandant's tit for tat and ill-informed questioning, Sebastiani cut in. 'On this point you're telling the truth. Your brother, Angelo Grizafi, was not in the barracks when the helicopter went down. The guardroom log shows that he left the barracks late that afternoon. You were also not at the barracks when the helicopter was sabotaged. I've got you and your brother Angelo Grizafi located at Viterbo at that time.'

'That's right, sir. So we could not have caused the sabotage.'

'You didn't need to be in the barracks to organize the sabotage. You knew that if you didn't act, you would be in trouble. Giulio Gagliano was on the point of giving evidence to the military about your involvement in aiding others to bomb the Vatican.'

'We didn't do it.'

'You were part of the team that organized and set the explosives. What do you say to that?'

Domenico didn't answer

Sebastiani wondered about the suspect's background. He would never know the confusion of associations and events that had brought Domenico and his brother to this point. The way his mother, then a call girl, had induced his father, a clever but crooked accountant, into corrupt business. It was inevitable that they would come to a bad end.

Sebastiani folded his arms and stared at him. 'Which brings us back to the helicopter. You had to get Gagliano out of the way. Sabotage his helicopter or kidnap him. It didn't matter which.'

Grizafi stared stiffly at the wall. 'It's not true.'

'I assure you, the evidence is conclusive.'

316

Grizafi bit on his lip. 'Sir, I didn't do it.'

'Rico Tamburo provided the explosives and you used them for the Vatican and the helicopter. Why did you have him killed after he did all that work for you?'

Sebastiani picked up the stunned surprise in Grizafi's eyes.

'Sir, I don't know that name.'

'A certain Doctor Bonni has identified you as the one paying him to falsify Tamburo's death certificate.'

'Sir, I don't know Tamburo or Bonni.'

'You idiot! Your lying is pathetic. But we'll get the truth out of you. You've let a chance worth years of your life slip out of your hands. Some of the men killed in the helicopter were your friends. You killed them. How could you do that?' Sebastiani drew it out as though preparing to vomit.

Grizafi closed his eyes and shook his head frantically, but said nothing.

Sebastiani turned to see the commandant peering at him with old man's baggy eyes and creased forehead. He continued regardless.

'Domenico Grizafi, what's your relationship to General Conti?'

'He's the head of national counter-terrorism, sir.'

'Right. And you and I are under his charge. But your relationship to him is a lot more personal than that. Am I right?'

'I don't know what you mean, sir.'

'Isn't he special to you?'

The young officer turned from Sebastiani, his face coloring.

'I think your trying to deny the way you feel about General Conti. You call him Ferdi.'

Grizafi wrapped his shackled hands over his face and wept loudly, embarrassingly loudly, for many minutes. And then barely audibly amidst sobbing, he said, 'He loved me. He's abandoned me.'

The commandant's jaw dropped as he gaped at Sebastiani in unfeigned astonishment, and he still gaped when he returned his attention to Grizafi.

In a tone of contempt, Sebastiani said, 'Return this man to the cells.'

'Colonel, we haven't questioned the brother yet.'

'We don't need to. He's a suspect. I don't want to give him chance to run.'

'I'm amazed about Conti. How did you know that?'

Sebastiani took the list of text messages between Conti and Domenico Grizafi from his pocket and flattened it on the table in front of the commandant.

The commandant leaned forward to read the paper and then suddenly shot bolt upright. 'My God.'

Sebastiani had spent yet another sleepless night, churning over in his mind the shock disclosure of the good Ferdinando Conti turned bad for the sake of money and his homosexual love. Also, Conti had disappeared.

The colonel pressed at the sides of his closed eyes with fingers and thumbs to get a sense of the intensity of the ache behind them and breathed a muffled question down into his hand, which the young officer standing in front of his desk bent forward to hear.

'So, you say the pay office has had the August transfer to his account rejected. Does that mean he no longer has an account with that bank?'

'Sir, the pay office had not checked when I asked them. They said it's too early to go raising questions about an officer when he's been absent for only three days. Might just have been taken ill somewhere, they said.'

'You told them you were making enquiries on my behalf?'

'Yes, sir.'

'Go on. Tell me what else you've got. Did you check his bank?'

'Yes sir. I checked with the bank. They wouldn't tell me if he'd had an account or not.'

'To be expected. And his home? What about his home?'

'Until six days ago he was living at home with his wife in the Via Bradano. I spoke to her but she told me to speak with their son.'

This brought a spark of interest to Sebastian's face. 'I didn't know he had a son. Did you speak to him?'

'Yes, sir.'

'And?'

'He said his father packed two suitcases and left for a trip but didn't know where. Left his car in the garage. I checked all the airlines. No record of a Ferdinando Conti travelling by air in the last six days. They did an Italy-wide enquiry.' The young officer dropped his head to one side to catch Sebastiani's eyes. 'Could've gone by rail, sir.'

'Yes, yes. Or taxi. If at all. Anything else?'

'That's all so far, sir.'

Sebastiani let his aching arms drop down to the sides of his chair as if they had suddenly filled with lead. It was probably going to be flu after all. 'Now what are we going to do?'

'Shouldn't we now put out an all-stations alert for him?'

'Not yet. I need to speak with Commandant Franchi and his committee first.'

Back at the office of the internal security agency, things had moved on and Sebastiani sat across from Ricardo Da Corte dabbing a finger into the cleft in his chin and listening for new intelligence about General Ferdinando Conti.

Da Corte took a letter opener from its stand and tapped his fingers with it. 'He's got a day's start on us. He seems to have cleared out as soon as he heard we'd latched onto Robert Colonna.'

'He'll know Colonna's dead.'

'Who doesn't?' Da Corte replaced the letter opener. 'So, you think Conti might have flown. Is he a pilot?'

'I don't know. I remember him talking about giving up tennis because of the pain in his arm. Said he'd have to stick with the flying club. I went through his offices, both of them. His personal papers had been cleared out. HR records didn't mention flying.'

Ricardo turned to the third pair of ears in the room, a lead spy in his organization. 'How many flying clubs in Rome, Filippo?'

'Don't know. Might not have been Rome.'

'Right. Oh God. Then where?'

'Wouldn't be far away,' said Sebastiani. 'Try Rome first and work outwards. There won't be many.'

Filippo went off to his computer.

'You do know he's got relatives in Rome, Fabio?'

'He's married and got a son.'

'Right. Son doesn't know where his father is. He also has two sisters here in Rome. They don't know where he is either. I've posted watchmen at all their addresses. But he won't go near them.'

'He's not that dumb.'

'Flying out would be risky. He'd need to file a flight plan.'

Filippo returned with documents in his hand. 'He's a member of the military flying club at Viterbo.'

'Of course. Where our sabotaged helicopter came from,' Sebastiani reminded his spy colleagues.

'Viterbo flying club have not seen him,' said Filippo. 'They know Commandant General Franchi is after him.'

Sebastiani grimaced. 'We're all bloody after him.'

'Viterbo put out an immediate alert to all affiliated flying clubs. We'll see what they come up with.'

'Good, Filippo. Thanks.' The moment Da Corte excused Filippo, the warning light on his red telephone blinked and he put the phone to his ear. A grin filled his face as he slapped the phone back on its cradle and stood. He threw his jacket on and shouted toward the door. 'Filippo. Get back in here right away.' He picked up Sebastiani's cap from the desk and handed it to him. 'It's Conti.'

Da Corte took a gun from his desk drawer and stuck it into the holster that was belted to his torso. 'Filippo. Get a couple of your young guns and follow me.' He felt for the car keys in his jacket pocket and made for the door. 'Fabio, you're in my car. Let's go.'

In the car, Da Corte hit Sebastiani with, 'Fabio, your daughter, Elaine Bruneau, is on the scene.'

'You're joking.'

'No joke.'

A mass of state police cars with flashing blue lights greeted their arrival at the National Gallery of Modern Art. Red and white tape cordoned off the area around the art gallery.

A totally bald, black man dressed in a light-grey suit, grey shirt and tie flashed his ID badge.

Sebastiani studied it and the Frenchman's face. 'French secret service.'

'*Oui.*' The Frenchman shrugged his shoulders. '*Non-capisco italiano.*'

He spoke to him in French. 'Where's Elaine Bruneau?'

'Come with me, please.'

They followed him up broad marble steps at the left of the art gallery. At the top of the steps, a state police officer saluted and addressed Sebastiani, the only one of the group in uniform. '*Buongiorno*, Colonel. We have an armed standoff with a young French woman. She's holding General Conti hostage and threatens to shoot him. Come with me.'

The group hastened through shrubbery and into a sandy clearing where police aimed their weapons at Elaine Bruneau. She had her back against a tree and held Conti in a one-armed stranglehold with the barrel of her gun against his head. Blood covered the lower part of Conti's face and his sports shirt and white trousers.

Sebastiani rushed forward with his head shaking and his arms beating the air. 'Don't shoot, don't shoot. She's my daughter. Don't shoot.'

'Go away, Fabio,' she shouted. '*Cet homme est un traître.*' She pulled on his throat. 'They were going to hang me. They told me my betrayer. Conti, Rome police. *Traître.*'

She turned Conti round, kneed him in the crotch and when he bent double she held his hair, kneed him in the face and then let him drop.

She pointed her gun at his head.

'Elaine, stop it. Stop it, do you hear me?'

'Go away, Fabio. They tortured and raped me.' She bent to Conti's ear. 'You're going to hell, bastard.'

Sebastiani moved toward her and she pointed her gun at him. 'I'll shoot.'

'Elaine. Elaine. You've got him. I'll deal with him. Come on. Come with me.' His fear of losing her slowed his pace. 'You're my daughter. I want to take you home.'

But she screamed. 'He betrayed me. They were going to hang me. They told me, Conti.'

When he got close to her he could see wounds on her face. He wrapped his arms around her ever so gently, fearing to hurt those wounds he could not see. He kissed her cheek. 'We've got him now.' He closed his hand around the gun and lifted it away.

She dropped her arms and wept bitterly.

Da Corte's men raised Conti to his feet, manacled his wrists behind him and took him away.

'Elaine, what's happened? What's the Frenchman doing here?'

'Leon. A colleague. As soon as I got back to Paris, I asked him to tail Conti. He would be sure to run when he found out I was freed. Leon called you when I threatened to kill him. Her beaten face raised a smile. 'I didn't do that but I beat him up good, didn't I?'

Sebastiani ordered the duty brigadiere to stand against a wall and then slumped into the large, old wooden chair that some thoughtful soul had placed in the corner behind the stand-up duty desk. He glanced through the iron-barred cell door but did not look at Conti's face. He folded his copy of *Le Figaro*, creased it between thumb and forefinger then reached forward and laid it on the desk. The colonel busied his mind with how he fell for Conti's sham, all those meetings, all those status reports and Conti's drive to find the culprits. How could he not see through the deceit? Because he didn't want to, he realized.

Sebastiani gave Conti credit for his clever acting but his mind struggled to dam up the deluge of rage for the traitor in the cell.

Conti, wounds cleansed and dressed, sat on the side of the utility camp bed in an officer's white shirt and black trousers, but without shoes, tie or belt. He turned to Sebastiani and waited as though expecting to be instructed on the theme of the visit. '*Buona sera*, Fabio.'

But Sebastiani remained silent.

'I understand,' said Conti.

Another long silence followed.

'I tried to commit suicide but that's not easy when you're rational. Anyway, I have a lot of personal things to do before I die. That's the reason I didn't pull the trigger. You see, I'm totally lacking honor.'

Sebastiani remained silent and motionless, and this stirred the confession.

'Why did I do it? Two reasons: the love of a young man and money. It's incredible to think now how I got wrapped up in this business.'

'Tell me.'

'It started in a confessional.'

'A confessional? You confessed to a priest?'

'Not me. I do not confess to priests. Domenico.'

'Your lover?'

Conti stood slowly, grimacing and holding on to his knees, causing Sebastiani to wonder if Elaine's battering had damaged his legs. Conti closed his eyes and dropped his head forward. 'The confessional was just an artifice. A place for transferring information. He talked with an American priest from France.'

'Bishop Francis Sinclair.' At the back of his mind, Sebastiani was tying names to the initials given in the Sinclair diaries.

Conti smiled and nodded. 'Domenico knew I was losing money. He told me I could be rich right away if I played a part. There would obviously be a Carabinieri investigation. All I had to do was divert it. I agreed. It was irresistible. I was close to financial ruin. Wrong investments, Fabio.'

'Tell me about Sinclair.'

'He was at the center of the plan. Agent provocateur, if you like. Had access to huge amounts of money.'

'Whose money?'

'An American tycoon. Robert Colonna. Religious fanatic. Wanted to destroy the Roman Catholic Church. As far as I know, that's what it was all about. Sinclair routed Colonna's money to willing people.'

'And you were one of the willing.'

'Not quite true. I just couldn't see them doing it. So much destruction. Killing so many. But as soon as Sinclair got my agreement it got passed up the line.'

'The chain of command. Their names?'

'Oh, Colonna I suppose. I never met him. Or Sinclair for that matter. But it was made clear I was in the game. They discovered I was susceptible over my homosexuality. Through Domenico. Unintentionally, of course. He was distraught about disclosing me.'

'Being outed is not a problem for most these days.'

'It was for me. You cannot deny there are problems in the Carabinieri. And my wife and son knew nothing, you see.'

'What about Archbishop Collineau? What was his part in the plan?'

'I'm not sure how he fitted in with the bombing. He had something to do with it, of course. But his mother, Yvette Collineau was definitely in the decision team.'

'I know. Kept good records did Bishop Sinclair. Identified all the bombing conspirators: you, Robert Colonna and Yvette Collineau. Sinclair was not a worthy crook, in my opinion.'

'It was Sinclair who organized Gagliano to kill Ricci. For Roger Collineau.'

'And you kept all this secret.'

He shrugged. 'I was threatened with the Gagliano treatment.' Then he closed his eyes and shook his head. After moments, he asked, 'Is that everyone taken care of?'

'Almost.'

'I'm impressed.'

'You're going away for a very long time. You know that.'

'Yes, I know.' Conti stood silent for several minutes, mostly looking down at his socks but occasionally giving Sebastiani a sideways glance. 'I believed your daughter would die in Tunis. I had the task of getting her arrested and convicted.'

'Sinclair paid you to betray Elaine Bruneau?'

'I didn't want to but by this time I was threatened with blackmail. Well, death, actually.'

'You're a despicable coward. I hope she's right about you going to hell. You've got a lot of crimes to answer for.'

'The helicopter. Are you going to ask me about that?'

'Don't need to. I know who arranged it and how. Modern telephone systems have powerful records retention. The Grizafi brothers are in prison. You're all in it up to your necks.'

'Domenico's friends listened to you all the way. They knew very quickly your exercise was to get Gagliano away. He was a big risk. We had to get him one way or the other. Alive if he was lucky or killed in the helicopter. If they had not got Gagliano they'd have shot down the other helicopter too. Everything covered.'

'Domenico Grizafi. I suppose you won't ever be seeing him again.'

Tears formed in Conti's eyes. He pulled his shoulders back, stood erect and looked upwards while struggling to fish a handkerchief from his pocket. A silence of several minutes passed before he spoke again. 'You suspected someone from our ranks from the beginning.'

Sebastiani looked at the cell's barred window and idly reassured himself that no one could stick their gun in and shoot Conti dead. At last he turned to Conti. 'Yes. At one point Ferri suspected you. Without your involvement, or his, or mine for that matter, the sabotage was impossible. I suspected him for a while.'

'I thought we'd got away with it. But as soon as I found out about your daughter's release, that's when I knew it was time to run.'

'As far as I'm concerned, that leaves just this.' To pose the question, Sebastiani stared all the time at his witness, the *brigadiere*. 'After standing down surveillance on the four Milan bombers, did you set the Grizafi brothers onto them? To kill them?'

'Yes.'

The *brigadiere's* iron face stared wide-eyed at Sebastiani.

'Look at this, you gutless bastard.' Sebastiani took up his newspaper, unfolded it and held its front-page picture up to the bars. 'Take a good look. Front page news a couple of days ago. In all the French newspapers.'

Conti turned away from the picture in horror.

'My new-found, beautiful daughter, Elaine. Looks different now. She'd been badly tortured. It'll take a long time for her wounds to heal. It'll take even longer for her mind to heal. If at all.'

Conti sunk his ashen face into his hands and wept.

'I could kill you, you fucker. The French secret service had a shortlist of three. Are you listening? Three possible traitors. You were top of their list. They arrested her as soon as she stepped off the fucking plane. You bastard. Frightened she'd break up the grand scheme. You're filth Conti. She came close to killing you. But if I have anything to do with it, you'll die in prison.'

He stood outside the prison building, took out his notebook and flicked through its pages, stopping at an entry that he had struck through: Fr Cantello, Barbentane. Then he remembered Moulard had promised to talk to Cantello about the Rome bombing, so he called him.

'Sorry Sebastiani. Up to my neck. Spoke to the man. Very old and dement. Been in France twenty-five years and can't speak the language.'

'Doesn't need to. All Catholic priests speak Italian.'

'My detectives don't and I can't afford interpreters. You'd better come and speak to him yourself. I'll take you.'

'Fine.'

Then, without having any particular reason, Sebastiani phoned Luisa Fabian. 'Luisa, hello.'

'Fabio. How are you?'

'I'm fine. I need to go to France. Well, Marseille. Maybe Avignon. Can you come with me?'

'Of course. Just tell me when.'

'Tomorrow. I'll book the flight and hotel.'

'Get a hotel in Avignon.'

CHAPTER TWENTY-FIVE

In the taxi from Marseille Provence International Airport, Luisa hung onto Sebastiani's arm and rested her head against his shoulder. The soft whoosh, whoosh noise reflected back to the taxi from regularly spaced poles at the side of the motorway recalled to her mind her many trips along this stretch.

'This is so nice,' she said.

'I was hoping you'd come to Nimes with me. You know Father Cantello; I think you should come.'

'I don't want to go to any prison, thank you,' she said, with mock indignation. 'And I don't want to travel with *Monsieur* Nicotine Moulard. I'd rather stay in Avignon and try to find the Archbishop.'

'Do you believe he knows where the stone is?'

'He knows Jean Collineau's French version of the text because it's at his mother's home. I think that's certain. That means there's a good chance he knows the Latin text. Ergo, if there is a stone he probably knows where it is.'

She laid a hand on his chest and snuggled up closer unaware of the arousal this caused in him.

'Will he be arrested?'

'Already was. Well, not arrested. Questioned. There's nothing to show he was involved in any crime. Moving the church is not a crime. Any religion can do that.'

'He's broken from Roman Catholicism. He's created a schism.'

'In Europe, that's not a crime.'

'Fabio, he's gained immense power. Maybe that's all he wanted.'

'I don't know. He's a criminal. He let Robert Colonna go along with his plan without saying a word. I'm pretty sure he knew what was going on. It's difficult to bring charges for his silence. And the police tread carefully when they're dealing with the head of the Church. I suspect he had a direct hand in the Rome bombing but you've got to have evidence. Moulard's put a tail on him. We'll see what comes up.'

What's more, I can't stand being near Moulard and his stinking cigarettes.'

Sebastiani frowned. 'That's a non sequitur. You're usually so logical.'

'You do this to me.'

Moulard screwed up his face like a maniacal demon. He shuffled papers about in the glove compartment of his grubby Peugeot, grunted, added to the disorder on the back seat by throwing odd papers over his shoulder and, looking only spasmodically at the E714 motorway stretching ahead of him, scaring the life out of Sebastiani sitting in the *place du mort* next to him. 'I have lost my fucking cigarettes.'

Sebastiani gripped the sides of his seat and forced himself to speak calmly. 'Stop somewhere. I'll buy you some.'

Moulard's agitation abated. 'Good, good. Thanks.'

Although new, Moulard's car already had all the characteristics of his office: in total disarray, stinking of nicotine and its once cream upholstery a grubby, brownish yellow.

Sebastiani turned his face to the fresh breeze pouring in the open window on the passenger's side, which fought back the beads breaking out on his forehead. Luisa had opted to stay in Avignon because of Moulard's chain smoking, he reminded himself, but she would not have appreciated his crazy driving either.

The Frenchman talked away unaware and unconcerned about the danger of driving at 110 kilometers an hour while mentally and physically distracted. 'Big pedo ring, Fabio. Politicians, police, priests. We've got them. I will bet you a peso to a pinch of dog's shit they will get life with hard labor. Lot of kids.'

'What are you going to do with them all?'

'No idea. Somebody else's problem. My problem is where they've put the pedos. French prisons are a disgrace. Old and bursting. We spread them around Avignon, Nimes, Montpellier and Marseille. It's a job to know where they all are. But your man Cantello is in Nimes. That I do know.'

'What's he charged with?'

Sebastiani regretted asking the question because it sent the Frenchman back into distracted mode. Moulard fished around the convenience tray between the two forward seats until he found the piece of card on which he had written the name. Sharing his vision between the card and the road ahead, he said, 'Father Cantello. Gendarmerie still working on the charge. Funny old guy. Gave himself up. Didn't have to. I guess we'd have come round to him at some time.'

The prison guard deposited Father Cantello and a recorder in the gloomy, windowless interrogation room where Sebastiani sat under a single, dim light bulb, pressed a button on the recorder and then disappeared.

'*Buongiorno*, Father Cantello,' said Sebastiani. He gave up the only seat in the room to the old man and sat, arms folded, on the edge of a sturdy tubular-framed table across from him.

In his tatty monk's habit seemingly worn out by the same hard years as its wearer, Cantello looked life-weary but cheerful. Wispy, long white hair hung from the edges of his baldness and a matching goat's beard drooped lifelessly from his chin. 'It's nice to be speaking Italian. You're from Rome.'

'Yes.'

'I've not been charged with any crime.'

330

Sebastiani looked Cantello over, wondering how this eighty-five-year-old Italian priest had come to be in such a pathetic state. 'They're working on your case.' He realized that his questioning would need to be gentle, coaxing and time-consuming.

'I'm in a cell with three other people. The cell has three bunks.' Cantello screwed up his face and rubbed the backs of his arms. 'I sleep on the floor.' A weak smile created yet more creases in Cantello's already corrugated face. 'What's your name?' He placed a finger on his lower lip and frowned. 'Have you told me already?'

'Colonel Sebastiani. Carabinieri.'

'Oh yes, good. Ah, colonel. Sorry.'

'It doesn't matter. I need your help, that's the important thing.'

Cantello stared wide-eyed at him, his mouth open. After several seconds of flicking his tongue along his lower lip, he said. 'How can I help?'

'Do you know Cardinal Sinclair and Cardinal Ricci?'

'Sinclair and Ricci,' said Cantello, frowning. 'Aldo Ricci? Is that Aldo?'

'Aldo Ricci and Francis Sinclair.'

'Yes, yes. What about them?' He clasped his hands together on his lap.

'They are both dead, did you know?'

'Yes. I'm very sad about my friend, Aldo.'

'What about Bishop Sinclair? Not a friend of yours?'

Cantello sank his chin onto his chest and sat quietly, lips pressed together, giving Sebastiani to believe he feared to answer the question.

'What work did the bishop do at the Barbentane seminary?'

Cantello's hands trembled. 'I don't know. Staffing the teaching faculties and reviewing curricula. That was his job. But he didn't do that. Didn't do anything for the school.'

'What did he do?'

Cantello's mouth sagged open and he stared up at the light for a whole minute, apparently looking for an answer in its glow. Then he turned to Sebastiani, mouth twisted by an angry scowl. 'He was a child molester. Couldn't keep his hands off the boys. He told me.' He

331

put his fingers to his mouth. 'I'm ashamed I didn't report it. They would have tortured me.'

'Did Sinclair threaten you?'

'They all did, those perverts. Plenty like him at St Alphonsus.'

Fewer now after Moulard's visit, thought Sebastiani. 'Does the name Robert Colonna mean anything to you?'

'The American. Very rich. Sinclair was always talking about him. Wanted his money.'

'Just his money?'

'Oh no, no, no.' Cantello swayed from side to side in silence and then looked up. 'You know, *Signor* Sebastiani, it was Bishop Sinclair who started all this.'

'The abuse of children?'

'Not that. He told me many times about his calls to Mister Colonna. The day for action is near, he used to say, and it was Colonna's duty to kill the pope and destroy the Roman Catholic Church. End the persecution. I didn't know what he meant by that. Sinclair was mad so I took no notice.'

But the old man had confirmed Luisa Fabian's vengeance hypothesis. Sinclair had stirred up religious fanatic Colonna with the Collineau oath, and Colonna's men had organized and carried out the bombing, killing the last of the Gaetani family, Pope Boniface X, thereby dissolving the excommunications that barred the Colonnas and their offspring, the Collineaus, from paradise.

'Bishop Sinclair was killed when the Basilica was bombed. Do you know if anyone had threatened to kill him?'

'To keep him quiet, you mean?'

'For any reason.'

'I don't know. But Sinclair was a bad man. He was with bad people. Sending children to evil places. He had rich customers. I don't know who and I don't know where.' Father Cantello raised a secretive finger to his lips. 'Pope Boniface was out to get him and all the other child molesters in the Church. Barbentane was his first target.'

Cantello strayed off into silence and stared at Sebastiani. Suddenly, his face lit up. 'I knew what they were speaking about. Sinclair and the Archbishop.'

'What archbishop was that?'

But Cantello sauntered on. 'Some people in the group didn't want it. Sinclair was all for it.'

'Father Cantello. What archbishop?'

'They talked about bringing the Church to France. The Archbishop and Sinclair.'

'Father Cantello, listen. What archbishop?'

'Collineau. Didn't I say?'

New evidence! Sebastiani's eyebrows arched. 'And you heard them discussing this? Were you always at their meetings?'

'I was Sinclair's run-about. Kept me on hand the whole time.'

'What about Cardinal Ricci? Did he visit Sinclair?'

'He always came with the Archbishop.'

Cantello suddenly looked troubled and distant. Sebastiani let a long pause dissipate naturally until the priest's attention returned.

'When did the visits start?'

'I'm not sure. About two years ago and they were always to see Sinclair. Other than that, I'm not sure.'

'What about Cardinal Ricci?'

The old man beckoned Sebastiani and when he moved to him, grabbed his arm and pulled him closer and whispered. 'The last time I saw him, he told me he was working with Americans. He was very upset.'

'What Americans? Colonna?'

'No, no. He was very frightened. Two Americans.'

Simms and Barnes, thought Sebastiani.

'That's why he told the Italian police. He was so frightened.'

'He told the police? State police? Carabinieri?'

'I don't know. He told me they didn't believe him.'

Or perhaps they did and marked him for Gagliano to deal with. 'Were Archbishop Collineau and Cardinal Ricci involved in child abuse?'

333

'The Archbishop, I don't think so. Ricci, yes. But that was Sinclair's fault. I should have told someone but… Oh my God. For this sin I should die. Sinclair had a gang of bullies in Avignon. They threatened me with torture and death. I'm an old man, *Signor* Sebastiani.'

Loud thumping on the door presaged Moulard's arrival and evaporated to the air Sebastiani's intended final words to Cantello. They would have brought little more useful information.

Moulard poked his head round the door. 'You ready, Fabio?'

He pressed stop on the recorder and ejected the cassette. 'Take this, Simon. Get it translated and listen carefully. You need to make another arrest.'

Sebastiani retrieved the lipstick that Luisa Fabian had dropped on the floor of the taxi and then held it for her to take. 'You don't need this. You're beautiful without it.'

He found it easier now to say those personal things naturally, without the need to overcome the stress hurdle that tied his tongue just days ago.

'You're so kind, Fabio. Thanks, but I feel dressed with it.'

He watched her apply it and reached over and kissed her cheek.

She smiled and snuggled into him. 'I've been thinking. How'd you like to move in with me? In my apartment in Rome?'

The question hit him like a bolt out of the blue. 'You need to warn me before asking questions like that.'

'Come on. What do you say?'

He dropped his head back and closed his eyes. 'I'd love to,' but the fall of his voice suggested his mind had filled with reasons why he could not.

'I know you well. We could have a wonderful relationship. I'm not after marriage, just a man I know I could be with and turn to when I need to.'

'I'm always away from home.'

'So am I. I travel all over the place. This would work perfectly.'

'I'm much older than you.'

'You're just putting obstacles in the way.'

'I've got a daughter in hospital.'

'When we get back to Rome I can help you with Elaine. She could stay with us in my apartment.' Her eyes lit up. 'We could be like sisters.'

'That's impossible. There are other problems too.'

'I can help you with them.'

'This is not something I imagined when we set off together.'

'So? What do you say?'

'It would be wonderful...' He deleted the ifs and buts about to pour out of his mouth and left it as said. 'It would be wonderful,' he repeated.

She smiled up at him and then stared silently out toward the fields.

After many minutes she asked, 'How did the prison visit go?'

'What Cantello told me would have been useful earlier.' He shrugged. 'It makes Archbishop Collineau a suspect in the Vatican bombing. I gave Moulard a tape of Cantello's evidence so he'll soon be knocking on the pope's door.'

The taxi stopped and they both lowered their heads to look out of the window toward the Popes' Palace.

Luisa got out and then looked back at Sebastiani. 'Don't you want to come with me?'

'I'll wait in the taxi.'

'I could be a long time. I don't know where his secretary is.'

'I'll be here when you get back.'

She checked through her handbag and then set off across the Place du Palais to the West Gate of the Popes' Palace. At the very moment she passed through the gate and out of sight, a recessed door further along the west wall opened. Sebastiani stared open-mouthed at the very tall man who came out of the door and stood for moments looking up and down the road. He wore a black suit, a black wide-brimmed hat and a priest's dog collar.

Sebastiani leaped out of the taxi and shouted back to the driver. 'I'm coming straight back. Wait.'

Walking briskly to the gate, he saw Luisa going from one door to another, still looking for the right entrance.

'Luisa. Quick.'

'What is it?'

Sebastiani kept his eyes on the tall man. 'Quick. Come here.'

'What the matter?'

'Look.' He pointed down the road. 'Your man is taking a walk.'

'Collineau. Taking a walk?'

'He's taller than everyone else. See him.'

'I see the tall man. How do you know it's Collineau?'

'Don't let him out of your sight. I'll pay the taxi.'

'Wait a minute, he's getting into a car,' shouted Luisa.

They scrambled back into the taxi.

'Follow that car,' said Sebastiani to the driver.

They sat forward, peering out of the windscreen.

'Are you sure that's him?' asked Luisa.

'Pretty sure.'

The car chase threaded a network of narrow roads and finally turned onto the Rue de la Banasterie where the priest's car stopped at a small church.

Luisa buzzed with excitement. 'I know where we are and I know this church. It's the Chapelle des Pénitents Noirs. Come on, Fabio, this is it!'

Sebastiani paid the taxi then joined her peeking round the corner of a stone-walled building and over a long line of parked cars toward the little church. Both drew back as the tall man momentarily looked in their direction, removed his hat and stepped through the church's terracotta-colored double door.

Luisa tugged Sebastiani along to the door.

He scanned the road for Moulard's man but saw no one he recognized. They entered the church and cool silence. In a large painting set in the richly ornamented wall above the altar, the crucified Christ looked heavenward while his only visible human subject, an old woman in the first row of the red bench seats, sat with head drooped and hands clasped together on her lap. Archbishop Roger Collineau, or whoever the tall man was, had vanished.

Luisa led Sebastiani along the aisle and through the door at the left of the altar. A spiral stairway she had no recollection of seeing on her one previous visit rose up to a door that was chained shut. She came out of the stairwell shaking her head. Then she went into an identical door on the other side of the altar but came out looking perplexed. 'I don't understand. This is the church. I'm certain of that.'

'Where's he gone?'

'I don't know.'

The old woman heard the Italian exchange, hobbled to the door and, brushing Luisa aside, went into an empty storeroom. She pressed a panel to the side of the door and pushed open a section of the wall. In French, she asked, 'Is this what you're looking for, young lady?'

Luisa cupped the woman's hand in hers. '*Merci, Madame.*'

Fabio said, 'I'll go first.'

They crept down stone steps and entered the murky greyness of a crypt. Murmuring indistinct figures moved about at the far end of the chamber. A scratching noise sparked itself into a small flame, turning the figures into ethereal beings whose faces mutated as the flame rose into the air. The burning taper cast a sinister aura around its holder, a silent, boyish acolyte in a hooded, white habit. As the candle he lit gradually raised itself to brilliance, the crypt came alive within Luisa's memory. A nervous thrill took hold of her inside and squeezed. 'This is it,' she whispered.

And he recognized the images she had told him about: the arches, the columns, the inscription in brass embossed on the age-old stone floor, the small altar and the large brass crowns hanging from the ceiling on chains. The sarcophagus of her memory lay against a wall. She held on to him tightly.

And the man they had followed, now in full-length scarlet gown and skullcap, conversed in hushed tones with two priests in brown robes. The lofty Archbishop Collineau looked at them briefly but

337

continued his conversation. Two minutes later, the priests shook his hand and left, ignoring Sebastiani and Luisa as they scurried to the exit.

'I need to phone Moulard,' said Sebastiani.

'Wait,' she whispered. 'Look. The stone above the altar. See it?'

Together they drifted nearer to Collineau who faced the altar chanting a liturgy.

'That's the covenant that Jean Collineau wrote in French in the Bastille,' she said. 'It makes sense because he lived in Avignon.'

'I must phone Moulard.'

'Shh.' She looked back and could see a very tall man standing near the steps dressed like the man they had followed to the church. The brim of his hat cast a shadow over his face.

'Fabio, look.' She pointed to the figure.

'What do you want me to see?'

'The man in black. I'm frightened,' she whispered.

'There's no one there.'

Clinging fiercely to him, she screamed at the specter. 'Get away from me.'

Archbishop Collineau stared at her. 'Your woman has gone mad. You should leave now.'

'Luisa, you're hallucinating. There's no one there.'

'Why can't you see him? He's standing just there.'

'Stop this madness. You are disrupting my service.'

'Archbishop Collineau, the murderer.'

'Just go away and take her with you.'

Luisa shrieked and buried her face in Sebastiani's chest.

'Luisa, listen. No one's going to hurt you.'

'Get out of here or I'll call the police,' said the priest.

'Go ahead. Then we'll watch as they arrest you.'

The archbishop snatched off his skullcap and stood silently for moments staring at the colonel. His eyes widened and he pointed a finger at him. 'I know you. The Rome interrogator.'

'There's an old priest in Nimes who is a witness to your crimes.'

'I have committed no crime.'

Collineau threw his cap to the side and shouted. 'Get out of here you crazy people.'

'Guilt getting to you, Archbishop?'

'Guilt? We laid the foundations of a pure church for the whole of mankind. That is not a crime.' Collineau turned his back on them, reached over the altar and laid his hands on the stone.

Let's go, Luisa. Moulard will deal with him.'

The archbishop turned to them, tears glistening in the flickering candlelight, voice breaking into a cry. 'It has taken seven hundred years and at last it is done. The Roman popes are dead and the Gaetani are dead.' He threw his arms up and cried to the ceiling, 'God bless you, Jacopo, your Covenant is fulfilled.'

Sebastiani took Luisa's arm. 'We'd better go.'

They had reached the steps when the smell of Moulard descended into the crypt with him and two gendarmes.

'Well, well. The colonel and his professor lady.'

'I was about to phone you, inspector.'

Moulard laughed. 'You just won't leave me alone.' He strode to Collineau with his badge in his outstretched hand. '*Monsieur* Collineau, you are to come with me to the police station. There are questions I must ask you.'

Collineau gripped his left-hand fingers in a bunch with his right hand but he could not stop them shaking violently. 'I am the pope of the Holy Catholic Church. I have committed no crime.'

'I have a witness and I have evidence. Please do not make trouble.'

Moulard flicked a hand and the two gendarmes rushed Collineau and grasped his wrists, but he yelled and fought with them.

The priest freed a hand and reached back to the altar, grabbed a ceremonial dagger and lunged at his assailants, stabbing one in the arm.

Moulard shouted. 'Leave him. Get back.'

Collineau panted, sneered and slobbered. 'Who do you think you are?' Then he raised himself erect and pulled back his shoulders. 'I am a prince of heaven. You will never put me in a prison.' He threw back his head, ran the blade across his throat and crashed to the floor.

Luisa buried her face in her hands.

Cold evil wrapped itself around her body and possessed her mind. She pressed her ears against the piercing scream of a mortal in pain. A giant with the head of a bull reared up and snatched at her with human hands. It roared the words of the Latin covenant and turned to the young girl she could see kneeling, head bowed, in front of the altar in a white communion dress. For just a moment it held an axe just above her neck and, with a fearful howl, raised it over its head.

Luisa ran up the steps and out of the church pursued by Sebastiani. Outside, she stood with her eyes closed, arms pulled tight to her bosom and her chin cradled on her fists.

'I'm sorry. That was a terrible thing to see.'

'What I saw you could never imagine. I know what it is and I'm all right.'

'Look, the taxi's still there. Go and sit in it. I won't be long.'

She didn't hear him. 'Why did he have a dagger?'

'I don't know. Ceremony, perhaps?'

'Jesuits practice a secret blood oath when a new leader is inducted. Collineau was a new leader. Maybe he was here today to take a blood oath.'

'I'm sorry Luisa, it means nothing to me.'

'I guess we'll never know.'

Moulard came out of the church grinning over his good fortune. 'Justice is done, colonel. And he's saved the French people all those legal expenses.'

'He might have been a useful witness for Italy but I can live without him,' said Sebastiani.

'I've arrested his mother. You must talk to her before you return to Rome, yes?'

'Soon as possible.'

A gendarme and the youth in the white habit emerged from the church and got into a police car.

'Fabio, that's Eduardo,' said Luisa.

'You know him?'

'That's Eduardo from La Calmette. What's going to happen to him?'

'That's Moulard's business. I'm off to Marseille prison to see *Madame* Collineau. If you come with me I can arrange for you to see her. What about it?'

'No thank you. I never want to see that evil woman again.'

Luisa Fabian would not have recognized the old woman, he thought. She looked as dull as the grey-painted and dilapidated interview room in which she sat at a bare table. Wearing a grey smock and with no makeup Yvette Collineau looked very old and pitiful. The intense flame of her yesterday's fire had been extinguished.

'French or Italian, *Madame*?'

'What do you want?' she barked in French.

'You are being extradited to Rome.'

'Why?'

'To face charges for bombing Rome and the Vatican.'

She raised her head back haughtily. 'Don't you dare throw that one at me. That was not my idea.'

'Ah. Whose then?'

'Not mine.'

'Cardinal Sinclair's?'

'Yes.'

She answered too quickly, he thought. 'How so? He died in the explosions.'

She sat back and glowered. 'I know he did,' she said, straining the words through clenched teeth. 'He was supposed to.'

'You organized the bombing with Colonna's men.'

She gave no denial. 'Robert Colonna was a good man,' she said in Italian.

'Innocent people died.'

'Innocent? They deserved it. They persecuted my family for centuries. This was revenge, do you understand? Revenge. It had to be. My son is the King of the Church. He will tell you.'

'Your son is dead.'

Her mouth dropped and her hands spread rigid before her.

'He committed suicide.'

'He was foreordained. The Collineau Covenant.'

'Believe what you want. After the Italian court has dealt with you, you return to France to face charges of transporting children for immoral purposes.'

She sank her head onto her outstretched arms and sobbed bitterly.

When Sebastiani arrived at the restaurant Luca Ferri was already there, sat in one of the six chairs placed around a large, fully decked out round table, the only one in the spacious room, studying a document. Seeing Sebastiani enter, he started to stand but Sebastiani patted down the air at him.

'*Buona sera*, sir.'

Sebastiani took a seat next but one to Ferri facing the arched entrance and scanned the room. 'Too upper class. Not my choice for eating with colleagues. But Da Corte's a regular here.'

'How's Elaine?'

'Getting better, thanks. She's moving into Luisa's apartment until she's well enough to live alone, then we'll see. But I'm sure she'll stay in Rome.'

Ferri sat back and pointed to the chairs. 'Set for six. You, me and Da Corte. Who're the others?'

342

Sebastiani pulled a sour face. 'I don't know. I was here a couple of times with him and his customers. I hope it's not them with their boring tales.'

'Do you know what it's about?'

'No, it could be social. We were at university together. Have I told you that?'

'No, sir.'

'Oh, for Christ's sake call me Fabio. We're almost friends after what we've been through together.'

'I got my promotion. Thanks.'

'You've earned it. I started the process months ago. I'm trying to think if I've seen you in civvies before. Nice suit, Luca. Looks expensive.'

Ferri touched the lapel of his jacket. 'Thanks.'

'How's your arm?'

'It's mending.'

'You were lucky.' Sebastiani looked around the room. 'Ricardo invited us so I suppose he's paying. But you never know with rich people. They like to pass on the bills.'

'Good evening, gentlemen,' shouted Da Corte, as he entered through the arch. They both stood and Sebastiani did the introductions. Da Corte's man, Filippo, came in after him, scanned the room and backed himself against a wall on their side of the arch with his hands at his crotch gripping a gun, finger on the trigger.

Sebastiani and Ferri looked at him and then at each other. As they sat, they both felt for the guns concealed inside their jackets.

'Good to meet you, Ferri,' said Da Corte. 'Heard a lot about you. Congratulations on your promotion.'

That surprised Sebastiani. How would Da Corte know that he had been promoted?

Da Corte took a seat opposite the two, put his briefcase under the table between his legs and tied the thin leather strap attached to its handle around his knee. 'It's just us three. Filippo will not be joining us at the table.'

The waiter appeared with menus and wine lists.

343

Da Corte looked up at him and then at his companions. 'Give us half an hour, Stefano. Just mineral water for now.' He checked Filippo over by the wall and then drew in his chair. 'I have important news that affects you both.' Ricardo looked for their attention. 'As of today, I am your new boss.'

Sebastiani arrested an urge to laugh. 'Well. Well…that's good news.'

'Your beloved Doctor Franchi recommended me to replace the disgraced Ferdinando Conti as national anti-terror boss. Got all-round approval from the ministry, apparently. So, I am moving up and out of the Internal Security Agency. Formal announcement tomorrow.'

'Congratulations,' said Sebastiani, now understanding why Da Corte knew about Ferri's promotion. And he's been reading my personnel file too, for sure.

In the short silence that ensued, Stefano poured out the mineral water as Sebastiani and Ferri darted looks at Filippo standing against the wall.

'It's a promotional move and I take the rank of General,' said Da Corte. 'This means you'll see me in uniform.' He turned to Sebastiani. 'My understanding is that the bombing investigation is not yet completely sewn up. Is that correct?'

Ah, a catch-up meeting before he moves into Conti's old offices, thought the colonel. 'All known living culprits are in high-security jails in Rome awaiting trials.'

'And the known dead culprits?'

Ferri answered. 'Some died in Robert Colonna's plane crash.'

'It's weird,' said Sebastiani. 'Just before it was shot down, traffic control heard someone in the cockpit behaving like a madman. From exchanges with the pilot, it was evidently Colonna.'

'Any clues why that was going on?'

'They haven't recovered the black box yet. Interesting that only Colonna's body was not found.'

'Yes, that's a bit of a mystery, Fabio.'

'One of several. We're pretty sure the Americans, Simms and Barnes planted the Semtex for the bombing. We're also of the belief

Simms murdered Barnes before the explosions. Simms's fingerprints were all over the murder weapon and he was psychotic. Witnesses say they argued in their hotel. This gives Simms a first-rate chance of being Barnes' killer. We know that the falling roof killed Simms but if he knew it was coming down, why the hell didn't he get out of there?'

Da Corte eyes widened. 'That is strange.'

'Bishop Francis Sinclair is another puzzle,' said Sebastiani. 'He was permanently assigned to a seminary in France but had duties for the Rome event. We have evidence he conspired with the Americans Simms and Barnes to bomb the Vatican so would know the timing of the detonations. The question is, why was he in the Basilica at the time of the explosions?'

'You'll have to set up an inquiry for that one. You know, with people like Sinclair, the Collineau woman and the Archbishop involved it could never have succeeded.'

Sebastiani screwed-up his face and sucked air through his teeth. 'In some ways, of course, it did. The papal seat is in Avignon and I can believe the French government is happy about that.'

'Will it not return to Rome when the Basilica's restored?'

'It was moved to France on the order of the acting pope. It will take a pope's decision to move it again. To…wherever. Perhaps Rome. Who knows?'

The sound of Da Corte's mobile telephone coincided with Stefano's return for orders and the half-hour limit the ex-head of counter intelligence had set on talking shop. Sebastiani looked at Ferri askance with raised eyebrows.

Untying the leather strap from his leg, Da Corte stood, picked up his briefcase, mutely excused himself and wandered to a far wall with his telephone against his ear. The waiter raised his eyes to the ceiling and disappeared.

Sebastiani peered at Filippo still standing ready for God knows what, and then at his new boss picking up urgency in his talk.

'Yes, yes. Right away,' said Da Corte. 'Okay, I'll be there with one man in support.'

He returned with a face affecting disappointment. 'I'm sorry, gentlemen, I have to go.'

'What's going on?'

'Espionage, Fabio. Probably my last act as a master spy. It's urgent. I trust you will understand.'

'I understand,' said Sebastiani, holding back the caustic smile pulling at one corner of his mouth.

Da Corte nodded once to Filippo who led the way out with his gun hand tucked inside his jacket.

Sebastiani stretched out his legs and sat back wondering what to make of Da Corte's dramatics.

Ferri said, 'I'm glad they've gone.'

'Oh, Luca. Why?'

He pulled the document he had read earlier out of his inside jacket pocket and flattened it on the table. 'I picked this up on the way here. It's from the CIA. I've only skimmed it. It's unbelievable.'

'What does it say?'

Ferri pushed the document to him. 'It's a letter Simms wrote to his sister Dinah about a week before the bombing. She gave it to the police in Alabama two days ago. Counter-terrorism routed it to Rome by e-mail.'

'Dinah took her time.'

'She didn't want to believe her brother could do such a terrible thing. That's in her statement at the back.'

After ten minutes of silent reading, shaking his head and re-reading, Sebastiani stared open-mouthed at Ferri. 'Good God. They planned to blow the Basilica when it was empty.'

'This one man killed over eight-hundred people.'

Sebastiani cited parts of the letter. 'Head pains, depression, unable to get his drugs. He even says that Barnes was threatening him. Simms wanted to commit suicide.'

'Probably why he stayed in the Basilica when his bombs went off.'

Sebastiani frowned and looked into the distance. 'The bridge was blown up at eleven and Pope Boniface was killed. That was the plan. But this says the Basilica was supposed to be blown up at two o'clock, three hours later. By that time, the Basilica would have been empty. Although I'm not sure about that.'

'No. You're right. The Basilica would have been empty mid-afternoon.'

Sebastiani tapped his lips with a finger. 'That explains Sinclair. He knew the plan but didn't know what Simms was up to.'

'How did a man like Simms get his hands on the detonator controller?' asked Ferri.

They answered the question together: 'He killed Barnes for it.'

Commotion broke out near the front of the restaurant. Staff members rushed by them and out through a door at the rear of the room. A large man burst in, coming toward them breathing as if an unfit, heavy smoker under physical stress. He pointed an automatic pistol at Sebastiani.

From the side, Filippo screamed loudly, 'Alfredo!'

Alfredo turned his gun to the shout but in a split second of intense noise he fell on his back blasting bullets into the chandelier, blood pouring from his head and chest.

'Game's over.' Da Corte strode in, grinning from ear to ear. 'Fabio, this was to be your dying day.'

'He was after us?' asked Sebastiani, astonished.

'They were after you, just you. Gagliano's friends, and there were three of them. Retribution, my friend. My listeners picked up they planned to kill you so we set this up.'

'Pointed them to me? In this restaurant?'

'You were the bait. We had to draw them out of the shadows. It was okay, Filippo was there the whole time.'

'That's made me feel really comfortable. And the other two?'

'On their way to secure custody. Best to get them out of the way.'

'I suppose you've saved my life.' Which is what everybody seems to be doing lately, thought Sebastiani. He turned to Ferri. 'What do you think, Luca?'

'I'm glad it's over.'

CHAPTER TWENTY-SIX

Sebastiani set off alone toward Dino Caso's grave. Walking slowly along the winding path, he felt relaxed within himself. No feelings of remorse or sadness. Just a strange awareness of the bright beauty of the graveyard with its carefully tended, white and black marble memorial stones adorned with colorful flowers, angelic sculptures and lofty poplars.

He studied the inscriptions and pictures on the headstones and considered his own mortality. We all die and my time will come soon enough, he told himself.

There was the grave, with a single vase of orange-red roses he supposed had replaced the by-now withered wreathes and bouquets.

The crunch of foot on gravel behind stiffened him. *Watch out Fabio, they want you dead.* He made no effort to turn. Eyes still closed, he waited for the sharp, hot pain and the unconscious eternity.

An arm wrapped itself around his shoulders. 'Gotcha.'

He recognized the voice instantly. 'Roberto! For goodness sake, don't ever sneak up on me like that again. How the hell did you know where to find me?' Sebastiani embraced his son fiercely.

'Luca Ferri dropped me at the gate on his motor cycle.'

'Oh, my God.'

'It was great. He promised to take me motocross racing.'

'Now wait a minute…'

'I just need a motorcycle. Come on, papa, I finished university. They're not so expensive. I can start work and pay you off.'

'Work?'

'Yeah, sure. No, wait a bit. I need to get a taste of life first. Travel for a year.'

Sebastiani burst out laughing. 'Slow down, slow down. All in good time. First I have more important things to tell you.'

'Yes, sorry Papa, I know you have been deeply involved in this terrible Vatican affair. How are you? You look very tired.'

'I am okay Roberto but it has taken its toll on us all. Despite that...'

'I'm serious...about work,' the youth added hastily.

'Well, let me give you some sound advice. Don't work for the Mafia or the Carabinieri. If you join one you'll get trouble from the other for the rest of your life.'

They laughed and hugged.

'Roberto, there are a couple of wonderful ladies I want you to meet. Come on, let's go.'

Driving Roberto to the hospital, Sebastiani turned off Cristoforo Colombo and entered Viale dell' Umanesimo and the lush greenery of the wealthy EUR district in the southern part of Rome. The three-story terracotta buildings of the Ospedale Sant' Eugenio spread themselves expansively and expensively over a beautiful landscaped park that rose high on a hill.

When they walked into the hospital's reception lounge, Elaine Bruneau and Luisa Fabian were there together, arm in arm as though Luisa were supporting her companion. When they noticed the men, however, they separated and walked to them.

After handshakes and 'hellos' all round, and his father's introductions, Roberto said, 'I have never met either of you before but I suppose I should think of you as family.'

'I think that's a good idea,' said Luisa. 'One loving, happy family, isn't that right, Elaine?'

'Of course.'

Sebastiani hugged his daughter and said, 'You look much brighter now.'

'I feel better too. Oh, and thank you for the flowers, Fabio.'

The colonel frowned and stared at her. 'What flowers?'

'You didn't send them? Well, I know Luisa didn't, so who did? They're in my room, come and see.'

The four went to her room and when she opened the door, rich fragrance wafted out. A large bouquet of yellow English roses lay on the bed. It was professionally wrapped and bound, and according to the attached card, 'For Elaine Bruneau'.

'I don't understand,' said Elaine. 'You and Luisa are the only two who know I'm here... Aren't you?'

Sebastiani hastened to reception. 'Excuse me,' he shouted to the receptionist, a middle-aged well-groomed woman discussing a document she held with a younger colleague at a computer. She put on an ambassadorial smile to attend to him. 'Colonel Sebastiani. What can I do for you?'

'The flowers in Elaine Bruneau's room. Do you know about them?'

'Yes. As soon as they came I took them to her. She was delighted.' She raised her chin and looked around. 'I've sent someone looking for a vase.'

'Can you tell me who delivered them?'

'A young man wearing sunglasses. I asked his name but he said Elaine would know.'

He shrugged. 'Thank you.' When he turned from her his face tightened in concern.

As they walked to the car Sebastiani threw Roberto the keys. 'I want to see if you can drive as well as you say.'

'I'm fine, papa, just trust me.'

'Can we trust him, Luisa?'

'You're putting my life in his hands so I must. Elaine is safe in the hospital so she doesn't get a say in this.'

351

'We'll see how it goes.' Get him driving a car and maybe he'll forget that crazy idea about riding motocross motorcycles, he thought.

As Roberto opened the car door, Sebastiani snatched a card from behind the windscreen wiper. His heart stopped. He grabbed his son and Luisa and screamed, 'Run, fucking run!'

Once out of the car park, he breathlessly phoned Fontana. 'Marco. I'm at Ospedale Sant' Eugenio. Send a bomb squad down here. I want my car checked out.'

'What is it, Fabio?' asked Luisa.

He passed her the card, which had four words written on it: 'Boom! Sebastiani, you're dead.'

THE LATIN AND FRENCH VERSIONS OF THE COVENANT

Jacopo Colonna had this Latin text of his family's covenant engraved in stone in the year 1303.

Sciarra, frater noster carissimus, Gaetanum, regem romanum nefarium, in gehennam misit. nihilominus falsus pontifex odio ardens qui exsecrationes in familiam nostram cumulavit postero tempore revertetur. gladium iustitiae divinae tollite et coronam a Gaetano deicite qui dehinc et in saecula saeculorum junctim cum tota stirpe sua damnatus est. perniciem parate exsecrandae meretrici satanicae eius, familiae nostrae omniumque gentium perditori.

haec sunt verba Iacobi Colonnae. die xiiimo mensis novembris aD nostri mccciiio

Its sentiments are also embodied in the covenant hand-written in French by Cardinal Jean Collineau before his execution in the Bastille in 1628.

La hache cruelle enverra Collineau à son Dieu dans le Royaume des cieux. Cependant Rome et son roi diabolique Gaetano, le faux Pape de la haine brûlante reste. Soulever l'épée de la vertu et trancher la tête de son corps, maudit maintenant et pour toujours jusqu'à sa dernière génération. Faire périr également sa maudite prostituée satanique, l'ennemi juré de notre famille et de l'humanité.

Signé par moi-même, le cardinal Jean Collineau, en cette année de notre Seigneur 1628, le quinzième jour du mois d'octobre.

AUTHOR'S DISCLAIMER

The Collineau Covenant is a work of fiction. The obvious proof of this statement is the ever profitably functioning Vatican in Rome and its still-standing St Peter's Cathedral. Apart from some real historical figures (including Pope Boniface VIII, Sciarra Colonna, Jacopo Colonna, King Philip 'The Fair' of France and, later than them, Cardinal Richelieu) whose brief appearances in my book I have dramatized for particular effects, the characters in my story are totally fictitious and any similarity to actual persons, living or dead, is purely coincidental. It is important to stress this because of the unsavory nature of some of the characters portrayed in the story.

ACKNOWLEDGEMENTS

A number of people have helped me bring this book to life and I want to thank them by mentioning their names here. At the outset, my sons put in creative ideas that got me under way, so thanks Gary and David. Special thanks to my patient and sparkling wife, Basia, who gave me great encouragement. Many thanks to my daughter, Luise Habrowski-Steinkellner, and friends Dr David Bradford, Steve Foehringer, Bethanne Cellars, Joyce Cellars, Gerhard Nagl, Sophie Newton and Roger Blackburn, who so readily agreed to read my drafts and give me valuable comments along with a large measure of encouragement. Thanks also to Dr Silvia Hansjakob and Duncan Salter for, respectively, the French and Latin versions of the Covenant text. And absolutely not to be forgotten, special thanks to my agent, Dr Paul M. Muller (of lunar mascons fame), for seeing in *The Collineau Covenant* the promise of a good story.

Sam Clinton

Sam Clinton was born in Southampton, England but has been living for the last twenty years in Austria with his second wife, Basia. On leaving the Royal Navy's Fleet Air Arm after completing seven years' service, Sam became a technical writer documenting civil aircraft flight control instruments. He has, however, spent most of his working life in software information development as technical writer, technical editor, information planner, and documentation manager for IBM. Later, he acted as consultant through his own company, which provided various professional computer and language skills to large account clients.

Author's website: www.samclinton.com
Aaurau Literary Agency address: www.aaraulit.com

Made in the USA
Charleston, SC
10 June 2013